THE WAYS OF WINTER

Karen Myers

THE WAYS OF WINTER

THE HOUNDS OF ANNWN: 2

Karen Myers

PERKUNAS PRESS • Hume, Virginia

The Ways of Winter
The Hounds of Annwn: 2

Perkunas Press
12142 Crest Hill Road
Hume, Virginia 22639
USA

PerkunasPress.com

Author contact: KarenMyers@PerkunasPress.com
Cover illustration: Larissa Kulik (Ann Mei)

Trade Paperback
ISBN-13: 978-0-9635384-3-7
ISBN-10: 0-9635384-3-8

ALSO BY KAREN MYERS

The Hounds of Annwn (series)

To Carry the Horn
The Ways of Winter

CONTENTS

Chapter 1	1
Chapter 2	13
Chapter 3	21
Chapter 4	30
Chapter 5	43
Chapter 6	57
Chapter 7	65
Chapter 8	74
Chapter 9	86
Chapter 10	99
Chapter 11	111
Chapter 12	131
Chapter 13	136
Chapter 14	142
Chapter 15	146
Chapter 16	158
Chapter 17	167
Chapter 18	178
Chapter 19	190
Chapter 20	198
Chapter 21	207
Chapter 22	212
Chapter 23	219
Chapter 24	228

Chapter 25   236

Chapter 26   244

Chapter 27   252

Chapter 28   259

Chapter 29   264

Chapter 30   273

Chapter 31   281

Chapter 32   290

Chapter 33   298

Chapter 34   303

Chapter 35   310

Chapter 36   319

Guide to Names & Pronunciations   329

If You Like This Book   337

Excerpt from King of the May   339

About the Author & Perkunas Press   348

CHAPTER 1

I'm sorry I ran away, Mother. I want to come home now.

Seething Magma raised her mantle in the dark underground cavity and interrupted her meal of crushed rock. At last, she thought, relief flooding her limbs. It had been almost a thousand years since she'd heard from her youngest child.

Where have you been? she scolded, then emended, *Never mind, just come home.*

I can't! He won't let me go. Granite Cloud's wail roused her mother's alarm. Nothing could hold an elemental.

I'm coming to fetch you, Seething Magma projected decisively. She shook herself and prepared for travel, pinpointing her daughter's location from her thoughts.

No, you can't. He'll get you, too.

Seething Magma settled back down thoughtfully. *Maybe you better tell me all about it. I'm sure we can find a way.*

⌒‿⌒

George kept Angharad company at her kitchen table as she prepared the crust for an apple pie. Almost a month of marriage hadn't diminished her charm for him in the least, but he couldn't spend the whole afternoon just watching her. Too bad.

It was the inactivity, he thought. The second of the early winter storms had ended this morning, after two days of snow. Hunting had been stopped since the first days of December. At least that allowed him to be more flexible in his domestic commuting schedule. His young junior huntsman Rhian had been handling hounds on Thursday mornings for hunting, and Sunday and Monday mornings for the hound walking, allowing him to come from Gwyn's court into Greenhollow and spend time with his wife (I can't believe it, my wife!) three nights a week. He was grateful Rhian was gaining confidence with handling the pack.

Now, with hunting stopped from the snow and hound walking restricted to the front grounds of the manor house, his hunt staff

1

had conspired to give him a full week off. He'd just arrived yesterday, anticipating at least a week of delayed honeymoon. His own dogs, coonhound Hugo and Sergeant, the yellow feist, were settled near the kitchen woodstove, but he knew Angharad's terriers Cabal and Ermengarde would roust them if it looked like the people were going to play in the snow.

Angharad broke the silence. "Did I tell you how well I liked your grandparents? I'm glad I had the chance to meet them."

"What about your family? You've been promising to tell me more about them."

"You'll have to wait for a visit to Gwyn's father in Britain. They're all in the old world, around the court, even the children."

George had a hard time getting used to the notion of her having several children, all of them older than him. At thirty-three, he was a well-grown human, but she was a fae, more than 1500 years old, and had lived many lives by his lights. He had blood ties to the fae himself, but no one yet knew if he had their gift of longevity, if he would be more than a brief interval in her life. It was an unstated worry that brought a note of urgency into their relationship.

He still thought it a miracle that she wanted to be with him anyway, given their relative ages. She'd settled into a solitary life as an artist when he met her, a self-sufficient existence, but he seemed to have jolted her out of that. He didn't quite understand why, lacking her perspective on extended life, but he was grateful and disinclined to question his good luck.

"Have you found a new apprentice yet? I know you asked your mentor Bleddyn about it," he said.

"These things take time, often many years. I've just let it be known I was available if anyone was seeking."

She'd been painting up a storm since they'd met, revitalized, and was offering to share that with someone, as masters did.

She filled the pie dish with sliced apples and sealed the upper crust in place. Having popped it into the oven, she washed her hands and walked over to join him at the kitchen table, patting him on the shoulder as she went by. He grabbed her with one arm around the hip and held her there, tight to his side, breathing in her scent and the overlay of apples, cinnamon, and dough. She melted against him and looked down at him suggestively.

The pounding on the door was very unwelcome, just then.

Angharad sighed and opened it, letting in Thomas Kethin, Gwyn's head ranger. He stamped the snow off his boots on the doorstep and unwrapped the wool muffler from his dark and weathered face.

"I'm sorry to disturb you two, I am, but we have a situation and I need George's help."

She offered to take his coat, but he refused. "The latest batch of Rhys's invitees has just arrived at the Travelers' Way, and the inn is full up and can't accommodate them. We've got to get them up to the manor."

"I feel for you, in all this snow, but what can I do about it?" George said.

"They're not exactly a cooperative group," Thomas said, wryly. "We have fae masters of several crafts, each prouder than the next, and quite a few korrigans. They're not getting along with each other, and the fae in particular aren't inclined to recognize my authority. I don't fit their old world ideas of a proper welcome."

"But I'm just the huntsman," George said.

"You can use Gwyn's authority as part of the family, and I think that would do the trick."

George was reluctant to leave his warm nest but he recognized that Thomas had a point. He pushed back his chair and stood up. "Sorry, sweetheart, but I think I must.

"Of course you should," she said. "There'll be other times." Ignoring Thomas standing by, trying to look anywhere else, she gave him a hug and a long, long kiss.

"There. Something to remember me by."

And if I can make my legs work again, I'll just walk on out of here, George thought, dazed.

In a few moments he'd assembled what he needed for a couple of miles of riding through the snow. He spoke to Thomas as he gathered up his gloves. "Do they all have horses?"

"There are seven wagons, carrying equipment and a few passengers. The rest are mounted, even the korrigans. I think we might as well sweep up all the other folk from the inn while we're at it, in case the snow gets deeper."

George whistled up his dogs and plunged out into the dark afternoon, plowing through the path to the stable to saddle his horse.

George looked up at the dark sky with its threatening clouds. The snow may have stopped but more was clearly on the way.

The two of them had the street to themselves at the moment and were able to ride side-by-side down the shallower snow in the middle, where the villagers had organized a log drag, a pole pulled behind a pair of horses that swept the top layer of snow to the side. They'd been sending a team out for the village streets every few hours for the last several days, and already the difference between the dragged and packed path and the untouched snow was a few inches. The full depth was approaching eight inches. Householders had cleared their own paths but were having a hard time keeping up with the persistent snowfall.

George had seen heavy snow occasionally in Virginia near the Blue Ridge, but even here in this otherworld version of the landscape, this much snow this early was considered unusual.

He stopped briefly at the Horned Man inn on the corner by the bridge to speak with Huw Bongam, the innkeeper. He gave his reins to Thomas to hold and stamped the snow from his feet before going in.

The main room was packed and noisy. The more fastidious fae were off in a group along one side, but the noisiest part of the crowd were korrigans. George had never seen so many of the dwarf-like folk all in one place. He'd only met the smith and his family at Greenway Court and a few traders as they came through.

Not many of the fae were as tall as George, at six foot four, and none were as broad. Huw Bongam had no difficulty spotting him as he came in, and made his way through the crowd. "Go back out on the porch, huntsman, or we'll never be able to hear ourselves." He pulled a cloak around himself and both stepped outside, where Thomas was waiting with the horses.

"I'm on my way to help Thomas with a new group at the Travelers' Way," George said. "Thought we might bundle up some of your guests and bring them with us, the ones who're headed for Edgewood."

"Well, you'd be doing me a favor, and that's no lie. I've got more than I can handle. I'm used to housing folks who are snowbound for a day or two, but this call of Rhys's for skilled craftsmen at Edgewood has brought out all the ambitious folks from Gwyn's domain, and a few from the old world, too. Do you know, I've even got lutins, looking to expand their opportunities?"

4

"Where are you putting them all?"

"It'll be the hayloft soon, if you don't take some of them with you."

"Alright, I'll go on and see what's come in at the Travelers' Way and get them ready to move out immediately, without stopping here. If you could sort out your 'keepers' from the ones that want to get one step closer to Edgewood, tell them I'll be back in about an hour with Thomas to lead them to Greenway Court."

"I'll do that," Huw replied.

Thomas spoke up. "Not all of the newly arrived people are prepared for this much early winter. Can you spare the loan of any blankets for the trip to the manor house?"

George added, "What about horses or wagons for the folks here? They'll have trouble walking in the snow, even if we help break more trail."

"I'll sort out some transportation and wraps for the journey, as much as I can spare, if you can get it back to me as soon as you can," Huw said.

"Much appreciated," George said. "If you can provide your own drivers, we'll house them and they can bring back the empty wagons with your gear, weather permitting, plus any villagers who might be feeling trapped at court."

With a nod, Huw went back inside and George remounted.

He rode with Thomas past the crossroads with the stone bridge on the right and turned into the cul-de-sac on the far left that led to the Travelers' Way. All the peace and quiet of the snowy streets fled as they heard the raised voices and clangor of the expedition, fresh from the more civilized old world of Gwyn's origins.

George hung back for a moment as Thomas rejoined the party. He saw seven wagons with goods and people, now shivering in the cold. There were a few fae on foot, and a couple of korrigans, but most of the travelers had heeded the instructions to come on horseback or with transport, and even the korrigans were mostly mounted on sturdy ponies, though they didn't all look like seasoned horsemen. To his dismay, he saw what must be wives and families for a few of the travelers, so there were several children to think of.

Thomas's reappearance drew the loudest speaker like a lodestone draws iron.

"A fine welcome this is, no one from the court and a foot of snow. How are we supposed to proceed?" This was from a tall fae, on the older side of middle-aged.

He put himself in front of the other fae as if he had taken charge of them, and they seemed to permit it, though George thought he detected hidden smiles as he continued to make a fuss. "We require some shelter in this wilderness. This is not what we were led to expect."

Thomas said, with great self-control, "My lord Cadugan, allow me to present George Talbot Traherne, the great-grandson of our prince Gwyn ap Nudd." He bowed from the saddle, and beckoned George forward.

"At last," Cadugan said, gratified. "His brother Edern ap Nudd summoned me as steward for the Edgewood lands, on behalf of his grandson Rhys. I'm eager to see that all of us get there as quickly as possible."

"I am pleased to meet you, sir, and all of you here," George said in his best political voice. "I apologize for our unseasonable weather, but we have yet to find a way to keep the snow from falling." This mild quip broke some of the tension, and the fractious crowd started to relax now that someone had appeared to take charge of them, someone acceptable to their leader.

One of the korrigan elders, a bearded man in practical woolens over a blue silk waistcoat came up to join Cadugan. He bowed. "I'm Tiernoc, elected leader for the journey for my folk." He offered his hand up to George.

George didn't dismount because he wanted the height to help direct the crowd, so he bowed low over his saddle to shake hands with the korrigan—very low, since Tiernoc was less than five feet tall.

"Are the two of you the leaders of everyone here, for now?" George asked.

"That's right," Tiernoc said, and Cadugan nodded.

"How many are you, including everyone?"

"Twenty-two fae," Cadugan said.

"And seventeen of my folk," Tiernoc added.

"Alright, here's the situation. We can't put you up at the inn because it's full with other snowbound travelers, and you're too many to just try to house in Greenhollow's homes. We're going to take your group and a party from the inn which is also headed to

Edgewood and bring all of you up to Gwyn at Greenway Court. From there you'll be able to get to Edgewood via the Guests' Way and a brief overland road to the Edgewood Way."

"How far is Gwyn's court?" Cadugan said. "We're not prepared for this weather."

"It's two miles, and the snow is deep. We have more wagons and horses coming from the inn, and as many blankets as they can spare. We'll organize trail-breakers in front. Everyone who can't ride will need to be in wagons so that no one's on foot."

Cadugan looked unhappy at this. "Can't we stop and warm up first?"

"I'm sorry, but the snow could restart at any time—look at the sky. Better to do one last push and be under sure shelter no matter what the weather brings next," George said.

He walked his horse back to Thomas who was issuing instructions to the four rangers with him. "You were right," he said privately, "like oil on troubled waters. Here you have two centuries of experience, and they wanted a member of the family instead." He shook his head.

"I'm headed over to the inn to get that batch organized. If you'll give me two of your men and keep two for yourself we can each arrange our groups into a trail-breaking order and then shuffle them together as they cross the bridge. What do you think?"

"That'll work," Thomas said. "Heavy horses in front to break trail, then light horses, wagons, and ponies at the rear. Don't forget blankets for this group, I don't like the looks of some of them in the wagons. And don't delay, that snow won't hold off forever."

Before entering the inn, George set Thomas's two men to sending on one of Huw Bongam's wagons to the other group, then coordinating the wagons of the inn's party. They'd line those up in the road and free up some space in the stable yard to maneuver the horses. George had a private word with one of the grooms to hold his horse tacked up but under shelter to spare him as much of the cold as possible.

He walked into the inn's main room, bringing his dogs with him, and beckoned Huw over. "Do you think we could send some hot tea and maybe something stronger down to the Travelers' Way? There are about forty people in the snow and some of them are shivering with the cold."

7

"I've already taken that in hand. The wagon they're getting carries fifteen blankets, three gallons of tea, and a nice hot toddy for any who wants it. Let me go see about the rest of the preparations in the stable yard."

"Good work."

Many of the crowd had turned to watch him standing in the entrance. George knocked loudly on the door frame for silence and addressed them. "In one hour we'll lead a party from here with a group from the Travelers' Way up to Greenway Court. If you're trying to go on to Edgewood, I strongly advise you to join us, since the snow could start again at any time. We can house you at the court until the weather allows you to continue your journey."

"Be warned," he continued, "The snow is deep and it's about two miles. We'll break trail for the vehicles as we go and there should be a place in the wagons for anyone who isn't mounted, but I urge you to ride if you can to leave room for others. Can I see a show of hands for anyone who plans to join us?"

A rising hubbub filled the room at the news, though George didn't doubt that Huw Bongam had already warned them this was coming. About a dozen fae raised their hands, and many more korrigans. Five lutins made their way through the crowd to the front, too, all dressed in red and a bit shorter even than the korrigans.

George called again for silence. "If you don't have a mount and need a place in the wagons, come up to me now for a moment. I'd also like to see a leader for each group, someone who can keep track of its members before and during the ride so that we don't leave anyone behind. Everyone else, start packing. And be quick about it."

Two fae and a korrigan joined the lutins in front as most of the rest of the crowd dispersed to pack their belongings.

The elder fae spoke first. "I'm Meilyr. All of us are from elsewhere in Gwyn's domains and came at his call. We have four in our party who are traveling to Edgewood as masters in their crafts. One of those is a colleague of Ceridwen. There are seven others who are seeking family long lost to them. I'm one of those."

"Will you hold yourself responsible for their names and making sure of their whereabouts for our journey to the court?" George asked.

"I will."

"Do any need wagons?"

"The craft masters brought equipment but we have our own wagons to haul it. All are mounted."

"Thank you. Please assemble your wagons on the party already out front and take your instructions from the rangers there."

The lutins came forward, led by one middle-aged lutine. She said, "I'm Rozenn. Some of us are looking for lost family, and others are seeking employment. I'll be responsible for our names and well-being, but we'll all need places in the wagons, with our goods."

"Thanks, Mistress Rozenn. Please bring your people and your goods to me here. I'll hold all the wagon loads in one place until we're sure how many will be required."

As she left, Huw Bongam returned. "How about it, huntsman? Do you know how many wagons you'll need from here yet?"

"So far, it looks like there are five lutins and their gear who will need transport, but the rest are accounted for. So, just the one wagon. What's the news from Thomas?"

"He thinks he only needs the one wagon I sent him for his group, so it's not as bad as I feared. I'll send out two drivers who can bring them back when the weather permits." He sighed. "It makes me think of Isolda, your party of lutins needing a driver. I can't get used to her being gone. She'd have loved the adventure."

George frowned and gripped his shoulder. He turned back to the senior korrigan who was waiting patiently to speak.

"I'm Broch, and I'll take charge of the fifteen of us from Gwyn's domains. We, too, are craft masters and traders, hoping to re-open the route to Edgewood. We've brought our own wagons, and a few of us are riding as well. I've already sent our folks to assemble in the road with the others."

One person was left waiting near the door, a fae who looked a bit younger than George. Unlike almost all the dark-haired fae George had met, he was redheaded and freckled.

"Not part of Meilyr's group?" George said.

"No," he said, smiling sardonically. "I'm just a lowly provincial musician—Cydifor. But I have hopes. No one said anything about Rhys Vachan having any musicians at Edgewood."

"I've been there and I don't remember any. But, you know, his cousin Rhodri is one, himself?"

Cydifor's face fell, and George laughed.

"Don't worry. Rhodri's not there to stay for the long-term, and in the meantime he's likely to prove a friend. I imagine he's tired of playing by himself for his own amusement. Do you need transport?"

"I have a horse, but I'd appreciate space in a wagon for my gear, to ease the burden on her."

"No problem," George said. "Bring it here with the lutins' bundles and then go mount up."

Cydifor looked at George with unapologetic curiosity. "Did I hear Huw Bongam call you huntsman? Are you Gwyn's new huntsman? I came through Danderi just after the great hunt and heard all about it."

"I'm sorry, I didn't introduce myself properly. I'm George Talbot Traherne, Gwyn ap Nudd's great-grandson and, yes, his new huntsman."

"I heard that someone died at the start," Cydifor said, tentatively.

"That was Isolda of whom we were speaking. She had just started working as a driver. She was only eighteen and newly-betrothed, and she gave her life to save Gwyn's foster-daughter from death at the hands of Cyledr Wyllt."

"Who became the quarry of the great hunt."

"Yes. He's gone now." There was satisfaction in George's voice.

"Excuse me, but someone said you were human."

"It's true, more or less. I was brought here when the old huntsman was murdered. It's a long story, for another time."

Cydifor persisted. "They also said you hunted as the horned man."

"As I said, a long story. We can speak at the manor house later."

Cydifor took the dismissal in good humor and went off to gather his possessions.

George took a look around as he hurried off. He waved a hand at the locals who were left in the inn's main room and went off to check on the assembly in the road.

❧

George and his men finished loading the borrowed wagon and helping the smaller lutins scramble in. Their driver hastened out to join them, still munching the end of his meal and fastening his coat.

As he mounted up to ride the length of the group standing in front of the inn, George considered how long it would take to get the two groups together and then up two miles of snowy road before dark or the next storm. Probably about two hours, if nothing breaks down. He pulled out his pocket watch on its chain and confirmed that he had about that much daylight left. It was going to be close.

He spoke to Meilyr and Broch as he passed and got their assurance that everyone in their groups was accounted for, waved at Cydifor, and checked with Mistress Rozenn that all the lutins were set, with blankets piled around them, Cydifor's instruments, and George's dogs at their feet, to keep them out of the way.

"Alright," he called to Thomas's men. "Let's move 'em out."

The horses at front of the line, including his own heavy Mosby, started out first, packing the snow down more tightly for the wagons that followed them. The korrigans, on their smaller horses and ponies, followed behind the heavier horses. The squeak of the dry snow combined with the rumble of the wagons and the creak of the horses' saddles and harnesses to make it a noisy departure. Some of the drinkers at the inn waved from the doorway as they pulled out, the light behind them shining out onto the road under the darkened sky.

They didn't have far to go. George held them short of the bridge and saw Thomas leading his group out of the gloom from the left. All the riders were as well-bundled as possible, and the people on the wagons had made good use of Huw Bongam's blankets.

George walked Mosby over to confer with Thomas. "How do you want to do this?"

Thomas said, "Two of my men at the back, two along the sides moving up and down to keep them moving, and the two of us in front. I'll have one of them do a count as they go by, so we know how many wagons and riders. Let me start out ahead to make sure there's no special problem with the road. You come along on your horse at the head of the line to reassure them as we go." He gave some last instructions to one of his men, then wheeled his horse around and crossed the bridge.

George turned back to the foot of the bridge, a grin tugging at one side of his mouth. He was going to be the master of a wagon train, if only for a couple of hours. Too bad he didn't have a cattle herd to go with it and a good Stetson hat.

He faced the two lines of riders and wagons and raised his hand for attention. The groups quieted.

"Listen up. We have about two hours of daylight and it should be enough. We're going to cross this bridge and go up the road on the far side of the stream, to the right. It's a gentle slope, but uphill all the way. At the end is the lower gate of the manor house and one more brief climb up to where we'll unload and get under shelter.

"Keep track of your neighbors. Don't leave the line under any circumstances. If anything happens, a child falls overboard, anything, call for help from one of Thomas Kethin's riders. Make sure your group leaders know where you are and, leaders, keep track of your people. It's not that cold, but you don't want to be outside overnight, wandering in the dark.

"We're going to line up in sections. All riders on larger horses first, beginning with the group from the inn, then those from the way. Stick together with your group. The riders on shorter animals next, both groups. Then the wagons, starting with the lutins from the inn and then the rest of the inn party, and last the other wagons," gesturing at the group from the Travelers' Way. "Try to spread out on the road several abreast with your horses so the wagons behind you have better traction for their wheels. We'll swap the leaders as we go so your horses can get a break."

He paused. "Any questions?" No one replied.

Thomas trotted back over the bridge and joined him. "There are footprints, someone small, headed up the road since we came through earlier. Keep an eye out for him."

CHAPTER 2

Maëlys looked up at the sky and despaired of finishing another mile and more before darkness fell. She hadn't expected the roads to be so deep in snow, dragging on her skirts and her cloak and making each step a misery.

She'd started south of Greenhollow at mid-morning. It was only five miles and she'd been sure she had plenty of time, but it was getting harder and harder to move her feet, and she was worried about being trapped on the road at nightfall with nowhere for shelter.

This is what comes of refusing to listen to Brittou, she thought, and waiting for the roads to clear. The farm manager for Iona's stock-raising operation south of the village had been kind to her after her husband Luhedoc was given up for missing in that last sweep of lutins into Edgewood, and she was grateful. He'd recently proposed marriage, at this stage in their lives, but she couldn't make him understand that she still felt bonded to her husband, even after eighteen years. Now that the holder of Edgewood had been unseated, she had to find out what had happened to him, to all the lutins who didn't come back.

She could picture his crooked grin even now, the one he wore when a trick he'd set up succeeded. She wanted his biggest trick to have been survival, whatever was wrong with the place that had trapped him.

She heard a panting noise behind her and turned. Out of the mist, a great beast came lunging toward her through the snow. She lifted a foot to run, and then realized it was just a big hound, baying with delight that he'd found her and dancing around her in exuberance.

❧

"Get back here," George yelled at Hugo as the hound leapt from the wagon of lutins and dashed up the road into the gloom, but before he could reinforce it with a mental call, he felt what his hound had smelled, a presence up ahead. He pushed forward at a trot on Mosby, his big gray Percheron/Thoroughbred cross.

He'd expected someone on the road ahead from the footsteps crossing the bridge, but he was unprepared for a middle-aged lutine, wet and exhausted, pestered by a hound almost her own size. "Good boy, Hugo. Now leave her alone," he said to his dog, who settled down with an air of pride in his find.

"Sorry about that, ma'am," he said. "Headed to the manor house?"

She nodded wearily.

"You must have just beaten us to the bridge. Let me give you a ride on one of the wagons."

With that, he reached down to her upraised hands and lifted her up, pack and all, to a seat sitting sideways behind him. She wasn't big enough to reach around his waist, so he swept his left arm behind him awkwardly to hold her and turned his horse back through the rest of the horsemen to the first wagon. Coming alongside the stopped wagon of lutins, he carefully lowered her down again, not releasing his grip until he was sure she was standing firmly on the wagon bed.

"Thanks for holding onto my other dog," he said to one of Rozenn's party who had a firm grip on the smaller feist. Hugo," he called, "Get over here." He dismounted to lift the heavy hound into the wagon, brushing off as much of the snow on him as he could reach to spare the other passengers.

"I'm Gwyn's huntsman, George Talbot Traherne," he said to the rescued lutine, as he remounted.

"My name's Maëlys. I've come from Iona and Brittou, seeking my husband in Edgewood."

Rozenn put an arm around her and sat her down in the midst of the warm nest of blankets. "Many of us are looking for family, too," she told her.

As he left to rejoin the head of the wagon train, he called down to her, "If you have any trouble finding housing when we get there, ask for me." Behind him, the wagons started forward again.

c⁓ɔ

A knock on his door warned Madog of the entry of a servant bearing mulled wine. The man bowed low, placed the tray on a sideboard, and left silently.

Madog took advantage of the interruption to lay his pen down and rise from the table, scattered with papers, that occupied the back half of his private study. Warming his hands with a cup of the wine, he walked over to the windows and looked to the east.

He never tired of this view. Naturally, nine hundred years ago, he had caused his court to be built defensively high, up the steep trail from the valley floor, right on the northern tip of the mountain keel that bisected the broad valley of the Horse River, the Dyffran Camarch. His special discovery later made this physical defense unnecessary, but he admired the prospect of the Blue Ridge to his east from this height so much that he determined to live with the inconvenience of bringing goods and people up the mountain to keep his court there. It represented his ambitions and reminded him, constantly, of Annwn, just over the deadly ridge he couldn't cross directly.

After all, he was not the one discommoded by the location, not since his little find. He glanced at the corner of the room, where his way-adept senses easily detected the entrance of his small personal passage to the village at the bottom of the trail. That was a successful creation, he thought, not like some of the other earlier ones, while he was still learning what he could achieve.

Creiddylad would miss this snow, he thought. He was surprised at how she'd grown on him, now that they were forced together, her pride of birth humbled by the renunciation of her brothers Gwyn and Edern. When she finally saw his court for the first time and realized his strength, that he wasn't just the obliging and cunning younger adviser she'd thought him, she was both grateful and gratified, inclined to meet him on equal standing, her age and birth against his new world power.

They restructured their alliance, sealed at last by consort status since they had lost the need to keep up pretensions. He'd have to be careful about that as always. He intended to raise no other way-adepts here, not even of his own blood. It was pesky the way that skill cropped up every now and then and had to be eliminated, even after all this time, but he prided himself on his thoroughness.

Creiddylad was no longer constrained by family squeamishness and was fully behind his plans to unseat her one-time brother Gwyn. Madog was glad, now, that he'd taken her with him after she'd backed him at the great hunt, even though that plan had failed.

Right now she was reveling in her new freedom. Though still under banishment by her grandfather Beli Mawr for her old role in creating the feud between Gwyn and her ex-husband Gwythyr ap Greidawl, she had perfected the art of traveling under a glamour and thought the risk of detection was low. Gwyn couldn't touch her here and, if she was discreet, no one would notice her in Britain.

He frowned at that. His way to Britain, the one he'd found nine hundred years ago from the other end, was still a closely held secret. It wasn't enough that he controlled its use through the way-tokens—he didn't want its location, or even its existence, generally known. If Creiddylad's glamour were detected, it would raise many questions about how she'd gotten there. She knew this, but he wasn't confident it would make her more cautious. What will she do if she runs into some of her old friends? Will she try and spy on Gwythyr?

Well, he couldn't do anything about her from here. He had his hands full with the new situation at Edgewood, working out what could be salvaged from the wreckage of his prior plan.

He took another sip of the heated wine, the spices tingling in his mouth.

Can my work go forward? Well, why not? Gwyn may know more about me now, I've lost that element of surprise, but what can he do about it? None of them can reach me. I control all the ways into the great valley of the river, and none of us can't cross the ridge overland. With my barrier in place, they can't even go around the long way.

The barrier I built at Edgewood for Creiddylad is still working, and the little beast grows stronger every day. It was stubborn this morning, but unable to resist his will. I wonder what else I can do with it? How big will it get?

What could stop me? That Rhodri there, Gwyn's way-finder, he's no threat, I think, and Gwyn had very limited powers with the ways himself.

The huntsman's a puzzle. My spies insist he's the one who shut down the Hidden Way after the great hunt, though they don't talk much about it over there. It's hard to believe, he's just a human distantly descended from Gwyn. It was odd how Cernunnos rode him at the great hunt. That didn't happen to the old huntsman

Iolo. Maybe it only happens with human huntsmen, because they're weaker than true fae.

There were very few humans in his domain, since none of his ways went to their world. The few he had were taken from Gwyn's domain, for his research. He'd experimented with breeding here, and verified that the powers always declined with human blood in the mix, usually in the first generation. It satisfied him to have information he could count on, rather than just relying on the writings of scholars. Always better to know for sure, and the fields always needed more workers.

Still, the Hidden Way that he'd created so long ago was truly gone, and no other explanation seemed to be available.

I can't destroy a way. Did the huntsman do that? Was it Cernunnos, riding him? Can I learn it from him or is he just some sort of freak?

It seemed to be common knowledge there that he sealed the way to Edgewood at the river meadow, the one I built for the ambush on Gwyn. It was a good idea, too, would have worked if the huntsman hadn't disrupted it. No matter—I may have lost control from the Daear Llosg end at Greenway Court, but when this snow lets up, I'll go back and close the other end, at least. It bothered him that it was still open, an untidy loose end from the older plan.

And either the huntsman or Rhodri destroyed the Court Way outside Edgewood's manor. Lot of good that'll do them. I just made a new one. That should keep them stirred up. He grinned. *Still, we can't have that going on.*

The Trap Way should close the gate nicely, keep them all corralled up into a single pen at Edgewood. He'd refined the process since the capture of Rhys ap Edern and his consort Eiryth and their retainers twelve years ago. That had been riskier, he'd had to bring the little beast with him all the way to Britain, and it turned out he couldn't control things well enough to keep his captives alive, though Gwythyr made no complaints.

This time, he'd try for Rhys's son, the one he'd missed twelve years ago, and keep him alive, if he could. He'd launched the first step this morning, despite the beast's odd resistance. *Let's see how they like that.* Clean up a loose end and take a hostage to manipulate Gwyn. Scilti would no doubt appreciate someone new to play with.

No mistakes this time.

⌒⌒⌒

"I think there'll be at least forty in this party that Thomas Kethin went to fetch," Gwyn said to Ifor, as they stood outside the main stables at Greenway Court.

"Where will we put them all?" his steward asked. "The stables are mostly full up, and the barracks are getting crowded."

"We'll take the warehouses nearest the balineum and turn them into impromptu barracks. That way they can use the baths across the lane. Anyone who finds that beneath his dignity for a night or two can look for individual hospitality at dinner."

"That would work, especially if we stand the wagons they'll be bringing right next to the buildings, to minimize the work of loading or unloading."

"Better leave them loaded if we can, and tie down covers over them in case of more snow," Gwyn advised.

"Alright, my lord, so much for the people. But what about the horses?"

"The stables are large, if overfull. We'll tie them in the aisles for now, it'll have to do."

A guard appeared on foot at the gate in the south curtain wall, breathing hard from a run up the cleared but uphill path. Ifor waved an arm to catch his attention and called him over.

"What news?" Ifor said.

"Thomas Kethin just rode ahead to meet us at the gate, sir." The guard paused to take a breath. "He asked me to let you know that he and the huntsman are bringing in two groups at once, one from the Traveler's Way and one from the inn. I'm to tell you that there are altogether thirty-four fae, thirty-two korrigans, and six lutins, with fourteen wagons, two of which belong to Huw Bongam, and he sent two drivers for them, too. Oh, and there are families and children included."

Ifor did a quick estimate. "That's got to be at least eighty or ninety horses, my lord. We'll need all the stable hands out just to keep track of them for a day or two."

Gwyn said, "Off you go, then. You organize the reception as they come in. Set someone to find Idris for me, and send me our people and the leaders of the travelers' parties. We'll set up food and drink in the great hall. And don't forget those covers for the wagons."

George stamped into the entry hall at the back of the manor through the double doors, shedding the snow from his boots. He found Rhian patting herself to make sure everything was in place. He assumed she'd just changed out of kennel clothes into something better suited to Gwyn's foster-daughter.

She turned as the rear double-doors thumped open. "Cousin," she said, "You're not supposed to be here. Where's Angharad?"

"Tell me about it," he said, wryly. "Not easy to get a honeymoon going."

"What's this group like?"

"A mixed bag of all sorts. I'll stick around to help with introductions."

She flashed him a look of gratitude. At fourteen, she was young to stand there alone as hostess on her foster-father's behalf and was glad of the support.

George took a moment to park his dogs in front of the fire in the hunting room that opened off the back entrance. They'd wait for him there, warm and out of the way.

The first travelers began to trickle in. Rhian took the lead in greeting them, and George ferried them to the comfort rooms on the side of the entry hall or to the great hall beyond, with its crackling fire and platters of food, depending on their most urgent needs. The three-story cavernous hall was relatively warm with its constant fire, the raised dais at the north end making it clear where the family took its meals.

When Huw Bongam's two drivers came in, he pulled them aside.

"Do you want to try and return tonight, or wait for morning?"

One looked at the other. "If you can put us up, I think we'd rather do it in full daylight, huntsman."

"You could get trapped here, if the snow returns," he warned them, but they shrugged.

"Alright, then, but better collect Huw's blankets now, before stopping for the day," George said.

A pile of personal belongings had begun to accumulate in one corner of the great hall, whatever had been carried with them on horseback for those who rode.

The noise of more than sixty people relaxing and eating filled the lobby as well, conversations rising as everyone warmed up. The sound of children, even crying, was more welcome than silent, shivering faces, George thought.

He walked into the great hall with Huw's drivers and raised a hand for attention. "If you borrowed some of the blankets from the inn, please return them to these men here. If you left them in the wagons, tell them so that they can fetch them in the morning." Privately he said to the drivers, "If you come up short, let me know."

"Group leaders, please come with me," he continued, operating under Ifor's instructions. "Rhian, you, too," he said. He walked through the crowd and singled out Maëlys and Cydifor, traveling without leaders, and brought them along with him, ushering the whole group into Gwyn's council room through the doorway on the other side of the raised dais.

CHAPTER 3

Gwyn glanced up from his conversation with his steward Ifor as George brought in the leaders. Idris and Thomas Kethin were already seated around the long table in his council chamber, having delegated most of the tasks of seeing to the travelers to their subordinates. A fire warmed the room behind him, near his desk. Ceridwen walked about the large room while waiting and returned to the table as George came in.

His foster-daughter Rhian slipped in behind George's group to take her seat next to Ceridwen. She's still not certain I won't revoke the privilege, Gwyn noted with amusement, after I let her start attending these sessions a few weeks ago. George remained standing with his people, waiting for everyone's notice, and Gwyn took advantage of the moment's delay to look them over. Three fae, two korrigans, and two lutines. That older fae must be Cadugan, the steward his brother Edern sent for. I hope he's more useful than he seems, Gwyn thought, as the fae stood there impatiently waiting for attention.

He nodded at George to proceed.

"My lord Gwyn, let me present a few of your guests. This is Cadugan, come at Edern's invitation to help Rhys at Edgewood." The fae executed a credible court bow and straightened up stiffly. "He leads a party of some twenty-two fae from Britain."

"Next to him is Meilyr, leading eleven from within your domain." Meilyr made a respectful bow, but without the old world flourishes.

"I've included Cyledr, from your domains, who is traveling by himself, a musician." Cyledr, much abashed in this company, managed a jerky dip of his head.

George moved on to the korrigans. "May I present also Tiernoc, leading seventeen of his folk from Britain, and Broch, with fifteen from your own domain." Both executed similar formal bows, sweeping their hats off at the same time.

"Finally, this is Mistress Rozenn with a group of five, and Maëlys whom we picked up on the road, all from Annwn." The two women curtsied.

George turned to them all and said, "This is my lord Gwyn ap Nudd, Prince of Annwn, whose guests you are. You've met Thomas Kethin, his head ranger, and Rhian, his foster-daughter. Here also are Idris, his marshal, Ifor Moel, his steward, and my lady Ceridwen, his scholar and healer.

Gwyn stood. "Welcome to all of you and thank you for coming. Please find seats. I'm sure you're weary from your travels, and I'll try not to keep you long."

He reseated himself and waited for them all to settle.

"Please be assured that we'll be glad to house and feed you all until you can move on to Edgewood. You won't be going any further this evening, and the weather controls what will happen next, but the remainder of your journey should be easier."

He pointed to the southeast. "Our Guests' Way entrance is just outside the manor gates you passed through. It will take you to our Eastern Shore estate, and within a couple of miles of easy ground with little snow, you will find the entrance to the Edgewood Way, which exits right at the court. There will be snow at Edgewood, as here—it's about fifty miles due north of us—but I understand the ground around the buildings has been cleared."

Thomas Kethin added, "Those of you who were on borrowed wagons, we'll be returning those wagons tomorrow but we'll supply you with substitutes."

Cadugan spoke up impatiently. "Can't we start sooner? I'm eager to begin work after all these delays."

Gwyn raised an eyebrow, but Cadugan stood his ground. "Let me suggest that you use this time to meet with your counterparts here and start to forge those alliances you'll need to be effective." Cadugan reluctantly nodded.

"Please let me explain to you what you'll be joining," Gwyn said. He leaned back to begin the familiar tale he'd told to two previous bands of travelers.

"Soon after I removed Annwn to the new world, about 1500 years ago, I granted my exiled sister Creiddylad an estate of her own, to spare her living forever at our father's court." The guests nodded their heads; most had heard the tale before.

"Edgewood had only one way, and I controlled the tokens, of course, so it was easy to keep her confined. She, in retaliation, prevented her own people from using the way, too, and so they were shut off from the rest of my domain. From time to time, she allowed settlers to enter through the way, but no one has returned for a very long time." Everyone listened attentively.

"Overland travel was always possible, of course, but we've met no settlers from Edgewood outside those lands, and none of the people we've sent there to investigate in the last several hundred years has come back.

"At this most recent Nos Galan Gaeaf, at the end of the year, we held the great hunt with my kinsman and huntsman," he pointed his chin at George. "For good and sufficient reason, my brother Edern and I renounced our sister afterward and banished her from my domain. Therefore, Edgewood has been free of her for just five weeks after all this time and, as you've heard, I've appointed my foster-son Rhys, my brother's grandson, to hold it and began to repair the damage she caused.

"Before you proceed, you must now hear that we have a newly unveiled enemy, Madog, a way-adept. He holds lands to the west of the mountains and for hundreds of years he has influenced Creiddylad and her doings at Edgewood. We believe she's with him now. He wishes me and mine no good and he may try to do harm here or at Edgewood—be warned."

He cleared his throat. "So much for the past. Let me tell you what we found when we reopened the closed way to Edgewood." He gestured to his marshal Idris to continue the tale.

"I'll just give you a summary since we're discovering more each day. To begin with, we can find no trace of the lutins or korrigans that we know were there at one time, some as recently as just a few years ago." This brought a gasp from several at the table. "Let me be clear, we don't know if they're dead, hiding, or captive, or even if they've somehow left the territory. In the case of the lutins, there's reason to think they're in hiding—there are reports of unexplained activities that remind us of the tricks they can play on humans." Gwyn saw Rozenn smile faintly at that.

"The fae that are there are... changed in some way. Craft masters have diminished and the levels of skill in all areas have deteriorated. Trade is minimal. The farmers on the outskirts of the land are worse, and there is some sort of barrier surrounding the lands. We don't understand it, but it's reminiscent of the barrier that marks the ridge line of the Blue Ridge mountain to our west. If you don't live locally, you may not understand the comparison; fae and others can't cross that line without damage or death." Gwyn noted Cadugan rolling his eyes, but Meilyr nodded thoughtfully. "The barrier at Edgewood wasn't there when the lands were first given to Creiddylad, and we don't know when it appeared or how it was made, but it may explain why there have been no known overland crossings in either direction."

Gwyn said, "Let me tell you what's been done in the last five weeks. My brother Edern is serving as Rhys's chancellor. I've provided a marshal, Lleision, and a weapons-master, Morial, from my own staff. I've also placed my kinsman Rhodri, a way-adept, on Rhys's council.

"At the urging of both Edern and me, Rhys has sent out an invitation to settlers and especially craft-masters to help restart the community. Those of you who will be settling in Edgewood will be holding Rhys as your lord. Some of you are planning only a temporary stay, and that's acceptable—no one will be required to stay if they wish to leave. That includes the current inhabitants, once we sort out the situation.

"We've also set up a courier service. Every afternoon, a rider bearing messages arrives at both Edgewood and here, one from each direction." At least, so far. Today's messenger from Rhys was hours late.

He paused to refocus his attention. "Would you please, each of you, tell us something about who you're bringing to Edgewood?"

To no one's surprise, Cadugan was the first to step forward. He said, "As you know, Edern has asked me to serve as steward. I would like to meet with you, Ifor, afterward," bowing to him, "to begin sorting out how the staff I brought with me should be arranged to cause the least disruption." Ifor nodded.

"I understand that there are three main villages in Edgewood, so I've recruited whatever craft-masters were willing to come without worrying too much about possible duplication." Gwyn thought that unusually practical for someone of his precise temperament. Perhaps he would prove suitable after all, ballast to Rhys's youth and inexperience. Edern was usually right about the staff he recommended.

"Some of our people brought their families, and perhaps they didn't understand the degree of danger involved. On the other hand, all are eager for an opportunity to prove themselves at a new court. Those vacancies are not easy to find, in the old world."

He turned to Ceridwen. "My lady, one of my party is for you, Eluned. I'll have her seek you out afterward."

Meilyr said, "Most of my group met for the first time at the inn. We've come from all over your domain, my lord," nodding to Gwyn, "some as craft-masters, same as Cadugan's, and several seeking kin lost to us these many hundreds of years. I, myself, am looking for one of my sons. I think more will continue to come in for a while, as the word spreads."

Tiernoc leaned over the table to face Gwyn. "Crafts we want, of course—smithies and iron work—but trade especially. Some of us have never traded in the new world at all, shame to them, and others just want a chance to see what opportunities are here. A few of us are miners in the old way, seeking to join our kinsmen, prospecting.

Broch nodded along and spoke to him, "We welcome you, friend. Let's meet afterward and discuss mutual ventures here." Turning to Gwyn, "And a few of us seek family and friends, too. There are many wanting to know what's happened to them."

Rozenn in her turn said, shyly, "Most of us are looking for our families, but some also want new opportunities. Many more wait at home to hear what we find and may come themselves, depending."

Gwyn glanced enquiringly at Maëlys, seated next to Rozenn. She said, quietly, "I'm searching for my husband, my lord, gone eighteen years. I'm from down the road, at Iona's place."

The last, Cydifor, gathered his nerve. "I'm from Tredin, my lord. Thought I'd see if your foster-son could use a musician."

Gwyn hid his smile. Tredin had perhaps ten families—large families, with a reputation for seeding their children widely all over his domain as soon as they could travel. Small wonder this one was motivated to try his chances elsewhere.

He rose to end the meeting. "We'll send you out tomorrow mid-day, weather permitting."

The travelers pushed back from the table and left, all except Cadugan whom Gwyn asked to stay behind. It was time to go into more detailed discussions about the situation, and Cadugan would need any information he could get to do his job for Rhys.

As things settled down, Gwyn leaned over to speak with George.

"I'm sorry to see you pulled away from Angharad again. I know how newlyweds like their privacy."

We should have done it in my world and eloped to Maui, George thought, but he contented himself with saying, "It couldn't be helped, sir, we understand. There were just too many people, and they needed reassurance."

Gwyn looked around the table. "I wanted to take this opportunity to bring us up to date together and to let Cadugan catch up. Idris, Ceridwen, please give us a summary of where we are right now."

Idris looked at Ceridwen and she gestured to him to start first, Rhian attentive by her side.

"We've got a working government established, with Edern as chancellor, Lleision as marshal, and Rhodri as an expert on the ways. The biggest concern is defense, with Madog still unaccounted for, and Morial has started recruiting and training. The fae furthest from the boundaries of the territory are most unaffected and are beginning to revive again, a little, now that they see hope and new life."

"That's the good news," he said. "On the other hand, we have hospitals that barely function, the schools are just... gone, and all the buildings and fields show the despair of centuries clearly upon them. We need basic crafts-masters, as Rhys has been recruiting, and education for such children as remain, and maybe for some adults, too."

George asked, "What about the fae with families?"

"A few have asked about their families elsewhere, which we take as a good sign, but we need a policy about opening the way altogether, not just letting the emigrants in but the residents out, and when. With a caution—what would happen if they all decide to leave, small blame to them?"

Rhian said, "What about the lutins? Has anyone found them?"

"Your brother Rhys has taken them as his special responsibility, with the korrigans, but there's no sign yet other than those I alluded to earlier: horses groomed in the stalls, lost cows restored, and so forth. The old tasks."

Ifor told Cadugan, "One other piece of good news—the crops did well at Edgewood and no one will suffer for a hard winter, if we can reach everyone. And we've sufficient here to support the visitors as well as ourselves, if we must."

Ceridwen filled in her part. "As Idris says, the schools have vanished, and most of the healers, too. I'm coming along on this next trip to re-establish everything again, and Eluned will be my delegate after I return."

Gwyn asked George. "Can you explain for Cadugan where we are with the ways at Edgewood?" He turned to Cadugan to elaborate, "My great-grandson has demonstrated some interesting way-adept capabilities since his arrival, but there hasn't been enough time to train him properly."

George leaned forward. "The Edgewood Way seems to be operating normally since Rhodri opened it and remade the way tokens. On my two visits he and I rode as much of the estate as we could reach in a short time looking for any other ways, especially the other end of the way that reaches to Daear Llosg, the Archer's Way, I think they're calling it now. That's still open but sealed at our end, and we assumed the other end would be open as well, since Madog didn't get to use it as an escape when he fled after the great hunt. We hope that it communicates with Edgewood.

"You may not have heard that we did find one small way not far from the house, one that hadn't been there when Edgewood was built. Rhodri and I decided to shut it down for greater security, Rhys and Edern concurring, and I collapsed it, like Madog's Hidden Way outside our palisade after the great hunt. We haven't found any other ways." Not yet anyway, he thought.

He caught Cadugan's skeptical glance. It wasn't supposed to be possible to completely eliminate a way.

"I felt a hint of something down at the southern end on my last visit, but we didn't get that far on horseback and I can't say for sure whether or not it's the end of the Archer's Way at the river meadow. I'd like to know; another access direct from here would be useful, even if it's some distance overland at the Edgewood end."

He sat back in his chair and summarized for Cadugan's benefit. "That's my highest priority task, on my next visit, to track down what I thought I felt at the south end of the estate. It's at least fifteen miles from Edgewood's manor, though, so it may have to wait until there's less snow on the ground."

Ceridwen broke in. "You haven't heard. Rhodri sent word yesterday that the way you destroyed has been replaced recently, however impossible that may seem. He says it's definitely a different way, a bit larger and not in exactly the same place. It's owned so he can't claim it. They have it under guard."

"Is it Madog?" George said, surprised. "Can he just make ways at will? I thought that couldn't be done."

"It does seem that our knowledge is... insufficient," Gwyn said.

George said, "I still don't understand why no one ever left overland to report on the doings at Edgewood."

Ceridwen said, "The fae who live closest to the barrier, whatever it is, are also the furthest from the manor, and Rhys has had his hands full, pulled in many directions. They just haven't investigated very far into it, yet."

Idris said to Cadugan, "Rhys and Lleision have been concentrating on defense, and this new way is a direct threat. I've been getting reports daily from Edern's couriers, what George here has been calling the Pony Express."

He turned to face Gwyn, "Do you have today's reports, my lord? In the confusion of the travelers' arrival, I haven't seen them yet."

Gwyn said quietly. "The messenger hasn't come."

Into the shocked silence, Rhian said, tentatively, "Maybe he's been delayed by the snow?"

Gwyn shook his head doubtfully.

A knock sounded on the door, and one of Idris's men stuck his head in. "It's snowing again, my lord."

Gwyn pushed back from the table. "It's getting on and you have tasks to occupy you. I'll see you all at dinner."

Dismissed, Cadugan and Gwyn's council members took their leave, Cadugan going over details with Ifor and Ceridwen as they clustered near the door.

George held Ifor back for a moment. "If there's any problem housing Cydifor or Maélys, assign them to me. They're each traveling alone and are probably feeling a bit lost, and I told Maélys I'd watch out for her."

He let Ifor go then but lingered on to speak with Gwyn.

"As long as I'm here anyway, sir, I should go with them," waving at the travelers in the great hall outside, "and see if I can help Rhodri with this new way."

"I was going to recommend that," Gwyn said.

"I have a question that's been bothering me about the ways, though. Perhaps you know the answer? I still don't understand what's normal, what to expect. I haven't been through very many of them yet."

"Yes?"

"What I wanted to know was, why do most of the ways have a passage, a little distance to traverse between one end and the other?"

"They all do," Gwyn said, puzzled.

"Well, no, they don't, not all of them. The one that you opened at the bridge for Nos Galan Gaeaf, for the great hunt, and the ones that Cernunnos opened during the hunt itself—those were all immediate, without passages."

"Yes, you're right. Those are exceptions."

"The one that brought me here, what Rhodri now calls the Huntsman's Way, has no passage, either."

"I didn't know that," Gwyn said slowly. "Perhaps Cernunnos has his own methods and the few scholars who write about the ways haven't attended the great hunt and seen them. It seems there's a lot we've been taking for granted about how the ways work."

He looked hard at George. "Given your presumed relationship, did Cernunnos open the Huntsman's Way, or did you?"

George said, "I have no idea how to open a way. I didn't know they existed, before I came here."

But since then you've destroyed two, enlarged one, and sealed one, he thought to himself. It's no surprise that Gwyn asks the question.

CHAPTER 4

"Alun?" George called as he opened the front door to the huntsman's house, along the lane nearest the kennels in the extensive grounds behind the manor. His dogs padded in behind him. There was no reply. Alun wouldn't have expected him back today and must be out on his own business.

I have just this evening to myself, he thought, before this batch goes off to Rhys and me with them. Unless it snows again.

He hung his outer coat near the back door and considered. If it snows, I'll get that Christmas tree I've been promising myself. That'll be a short jaunt into the woods nearby and I know just the little balsam fir to take, big enough for the central hall in this house, by the staircase.

He'd taken some ribbing when he first raised the topic. Most of his family and friends here had never heard of Christmas trees, and he had had to explain the custom as part of the winter solstice traditions of his human family—they could understand that. His recent marriage had made him think about how to pass along traditions to his own children, should there be any, and this was one he intended to keep. There were few Christians in the otherworld, just a handful of the humans. He didn't know where he stood on the subject of religion himself, but he was sure about the importance of family traditions and he meant to celebrate the season in his own way.

He lit a lamp to help dispel the winter afternoon gloom and took it with him as he walked up the stairs. A glint on glass caught his eye and he was cheered to see that Alun had started to hang some of his family photos along the hall, here upstairs where the phenomenon of photography would be less startling to his fae visitors. He lit the hanging wall lamps so that he could stand back and look at them.

On that first visit home a month ago, after his decision to stay, he'd had to decide what to bring with him from his human life, thirty-three years of accumulation. He'd settled on some clothes, a few keepsakes, the boxes holding his parents' materials (now piled in the library downstairs awaiting a free moment), and these photographs, many of which were recently blown up and framed for the purpose.

His grandfather had done something extraordinary. George was his only descendant, the son of his daughter, and he must have been seized with sentiment at his marriage and the possibility of great-grandchildren, for he'd taken the lead in arranging the selection and framing of the photos and, most surprisingly, had passed along the painting of the Talbot family arms, done for his own grandfather more than a hundred years before. That gleaming vision, the golden lion standing rampant on the red ground, had presided over George's meals in his grandparents' house for his entire childhood, and he still couldn't believe his grandfather had decided to part with it.

Here, now, in this fae otherworld, that heraldic lion came to stand for the most prominent human thread in his makeup, and he gave it a position of honor at the top of the landing where it presided over the hall.

The center of his family display was not, however, the photos, but a painting just hung that Angharad had made after her visit, of his grandparents, now in their late seventies. There were few elderly fae—George had yet to meet one—and she had dwelt perceptively and sympathetically on the changes of age balanced by the accumulation of experience. You could see Gwyn's features in his daughter's face, humanized and softened. This painting was very dear to him and he lingered over it now. After his parents' deaths when he was nine, his grandparents were the only human family he had. He smiled faintly, remembering—Rhian had never seen aged humans before and was frankly shocked when she met them, politely though she tried to hide it. He imagined this painting might disturb others here, too. Let them see what mortality brings, they'll experience it too if they live long enough.

He touched the framed photos of his mother. He was older now than she was when he lost her, and her young face from childhood on smiled from every frame. There were no pictures of his father; he hoped to learn more when he went through their papers.

He'd also brought back books and intended to bring more, but that was a topic which gave him difficulty. It was one thing to leave natural history references lying around, but what about books on technology that was out of place here? Or fiction that painted a story of a world alien to the fae, especially the twentieth century?

He'd made Alun a gift of Kipling's Jungle Books so that he could have a copy of his own and return Ceridwen's to her, but he was reluctant to contaminate this world with too much of his old one, despite Ceridwen's fondness for old-fashioned country house murder mysteries. On the other hand, who was he to decide what they should or shouldn't know? Nothing prevented the ones who were interested from traveling into the human world via a way, if they could find one. He intended to have a long discussion with Ceridwen about it, soon.

He went on to his bedroom to pull out one of his old sweaters suitable for tomorrow's excursion into the woods for a tree and to put on fresh clothing for dinner this evening.

He stepped back into the hall when he heard the sound of footsteps, and found Alun climbing the stairs. "I saw the dogs," he said. "You're back already?"

"I had to help Thomas Kethin with a big group of travelers, too many to house at the inn. Now I've been drafted to help get them to Rhys and look into the ways there, again."

"You should go somewhere they can't find you," Alun said sympathetically.

"That gets my vote," George said, ruefully. "Oh, we might be housing guests overnight. Two of the travelers are on their own, a musician and a lutine from Iona's place. If Ifor can't house them, I volunteered. I don't know yet what will be arranged, but wanted to warn you."

"I'll take care of it," he said. "I was just hanging these." Alun gestured at the wall. "Very strange, these photographs are."

"It looks fine, so far. A wall of pictures like this is very common, where I come from. Be sure to leave room for more from Angharad, as the spirit moves her."

"I suppose it's comforting, having a taste of home around you."

"I'm finding it so, though it's not my home any longer. This is. No regrets." He smiled, thinking of his wife and wishing she were here.

"Have you finished your work to cover your absence in the human world?"

George thought about his arrangements with Mariah Catlett, the human agent Gwyn used to coordinate his human holdings, such as the Bellemore property in Rowanton. As a whipper-in for the Rowanton Hunt, he'd known her only as a quiet middle-aged woman, always in the first field. After he took over as huntsman for Gwyn and decided to stay, he discovered that she'd been an agent for Gwyn for thirty years. She'd inherited the position from her father, who'd stumbled upon Gwyn's other life, back when he was impersonating a human in order to raise his daughter, George's grandmother, and see her married.

She knew what Gwyn was, and took George's revelations in stride, content with this unusual way of making a living. Gwyn paid her well, and the only condition placed upon her, other than discretion, was that she had to live in the caretaker's house Gwyn had built for her father, at the spot where the Guests' Way's hidden branch emerged on the Bellemore property.

She was widowed with one son, and George wondered if he would be initiated into the family arrangement, or if Gwyn and he would be seeking someone else eventually, but for now it was a stable situation.

"Mariah and my grandfather have arranged my bank accounts and set up the necessary paperwork to rent my farm and sell the things I won't be keeping, and to keep my human identity alive. They're telling my friends that I've sold my position in my company and am taking the opportunity to travel, a complete change of life." That's not so far wrong, he thought.

"Has it been hard, giving up the business that you built?"

"Surprisingly not. I feel like I've squeezed that life dry, and suddenly software and computers and email, they're not so important." He smiled at Alun's blank look. "I'll still buy a few things through her, I imagine." Giving up the Internet was one thing, he thought, but deodorant was another.

"This will all get more complicated when my grandparents pass on, but I hope that will be many years from now. If I have the long life, I suppose I'll eventually be a solitary on the human side, like Gwyn." It was a sobering thought, that he might have centuries yet to see how the human world advanced.

"Oh, well, " he summarized, "no gain without some loss. And speaking of concentrating on the here-and-now, if we can't travel tomorrow, I'm going after that Christmas tree. I'll need a pick, and ax, and a spade. I want to bring it back as a live tree, not a cut one, so I'll also need something to bundle around the root ball and not make a mess in the hall. The bottom half of a small barrel, maybe?"

"How will you get it here?" Alun asked.

"Good question. I wonder if anyone around here knows what a toboggan is?"

⌒‿⌒

The great hall was almost full, all of the tables set up for the unexpected visitors, amid a general air of jollity as everyone enjoyed a break in routine.

Ifor caught George as he walked in and asked if he were still willing to house Cydifor and Maëlys for the night. "It's been that difficult to get them all sorted out. Those two didn't say anything, but I could see they weren't comfortable just tagging along with the others."

"No problem at all," George said. "Alun's making the two rooms available, and I've planned to have a few friends over. Can you tell them to come to me at the end of dinner, and I'll bring them along?" Ifor nodded, and George went on to find Brynach, seated with his great-uncle Eurig in the position of an honored vassal at the front of the main hall.

"You're in the wrong place, young married man," Eurig teased, his walrus mustache waggling for emphasis.

"And don't I know it," George said. "Speaking of which, how is Tegwen managing in your absence, old married man?"

Eurig roared with laughter at the hit. "I'll find out soon enough when I go back home." Eurig's estate was just up the road a bit beyond the Daear Llosg, north of the manor.

George continued smoothly, "In lieu of married life, I've come to invite my whipper-in here to an informal gathering this evening at my house after dinner."

Brynach, with every inch of his seventeen-year-old dignity, rose and bowed. "I would be honored, huntsman."

George smiled and walked up the steps to the dais to take his usual place at the high table, next to his young cousin Rhian. "Come on over tonight, if you want," he told her. "I've invited the hunt staff, and we'll make some of these guests feel welcome. Benitoe said he'd come and we might even see Ives." That last was said with feeling. He'd dropped in on Ives at the kennels before dinner and had been sorry to find him still so disconsolate over the death of his daughter Isolda.

Rhian said quietly, "I think I remind him of her. I've been trying to keep out of his way."

George gripped her hand on top of the table for a moment. "It takes time, my dear, there's no hurrying it. Might be six months or a year before it stops stabbing at you with every recollection."

"So, tell me about the hound walking, now that the snow is so deep," he said, to change the subject. He helped himself to the beef, sliced on the platter, while he talked.

"We're following the new routine you suggested. We've got the run of the yards in front of the manor first thing in the morning. After we're done, the horses are turned out there for exercise. Between us, we keep the snow pounded down."

"Sounds like you've got it down to a system already," George said, and she nodded.

"We'll be fit to resume hunting if there's a thaw," she said. "We'll need you back, then, ready or not."

George sighed. Everyone felt free to comment on his lack of a honeymoon. "I'll take them out tomorrow, as long as I'm here. You can take a break from it."

As the meal wound down, Gwyn pushed back and rose to his feet. The crowd in the hall quieted.

"Our best prediction for tomorrow is that there will be more snow. I've decided there will be no travel Sunday for our guests. Please enjoy our hospitality for another day and prepare for the next stage of your journey." The noise in the hall resumed at a louder level, as the travelers, all together on one side of the hall, discussed this change in plan.

George looked simultaneously pleased and regretful. Rhian glanced at him quizzically.

"The sooner we get these travelers to Edgewood the sooner I can get back to Angharad, but if I can't, I have a fun project in mind," he said.

"Oh, you mean your little tree, don't you? Wouldn't it be easier to just bring a branch in?"

"It's not the same thing at all," he protested. "It has to be a tree, an evergreen."

"You're sure you're not some sort of druid?" she said, with a straight face, and he realized she was teasing him.

"Hey, this has been my family tradition for many generations. I bet I can convince you that it's fun, especially when I explain about Christmas presents."

It was an odd group that assembled on George's doorstep after dinner. He'd brought Rhian and Brynach along from the great hall, and Cydifor and Maëlys walked shyly in their wake, the two teenagers keeping the conversation lively for all of them. Brynach picked up Maëlys's pack as if it weighed nothing and carried it for her despite her protest.

When they came in they found Benitoe already there, talking with Alun. "Did Ives come?" George asked. Benitoe shook his head and George frowned. "It's not good for him to be alone so much."

"I usually spend part of the evening with him," Benitoe said, "but, you know, it's not easy for him to have me about, same as Rhian."

George recalled his duties as host. "Cydifor and Maëlys, Ifor will have told you that Alun here has prepared rooms for you. Why don't you let him show them to you and you can get settled. Come back down and join us when you're ready."

Alun led them upstairs, Brynach taking the steps two at a time to bring Maëlys's pack along for her. He returned downstairs in a few moments, followed by Alun.

In the meantime George had shooed everyone into his front study, the comfortable leather chairs reinforced by a warm fire and soft lights. His dogs made the rounds to greet everyone in their own fashion. "Drinks?" he asked.

Alun came into the room in time to hear that and took over the task. Soon everyone was wrapped around their favorite tipple, with cider for the youngest. Footsteps on the staircase announced the return of the two house guests, and Alun made quick work of serving them, too.

George made introductions all around. "Cydifor, Maëlys, let me introduce some of the hunt staff. You've met Rhian, Gwyn's foster-daughter. She's serving as junior huntsman. Brynach, here is one of our whippers-in, and Benitoe is the other." The lutin nodded at them. "Before his new duties at Edgewood, Rhian's brother Rhys served a term as whipper-in, as well."

He turned to his friends, "Please welcome Cydifor, hoping to find a place with Rhys as a musician, and Maëlys, from Iona's place."

Maëlys said, "Thank you for your hospitality, huntsman. I heard about you and Benitoe from Brittou, after your visit to Iona for ponies a few weeks ago." She addressed Benitoe directly, "I'm sorry for your loss, your betrothed. I myself am seeking my husband Luhedoc, vanished into Edgewood these eighteen years."

"Why were you on foot, coming from Iona's? Couldn't she spare you a pony?" George asked.

"I've never been much of a rider," she said.

"I can help you with that," Benitoe said. "It would be wise to improve, in case the journey makes wagons difficult. You'd have more options."

He turned to George, "I've been meaning to tell you. Since the hunting is shut down for the weather, I intend to join this next expedition for a short while, if you can spare me. I've been approached to try and find out what's happened to all of us there, the lutins, and to report back."

"Fine by me," George said. "If it turns out you're going to be gone indefinitely, let me know, but in the short term we can manage with Rhian and Brynach, if we must. I'll be coming along on this one myself."

Benitoe looked relieved and turned back to Maëlys. "I'd be happy to spend some time tomorrow with you on our ponies, if you'd like."

"That would be kind of you," she said, "but I don't have suitable clothes with me."

"I can find breeches to fit you, if you don't mind borrowed clothing, and you can even wear them under your skirts, for added warmth. Several of my friends have taken up riding. Come by the kennels in the morning after we've walked the hounds."

George was interested to observe Benitoe's courtesies to a woman old enough to be his mother. He was careful to keep her from being overwhelmed in the company of so many larger people and settled her on the couch next to him, where she curled up comfortably on the over-large furniture. He suddenly realized how much accommodation the lutins made in their coexistence with the larger fae here at the court, seeing it made manifest here. He also felt more conscious than usual of his own bulk, big even among the fae.

He turned to Cydifor. "And why have you decided to go traveling?"

Cydifor had taken a seat far from the fire and said little. Now he blushed to the roots of his red hair at the sudden attention. "Do you know my village, Tredin?" he asked George.

"Sorry, I'm new here."

"We're just a few families there, but they're very large families. It's a noisy life, and not everyone can work the land. If you can do anything else, why, you leave to make room for the others." Benitoe nodded at this, and George made a note to ask him about his family. He'd been very private in the two months George had known him, but if they were going to be traveling together to Edgewood, maybe this would be a good time to find out more.

"I was always wild for music, pestering my relatives for songs and tunes, and saving my money to buy instruments off the traders that came through. But loving the music is not the same as living by it, and there are few opportunities for that, no empty positions at the courts or grand estates for professionals. When we heard about my lord Rhys's call for settlers and experts, my dad told me 'Now's your chance, seek him out before someone else does.' And that's what I'm doing."

"I'm sure his kinsman Rhodri will be glad to see you," George reassured him, "and what he likes will probably do well with Rhys."

Rhian chimed in, "Rhys loves music. I doubt he's had time to even think about it, but that won't last."

"Thank you, my lady, that's good to hear."

George hid a smile at this careful display of manners to a potential royal patron, however young.

"I had already heard of you, huntsman, as I told you, coming through Danderi. It was just after the great hunt, and they were full of the story. But I could make no sense of it. Forgive me, I mean no offense, but are you fae or human, or something else?"

"Yes," George said, with a shrug, "it's complicated. The others know the details, of course, and I don't want to bore them with it."

"Ah, but you said you would tell me later, and later it is." George demurred, but the others urged him to it, and he'd had just enough to drink to give in.

"Well, to keep it brief…," he began, "I was a human, a whipper-in to a foxhunt in Virginia, and jumped my horse through a way, as I later understood, to Gwyn's domain just at the moment when Iolo ap Huw, his huntsman of 1500 years, was murdered. This was a couple of months ago, just two weeks before the great hunt at Nos Galan Gaeaf. I was no random visitor, for Gwyn was my grandmother's father, and so I call him kinsman. More to the point, my own father may, or may not, have been some descendant or avatar of Cernunnos, the beast master, the horned man. You know him?"

Cydifor nodded.

"We think he arranged my arrival, and perhaps my, um, breeding, to help defend this domain. With a great deal of help," he gestured around to his hunt staff, "I took over as huntsman, and we judged the murderer at the great hunt."

Benitoe said quietly, "That's where my betrothed Isolda was killed, by the same hand."

Brynach said, "He tried to kill Rhian, too. He would've succeeded, if George hadn't stopped him."

"Isolda stopped him first," Rhian said, sadly.

Cydifor looked from one speaker to the next. "He hunted as the horned man, they told me."

"Cernunnos and I have a sort of… arrangement," George said. "Sometimes he breaks free." This was more personal detail than he'd ever shared before with his hunt staff. Perhaps it was time for them to know more fully what had happened. "I can call up the forms of the horned man and Cernunnos, but they're usually just that, empty forms. During the great hunt, Cernunnos was manifest, and I had to fight for control."

It made him uneasy to admit all this, but the acceptance he saw on the faces of his friends, the ones who had gone through this with him, was comforting.

Maëlys asked, shyly, "What does he look like?"

Oh, no. Well, he'd opened this door himself. "Cernunnos is a great red deer, head and antlers on the body of a man. The horned man is the same, but with a man's head."

"Show her," Benitoe said, quietly. "I think we all want to see, now that the great hunt is over and they are empty forms again."

But they're not empty all the time, he thought. He should quell this, before they became afraid of him.

The trouble on his face must have shown because Rhian leaned over and said, "Go ahead, kinsman. It'll make it easier next time."

She was right, there would be a next time, a great hunt every year.

He stood up, spreading his feet wide in anticipation of the weight. He called up the red deer's form, his posture changing as he dipped his chest out and then up, the muscles shifting to support the head and its heavy antlers, hanging three feet behind him with many tines. As always, the objects in the room lost most of their color but the scents intensified greatly and his ears swiveled to follow every sound. The clothing on his upper body resettled, accommodating the narrower shoulders and thicker chest muscles and fur that he knew reached halfway down to his waist.

His guests and the hunt staff were frozen in place but not... alarmed. They trusted him, that it was still the man they knew and not some monster. He pulled back the form of Cernunnos to the horned man, the head unnaturally large to support the antlers, and let them get a good look. He knew the face didn't resemble his own. Then he pulled that form back, too, and sat down.

Alun brought him another drink, and there was silence for a moment.

Cydifor regarded George soberly. "And so, not quite a human after all? Not entirely."

George nodded.

"I see you decided to stay. Was it not hard, leaving your human family and friends?"

"Yes, indeed, very hard."

Benitoe said, "You've never told us what that meeting was like."

George was surprised. "Rhian was there." He glanced at her.

She looked down. "It was your story to tell, not mine."

"Ah." Well, why not tell it now? He took a good swallow of his drink before he began. He stared into the fire, glancing at them from time to time as he spoke, but mostly averting his gaze.

"When I decided I would stay, after the great hunt, I went back and told my grandparents what had happened during the two weeks I was gone. They're the only family I have, in the human world. After that, I went back again briefly to arrange my affairs." He didn't want to speak about the details of Gwyn's and his own contacts between worlds.

"Then, two weeks ago, I took my formal leave of my grandparents. I met them on Gwyn's human estate, where my grandmother was raised, and I brought Gwyn, Rhian here, and Angharad, my new wife, with me." He couldn't keep the warmth out of his voice at that last, or the smile off his face, and didn't try.

"Gwyn went off with his daughter for a long private conversation. I don't know what they spoke about, but my grandmother looked at peace afterward. She'd thought he'd died soon after her marriage, a deception he'd arranged. She was glad to see her father again, in any form.

"Before they were done, Gwyn asked my grandfather to join them, thanks, I think, for looking after his daughter." He cleared his throat. "It was very kindly done of Gwyn. He could have avoided the meeting, as the fae usually do for their human descendants with their short lives." He meant that, he'd been surprised Gwyn wanted to accompany him.

"When they all came back, I introduced them to their cousin Rhian. Her brother Rhys was already at Edgewood, of course."

He glanced, amused, at Rhian, "You'd never seen elderly humans before, had you?"

"Forgive me, cousin, but I didn't realize anyone could be that old," she admitted.

"And yet, with luck, they may live many years more. You should go upstairs and look at the pictures of my grandmother as a girl. You'll find Gwyn in her face, well enough."

He continued, "It gave me great pleasure to introduce Angharad to them." He smiled privately. His grandmother had brought her some oranges, a private joke between them. She'd given him oranges before, a courtship gift he'd presented to Angharad when they agreed to marry. The gift this time broke the awkwardness and Angharad had hugged her warmly. George was sure he'd seen tears in his grandmother's eyes.

He continued more briskly. "My grandfather is a Master of Foxhounds for the Rowanton Hunt, and I brought back two of our hounds to show him, Dando as an example of a great all-around hound, two generations from outsider blood, and Cythraul as the type of a first generation outsider hound, the new blood that keeps the pack healthy." He looked at his guests. "We get hounds like Cythraul as whelps on Nos Galan Mai, when Gwyn wins his annual contest against Gwythyr. That's another long story, for some other night."

There was silence in the room for a moment, and the crackling and popping of the fire absorbed George's attention.

He caught sight of Brynach suppressing a yawn, and stood up, breaking the mood and pulling out his pocket watch.

"Alright, we might not be traveling tomorrow, but I have plans for the afternoon if we're still here and the weather looks promising. I'll tell you all about it at lunch."

"It's that little tree," Rhian told Brynach, with a grin.

"Never you mind. Let's give our guests an opportunity to rest tonight. They had a long trek through the snow."

He bundled them out of the door, Benitoe taking the back way toward the kennels.

"Now," he said, turning back to his two house guests, "is there anything Alun or I can get you to make your stay more comfortable?" They shook their heads and climbed the stairs slowly, and George sent Alun to bed.

He turned down the lamps in the study and spent the next half-hour staring into the fire with a drink in his hand and his dogs curled up at his feet, wishing Angharad were there and missing his human family.

CHAPTER 5

George took the pack on another circuit of the grounds below the manor in the early morning. Rhian was right—between the hounds and the horses getting their exercise here, the depth of snow was much reduced. Benitoe whipped-in on the left, and Brynach on the right, in Rhys's old spot.

Brynach was coming along nicely, for all that he lacked George and Rhian's special gift of bespeaking the hounds and other beasts. He was picking up the job in the old way, the one which George was familiar with in the human world, observing each hound and learning its behavior, anticipating what it would do. Benitoe operated in the same style, for the same reasons, and they made a good pair, with Benitoe's experience matched to young Brynach's steadiness and eagerness to learn.

Still, they were short-staffed. It was time to find another whipper-in or two to bring along. He'd have to speak to Gwyn about that.

Alright, he decided, he'd come out here for some exercise, and this wasn't really enough. "Let's take them up to the orchard and get them nice and tired," he called to his whippers-in.

He used his horn to get the attention of the hounds. "Pack up," he said, firmly, and they fell into place behind him in a close group.

He brought them through the north curtain wall past the manor house into the orchards at the far end of the rear grounds. Here the snow was almost undisturbed and much thicker. It wasn't a safe place for the horses to exercise, with so much of the ground invisible under the snow, but it wouldn't hurt the hounds any, and they could keep their horses to a cautious walk.

It didn't take too many minutes before even the liveliest hounds showed the effects of trying to breast that much snow. They turned when he called it quits and followed him happily back across the rear grounds to the kennels. He felt better himself for a bit of hard work.

A knock on the door of the workroom at the kennels brought Benitoe to his feet. "I lost track of time," he said to Ives, "that must be Maëlys."

He opened the door and found her on the threshold, hand raised to knock a second time. "I see you managed to find us."

"It was easy enough," she said. "I just followed the smell of the cooking."

The great cauldrons were simmering as usual, one with a warm porridge for the winter cold, and the other with boiling meat.

He introduced the two kennel-men, Huon and Tanguy, while Ives rose from the table. "And this is our kennel-master, Ives."

She curtsied to him. "Brittou asked to be remembered to you."

He bowed to her in turn. "I met your husband, Luhedoc, on his way north. They were all excited to visit Edgewood, the first lutins in many years, and would not be dissuaded. I was sorry to see our fears realized."

Benitoe admired her composure as she murmured, "We were all younger then, and more foolhardy."

He turned to Ives. "I've promised her a riding lesson this morning. Could I use one of the hound yards for a bit of privacy, do you think?"

"No problem at all," Ives said. He led her to the door. "You'll be wanting someplace to change into the breeches Benitoe brought you. Let me show you into the huntsman's office."

Benitoe scooped up the clothing he'd borrowed, two choices provided by his riding friends, and the three of them went back outside and across the inner yard between the pens to the matching entryway on the other side, where Ives showed her into the huntsman's office and sent her inside, warning her to draw the curtain.

Benitoe walked back out and took the blankets off the two waiting ponies, both of which had come from her own place, from Iona, provided by Ifor Moel for his use as a whipper-in. He'd brought Eleri for her, a kind bay mare, and the boss mare, gray Gwladus, for himself.

When Maëlys returned, he introduced her to her mount and encouraged her to pet her and make much of her. Then he showed her how to tighten the girth and let her do it herself. He gave her a leg up, pleased to find her wearing sensible boots. "My friends tell me that the easiest thing for you to do with a full skirt and breeches under it is to let nothing come between the breeches and the saddle. Let the back of the skirt drape over the pony's back, petticoat and all. It'll keep the pony warm, and you, too, once you get off and claim it back."

She stood in the stirrups and rearranged her clothing until she had achieved a comfortable result. Benitoe, still standing on the ground next to her, showed her how to adjust her stirrup leathers and let her do it.

He mounted his own pony and looked at her. "All set?"

She looked apprehensive, and he reassured her. "We won't be going anywhere without a fence, and no one can see you."

"Why are you being so kind to a stranger?" she asked him, forthrightly.

He was startled into an unconsidered response. "I like your courage, setting out on your own like this, and your loyalty seeking your husband and not just leaving him to his fate. Ives mentioned something of how Brittou has offered you his own home."

He cleared his throat. "I was raised by my mother's sister and you remind me of her. She would have done the same." He spread his hands and shrugged. "I can't see your situation and not want to help."

He rarely spoke of his family. For the clannish lutins, he was something of an odd character, content to be independent and observe his folk from the outside. But he also felt the estrangement and wanted the warmth of family for himself. He couldn't think of Isolda's death without a hitch in his heart, but he knew that in time the pain would diminish and he would want to try again.

For Maëlys's sake, he said, "I suppose I just miss my family. Shall I call you 'Auntie' for the trip?"

He smiled as he said it, to lighten the mood but was surprised when her face filled with longing. "I would truly like that, young Benitoe. I haven't had children yet, and I miss family myself."

"Well, then," he said, turning his pony and letting hers follow him. "Let's find out what you can do on a horse, Auntie."

❦

George mounted the sledge behind the manor and picked up the long reins looped around the pole on the front boards, waist high, standing with his legs braced. There were three or four inches of snow under the runners even here in front of the stables, and he gave an experimental cluck to the two heavy draft horses to see what they made of the weight and the whole contraption. They leaned forward into the harness and easily moved it a few feet before George stopped them again.

The head groom who'd found the old stone boat for him nodded with satisfaction. "I think this'll do fine, sir. With the snow under it, they should have no difficulty bringing that a couple of miles, even if you carry a person or two. Folk don't weigh like stones, after all."

He'd spent much of the morning after the hound walking trying to arrange a means of transport for getting to the nearby woods for his tree. This sledge, a bit larger than a single bed, would carry his tools and the small barrel end he would use for the tree itself, with the tree in it on the way back. In the deep snow, the runners reduced the friction and made it easier to draw.

The word had spread at lunch, and he'd found a couple dozen people mounted and loitering when he'd emerged, asking to come along for a break from staying indoors, now that the morning's light snowfall had stopped. He'd invited several of them himself, but at the sight of so many he ducked back into the manor and begged a large sack of apples from one of the cooks. He'd carry that out in the empty barrel end.

After his experiment with the full harness, he looped the reins around the pole and stepped down to face the gathering.

"Glad to see you all. I'm just headed to the woods to bring back a tree for the winter solstice, but I thought we could make a party of it since the snow has eased off again. We'll be going down to the manor gates, then up the nearby slope to the edge of the woods, maybe a total of a mile each way.

"The snow's too deep for walking, but the distance is short enough that you could ride double with some of the kids, maybe. I can take a couple of the small folk, but it could be dangerous without side rails. I don't want to try it with children. And coming back, with a tree, it'll get crowded.

"So, sort yourselves out. Who wants to come with me?"

The local folk, all mounted, stood off to the side. Eurig and Brynach were joking with each other, their cheeks already red in the cold, and Rhian joined them. Ceridwen had introduced George to her colleague Eluned at lunch, and the two women were sitting together astride their horses, well-wrapped against the chill.

Benitoe had persuaded Maëlys to come, mounted. George overheard him explaining that her pony could hardly run away in such deep snow. Kennel-man Tanguy had fetched Armelle, his betrothed, and now the two lutins came forward to join George on the sledge, neither one having learned to ride.

Only Broch and Tiernoc among the korrigans came along, on their ponies, but Cydifor and many of the other traveling fae had decided that this promised some fun, especially for the kids. The older children were mounted, and a few younger ones sat in front of a parent, wide-eyed.

George looked over the group and nodded. Before he turned to step up to the stone boat again, he caught sight of Cadugan walking by with Ifor, headed to a meeting with Gwyn. Cadugan was shaking his head at the spectacle, but smiling, too.

George asked the head groom for a short leather strap to buckle around his waist so that the two lutins would have something to hang onto, without a side rail to steady themselves. He knew it would be difficult to keep their footing standing up all the way.

He picked up the reins and clucked to the horses. They moved out at a slow walking pace, and his dogs bounded through the snow ahead of them.

⌐⌐⌐⌐⌐

It was tricky keeping his balance, but with a lutin on each side of him, holding to the front boards with one hand and his impromptu belt with the other, they worked out a method of swaying with the motion, knees bent, that kept them all upright. The horses pulling the sledge seemed to take its weight as inconsequential and were enjoying being outside. George held a light mental touch on them and felt their pleasure.

If he only had a red suit and a white beard, maybe a few jingle bells, the scene would be complete, he thought, smiling to himself.

The voices of the children behind him rose with excitement as they approached their destination.

He pulled the stone boat up in front of the small balsam fir he had in mind. Good, he thought, as he looked it over. It's still in fine shape. Before unhooking the horses, he looped the reins on the pole and hopped out to check its size, pulling a cord out of his pocket. He'd measured the ceiling height in the hall, and the width available, and knotted the cord appropriately. Now he stretched it against the actual tree. Seven feet tall, plus the root ball—should be fine.

"Alright, we're here. Let's bring the horses under the shelter of the trees so they don't have to stand in such deep snow."

He pocketed a couple of the apples, then unhooked the doubletree from the stone boat and led his team into the woods several yards, tethering it to a sturdy tree. They each took an apple delicately from his hands and munched appreciatively. When he returned, he found that everyone had dismounted. One of the fae borrowed his spade as a shovel and cleared a spot for a fire, in the open away from the trees, while others gathered fallen branches to use for fuel.

Eurig and Ceridwen took charge as hosts for the group, and George decided to get the tree sorted out right away before joining in. He reclaimed the spade, brought the pick and ax over to the tree, and untied the barrel end from the sledge and rolled it over up close.

Probing the ground with the pick, he was relieved to find it not as frozen as he'd feared—the winter so far was snowy but not very cold. He marked a circle around the trunk about the width of the barrel and began to drive the spade down.

He angled the spade inward as he approached the maximum depth the barrel end would hold but encountered a few tough deep roots that resisted his tool.

The snow squeaked as the two korrigans walked up. "Stand aside and let me show you how we deal with this," Broch said, picking up the ax. Tiernoc tilted the loosened tree to supply tension, and Broch applied two precise cuts with the ax that broke the first root free. They made short work of the remainder, George standing by in admiration at their expertise.

Now that the tree was completely liberated, he squatted down to grasp the trunk near its base and lift it. The root ball added significant weight but he got his back into it and hoisted it out of the ground. He dropped it next to the hole, still upright. The two korrigans leaned down to inspect the evenness of the bottom part of the cut and added some loose dirt to the empty barrel to give the root ball something to expand into. Then George picked it up one more time and set it in the barrel end, holding it upright while the korrigans filled around the edges with dirt and the occasional rock, tamping everything down solidly.

"I'll need some help lifting this to the sledge and tying it down," George said, eying the ten feet of distance. A snowball took him fair on the cheek, and he spun around to find himself under sneak attack by Rhian and Brynach.

"Oh, yeah?" he said, mock ferociously, and set off after them, stooping to gather and pack snowballs as he ran. They lured him straight into the middle of a group snowball fight where this presentation of a new, large target, barely whitened at all, proved irresistible, and he was pounded on all sides until he fled down the slope to recoup.

The youngest children were playing there. He smiled at one of them, a little girl maybe seven years old. "Have you ever made a snow angel?" he asked. She looked at him blankly, and he rephrased, "I mean, a snow lady?" She shook her head solemnly. "Here, I'll show you."

He took her by the hand and led her a few feet away to an untouched stretch of snow. "Lie down on your back, like you're going to bed. Now put your arms out sideways and move them back and forth." He demonstrated for her. "Do the same thing with your legs." He reached down and gave her a careful hand up. "Now turn around and look at the picture you just made in the snow."

It was a perfect snow angel, and she squealed with pleasure. At once some of the other youngsters surrounded them and started their own experiments. He glanced up at one of the parents who was keeping an eye on them and winked, before walking back up the slope to the fire.

Eurig and Ceridwen greeted him. "What do you think?" George said. "Shall we give them a few more minutes before heading back?"

Ceridwen beamed at him. "It's been so long since most of us were children, you can't imagine how a scene like this feels to us. I hate to stop."

"Well, alright then, I have a family game you might like," He walked a few feet from the fire and called out. "We're going to have a couple of rounds of "Statues" before we return. Everyone can play. Kids, too."

Most of the people came over to find out what this was.

"Here's how it works. Someone is 'it' and stands over there facing the woods." He pointed to the top of a small open space before the trees. "Everyone else lines up at the foot of the hill. The goal is to tag the person who's 'it.' When he turns his back, you can move. When he turns around, without warning, you have to freeze, like a statue. If you move and he sees it, you have to go back to the start of the hill and start again. He can try and make you move, too, as long as he doesn't touch you. The person who tags him while his back is turned becomes the new 'it.'" He glanced around. "Clear?" Heads nodded.

George walked up the slope and looked down at the crowd about twenty yards away. "Alright, here we go." He faced the trees for about five seconds then spun around.

"Benitoe, Rhian, Tiernoc—I saw you. And you, there—sorry I don't know your name." He pointed at five more who went sheepishly back to the start. Broch and Eurig had covered a surprising amount of ground, and where was Ceridwen?

He faced the tree again, pretended to turn, then turned for real. As he'd hoped, some of the bolder ones had restarted and been caught. "You again, Rhian?" This time he saw Ceridwen, flanking him where it was hard to keep an eye on her. Eurig gave him a grin but didn't move any other muscle. Some of the teenagers were getting fairly close, and Brynach was right next to Eurig.

He turned away then spun back. Eurig and Brynach were three yards closer, but when he looked away from them for a second to check on some of the others, he heard a noise and glanced back. Brynach had somehow tripped and was glaring at Eurig maintained a serene expression. Tanguy and Armelle in with the spectators were laughing, and those of the players who couldn't keep a straight face joined Brynach as he trudged back to the start.

Once again, he faced the woods but before he could turn he was tackled by Eurig who laughed down at him. "Reminds me of my warrior games when I was a lad." Brynach and Rhian charged up the hill and piled on. They rolled him down the slope and his dogs barked and chased after them.

Eurig took the new 'it' position and George retired to the sidelines to watch.

This is a kids' game where I come from, he thought, but look at how the adults are treating it as an opportunity to practice battle tactics. Ceridwen moved fluidly and surefootedly up the slope, along one side. As she got closer, Eurig concentrated on her more as a threat, but then Eluned, on the opposite side presented herself as a target and made enough of a distraction for Ceridwen to sneak in from the side and tap Eurig as he turned back. Teamwork, George thought.

While they played a couple more rounds, he went and fetched the sack of apples for everyone and their horses, keeping back a couple for his own team.

After the horses munched their treats, the riders mounted up. Eurig helped George lift the upright tree in its barrel end onto the back of the stone boat where they tied it down with ropes.

The branches reached out and tickled George from behind as he took up the reins again and it was a crowded ride for them all, but the whole party hummed with jokes and laughter as they headed home.

❧

With a flourish, George pulled the sledge up to his own front door and halted before the steps. Tanguy and Armelle dropped off on either side and thanked him, then headed off arm in arm. Benitoe and Maëlys brought their ponies up, and Maëlys carefully dismounted. George was watching for this and had a hand under her elbow before her knees had quite started buckling from the sudden change. "Long day?" he said.

"I never would have thought I could ride for several hours," she said. She looked up at Benitoe who had taken the reins of her pony. "Thank you for taking such good care of me."

"My pleasure, auntie. I'll see you at dinner." He turned and led her mount down to the stables.

"Auntie?" George asked, looking down at her.

She colored faintly. "We got to talking about families," she murmured.

"I see," he said. "You're going to be sore. I recommend a good long soak in a hot bath, right away."

"Wise advice," she said, as she took a few experimental steps.

Brynach, Rhian, and Cydifor had followed George on foot from the stables. The two teenagers were trying to put Cydifor at his ease, rubbing off his country shyness, and it was beginning to work. George spotted grins on all three faces as they recalled the afternoon events.

"Why are you two hanging around?" he asked. "Cydifor lives here, so he's got an excuse."

Brynach said, "My great-uncle told me to come and make myself useful with the tree."

"Good of him," George said. "Better, of you—you're doing the work. Well, let's get the darn thing into the house." He bent to start removing the ropes.

Rhian ran up the two steps to get the door. When she opened it, George's dogs dashed by her to be greeted by excited barks as Angharad's terriers rushed to the defense of the house.

George looked up, dropped the rope, and took both the steps at once, passing Rhian into the hall. Angharad was just coming down the last treads of the stairs. He swept her off the final one into his arms and took advantage of the momentum to swing her around before setting her down. "You came!"

She smiled at his enthusiasm. "Better finish bringing your tree in, dear."

With a start, George recalled what he'd been doing, and their interested audience. He gave her a mock bow with a quirk of his lips. "Yes'm."

He walked back out, past the grinning Rhian who was still holding the doorknob.

With Brynach's help he lifted the tree in its barrel end to the top step and knocked the last of the snow off of its branches.

"All ready in there, Alun?" George called.

"I suppose so," came the reply.

With one final effort, they duck-walked the tree into the hall, keeping it as low as possible to clear the ceiling, and dropped it on the round mat that Alun had prepared for it, next to the study door and opposite the bottom of the stairs.

George straightened up with a creak. "Handles on that barrel next year," he said, holding his back. After a few rotational adjustments to present the tree's best side, he backed up to get a good look, snaking his arm around Angharad's waist in the process. "So, what do you think?"

"I think we have a forest in our house," she said. "Nice aroma, though."

"You just wait until it's cleaned up and decorated. You'll see."

From the doorway Brynach said, "I'll take the sledge back to the stable."

"Have you ever driven two horses in harness like that?" George asked.

"No, but Rhian can help explain it to the horses. It'll be fine."

"Alright. Thank you, and thank them all for me at the stables. And make sure those tools get back to where they belong." They ducked out, leaving Cydifor and Maëlys standing in the hall.

"George, will you introduce me?" Angharad said.

"Oh, sorry. These are our guests until the traveling parties move on. My lady, may I present Cydifor, a musician from Tredin, and our neighbor Maëlys from Iona and Brittou's place, seeking her husband." To the guests he said, "This is Angharad who has recently done me the honor of becoming my wife."

Cydifor bowed low. "My lady, even in our little village, we have heard of your work."

George turned to Angharad, "I don't understand how you managed it. How long can you stay?"

"I had Huw Bongam send me the wagons when they returned this morning. He and I have an old arrangement for when I travel." She looked at him sternly. "I do travel sometimes, you know. He holds the materials that don't do well in bitter cold, keeps them for me in his attics. The finished works are preserved—a little chill won't hurt them. All I had to do was refresh the spells and pack up. Empty the water from the pipes, and I'm done. I brought plenty with me to keep me busy."

She laughed at George's look of confusion. "I'm here for the season, dear, or at least as long as this stretch of bad weather lasts, where travel is so difficult. Horses in the stable, dogs and cat here."

He could feel the smile beaming across his face. "Wonderful."

A sudden thought struck him. "Where will you work? Shall I clean out a room?"

She shook her head. "I spoke with Ceridwen. She's put aside an unused space beside the infirmary where my noises and stinks won't bother anyone. It's large enough for my needs and well-lit. All I need do is walk across the lane. I'm already moved in there."

He looked at her admiringly. "I think I'll have you do all our travel planning. You've thought of everything."

Maëlys excused herself to change clothes and, George expected, soak away some of her unaccustomed exertions on pony-back.

Alun brought bread and cheese from the kitchen, along with hot cider, and took it into the study. Cyledr followed him closely as if physically pulled along by the aromatic scent of cinnamon and apple.

George joined Angharad and Cyledr in the study room and took a mug of hot cider from Alun. "Where do you all get cinnamon?" he asked.

"It's another import, of course," Angharad said. "Much easier to buy from the human world than from our old channels to the far east."

"Yes, I imagine so. These things are so familiar to me I forget how exotic they must seem here."

A knock at the front door sent Alun back into the hall. He returned with Ceridwen and her newly arrived colleague whom she introduced to Angharad and Alun.

"Eluned is going to Edgewood to take over the school and hospital arrangements there, and to do some research of her own once that settles down. I'll be coming with her to help get things started again."

She turned to George, "Thank you for organizing that trip today." She turned to Angharad. "You heard about it? We had many children, so much laughter."

Any human outdoor party like that would have had even more, George thought. Once again it struck him how few children there were in the lives of the fae. Over their long lives they might have many, but they were spread out over centuries and only young for a relatively brief time. There were proportionately so many more children in the human world. Only the special nature of these travelers, emigrating with families, would have concentrated even this many children into a small group.

He wondered if the old slanders about the fae kidnapping human children had any truth behind them.

Angharad replied, "I've only heard a bit about it so far, and the results are sitting in our hall. Come tell me more. I'm sure Alun would like to hear, too."

Ceridwen launched into a summary of the highlights, Eluned and even Cydifor chiming in from time to time. George watched them all silently, made sleepy by the warmth indoors. The smell of the fire, the cinnamon, and the tree, beginning to warm up and give off its sweet balsam scent, all mingled to give him a vivid feel of the season. Even the light from outside, glaring off the snow, felt right.

He'd be spending Christmas here, in a couple of weeks. For the first time since he was a child, when his grandfather brought him back from Wales after the death of his parents, he'd be away for the holiday. It made him uneasy. At their age, each Christmas for his grandparents might be their last.

"George?"

He looked up as Ceridwen spoke. "Hmm? You were saying?"

"I said, please explain to Eluned about this winter solstice event you're celebrating."

"This will be hard to do briefly. It's all tangled up," he said, straightening in his chair. "It's a German custom," he glanced at her to see if she understood the human geographical reference. "A few hundred years ago, a long time for us humans, people in Germany started setting up trees to celebrate Christmas, December 25."

"That's a Christian holiday, isn't it?" Eluned asked, her deep voice contrasting with her fair blond face.

"Yes, the traditional date of the birth of Christ, but then Christianity only goes back 2000 years, and as it spread the founders were careful to associate it with older pagan holidays to encourage conversions. It's not a coincidence that the conventional date is so close to the winter solstice of December 21. The actual date's unknown. It's not clear if the tree is some sort of pagan echo or if it represents some Christian symbolism, now obscure.

"The German custom became popular all over northern Europe and then spread widely to all Christian countries. In my native land, families have been doing it for generations, unless they adhere to a religion that considers it unsuitable. For most of us, now, the tree is a secular expression of the season. The date still has religious overtones, but not the tree itself, by and large.

"It's very much a family thing, with customs that differ in each family. It's especially important for the children, the thing they long remember from their childhood. We give each other gifts, prepare a feast, and build family rituals around the 'proper' way to set up, decorate, and take down the tree and the memories of individual ornaments and what they commemorate. It's all in fun but, like all rituals, these things take hold and give us comfort in our lives."

Eluned nodded.

"After this tree settles in, I'll start decorating it, and the house, too, with garlands on the banister and the mantles, and holly branches. They're all green in winter, you see, part of the winter life renewal aspect of the solstice, pagan in feel if not in origin. We don't have children, yet, but it'll be like a rehearsal, figuring out what works here and for us."

"How long do you keep the tree?" Eluned asked.

"Well, religion comes back into that. The traditional date is January 6, which we call 'Twelfth Night,' the twelfth day after Christmas. That's Epiphany in the Christian calendar, when the infant Christ becomes manifest as a god in human form. Religiously or not, it marks the end of the Christmas season, and there are customs about making sure all the special decorations are removed by then."

Cydifor ventured a question. "Are you then a Christian? Won't that be a problem for you, living here?"

George rubbed a hand over his chin. "Well, I was raised one, most of us are, where I come from. How much I truly believe, I don't really know myself. I'll just say that this is a pagan tree for the season and not a religious expression, and no one should be concerned about it, one way or the other."

Eluned took the hint and changed the subject. After a few minutes, Ceridwen gathered her up. "See you at dinner," Ceridwen called from the front step as they left.

Cydifor bowed to George and Angharad in the hall by the fresh tree and went up to his room, and they were finally alone together.

He said to her, quietly, "You know I have to go out to Edgewood again, to see about this new way that's appeared where I shut down the old one? I'll be back as soon as I can but I'll probably be leaving tomorrow."

"Yes, I heard about it. Never mind, we'll take it one night at a time."

"I'm sorry about the guests. If I'd known you were coming I'd…"

"Doesn't matter. Our door has a lock." She smiled at him fondly.

"We could always go up to change for dinner early, and test it," he proposed.

CHAPTER 6

Gwyn stood by as Idris dispatched today's courier to Edgewood. The stable area was crowded with people just returned from George's Christmas tree excursion. Brynach and Rhian drove up the horses with the stone boat George had used to carry it, and joined the group. They all seemed reluctant to break up the after-party and return to their normal lives.

Gwyn was surprised how pleased everyone was for the simple change in the routine, a chance to get out in the snow. We seem to have generated an unexpected bonus of goodwill, he thought. Even Cadugan had unbent enough to praise it as a way of bonding the travelers into a stronger group.

As he walked back into the manor, he made a note to come look at George's tree in a few days. He knew Christmas trees from his years living as a human, and he thought it would be a fitting gesture to get George an ornament, something from him personally. What would be good? He wanted it to stand for their bond as family, and it should be something that would last, as a keepsake should. He'd have to think about it.

Still no messenger from Rhys or Edern, and nothing to account for it. He couldn't take his mind off of that.

With Rhys, Edern, and Rhodri at Edgewood, George found himself only one seat from Gwyn at dinner, Idris between them. When Idris stepped away for a moment, George got a good look at Gwyn and noted the worry on his face and his distracted manner.

He leaned across Idris's empty chair. "What's bothering you, sir?"

Gwyn looked up at the sympathetic voice. George could see him deciding not to fob him off with a meaningless assurance. "There's been no courier from Rhys, yesterday or today," he said. "I've sent mine, with instructions to find out what's going on, but I don't expect to hear back from him tonight."

He made a visible effort to lay the problem aside and smiled at George. "I've been hearing about your Christmas tree all afternoon. Seems to have been quite a party."

"Well, you know how it is, you've lived in the human world at Christmas," George said.

"Indeed. I look forward to seeing the results. And to hearing you explain the custom."

"I had a dose of that already this afternoon, with Ceridwen and Eluned." He pointed his chin at the two of them seated beyond Gwyn, on the other side of Cadugan and Ifor. "Everyone seems to find it very odd."

"Don't let that stop you," Gwyn said. "It'll do them good to shake them up a little with different customs."

Angharad on George's other side touched his arm to draw his attention. Idris had reentered the hall, bringing a snow-covered rider with him.

Gwyn rose, recognizing the messenger he sent out a couple of hours ago. They came up the steps of the dais and stood in front of the table, facing Gwyn. Everyone stopped talking.

"My lord," the courier said. "I couldn't get through. The way is barred somehow, at the Edgewood end."

⸻

George wasn't surprised when Gwyn didn't stand on ceremony waiting for the meal to properly conclude. He swept his family and council from the high table down the steps and into his council chamber, bringing the courier along. Before he entered the room, he paused seeking Thomas Kethin in the great hall. When he caught his eye, he beckoned him along.

Everyone took a seat along the table, and the messenger placed himself in front of the seated Gwyn, Idris standing behind him for support.

"Now tell your tale in full and spare no details," Gwyn told him.

"My lord, we all knew there'd been no courier from Edgewood yesterday. The one you sent in would've been the next one to come back in our rotation, and when they told me at Eastern Shore that no one had come from Edgewood today either I was well and truly alarmed."

Gwyn gave him his complete attention.

"Before entering the way, I dismounted and found a long stick. It's dim in the passage, as you know, and I used the stick as a blind man does, feeling the ground before me and leading my horse slowly. I also took the precaution of tying a rope around me that the guards outside held."

"What happens when you do that?" Gwyn said. "Isn't it severed partway through?"

"No, my lord. We couriers have done many experiments, professionally. We go through ways all the time for our work, and so we've accumulated some bits of knowledge that maybe others don't have. The actual transition doesn't happen until just before the passage stops. The end of a way passage after the crossing is always no more than a yard or two in length, however long the interior, and we know the lengths of the interiors of all the common ways we use, and how they bend, if they do."

"I never thought to ask. I'll talk more with your colleagues about this later. So, what did you find?"

"I thought if I reached the transition point, I would untie the rope and the guards would know. If I was taken by surprise, it would come back cut. Thus there would be at least some information no matter what happened."

Gwyn nodded his understanding.

"Of course, I wanted no surprises, my lord. I probed cautiously as I went along. As I approached the end, I knew I was still a couple of yards short and I looked very carefully. This was the point where I should have been able to see Edgewood clearly, just before crossing over. Instead I saw a dark place with a flicker of light, as if torches were somewhere nearby. It was not the grounds of Edgewood Manor. My stick, pushed along the ground, sank before the end crossed over and it was pulled from my hand. There is no change in level at the end of the way to Edgewood."

He let that hang in the attentive silence for a moment.

"I backed up, turned my horse around and went back out as I came in. The guards knew I was coming by the slackening of the rope that they pulled in as I approached. I told their sergeant to block the exit of the way from their end and to set a guard and watch for a possible attack. If any of our people came out, they should send to tell you, or escort them to you. But I wanted to bring this news to you myself without waiting for morning. The roads weren't long, and the snow on the ground reflected enough light to make it possible."

He stopped and stood composedly, waiting for Gwyn's further questions. George admired his quiet professional competence.

"Very well done," Gwyn said. "You have our thanks." His eye caught Idris, who nodded.

A promotion coming, George thought. And well-deserved, too.

Gwyn digested this all in silence for a few moments, and his council waited for him.

"So, what does this mean? And how was it done?" he asked them.

George ventured, "Wasn't the way that trapped Rhys ap Edern years ago an opening slipped in front of a normal way's opening? Maybe this is what it looks like. Madog's signature?"

"Where would it lead?" Ceridwen said.

"Nowhere good," Gwyn said. "We never saw Rhian's parents again."

George saw Rhian struggling not to react to this impersonal discussion of the death of her parents when she was a very young child.

"Could we just shut it down?" Gwyn asked. "Could George enter the Edgewood Way as the messenger did and kill the intrusive way, if that's what it is?"

George said, uneasily. "I don't know much about ways yet, but something tells me that collapsing one way while standing inside another might be a very bad idea."

Ceridwen nodded, and then Gwyn joined her, reluctantly.

"What are our choices for finding out what's happened at Edgewood?" Gwyn said.

Idris said, "We can send someone overland. But it's a long distance and would take several days, and you know we've had no success getting them back."

"What about the Archer's Way?" George said.

Cadugan spoke for the first time. "What is this Archer's Way that I've been hearing about?"

"You know about the burning ground for our funerals, the Daear Llosg just north of the grounds?" Gwyn asked.

"I've been told," Cadugan said.

"When we held the ceremony for my murdered huntsman Iolo a couple of months ago, a way was opened there and an ambush attempted by a mounted bowman. George interfered and chased him to the other side, and I followed to bring him back. It ends in a river meadow, and several of us assume, for many reasons, that it's somewhere in Edgewood."

"How was the way made? Is it still open?"

"We think it's Madog's work, and we don't know how he does it. George, still untutored in the ways—our best expert, Rhodri, is with Rhys—came up with a novel method of sealing it that held against Madog's attempts to reopen it later, and it's still there."

"I have lots of questions, though," George said. "If I unseal it, as I think I can, will it be open to us to use? And if it's open at this end, what about the other end? If Madog built it and owns it, can I pass through it? Although I suppose I did it before, didn't I." He trailed off, puzzled.

"This can be tested," Idris said, pleased to find something practical to attempt. "We can bring an armed party through as a trial first. But if you do get to the other end, will you be able to tell if you're at Edgewood?"

"Maybe," George said. "The last time I was there, up at the north end, I thought I detected something way down south, but I can't know if it's the same way. It must have been ten or fifteen miles away at least, I think, whatever it was."

"But still within the barrier?" Idris asked.

"Yes, I think so. I can very dimly feel the barrier, and the nearer curves of it implied a loop that would be further yet."

"So, if this is the same way, you should be able to detect the Edgewood Way from its exit point, right?"

"I presume so."

Ceridwen said, "Wouldn't there need to be tokens? George doesn't know how to do that."

"That wouldn't work anyway, since Madog may still be the owner," Gwyn said. "But I don't think it matters, I think George might be able to take some of our men through directly, as a guide."

He told Idris. "Better not lose him, you might not be able to get back without him."

George gave an uneasy laugh and Angharad looked alarmed.

"In fact," Gwyn said, "I'll go with you."

"Not all the way through, my lord," Idris protested. "We don't know where it goes."

"No, but I want to see the situation for myself."

Idris said, "So, it's decided. We'll send a small armed party to Daear Llosg and the Archer's Way in the morning. George will try to unseal it, and then we'll see what we can see. If we get through and if we're sure it comes out in Edgewood, and if there's no obvious hazard, then the travelers' expedition will follow the next morning."

"Why not right away?" Cadugan asked.

Thomas Kethin spoke up. "Because if George is right, it may be ten or fifteen further miles overland, and they'll need to prepare for that and start early in the morning. They might have to camp out for at least one night. And if George is wrong, or we can't get through the way at all, then there's no sense stirring up the whole expedition just to send them back here again."

There were no more objections.

Gwyn stood up, and the council rose with him. "Idris's troop will depart immediately after breakfast, whatever the weather. Cadugan, please spread the word to the expedition leaders about our plans and coordinate with Ifor here about supplies and equipment."

⁓

Madog walked up the stone steps of his keep, out of the light of the flickering torches. A stumble on a dimly-lit step had him swearing, renewing an old vow. First thing I'll do when I have Gwyn's court in my control, I'll take over their human trade and start bringing in oil lamps, like the ones he uses so profligately.

And why stop there? Everyone says the short-lived have many conveniences, and I mean to have them all. That's the one real problem with the beast, he'd never been able to convey the notion of the human world to it, as a destination. He'd have to wait and take over Gwyn's ways instead.

Scilti seemed pleased with his work. Madog thought it a waste of time to indulge in such bloody pleasures, and a weakness, but his desires made him easier to control so he permitted it. He'd gotten what he could from that ruin of a courier, ordinary news from Gwyn about new arrivals, lists of names and skills. Nothing useful.

There was that odd report from the guards he'd posted at the end of the Trap Way. They said a stick just appeared, clattering down onto the stone. He wasn't sure whether or not to believe them, but he didn't think they dared lie, not after that last example he'd made. The Edgewood Way passage isn't very long, and neither is the Trap Way, he considered. I suppose the wind could blow something through if it caught it just right, though I've never seen it happen before.

Too bad I can't just shut the Edgewood Way altogether, but Gwyn's ownership claim makes that impossible. Still, blocking it like this is almost as good and it has the benefit of catching whatever tries to get there. They may figure that out eventually, but what can they do about it? When traffic stops coming through, I'll reverse the effect and start sucking them in from the other side. I'll close it in both directions, first, and block the Edgewood Way completely.

Let them stew for a while, and they'll be all the more eager to use it when it mysteriously reopens again.

❧

Angharad walked through the huntsman's house, turning down the lamps before joining George upstairs.

I move here, she mused, shaking her head, and he goes... somewhere else. Well, it's not his fault, and he'll be back tomorrow night anyway. None of the scenarios they'd sketched out had him staying overnight, even if it was all successful and they reached the Edgewood territory.

But then she'd lose him for the expedition on Tuesday for several days.

The courier's description of the trap at the end of the Edgewood Way made it only too clear that Madog was active again. Better then for everyone to come in via the Archer's Way, if it worked, and stay out of his reach.

No one said anything, but they're all assuming that first courier is dead, and they're probably right. Who's been lost from the Edgewood end, I wonder.

The house will be quiet once everyone's gone. Just me and Alun.

Her cat curled around her ankle. Alright, and the cat and dogs, too, she smiled. Just like my home in the village.

She'd taken over the bed linen duty from Alun for the master bedroom, and now she was glad of it. The sheets would still bear the scent of George for the few days he'd be gone, to keep her company. The thought made her hasten to finish her task and head up.

She paused in the hall, her foot on the first step. I do like the smell of this tree, the balsam rising into the air as it relaxes into the warmth of an artificial spring. It's good that George wants to set a family tradition like this, to put a personal stake into this alien land, and I'm not too old to learn a new custom myself, for the sake of whatever children may come.

A thought had occurred to her during the afternoon's conversation with Ceridwen and Eluned. She'd decided to make small ornaments for the tree, as Gwyn had described to her once before. Let the family collection begin with that. I'll show them to him when he returns, and he'll be glad, one for each day.

I should have included small carving tools when I packed, she thought, but Iolo's workshop looks like it has most of what I'd need. Alun showed me what he had there, and it should do.

I could make him something tomorrow, maybe, to take with him on Tuesday.

And something for the mantle in the study. Maybe with oranges as a decoration. She smiled at the memory and hastened up the stairs.

CHAPTER 7

George looked around him again one last time at Daear Llosg. Idris and Thomas were behind him with a band of about twenty, well-armed and prepared for a stay of a few days if something should go wrong. Seems like overkill, but I guess there's just no way of being sure, he thought.

At his right hand stood Gwyn, both of them dismounted, their horses held by one of the guards staying behind with Gwyn.

Before them was the end of the Archer's Way that he'd sealed almost two months ago. He'd marked the location of the entrance by shuffling through the snow, to keep the riders away from something they couldn't see.

"You remember asking me if I could unseal it again at the time?" he said to Gwyn.

Gwyn nodded.

"Can you see what I do, a woven web holding it together?"

"Yes, I see it."

"Well, there's this sort of tab in the bottom right that I'm going to, um, pull on."

Gwyn said, "I don't see that feature. It must be visible to you because you made it."

George shrugged and took a mental grip on the piece he'd described, and gave it a gentle tug. Slowly, like an unraveling sweater, the web began to pull apart. As the first strands worked loose, he felt a presence on the other side.

"Watch out, there's something there," he called. He stumbled through the snow and pulled Gwyn out of the direct path while the seal continued to unweave, and the guards drew their swords. When the bottom seam gave way, a sleepy and irritated black bear rolled out, and some branches with her. She sat up and blinked, then offered them a half-hearted growl. The relieved laughter of the guards in reply intimidated her, and she rumbled to her feet and made for the woods upslope, scattering drifted snow behind her.

Even the sober Gwyn chuckled. "Well, I guess that answers the question of whether the other end is still open," George said.

They retrieved their horses and mounted up.

"You'll be staying here, my lord, yes?" Idris said.

"That's my intent," Gwyn said, patiently. Idris accepted the ambiguous reply with a skeptical glance but no comment.

George and Idris entered the way side by side, and the troop followed in pairs. The passage was short, the featureless gray broken by the vegetation the bear had brought into her winter den and by drifted snow at the end. As they emerged, George stood off to the side to let the riders by.

The way was obvious to him, and the marks in the snow of the riders starting seemingly from nowhere was a good enough indicator of its location for everyone else, for now.

Idris rode up to him. "I want to send a rider back immediately to Gwyn, and then have him return here. Let's see how open this way is."

He sent one guard back in, but the way was closed to him and he just passed through the spot.

George joined him, and he tried again. This time they both rode through.

He called to Gwyn, sitting his horse with the two remaining guards. "We're reporting back, at Idris's request. The way is just as we left it, with no one around. We've tested, and it looks like they can't get through without me, which we thought might happen."

"Can you find the Edgewood Way?" Gwyn said.

"Don't know yet. We're taking this in small steps. I'm headed back."

George turned his horse and brought the guard back with him to rejoin Idris.

Idris had already deployed his men in a semicircle around the way in the otherwise unbroken snow of this river meadow and was standing by, waiting for them to return. George noted that even the bear had left no tracks. She must have been denned up there since before the last snowfall.

"I'm going to see what I can find, now," George said. "If Mosby will stand still for me, I'll try to stay mounted. May take a few minutes."

Idris said, "I'll wait until you're done to send out scouts, in case they stir up something that interrupts you. Identifying the location is the highest priority."

George pulled out his brass compass from his vest pocket, where it was attached to the other end of his watch chain. On this overcast day it was difficult to see the sun to judge direction, and the Blue Ridge wasn't visible from here.

He found magnetic north and used that as his first search priority, still operating on the assumption that they were at the south end of Edgewood.

He faced north and reached out to see what he could find. He was startled to feel something behind him first, a very long thin faint trace that ran from east to west, nearby, with a hint of a curve, as though it were the bottom of an oval, opening to the north. We must be close to the barrier, he thought.

He turned his attention away from it and resumed his search. At the extreme distance, a bit blurred, there were two, no, three presences. One was a way, definitely, north and a little west, and then an odd sort of double impression straight north. He tried to focus more strongly on the latter, and thought, what if this were the Edgewood Way and some kind of trap way together? That made sense out of what he picked up.

He opened his eyes to find Idris watching him intently. "What did you find?" he asked.

"You understand I can't be certain. But I think I've found the new way that appeared west of Edgewood Manor, and the Edgewood Way itself with some other sort of way tied to it. They're at the limit of my range but I can't judge distance well. I still think it's ten or fifteen miles."

Idris turned as if to send out his scouts.

"Wait," George said. "I believe that barrier everyone talks about isn't far away at all. I think we should take a look at it, don't you?"

Idris paused in thought. "Thomas," he called. When Thomas Kethin came over, he continued, "I'm going to divide us into three groups. I want you to take three pairs of scouts and send them north, east, and west a little distance. We're looking for roads and settlements. George thinks we're in Edgewood so probably it's safe enough, but don't count on it. We'll meet up again here in one hour."

Thomas nodded and rode off to select his men.

Idris beckoned George. "Please go one more time, huntsman, and report to Gwyn this latest and warn him we'll be an hour or more. When you come back, I'll have a group ready to go with you to the barrier."

George popped back out through the way to update Gwyn. The relief at the news that this was almost certainly Edgewood was visible on his face, and he endorsed the investigation of the barrier.

"We'll wait for your return," he said. "It will do us all good to take a little exercise with our horses in the snow here."

When George returned, he found that Idris had set a small group to hold the way's exit point, and a larger one to follow George to the barrier.

"So, which direction?" Idris said.

George looked over the landscape and matched it to what he could feel, looking for the easiest route. "I think if we ride up out of this streamside flatland we can get out of the tangle of the vegetation more easily."

Idris gestured for him to take the lead. George picked his way carefully, the footing hidden by the snow, and ascended the meadow's margin at a diagonal. At the top he found his guess had paid off. The ground was open, only sparsely interrupted by trees. There was no sign of habitation. He waited to make sure everyone had gotten up the slope without mishap, then walked off with Idris to the south.

Before they had crossed as much as half a mile of this terrain, George brought them to a halt and dismounted, giving his reins to a guard.

He walked through the snow about ten yards further. "There's something here. It's not strong and I get no sense of danger, but it's a long, long line and extends further than I can see." He gestured with his arms to try and mark the trace.

He said to Idris, "Just because it doesn't feel dangerous to me doesn't mean I'm right. I felt something like this along the ridge line of the Blue Ridge one time out hunting, and one of my hounds came back hurt after crossing it." But the two outsider hounds crossed and came back without any harm, he thought. How did they do that?

Idris dismounted and made as if to join him but stopped partway. "I can feel something, and it's not pleasant. We know that people cross the line, but we don't know what happens when they do. All we know is they don't come back."

One of his guards, young and grim-faced, rode up to Idris. "Sir, I lost my father to something like this, or at least I never got him back. Give me a rope and I'll try crossing it to find out."

George protested, "You might never recover."

"I'll take that chance. I want to know what happened to him."

"You're not going to let him?" George asked Idris.

"It's Emrys's choice, and a valuable one," Idris said. He called for rope.

With one end held by Idris and another guard, and the other tied around his waist, Emrys was ready to cross. George went with him step by step, but he halted well before the line, his face in a sweat.

He took a running lunge at the invisible barrier and charged through on pure momentum. As soon as he crossed, he gave a loud cry and fell.

George swore and charged after him, ignoring the protests behind him. He felt a tingle all over as he crossed the line, but no other ill effect.

He bent down and picked the man up in his arms, staggering back across the barrier with him and lowering him to the ground well away from it.

Emrys shivered and shook, incoherent. Idris pried his lips open and poured in a mouthful of something from his flask. George could smell the fumes of brandy. They untied the rope around his waist and hauled him to his feet where he swayed.

Idris pointed at two of his men. "Get him on his horse and ride beside him to keep him there. Tie him on if you have to. We're going to take him home."

They made the best time they could back to the exit of the Archer's Way, and George brought that detachment through to Gwyn so they could take Emrys to Ceridwen for treatment. He returned to wait with Idris for Thomas to bring back the scouts.

As they slipped into the meadow in pairs, Idris looked to Thomas for news. "Not much found," he said.

Idris said, "We're leaving. We'll discuss it on the other side."

George brought them all back to Daear Llosg, and resealed the way behind them.

Seething Magma felt a group of people emerging from a way within her range. Normally she ignored this sort of thing but this time she reconsidered. She hadn't thought about seeking help from the surface folk, but now one of them held her child. Maybe the remedy lay with them.

She made a way to the surface and cast about for a better feel. There was one in the group that tasted different, like her new neighbor, the horned man. She watched him from afar every year as he marked the season with his own ways. Odd behavior, but he cleaned up after himself and they had no conflicts.

This one should know about the ways and understand her child's captor. Maybe he can help. As she started to make progress in that direction, she felt him vanish to her senses twice, briefly, and reappear. Then he was gone.

She continued on to the spot anyway, where she found the anchored end of a way made by Granite Cloud and tasted it. Maybe he'll come back. I can wait. She thought about his flavor, turning him over in her mind.

Mother, when are you coming?

Seething Magma settled down in the snow and made herself comfortable, like a cat at a mousehole. *Patience, child.*

◡﹏◠

Ceridwen hastened into Gwyn's council chamber to join the meeting just starting, followed closely by Eluned.

"How's Emrys?" George said.

"We've got him settled. He's chilled to the core, but he's talking and coherent. He's very grateful you went after him, George."

"When we lost that hound over the ridge line, Aeronwy, she made her own way back across but she was cold and shivering. We settled her in some straw with a couple of warm packmates and fed her hot broth. It took a week, but she eventually recovered."

"That's more or less what we've done for him, minus the straw," Eluned said with a quirk of the lips. "If there's no one there to help, though, I wouldn't be surprised if the shock were fatal."

Idris caught George's eye and touched his brow to thank him. George nodded back and waved his hand dismissively.

"We're all glad the guard will survive." Gwyn said. "The obvious question is, why didn't it bother you, kinsman?"

George said, slowly, "I've been chewing on that all the way back. All I can offer is a theory… You know, the outsider hounds, the ones brought back as whelps from Cernunnos, they weren't damaged when they crossed the ridge line, the way Aeronwy was. And as far as I can tell, wild animals aren't either. So, tell me if I'm wrong… All people who cross the ridge are hurt, yes?"

"All of them," Ceridwen said, "as far as we know."

"Fae, lutins, korrigans?"

She nodded.

"What about ordinary humans?"

Silence. Very few ordinary humans lived here. Mostly they were of mixed stock, but occasionally one stumbled into a way or a spouse was brought back. George hadn't met one yet.

"I don't know," Ceridwen said. "I've never heard of that, one way or the other."

"Here's my theory. I think the barrier acts on those who are in some sense, excuse me, unnatural, that is bearers of magic or otherwise, um, enhanced. I think that natural animals, like wild animals, and maybe ordinary humans, are immune.

"What would make the outsider hounds different, and maybe me, too, is that we come fresh and direct from a source, like Cernunnos. Only as the blood dilutes does the barrier get a hold on it, as it did on Aeronwy."

He turned to Gwyn. "Cernunnos has expertise with the ways, sir, but it's different from yours, and the ways he makes are also a bit different—no passages, remember, as we discussed? Maybe I'm really like him that way, and not like you. Maybe that's where my way-handling comes from. Maybe my beast-sense is his, too. Maybe it's really all his, not so much yours. That could explain why I'm stronger in these aspects than any third-generation descendant of the fae should be."

And maybe that means I don't have the long life, he thought. But maybe I do, though—I can work a glamour, if not very well, so at least some of Gwyn's blood has survived in me. But it isn't going to save my grandmother, is it. Well no sense worrying about it. I'll know eventually.

Gwyn mused for a moment. "I'll think about what you've suggested. In any case, I don't see that it matters much right now. We've proved as well as we can that the Archer's Way leads to Edgewood. It's time to get the expedition ready for tomorrow morning."

Idris told Cadugan, "Warn them that they'll be going overland and to put as much as possible onto horseback. We can supply pack horses."

Gwyn asked, "Did you find any roads, Thomas?"

"Only the one, and it narrow and snow-covered. No habitations. Even if we find a village it won't be able to house so large a party. We must be prepared for one or two nights camping, at least, as we move north."

Angharad sat in one of the soft armchairs in front of the fire in the bedroom while George roamed around, rummaging through wardrobes and drawers, looking for anything critical he'd forgotten to pack. George looked over at her and admired her calm. He was too on edge to sleep right now, and not the least of it was the knowledge that he'd be away for several days, a week or more, helping Rhys with some unknown situation, instead of here with his new wife.

She patted the chair next to her. "Come sit down for a moment and relax. I have something for you, to take with you while you're gone."

He came and sat as bid, grateful for the distraction, and always happy to just look at her. Tonight, with the firelight soft on her face, her long auburn hair loosed from her braid, she filled his eyes.

"When you come back, you can hang it on the tree," she said.

She reached over and took his hand, turning it up to hold something. Then she placed a small pendant on a cord in it.

He held it up to his eye. She'd given him a wooden arrow, about two inches long, sturdier than a real one would be and heavier than seemed right, for wood. It was delicately carved and tinted green overall. A thin green braided silk cord was attached at the midpoint on a swivel so that it could hang levelly and turn.

"It's lovely," he said.

She pushed his hand at him. "Hang it round your neck."

Obediently he passed the cord around his neck and let it fall on his chest, over his shirt. "No, against your skin," she said.

He decided to take advantage of that instruction, here in front of the warm fire, to remove his shirt altogether rather than just tuck the pendant under it. He had plans for later in the evening. When the arrow touched his skin, it vanished, with the cord. "What?" he said, surprised.

72

"Now take it off again and hold it suspended."

Focused now on the gift, he removed the pendant, and it reappeared. He held it by the cord, the arrow pointing at Angharad.

"Watch the arrow." She stood and walked around the room. The arrow swiveled on its cord to follow her movements.

She came back and stood by his chair. "It's a simple finder spell, enhanced with a bit of silver for permanence, combined with a see-me-not. While you wear it, none can see or feel it, only you. When you hold it like that, it'll point to me, wherever I am. Should work for a good long distance."

He smiled at her and put it on again. "As if I needed any help finding you," he muttered, as he rose to enfold her in his arms, shivering at the touch of her hands moving on his bare back, heated by the flames.

CHAPTER 8

George and Thomas Kethin sat their horses at the head of the expedition, just before the sealed end of the Archer's Way, while Idris and his men went over the long train behind them to make sure everyone was ready. The way wasn't much wider than a wagon, so the whole group would have to come through more or less in single file.

Gwyn stood with them, though he wasn't coming. George asked him, "How will you close the door behind us? I won't be back for at least a few days."

With a wave of his hand, Gwyn dismissed the concern. "We'll mount a guard, but I doubt Madog will be coming from this direction, and it doesn't seem like anyone else can use it, besides you."

George thought to himself, I suppose he knows what he's doing. George would be heading the line as way-guide, with Thomas and some of his rangers who would immediately disperse as scouts around the exit point until Idris's men could join them. He'd also bring two of Idris's people at the head of the line with him, to direct and organize the traffic at the other end.

"How long will the guide effect work? Will I be able to pull the whole expedition through the way, the long line of it?"

Gwyn said, "I've never heard of that being a problem, but then I haven't often seen a group this large attempt a single passage. The last one was the night we brought Annwn to the new world." He paused in reminiscence for a moment, then said, briskly. "If you find your party is incomplete on the other side, you'll just have to come back to start the next segment along. Should be fine."

From his vantage higher up on the slope, George looked over the long serpentine line. Ceridwen, Eluned, and Cadugan made a tight knot nearby on horseback, occupied in their own tasks of counting the groups.

The wagon of lutins was near the front of the line, but George saw that Benitoe had persuaded Maëlys to ride with him on ponyback, with the other riders. Despite the addition of food and camping gear, the lutins' wagon was still one of the lighter-weight vehicles and would be used to test the difficulty of the terrain in Edgewood. Anything too difficult to get that wagon through would automatically rule out the rest of them.

Overall, the number of wagons had been greatly reduced, despite the extra shelter for the expected one or two nights out. As much as possible had been added to pack horses, leaving only the heaviest and most unwieldy equipment on wheels, along with the very young children and a few others. Still, getting these six wagons through to the manor would be tough in several inches of snow. Idris had made quite an effort yesterday insisting they were as lightweight and small as could be, for ease in man-handling.

Ifor rode up to Gwyn. The steward looked as if he hadn't slept all night and, for as busy as George had seen him yesterday, he supposed that was entirely possible. "We're ready, my lord."

Gwyn caught Idris's eye, halfway down the line, and Idris nodded.

Gwyn turned his horse to the crowd and raised his hand. The voices quieted as he got their attention, until only the squeak of horse hooves in the dry snow and the rattle of chains remained to disturb the silence.

"Our thanks to all of you who are undertaking this journey. You have our blessing and good wishes, and may fortune attend you."

There was a general, but subdued, cheer in response, and Gwyn gestured to George to lead off.

George turned Mosby to face the way and unsealed it again. No bear this time—that story had spread and everyone near the front watched to see if there would be any new surprises. He set off at a walk with Thomas and his men, wondering if they could reach Edgewood Manor in a single day. Highly doubtful, he thought it.

As the creak of the riders and wagons followed him, he smiled and muttered under his breath, "Git along, little dogies."

As soon as he cleared the exit, George pulled aside and waited, watching them all emerge. He assumed that staying close to the way would help the way-guide effect, however it worked. Idris's men lined the travelers up in an orderly manner as they came through, and then Idris himself took over as he emerged, with Cadugan helping.

Thomas came back and stood next to George, having dispatched a screen of scouts ahead of them. "We'll need you at the front when this part's done," he said to George, "You're the one who knows the exact direction."

"Yes, but straight north in any case, unless we find a road that can help," George said.

Benitoe had taken his place beside George automatically, as if they had a pack of hounds to manage, and Maëlys sat quietly beside him, warmly wrapped.

They watched the korrigans, well past the halfway point of the long line, coming through as a single group, excited and talking together.

Suddenly, like a clap of thunder, George was deafened by a voice, a sort of pleased *THERE YOU ARE!* It exploded in his head, with the scent of hot lava and cinders and a flash of red-orange light. He flinched away from it and never felt himself topple from his horse bonelessly into the snow.

⤻

Benitoe saw George's head jerk back, as if he'd taken a blow, but couldn't reach him quickly enough to help break the fall. He dismounted and gave his reins to Maëlys.

Thomas joined him on the ground and they bent over George, checking for injuries. Broch pulled out of the group of korrigans to join them.

The disturbance caught Idris's eye, and he rode over. "What happened?"

"I don't know," Benitoe said, straightening up. "It looked as if something hit him, but I couldn't see anything."

As Thomas finished looking for broken bones, George opened his eyes and sat up. He leaned forward, and held his head in both hands between his knees, covering his ears. "Ow, ow, ow," he said, unhappily.

"What was it? Are we under attack?" Idris asked.

"I don't know," George said. "I don't think so." He stood up carefully and brushed off the snow. He leaned against Mosby and delicately shook his head, using his stirrup for support.

⤻

The voice returned, cautiously.

Sorry.

This time it was much quieter. George lifted his head and looked west. "Who are you?"

Behind him he heard Benitoe quietly asking Thomas, "Who's he talking to?" He ignored them.

Friend. Coming.

George said over his shoulder, "I think we're about to get a visit from something very strange." In an aside to Thomas, he said, "Help me get back on my horse." He accepted a boost and resettled himself on Mosby.

"It's talking to me, sort of, more like concepts and pictures instead of words. I think it was just too loud the first time and didn't mean to hurt me," he said. He reached over and gripped Idris's arm. "I don't think it means us any harm, don't let the guards get carried away."

"Alert," Idris called to his men. "No shooting."

Behind them, the rest of the expedition was still coming through the way, just reaching the end. The korrigans had pulled out of line, not to leave Broch behind.

The sound of branches cracking was audible from the woods on the western edge of the river meadow, and everyone turned to face it, silence spreading in the group as they realized something unusual was happening.

George walked his horse forward to meet it partway, Benitoe at his side. Idris and Thomas came with him, and Broch, curious.

Out of the trees flowed some sort of creature, the size of a pickup truck, to George's eyes, and not a small one. There was no obvious head or tail, no eyes. It was shaped like a long, heavy slab, colored rock-gray, but it was flexible and the form seemed to be malleable. He couldn't see how it moved, exactly. Some indeterminate number of short and stubby pseudopods appeared to be propelling it along. If rock could be alive and mobile, then this is what it might be like.

Moving slowly, it flowed forward to meet George who waited for it on Mosby. The horse was surprisingly calm about it. George got no sense of "predator" from him. Probably doesn't smell like an animal at all, he thought.

Benitoe asked, "What is that?"

Broch walked his pony past him and stopped just short of George. "One of the Old Ones," he breathed. "I never thought to see one, in my life." He looked at Benitoe, "An elemental, a rock-wight." He dismounted, swept off his hat, and bowed deeply to it. Behind him, several of the korrigans had come up and joined him, hats off and bowing, on foot and holding their reins.

George heard them but was concentrating on trying to understand the creature.

Picture of creature and George meeting. Approval.

"Yes, greetings to you, too," he said. "Happy to make your acquaintance."

Picture of George. Question?

"My name? I'm George Talbot Traherne."

Picture of horned man. Question?

"That's Cernunnos, in one form. He and I are... related."

Satisfaction. Picture of creature, pool of bubbling lava.

George was puzzled. In context, perhaps that was its name. "Is that your name? Boiling Rock? Hot Lava? Seething Magma?"

At the last of these, the response was *Approval.*

"Glad to meet you, Seething Magma. Mind if I call you Mag? It's a little easier to say."

Amusement.

"I'll take that as a yes."

He turned to the people who had been gathering behind him. "Folks, let me introduce Seething Magma." There was a general low response, and a high-pitched child's voice asking what it was.

"Yes, I'd like to know that, too. Can someone explain to me what's going on? Can anyone else hear it?" Heads shook in denial.

Ceridwen rode to his side. She said, astonishment plain in her voice. "This is something out of legend. I thought they were all gone. We met them long ago in the old world, especially in the far east, where some called them dragons. They live in the rock, somehow, inside the mountains."

Eluned added, "They get to be very large, much larger than this, and they are very old, even by our standards, perhaps immortal."

Tiernoc said, "We live all our lives never expecting to meet one, even though many of us delve in the mountains. No one can name the last before us to encounter one. Why, we'll all be famous..."

"Anything we can do for it, we will, all of us," Broch said. There were murmurs of agreement from the other korrigans. "Find out what it requires of us."

George could hear religious awe in their voices.

He turned back as Seething Magma resumed the conversation.

Urgency. Picture of Blue Ridge, opening like a cutaway drawing. Picture of Mag deep within.

"You live inside the Blue Ridge," George translated out loud, for the benefit of the bystanders.

Picture of Mag, budding like a cactus. Bud breaks off, moves.

"You have a child! Oh, you're a 'she'—sorry, ma'am."

Amusement. Picture of child, dark gray, solid rock, clouds in the sky.

Oh, no, George thought, another name. "Her name is, what, Gray Cloud?"

Picture of lava rising inside a volcano, solidifying to rock.

"Oh. Basalt Cloud? Granite Cloud?"

Approval.

"Alright, folks. Mag here has a child, a daughter I guess, named Granite Cloud."

Picture of child, moving away, gone. Child caught by something, struggling. Child reaching toward Mag, Mag reaching back.

"Cloudie went away, did she? And something caught her. And you can't get her back."

YES, YES, YES.

George winced and held his head. "Ow, too loud, Mag."

Sorry.

"That's alright. What do you want from us?"

Picture of child.

"You want us to help get your daughter back."

Yes.

The great rock-like creature moved back and forth almost as if dancing at her success in conveying her need.

"Hold on a moment," George said.

Idris said, quietly, "We can't keep everyone here like this. We have to get to Edgewood."

Broch protested, "This is more important than anything else we had planned. We can always find work and homes. An Old One asks for help. We must provide it."

George could see trouble brewing, and feared the journey they still had ahead of them today. He held up a hand to interrupt them and turned back to the creature.

"Mag, we're cold and we have young ones with us. We must get to shelter tonight, and then to Edgewood Manor. That's a long distance for us."

He pictured it to her as a map with their location and the ways marked, out of habit, since he was always conscious of them. To his astonishment, she echoed it back with a much higher level of detail, and Edgewood Manor's location was emphasized.

There? Your intention?

"Yes, that's where we're headed. Can you come with us? It might take a day or two."

Picture of Mag moving abruptly through space, coming out at Edgewood Manor. Picture of people following.

George blinked. "You can make a way? You want to take us there?"

Yes. Simple. Waiting.

He paused to readjust his plans. "Folks, I think I've found us a ride. She's just offered to make a way to Edgewood Manor and bring us along."

Eluned said, "That's what the legends say. It's supposed to be how they get through the rock they live in. Might even be how they eat it, for all we know."

Idris said quietly, "Do you trust her, huntsman?"

"Yes," George said, slowly. "I do. She might make a mistake, like not notice how fragile we are, but she doesn't mean us any harm. I think we should do it."

He told her, "Thanks for the offer, Mag. Hold on while we organize things, please."

"This is our last chance to send a message through to Gwyn easily. I can carry it, but what on earth would I tell him?" George said.

Ceridwen replied, "I'll write a quick note to try and explain, though it's probably a waste of paper—he'll never believe me..." She scribbled on a sheet in her pocket notebook and tore it off for George.

He looked at Idris who nodded and said. "Yes, be off with you and I'll get things ready."

George bowed to Seething Magma from the saddle. "I'll be right back, don't go away."

Yes.

George popped back through the Archer's Way and surprised the guard standing there. The Greenway Court people had all started home after the last wagon went through.

"I have a note here for Gwyn. I can't wait. Tell him we found an unexpected and impatient ally."

He turned and rode to the other side.

⌒〜〜⌒

The expedition reformed on Idris as Thomas gathered the last of the scouts back in. George, at the head of the line again, walked Mosby up to Mag. "We're ready. Remember, it'll take us a while to go through, all of us."

She turned and faced the woods. George had taken to identifying her leading edge as her front, though he'd already noticed that she seemed to move in either direction without preference. She made a small undulating motion and a wide way opened in the clear space of the meadow before them. George could dimly see buildings on the other side, through the passage.

The korrigans had seized the position immediately behind George, as if providing an honor guard for the creature.

There. Picture of Mag and George entering together.

"Thank you. I'm coming." They walked through the entrance, and the korrigans followed.

She kept pace with his horse as they went. *Picture of horned man and deer, talking. Picture of George and deer. Question?*

"Cernunnos talks to beasts, yes. I can, too, some."

Picture of Mag and George, talking. Question?

"Is that why we can talk? I don't know. I suppose so. But you're intelligent, not a beast."

Picture of mouse, deer, man, Mag, horned man.

"All a matter of degree, you mean. True."

They approached the transition point and emerged onto the main terrace at Edgewood Manor. George pushed to stand in front of Mag as people scattered out of their way. "It's alright, we've come from Gwyn," he shouted, hoping to forestall any accidents.

Rhys's guards, running to the defense, slowed as they recognized both Idris and Gwyn's huntsman. Idris rode up to the first guard. "I've got a large party coming through. Where can I put them?"

The guard sent two of his troop to lead the riders down the terrace steps into the grounds where they spread out as they emerged.

Edgewood Manor was a long, low, two-story stone building on a low prominence, surrounded by many terraces and farm fields beyond. The small market village was just out of sight to the south, though George caught a glimpse of buildings through the trees now that the autumn leaves had dropped.

The wagon drivers remained on the terrace level as they emerged, there being no simple way to get the wagons down from there without a ramp over the steps.

About a dozen of the korrigans kept together to stay with Seething Magma. Idris took one look and visibly gave up on the notion of parting them, even as the terrace was filling up. George held his position at the front with Mag and a few of the others.

The main doors of the manor opened and Rhys strode out to greet them, followed closely by Edern and Rhodri. George thought Rhys looked tired and a bit worn, feeling the responsibility and uncertainty of rule, perhaps. He dismounted to greet them properly.

"Good to see you, cousin, and all your..." Rhys said. He broke off at the sight of the rock-wight.

Rhodri walked over to embrace George about the shoulders, but practically tripped over his feet getting there, not being able to take his eyes off of Mag as he went by.

George said, "My lord Rhys, Rhodri, my lord Edern, allow me to present a guest. This is Seething Magma. She has urgent business she wants our help with, as soon as we can take care of these travelers." He smiled privately to see that even Edern was taken aback at the surprise.

Before they could respond, Cadugan walked forward and bowed to Edern. "My lord, I've come as you requested. I have much to do to settle these people, and would like to get started."

"I am pleased to see you again, Cadugan," Edern said. "Thank you for accepting this task. This is Rhys Vachan ap Rhys, my grandson and Gwyn's foster-son, on whose council I serve."

They bowed to each other. "I look forward to receiving the benefit of your wisdom, steward," Rhys said.

"And I to serving you to the best of my abilities," Cadugan replied.

Edern beckoned over a woman with the keys of the head housekeeper. "Let me introduce you to someone who can help you get everything coordinated." She walked off with him, responding laconically to his many probing questions as he headed to the edge of the terrace to begin organizing the travelers.

This left the korrigans unaddressed. George turned to Broch and Tiernoc. "I understand your reverence for Mag but we must get you settled before we can do anything else. Will you content yourselves for now with sending one of you to our council to hear more about what she has to say?"

Broch said, "I'll stay." Tiernoc looked as if he wanted to contest this, but Broch repeated, "I'll stay," and quelled him with a raised eyebrow.

Cadugan could be heard behind them, calling for planks so that the six trapped wagons could be rolled down the steps.

As the crowd on the terrace thinned out, George thought of his own responsibilities. He'd seen Benitoe take charge of Maëlys without being told, but couldn't spot Cydifor until he looked around and realized he was lingering discretely within earshot. He wasn't hidden, exactly. He reminded George of a child who was hoping to be overlooked when the conversation among the adults got interesting. Come to think of it, he'd kept himself close when Mag first greeted them, too.

"Rhodri," he called. "I've brought you something. Besides Mag, I mean."

His friend shook himself out of his fascinated study of Mag to give him some of his attention. "Hmm?"

"You'll like this," George teased.

Rhodri turned around altogether, and George waved Cydifor forward.

"I'd like to introduce Cydifor. He's come a long way to meet another musician."

"A musician!" Rhodri said, delighted. "How did you manage that?"

"He's come to serve Rhys and needs a patron." Cydifor bowed deeply from horseback.

"Assuming he can rub two notes together and not make them squeak, I'll be happy to see what I can do."

"For now, my lord," Cydifor said, "I just want to find out what this creature out of legend has to say. Think of the material."

"Arrange your belongings with Cadugan and come stay near me. You might have to leave if the council needs to be private but stick around as long as you can. Tell Cadugan to house you in the manor, at my say so."

An impromptu council was left on the terrace, as George, Idris, Ceridwen, and Eluned walked over to join their hosts, leading their horses. Idris said, quietly, "What's the situation?"

Edern replied, "The Edgewood Way's been closed since Saturday, marshal. We were suspicious of what might follow and set a guard around the entrance. How did you get here?"

"That's a long story," Idris said. "We started at the Archer's Way, but then the huntsman seems to have acquired a... friend, and she brought us the rest of the distance."

Rhodri frankly stared at her. "She made that way, didn't she? I felt it. I've read legends about this. Can I talk to her?"

"Yes, soon," George said, "but Rhys, we need to ask about Gwyn's courier, the one he sent Saturday. He never came back. Did he arrive safely?"

"No, we never saw him."

"We think Madog's back," George said.

Rhys decided he needed more information and, as George had seen his foster-father Gwyn do dozens of times by now, he stepped forward solemnly and said, "We'll meet on this immediately, as soon as your horses are stabled."

George stopped him, "I think Mag will have important things to say about this, and she's part of the news. Is there a room that can accommodate us all?"

"We'll use the room we call the conservatory, though there's nothing growing here now. It has double doors at the front which should be big enough. I'll have the fires lit there and food provided for us. Give your horses to the guards and they'll see to their comfort."

"Mag," George said, "will you join us at our council in a few minutes? Is there any refreshment we can bring you?"

No. Approval.

"Rhodri, would you like to show her how to get there? I think she can understand you if you speak to her, though I don't know if you can hear her replies."

"I'll figure something out," he said eagerly. "Won't you please come follow me, my lady?" This last in his most official diplomatic tones.

Amusement.

She glided off the terrace alongside her infatuated admirer.

Gwyn sat in his council room alone, reading Ceridwen's hasty note again and mulling it over. They found a *what?* An Old One, a rock elemental? Or, rather, it found them. No, he corrected himself, *she* found them. How odd to think of them as female.

This one needs something and offers alliance. A very rational behavior. We must seem to them as the humans seem to us, short-lived creatures, easy to ignore. What can she want that we can possibly provide?

His grandfather had met one, in the far east, but he himself never had. So we have them here, he thought, in the new world.

Elementals in the Blue Ridge, and a barrier on the ridge line. He didn't believe in coincidences, and wondered.

Ceridwen says the rock-wight will make a way for them. I suppose if that had failed, they'd still be there and able to send an updated message, so I must assume it succeeded. No one knows where the ways that are discovered come from. Have we just found an answer?

CHAPTER 9

George and the others followed Rhodri as he led Mag to the room Rhys called the conservatory. This occupied the corner of one long wing and was generally used for games and recreation in the summer time, a place where people could gather informally.

It was little occupied in the winter because of the chill of its many windows and George hadn't had an occasion to use it before on his two previous visits. The external double doors faced the front of the manor but the terraces were not joined directly, only connected by a walkway. Watching from behind as Mag negotiated the snowy path, George could make no sense of her undercarriage, whatever it was that propelled her along. The blur left on the ground after her passage was no help either.

She paused while Rhodri opened the doors.

Watch.

She raised up about a quarter of her length, like a walrus, and let them look at her underside. Dozens of protuberances covered the surface. The longer ones were stubby and flat, reminding George of elephant feet, but much smaller. Others looked like they might be used for eating. Makes sense, he thought. Presumably she ingests dirt or rock. As they watched, fascinated, some of them withdrew into the body and re-emerged elsewhere, changing form. It was both disturbing and mesmerizing.

She resettled flat on the ground, and George was strongly put in mind of a dignified old lady resettling her floor-length skirt and petticoats.

"Thank you for showing us," he said. "I didn't want to be rude and ask, but we all wondered."

Satisfaction.

It hadn't escaped his attention that he hadn't spoken his curiosity aloud, that she must have seen his thoughts.

Concern?

No, it's alright, he thought to her. It's just that none of us are very comfortable exposing our raw opinions and inclinations.

She repeated the picture of mouse, deer, man, Mag, horned man.

Yes, we all think the same sorts of thoughts, in our own way, and have the same concerns. Nothing I can do about it anyway. *Picture of George and the horned man. Then picture of the horned man inside George.*

I can't hide from him, either, he agreed.

Amusement. Picture of child playing at hiding from parent.

"Yes, but we're not children." George forgot himself and spoke the last aloud, with some asperity. Ceridwen looked at him.

Sorry. Truth. Picture of child hiding dissolved.

"We're having a conversation about privacy," he said to Ceridwen. "I can't keep her out, but she's not prying, either." He shrugged.

Seething Magma checked her width against the double doors, open wide and pulled her sides in, raising her height in the middle to fit the opening.

"Good, just right," Rhodri said, as she flowed through onto the stone floor.

Amusement. Picture of Mag stretched thin and very, very long flowing through a mousehole like an endless snake.

George stumbled, laughing at the unexpected joke. "Rhodri, I don't think that was ever going to be a problem." He waved off trying to explain himself, some things were just too hard to translate.

He looked around with interest as he followed Mag into the large room. In keeping with its original intent as a conservatory, the floor was stone flagged and windows ran all around it, down to waist height. Some later builder had added wooden paneling to the interior walls and built in seating with cupboards beneath all around. The contents were in something of a jumble—clearly it functioned as a lumber room during the winter months.

Right now the servants were laying logs in the broad fireplace and clearing the furniture off to one side. Edern directed the staff to set up a semicircle of chairs facing the fire with a large open space for Seething Magma in front of it. At the end of the room nearest the inner doors of the manor, other servants set up food and drink.

Ceridwen sent one of them off on an errand, and soon both she and Eluned were set up with small tables and writing materials near the fire which was taking the chill off the room. As Cadugan returned from his initial arrangements outside, she beckoned him to a seat beside her, and they shared the table. George watched this byplay and thought, she knew he'd want to take notes and planned the courtesy.

Eluned stood to introduce herself as Rhys approached his own seat, next to Rhodri. George was struck by the resemblance between them, both blond in this room of dark-haired people.

"My lord, I'm Eluned, come to help you as Ceridwen has helped your foster-father."

Rhys bowed. "I am honored, my lady. Please be welcome."

"You know, we're kin," she said. "I was your mother's great-aunt, her grandmother's sister."

Rhys stiffened. "No, I didn't realize. Did you know her well?"

"Only as a child. My travels took me far away in the early years of her marriage, and then it turned out there was no more time."

Rhys lowered his head at the thought of his mother Eiryth, abducted with his father by Madog when he was ten years old, and killed.

Edern stood and bowed to her as well. "Welcome, kinswoman." She nodded in reply and reseated herself.

George anchored one end of the semicircle, to help as Seething Magma's translator. Broch set himself next to him, as close to her as he could get, and never took his eyes off of her. Idris sat beside him, and next to him, Rhys's marshal, Lleision.

Cydifor found a seat behind Rhodri and made himself as unnoticeable as possible.

Rhys took charge of the meeting. He's come a long way in a few weeks, George thought, as he watched the young man. He's done well to take his foster-father as a model.

"We are here assembled with our council and our guest, Seething Magma. Before we hear her story, is there anything affecting our defenses that can't wait?"

Idris said, "Gwyn's greatest concern was the peculiar situation with the Edgewood Way and the disappearance of his courier."

Lleision replied, next to him. "We have the way entrance blocked and guarded, and we haven't seen any messenger since Friday."

Cadugan spoke up. "The travelers are being housed in guest halls and we'll be settling them in the Edgewood villages over the next few days, those that are come to stay. They're all taken care of for the present."

Edern summarized. "I see no reason we can't now spend whatever time is necessary to hear from our guest."

Rhys nodded. "Huntsman, are you the only one who can talk to her? Will you please make the introductions?"

George rose and remained standing. "It may only be me who hears her but I think she can understand all of us, words and thoughts. She doesn't speak to me in words, but in pictures and emotions."

He turned to her and bowed. "My lady Seething Magma, thank you for bringing us from the Archer's Way and for waiting so patiently. Are you comfortable? Is everything to your liking?"

Yes, thanks.

"Alright. Let me present to you Rhys, earl of this Edgewood domain under his foster-father Gwyn, Prince of Annwn. This is his grandfather, Edern, Gwyn's brother, acting temporarily as Rhys's chancellor. Their kinsman Rhodri, a way-finder."

Rhys and Edern nodded from their seats, and Rhodri grinned.

"Next to me are Idris, Gwyn's marshal, and Lleision, Rhys's marshal. Rhys has but lately taken charge here after a disastrous predecessor, and there is much work to do for the relief of his people and to welcome new settlers."

The two marshals nodded.

"You've met Ceridwen and Eluned, scholars and healers for Gwyn and Rhys, respectively, and Cadugan, Rhys's new steward." They nodded, each in turn.

"You've also met Broch, most eager to help, with all of his people. And behind Rhodri, just to be complete, is Cydifor, Rhys's new musician." Cydifor was aghast at the presumption and Rhys glanced back over his shoulder at him in surprise, but Rhodri next to him patted his arm and said he'd explain later.

Picture of George. Question?

"Oh, and I'm Gwyn's great-grandson and his huntsman, a way-finder like my kinsman Rhodri." And related in some way to Cernunnos, as we discussed, he thought to her.

"Please tell us who you are and help us understand what you need. We'd like to help, if we can."

Mag visibly settled herself in place as the crackling fires behind them began to warm the room.

Pictures of Blue Ridge cutaway, budded child, child reaching.

"She's asked me to summarize our conversation so far. Her name is Seething Magma. She lives inside the Blue Ridge, I'm not sure just where. She has a child, Granite Cloud. This child went away and is prevented from returning."

Picture of Mag, child budding, growing up, leaving, repeated several time. Picture of Granite Cloud reaching, still a child.

"She's had many children, all grown. This one's very young, her youngest."

Picture of Blue Ridge cutaway, view from higher, many miles long. Several creatures like Mag.

"There are more like Mag throughout the Blue Ridge. She showed me a picture, looked like it was maybe a hundred miles long or more. Are they all family, Mag?"

Yes. Picture of Mag, getting smaller, shrinking to a bud on another creature.

"Is that your mother, Mag?"

Yes. Picture of a pile of small rocks.

Another name, George thought. "Rock pile?"

Picture of river washing small pebbles, river vanishing, stones remaining.

"Pebbles? Gravel?"

Yes.

"Her mother's name seems to be Gravel," George told them. "She's bigger than you are, isn't she?"

Picture of Mag next to Gravel.

George swallowed. "Um, yes, her mother is larger than Mag. A lot larger. Like a small house." To Mag, he said, "Gravel seems like such a little name."

Amusement. Picture of Mag very small, picture of small red rock. Picture of Mag larger, picture of boiling lava. Picture of Gravel very small, picture of gravel pile. Picture of Gravel larger, picture of gravel pile.

"You change names as you grow up? What, Gravel is a baby name, like Sweetums?"

Yes.

The chuckles started with Rhodri but they spread until everyone, even Cadugan and Edern, were smiling. It broke the formal tension in the room, to think these ancient creatures would have baby names.

Picture of mouse, deer, man, Mag, horned man.

Yes, you're right, he thought to her. More alike than different.

Rhodri asked, "Is Granite Cloud her baby name?"
Picture of small bud, picture of granite, picture of cloud.
"Yes."
Picture high in the hills. Small bud makes ways that exit high into the sky, falls, makes ways to catch herself before hitting the ground.
George was stunned. "She gets her name because of how she plays, like a skydiver. She makes a way that exits far up in the sky, like a cloud, then falls, and makes a way she can enter before she hits the ground." He listened a moment. "Oh, it's the same way, catching and throwing her over and over until she stops."
He rubbed his face. "Why, it's like a children's slide. How old is she, Mag? Is she very young?"
Consternation. Uncertainty.
"I think I've asked a hard one," he told his audience.
Map of eastern part of continent as far as the Great Lakes. Recognition?
"Yes, I recognize that, Mag."
Picture of map, ice coming down from the north well past the Great Lakes. Recognition?
"Yes, I know about the ice ages."
Satisfaction. Picture of Mag, Picture of ice advancing and receding.
George said, slowly, "I think Mag has just told me she's seen the ice advance into the middle of this continent and then retreat. I'm not sure about the length of the previous glaciations and the interval before it, all I know is the most recent one retreated maybe twelve-fourteen thousand years ago. Without getting into actual numbers, let's just estimate that she's about a fifty thousand years old. Or more. And I got the distinct impression that her mother was still alive."
Dead silence in the room, except for the scritch of Eluned's pen.
Picture of the continent, east of the Blue Ridge. Question?
"Yes, I recognize that."
Picture of horned man, arriving with an expedition of people. Question?
Was that the arrival of Gwyn when he moved Annwn here, he wondered.
Picture of Granite Cloud as a very small bud.
"Looks like Cloudie was born not long before Gwyn arrived."
Wider picture, includes Shenandoah Valley across the Blue Ridge. Question?

"Yes, I recognize that, too."

Another expedition arrives, picture of north end of Massanutten mountain rising from the valley floor.

That's Madog's arrival, I bet.

Picture of Granite Cloud playing. Drops down to look at people on Massanutten mountain. Picture of child reaching.

"Alright. What I think she's trying to do is peg the dates by other events she thinks I'll recognize. She saw Gwyn's arrival when he moved Annwn, though it's Cernunnos she noticed. She saw an arrival over in the Shenandoah Valley up on top of Massanutten mountain, I don't know what your name for it is, the one that rises like a keel from the valley floor, maybe thirty miles from here on the other side of the Blue Ridge. Assuming that's Madog's people, then that would be about eight or nine hundred years ago, yes? Cloudie went to see what was going on and was somehow caught."

He paused. "I think Cloudie's very young, for her kind, like a small child, and I think Madog's got her."

"How's he holding her, Mag?" he asked.

Frustration.

"That's too hard for her to explain with this limited method. We're going to have to break the question into pieces."

Rhys stood. "Let's take a moment to eat and discuss this. Maybe we can come up with some theories to test against her."

"Mag, we're going to pause and talk about it," George said.

Agreement.

They filled plates from the food the servants had brought in and took them back to their seats, pulling up small tables as necessary to hold them.

Rhodri and Eluned pulled chairs over to Mag while they ate. Eluned said, "I'd like to try a method for you to talk to more of us, if you don't mind. Can you make a rapping sound, like this?"

She knocked on her chair with a knuckle.

Mag answered with a chock on the stone beneath her.

"That'll do fine. First step: one knock is for 'yes,' two knocks for 'no,' and three for 'I don't know.' Clear?"

One knock.

"Can you understand us alright?"

One knock.

She turned to Rhodri. "You and I are going to need to put together some symbols to stand in for people and places. That way she can point to answers for 'who' and 'where.' Unfortunately, 'how' and 'why' are going to be much more difficult."

"Numbers would be useful, too. Here's how we count," she told Mag. She explained the decimal system, that a number like 234 could be represented as two hundreds, three tens, and four ones.

As she demonstrated on her fingers, Mag surprised them by creating a pseudopod on each corner of her leading edge, with five rods, like fingers.

"Yes! That will be a big help."

Amusement. Admiration.

"She's impressed by your skill in conveying all of this, Eluned," George said.

"Well, it's what I do," she demurred. "Though this is nothing like teaching a young student."

Picture of Granite Cloud running off to play instead of listening.

"She agrees," he said.

⁓

Seething Magma settled down to wait and occupied herself watching the busyness of these new allies. She'd never been close to one of the two-legs before, much less so many, in one of their hives.

She understood that the one in the middle, Rhys, was in charge here, as her mother Gravel made the important decisions for any clan members in range, but couldn't understand why he was so young, clearly the youngest in the room. Even in their short lives, their experience colored their tastes as the drips of dissolved minerals colored the taste of stalagmites, and so their relative ages were clear to her.

But still, the oldest of them—so young. She'd gathered from George's thoughts that many of them were younger than Granite Cloud, much younger. How brief their own childhoods must be, no time to savor the world, to try its many flavors.

The one she wanted, George, was also young but he tasted different. Must be the element of the horned man, the one he called Cernunnos. Too bad he can't understand me more clearly.

His thoughts revealed all sorts of interesting notions. It takes two of them to make a young one, how strange. That's much on his mind. And he himself is from somewhere else, that strange place that a way occasionally breaks into. It must be somewhere with a long memory—she hadn't expected him to recognize the pulsing of the ice.

We've never heeded these creatures who use the ways we leave behind, but we were wrong, she decided. One of them has paid too much attention to Granite Cloud. From George she saw that they had a name for him, Madog, and that he was not a friend. Enemy was an odd concept for her. With so few of them and an endless world to inhabit, what did her kind have to dispute about? But even they were not immune to personal quarrels, perhaps it was something like that. It must be worse, though—she saw in George's mind fleeting images of fights, wounds, deaths. They were very savage.

She was impatient to free her child, now that she knew of the problem, but she could see that they had many things to occupy them, lives of their own. They wanted to help, and she trusted that they would, she could taste it. A few days would make no difference, certainly less to her than to them. She'd learn what she could while they readied themselves.

She wished there were fewer of them in the room. Hard to keep the flavors of so many sentient beings separate, all in one place. How did they do it?

c—～o

As the council finished their meal and individual conversations, something about Seething Magma's posture caught George's attention. What's wrong, he thought to her.

Picture of each person in the room, moving around, mingling. Too much weight.

Overload, he thought. Yes, crowds can be exhausting. We're very different, but we all care about lost children.

Agreement. Picture of mouse, deer, man, Mag, horned man.

Rhys resumed the meeting. "We've heard much from our guest. Now we need to understand better what Madog has done, and how."

Rhodri said, "Ask her about the ways."

"Alright," George said. "Mag, you made a way for us this morning. Do all of your kind make ways?"

Yes. Picture of Mag, making a way in the rock to eat, making a way in the rock to travel.

"Apparently it's how they make passages in the rock, to eat and to move around."

"This would explain why so many ways are found in rock, one end or both," Ceridwen said.

He thought about Mag's pictures for a moment. "When you travel, the way starts, there's a transition, and the way ends. You've gone a good distance. When you eat, the way starts and ends, but there's no transition. Is that right?"

Same. Difference not important.

"So, the transition is an arbitrary element of the way, not an essential one," George said.

"All the ways we use have a transition—it's why they're useful," Rhodri said. "The ones that don't are no better than tunnels."

"How about it, Mag? Are your kind responsible for *all* the ways, both underground and above?" George asked.

Surprise. Thought. Tentative agreement.

"Yes, she says."

Into the silence, she added *No. Picture of horned man.*

"Alright, except for those made by Cernunnos."

Picture of way in rock, crushed if mountain moves. Picture of Granite Cloud's way in air, unanchored, dissolving. Picture of way on land. Anchored, slow to dissolve.

"This is complicated. Let's see if I have it right. If they make a way in the rock, it lasts until the movement of the earth crushes it. If they make one in the air, there's nothing to hold it, and it dissolves soon. If it's on the land, then it's anchored. I think it may eventually fall apart, but I can't get a sense of the time scale."

Ceridwen said, "All the major ways, we've been using them for thousands of years."

"That's not very long for our guest, is it?" Edern said.

"Can they destroy a way?" Rhodri asked.

Three knocks.

"She doesn't know," Eluned said.

Picture of George, picture of the Archer's Way exit.

"You want to know how we use the ways?"

Yes.

"Rhodri, you want to take this one?"

Rhodri walked over to stand near Mag and talk to her directly. "Most of us can't detect or use them. A few of us, like George and me, and Madog, can find them. We can see them at a distance. If the way is unclaimed, we can claim it."

Question?

95

George said, "She wants to know more about claiming, I think."

Eluned broke in, "Mag, can you make a different noise when you have a question?"

One knock. Scratch.

"The first way-finder to stumble upon a way can claim it," Rhodri said. "That means he, in effect, owns it, at least the end he located. What typically happens next is that he goes through it, up to the transition point, and tries to determine what sort of location the exit's in. Often the other end is in solid rock. I guess now we know why. If so, the way's useless to him. But if the end is somewhere on the surface, then he claims that end as well, and owns the whole way.

"The way-owner has special privileges. He can go back and forth at will. He can guide others through the way. He can create way-tokens, if he has the skill, and confer that ability on others, subordinate to his own control, and he can transfer that ability directly to others, permanently.

"What he does with the way depends upon circumstances. Private individuals can set up tolls for use and guide parties through the way, if their ruler permits. Way-finders working for the great lords can hand the ways over to them and make way-tokens for use. A way can be made public and open, for all to use, or it can be closed. It can also be hidden, so that very few even among the skilled can detect it."

Wait.

"Hold up," George said. "She's thinking about all this."

Picture of ways that George showed her, in the river meadow. Picture of ways she echoed back. Question?

"Not sure what you're asking, Mag," he said. "Is it that we saw the same ways from that location?"

Agreement. Picture of ways she echoed back, much more detail. The Blue Ridge a blaze of markings.

"When I tried to tell her we were going to Edgewood, I pictured a map with the local ways marked, and she echoed back something similar but in finer detail. Now she's shown me hundreds of ways, deep within the Blue Ridge. Not sure why." He asked Rhodri, "Can you sense them?"

"No. We've always believed rock is an effective mask against the detection of a way. How about you?"

"Me, neither."

Picture of Edgewood, barrier marked.

"What about the barrier, Mag?"

Frustration.

"There's something she wants to say about the barrier but it's too hard."

"Let's get back to Madog," Ceridwen said. "The most inexplicable thing about him is that he can apparently create ways. We know of at least the Hidden Way that George destroyed after the great hunt and the Archer's Way."

Seething Magma made agitated movements for attention and all eyes turned to her. *Picture of Archer's Way exit at river meadow. Picture of Granite Cloud.*

"Did Cloudie go through the Archer's Way, Mag? Is that what you're saying?"

Two knocks. No.

"Did Cloudie make the Archer's Way?" Rhodri asked.

One knock. Yes.

"How do you know?" George said.

Picture of eating rock. Picture of Granite Cloud.

George took a stab at the metaphor. "It... tasted like her?"

One knock.

"So, Granite Cloud made the Archer's Way for Madog," Ceridwen said. "We know she wants to come home and her mother says she's not able to. This sounds to me like Madog can make her do what he wants."

One knock.

"How can he control her?" George said. "How would you control Mag?"

They all looked at the massive form in front of them and shook their heads.

Picture of a way. Picture of a man touching it. Picture of Granite Cloud. Picture of a man touching her.

"No..." George didn't want to think he understood. "Madog can control Cloudie because she's *like* a way, fundamentally? He can claim and own her?"

One knock. Yes. Three knocks. I don't know.

George heard the exclamations of outrage rise in the room. He felt it himself—enslaving a small child for hundreds of years—and had to make himself walk away for a few paces to calm down.

He returned to her side and asked the room at large, "How does a way-owner lose what he owns?"

Rhodri said, quietly, "He gives it away. Or he dies without doing so."

Mag, you're in danger yourself, then, from Rhodri or me, George thought. You're not safe here.

Calm. Picture of George. Picture of Rhodri. Picture of window glass.

He rubbed his face. "I pointed out to Mag that she herself might be at risk from Rhodri or me, if this is true."

Edern said, dryly, "And yet she's still here."

"She, um, implied that the two of us were reasonably transparent to her."

Rhodri cleared his throat at that.

Rhys said, "So she trusts us because she can see into us well enough."

One knock.

"Well, that's a compliment, I suppose," Edern said.

Eluned made an observation that stilled the room. "You realize this rules out the obvious approach, of Seething Magma just making a way into Madog's domain to rescue her child directly. Madog could claim her, assuming she could even locate him."

"That's why you're looking for help?" George asked her.

Agreement. Picture of Mag going to Granite Cloud. Picture of Granite Cloud preventing her.

"Cloudie warned her not to come," he said.

Rhys rose from his seat and bowed to Mag. "My lady, I pledge our help for the rescue of your child from our mutual enemy. It make take us a few days to form a plan with some reasonable chance of success. Can you wait that long, working with us?"

She held herself still, lifted her front end slightly and dipped it. *Agreement. Gratitude.*

"Huntsman," Rhys said, "I put her in your charge to look after."

George nodded, and they agreed to reconvene to discuss the local Edgewood issues before dinner.

CHAPTER 10

It was a larger and more relaxed group that met with Rhys before dinner. Rhys had discussed the venue with Edern beforehand and agreed that keeping the meeting in the conservatory was advisable. They wanted George there, and Mag came with George, so best to use the room that could accommodate them all. As Rhys walked in and looked at the impromptu lineup of tables with chairs around the perimeter, approximating the long table in his council room, he was reasonably satisfied with the arrangement. He'd spent years watching his foster-father maintain the dignity of his station without pomp, and recognized that a formal table with a clear master at the top was part of the necessary trappings. People cooperated better when their expectations were met.

He stretched his hands by his side and shook them in the air as he walked to his seat, preparing to take charge of yet another set of complications at Edgewood. His great-aunt Creiddylad had left a thorough mess and people were suffering badly. It made a great deal of work for him and his staff, recreating an effective government from scratch, but he could feel himself running at his strongest for the first time in his life, eager to test his wings. His greatest fear before he arrived, that the task would be beyond him, was already long gone.

His council members and their counterparts from Gwyn's court were all there, as well as the leaders of this most recent set of settlers and a few others.

Seething Magma stood quietly in one corner of the room, and everyone's eyes slipped to her unobtrusively as they came in. George had seated himself away from the table to stay near her, and Benitoe kept him company.

Rhys took his seat. "Thank you all for coming. We need to coordinate the activities of the next several days so as to waste as little time as possible. I want to start with our chancellor's list, and if we've left off anything important, there'll be time for you to bring it up at the end."

He looked around the table, and heads nodded.

Edern said, "Our first order of business is to make sure the new settlers find appropriate destinations. The steward here," gesturing Cadugan beside him, "is coordinating all the lists of people and places. If you have a craft you'd like to establish, a farm you'd like to build, a family member you're looking for, he's the one you must speak with. He'll be available in the great hall, after dinner and after breakfast tomorrow, for everyone to come and speak to.

"As you know, we have two other villages here besides the one nearby, and all have both needs and opportunities for settlers. At mid-day tomorrow, and again on the day after, Lleision, our marshal, will escort the groups going to each one to make sure they reach their destinations without difficulty. When you speak to Cadugan, he'll help you sort that out.

"We have many abandoned farms, and ruined houses and craft shops in the villages, and these will be made available to you on very favorable terms. Our only requirement is that you help us by employing local workers wherever you can, and apprenticing them to your crafts where possible.

"It has not been hidden from you that something dire has happened to our residents. Many, perhaps most, seem deceptively normal if rather quiet, but further from the center, many seem almost sick or damaged, in mind if not in body. We're still seeking the causes. Those who have preceded you as settlers in the past few weeks have not reported any symptoms themselves."

Rhys noted the look of apprehension on Meilyr's face when Edern ticked off the ways in which the fae population seem to have suffered.

He took over from Edern for the next topic. "Ceridwen and Eluned will be reestablishing schools and hospitals as quickly as possible. Eluned is helping Cadugan compile the list of family members sought so, if you can't find Cadugan, speak to Eluned. They will be traveling to each village in the process of their work. If you or any in your party can help with schooling or nursing, please make yourselves known to them."

Meilyr spoke up. "We have several young children with us that need to continue their education. What should we do?"

Eluned said, "Identify yourselves to Cadugan or me, and let us know where you decide to live. We'll be arranging classes soon."

Rhys turned to Benitoe, sitting away from the table with George. "Benitoe, I understand that you've been charged by seniors among your people to find out what's happened to the lutins who were here. Your party are the first lutins to arrive since the succession."

Benitoe stood to face him, and nodded.

"If mistress Rozenn will permit, I'd like to task you with the leadership of that activity here, for all the lutins. Cadugan will share with you all the information he can collect, and provide whatever resources you need. The rest of the lutin party can follow the lead of the others in deciding where to live and what livelihood they want to pursue. Will you do that?"

"It's why I came. Thank you, my lord."

Rhys hated to be so formal with him. Just a few weeks ago they'd both been whippers-in supporting George as huntsman for the great hunt. He was cheered to see Benitoe give him a barely visible wink as he sat down again.

Edern took up the next item on the list. "Masters Tiernoc and Broch, those of you who wish to settle are just as welcome as all of these. I understand that you have some additional plans, however?"

Tiernoc said, "My friend Broch and I have discussed this and we propose the following. We came with four objectives, and now we have five. First, several of us just wish to take up their crafts, as the rest are doing. Second, there have always been special ore deposits known or suspected in this region, and some of us want to check on the mines that were started, to see what's happened.

"Third, we have those who seek family members and would greatly appreciate your help in locating them or in discovering their fate. Lastly, on our original list, we have several who do not intend to settle here, exactly, but who want to re-establish the trade networks that were disrupted so many years ago. Some of them may live here, as a headquarters, but others are already settled elsewhere and are looking to build local outposts."

Edern said, "Look to Cadugan for help with all of these things. The sooner we can establish reliable trade, the better."

"Thank you, my lord," Tiernoc said. "We also have a new request. Never could we have imagined that one of the Old Ones would make herself known to us and seek our help. There is none among us who would not willingly drop everything for this task. We'd like to be remembered in any planning that comes of it. If there is any way we can help, we want to know."

Rhys said, "We'll do so, and thank you for your offer."

He looked over at George. "George, please work with Rhodri to find out whatever you can from Seething Magma. We need a plan."

Eluned said, "I'll help when I can, just let me know your schedule as you work it out."

George said, "I think we need some practical experiments as soon as possible."

Approval.

He looked back at Mag and continued. "I was thinking that we could go back to the Archer's Way tomorrow to do that and, while I'm so close, there's no reason I can't guide anyone who wants to go back to Gwyn at Daear Llosg."

Idris spoke to that. "Rhys, if you can spare me, I'd like to get my men back to Gwyn. Lleision seems to have your defense well in hand, and my troop was intended just in case you were under attack here. I can give him a report to bring him up to date."

"Agreed," Rhys said. That would lessen the crowd in the barracks and they weren't really needed here.

"I'll write up something for him, too," Ceridwen said. "Get it from me before you go."

Rhys added, "We have messages as well, since the closing of the Edgewood Way on Saturday."

Idris looked over at George. "After breakfast, huntsman?"

A quick glance round to Rhodri, and George replied, "Fine."

Rhys caught Edern's eye. Edern said, "Anything else?"

The crowd was silent. As Rhys had planned, the appetizing smells of dinner had helped ensure the shortness of the session.

As the room emptied, Rhys saw Cydifor ask George a question and smile at the response. He lingered in the background, trying not to be noticed. He's persistent, Rhys thought to himself, and walked over to greet him.

"So, you're my new musician, are you?" he teased.

Cydifor blushed to the roots of his red hair. "My lord, the huntsman had no business saying so. I had only just spoken to lord Rhodri about the possibility."

"Don't worry, no harm done. George was just poking at me a little. I used to work for him," Rhys said. "Tell me about where you're from."

Oh, no, he looked panicked again. "From Tredin, my lord."

Rhys couldn't help himself. He laughed out loud. "I see. Couldn't get any further away, is it?"

Cydifor gave a sheepish nod.

"Well, relax. Maybe you and Rhodri can play for us all, later tonight."

Panic again. "We haven't practiced with each other at all, my lord."

"Do I look old enough to be able to tell the difference?" As they walked out together, Rhys reminded himself to thank George for sending him someone who could distract him from his work.

⌀⌀⌀

George sat alone in the conservatory with Seething Magma before going into dinner. Cydifor had asked if he could come along tomorrow, for the experiments, and George agreed. Now he watched him leave, chatting shyly with Rhys, and was pleased with the success of his joke earlier. He'd given them something mutual to complain about.

"Better, now that they've all left?" he asked.

Picture of a groove being worn into bedrock.

Hmm, that's a tough one. "They're wearing you down?"

Amusement. Two knocks.

"Um, a repeated action, a custom? Ah. You're getting used to it?"

Yes.

"Could you follow much of what's going on?"

Picture of little frogs lined up around the edge of a puddle. Big frog lands in the middle, little frogs scatter in all directions.

"Well, that's a bit unfair." He tried to use her methods: picture of a clockwork mechanism with moving parts and Rhys as a key turning it.

One knock.

"How will you eat? Can I get you food or a place to sleep?"

Not needed. Picture of Mag in woods, wrapped around a boulder.

"Well, as you like. You know how to find me." He tapped his head. "I need to go in to dinner soon. Come here after dinner, there will be music."

Question?

"Ah, you don't know it. You might find it interesting. It's one of our art forms, an entertainment for us." He thought of Angharad singing, for a moment.

Picture of green arrow pendant. Question?

Must be on my mind, he thought. "That's a gift from my wife, Angharad. Shall I show you?"

One knock.

He pulled the pendant on its cord out from under his shirt and lifted it up over his head. When he let it dangle, the arrow pointed almost due south.

"It's a little bit of magic. It points to her, to remind me of home."

Picture of George and Angharad, picture of little person. Question?

"No, no children yet. Soon, I hope. We're only just married."

Picture of George budding, picture of Angharad budding. Question?

He laughed out loud. "Angharad would be the mother, like you." He tucked the pendant back under his shirt.

Picture of brass compass. Question?

She follows all the references I think of. "I have a device from my world that we use to tell direction. Angharad's arrow reminded me of it."

He pulled the compass out on his watch chain and showed her. He pictured for her his best understanding of the spinning iron core of the earth and the magnetic field, how it occasionally reversed, and how the needle pointed to magnetic north.

She surprised him by extending the forward edge of her mantle to touch it. He relinquished it somewhat reluctantly, fearing its destruction, but she was very delicate with it, holding it in a sort of living cage as if to feel it from all sides.

She withdrew her mantle from it and let it fall into his hand again. *Picture of rocks, pointing one way, more rocks, pointing the opposite way, repeated.*

"Iron in molten rocks holds the magnetic signature of the era when they solidified and captures the pattern of reversals. Is that what you mean?"

One knock. Two knocks. One knock.

Picture of east coast and ocean and west coast of Europe, from very high up. Picture of same, but the continents visibly closer. Question?

"You're asking about continental drift? Plate tectonics? You know about that?"

Excited. Yes. No. Want. Question?

Oh my, he thought. I might be a little late to dinner.

❦

As the after-dinner guests continued to drift in, George let himself slump comfortably in his chair along the outer edge, keeping Mag company with a mug of warm cider in his hand. The fire in the conservatory warded off the outdoor chill, and George relaxed, looking forward to his bed in his usual guest room in the manor.

The tables had been separated again and were scattered about the room like seatings at a cafe, the people at each table sated after their roast beef and pie. The servants kept them well-provided with cider and beer. The one problem Edgewood didn't have was a shortage of food. The population seemed to have diminished faster than the food supply.

Rhys took a casual seat at the front. George knew how he enjoyed Rhodri's performances.

Those travelers who had instruments had been encouraged to bring them, and some of the residents came prepared as well. Many had brought children, some of whom were young enough to run up to Seething Magma and stare at her until their exasperated parents retrieved them, apologizing for their manners.

Picture of Granite Cloud. Picture of children. Question?

"Yes, those are children."

One determined little girl with brown curls, about five years old, crept up to George's chair and leaned on his knee, never looking at him. She couldn't take her eyes off of Mag.

"Hello. I'm Gwyneth. What's your name?"

Amusement. Picture of boiling lava.

George said, "You can't hear her answer but she said her name is Mag."

The child looked at him skeptically. Mag rippled the front of her mantle at her and convinced her he hadn't made it up.

"Where are you from?"

Picture of Blue Ridge cutaway.

"She said she lives deep in the Blue Ridge mountains," he told her, pointing to the west.

"Why did you come here?"

Picture of Granite Cloud, picture of girl, picture of Granite Cloud reaching.

"She said she has a little girl like you that's gotten into trouble."

This time she turned her head and looked directly at him. "You're going to help her, aren't you?"

"Yes, my dear," he told her gravely, "we're all going to help."

He spotted a woman standing and looking around the room distractedly, and ventured a guess that this was her mother. She came over to his raised arm with relief on her face, ready to scold her daughter.

Envy, worry, picture of Granite Cloud.

George forestalled the mother. "Mag says she envies you your daughter. She's looking for hers, much the same age."

The woman's face softened with a vision of how worried she would be if her daughter went missing. She curtsied to Seething Magma.

"I hope you find her, safe and sound," she said, then took her daughter by the hand and led her away.

The room quieted as Rhodri left the far side where the musicians had been tuning and walked to the front near the fire, holding a bowed instrument similar to a fiddle.

"We'd like to invite everyone to join us, as they wish, for our own mutual entertainment. Cydifor and I have a little something to get us started."

While he was talking, Cydifor came up with a similar instrument and stood beside him. Rhodri lifted his bow and began a stately dance tune in a minor key that put George in mind of a minuet, and Cydifor joined him in unison. The timbre of their instruments was mellow rather than harsh, somewhere between a viol and a violin.

As tune reached its end the first time, Cydifor began a series of variations around Rhodri's solid melody, first as a slow weaving around the harmony, then in later repeats as double-time embellishments and flourishes. They whipped the duet up to maximum complexity, never altering the tempo, then in the final repeat, it wound back down into simple harmony, ending in unison.

The room was silent for a moment, then burst into applause. George stood as he clapped, and Rhys rose from his chair to shake both their hands. He said something to Cydifor that George couldn't hear, but he could see his flush of pleasure all the way across the room. Looks like he's found a home, George thought.

Interest. Picture of lines rising, crossing, geometric forms and relations. Yes, he thought to her, music is closely related to mathematics. Do you know about harmonic intervals?

He told her about vibrating strings and overtones while other musicians joined the ones on stage to make livelier tunes and the audience grew more boisterous.

After one foot-tapping song that had the whole room singing along on the chorus, Mag asked, *Picture of people swaying rhythmically. Question?*

Not sure what you're asking, Mag, he replied silently. Is this something we do for social bonding? Yes. Is rhythm a part of music? Rhythm's even more fundamental to music than melody, certainly more hard-wired into what we are, as physical animals. He showed her dancers, marchers, sailors hauling a rope to a chantey. Rhythm entrains us to act together. It's hard to explain, we don't understand how it works very well ourselves.

George had studied music informally out of interest, as a casual singer. He'd always envied those with a special talent for instruments. Music theory and its relationship to mathematics fascinated him, before he was distracted by his work building a software company. He was deep into this silent conversation with Mag when he noticed faces turned his way.

Rhodri stood in the front with his eyebrows raised in question. When he saw he had George's attention, he said, "I asked, what do you play, huntsman? I've heard you singing to the hounds, so I know you can carry a tune."

George was startled, but game. He said, "I can sing for my supper, if you like." Rhodri beckoned him up.

George stood in front of him and the other musicians, and said to them, "I better do this one on my own since I don't think you'll know it." He waited a moment for silence and surveyed his audience, noting the attentive children. Behind him, Cydifor played a suggestive triad privately for his own ears, and he found it fit well enough with his range.

He launched into a comic performance of the old ballad "An Outlandish Knight," playing all the parts for maximum dramatic impact. First he was the seductive knight luring the maiden off with him, with her father's gold and horses. When the knight threatened her with robbery and death, he was the cunning maiden who plays modest and tricks him to his own death and then returns to her home, sneaking back in. He was her sleepy father wondering at the noise outside, and finally the nosy parrot, milking the suspense to see if he would betray her clandestine adventure.

Cydifor entwined his singing with a quiet high tenor wordless descant around George's baritone, once he caught the contours of the tune. He managed to enhance the comic effect greatly.

When it all came to a satisfying conclusion, he was gratified to see smiles on the younger faces. Rhodri said, "Always good to have a nice low voice to round out the singing."

Rhodri launched into an *a cappella* parody song about a clumsy warrior that Cydifor clearly also knew. George was put on his mettle to improvise a vocal "oom-pah" walking bass line beneath it in place of the missing instruments. He relished the way it required all of his attention to stay synchronized with the others as he came wheezing to the end.

He bowed to the humorous applause and returned to Mag.

Picture of instrument, picture of George singing. Question?

I'll assume that's not a critique of my performance, George thought to her, amused. We call the second type "song." It includes words with rhythm and rhyme. We have a non-musical version of the same thing for the spoken word, called poetry.

He filled out a basic musical education for Mag for quite a while before succumbing to sleepiness and heading off to bed, the party still going strong behind him.

Seething Magma watched the remainder of the entertainment, another hour or so of musical performances, and one comic recitation by a korrigan, which she understood was not exactly music, but similar.

What a very interesting thing the surface folk had made of rhythm and sound. She knew of rock formations that gave off a clear tone when struck, but music itself was wholly new to her. She found the mathematics of it fascinating, as well as the physics of the different instruments that were used by the performers. George had also tried to describe to her some of the art of it, the confounding of expectations with the unanticipated, the suspended resolution, the similarity to emotional narrative. She'd pursued the subject with George until he yawned in her face and put a stop to it for the night.

Sleep, now, that was another thing she hadn't thought about before. She knew that animals quieted sometimes without being dead, but the underground fish she was most familiar with never stopped moving, like her own people. George explained that to her, too—sleep was a time for the body to rest and the mind to "catch up," as he put it. She couldn't believe it, though—a third of each day, just for that?

They'd tried to explore their differences in minds and brains but couldn't get very far with the one-sided nature of their conversation.

She could feel the change in George's thoughts as he got sleepy, and she monitored him discretely in his room as he dropped off. He'd told her about dreams, and she found those very odd indeed. What an strange way to digest the day's events.

But then, what a surprise all these people were. She'd expected that some would be afraid of her, but mostly they were polite and helpful, and she could feel their genuine sympathy for her need. The anger she tasted from them when they realized what Madog must have done to hold Granite Cloud, why, they wanted to make it their own fight. She needed to explore this with George when she saw him again in the morning.

The biggest shock was George's casual revelations about the bones of the earth, what he could tell her about the movement of the lands. In just a few moments he had illuminated generations of speculation among her own kind. How could a creature so young know these things? She saw behind his explanation a dim image of hundreds of other people, all learning about the subject and contributing their knowledge into a great pile of glistening treasure. She knew he came from somewhere else, and that he'd learned these things as students do, not through his own expertise, but it was almost impossible to believe that any people so young could make that much sense of what had happened so long ago, and was still happening, to the rocks of the world. It was humbling. My kind may be the elder, but his people see further back in time. How unexpected.

There would be much to tell her mother and her kin when she returned from this encounter. She wondered if they would believe her? She'd always thought of herself as one particular bit of the gravel in the image that represented her mother's name. *Maybe I can make that piece shine like a jewel for her.*

She turned to the door and extended a pseudopod to open it, taking care to close it again after leaving, as George had told her. She'd spend the night foraging until they were ready for her again in the morning.

As she passed the barracks where the travelers were staying for the night, she caught the taste of a sleepy child and its mother. The mother was singing to the child, and it calmed and settled. *So that's another use of music,* she thought, *to capture the senses of a child and encourage it to rest.* She made a resonating chamber with a vibrating tongue and experimented with pumping air through it, humming the tune to herself as she entered the woods.

CHAPTER 11

George joined Idris and Lleision at breakfast just as they were getting started. "Sorry to interrupt, but it was occurring to me last night that I might be off in the south much of the day and I haven't yet looked at that way which appeared a few days ago, replacing the one I destroyed last time."

Lleision nodded as he chewed.

"I'd like to duck over there first, before Idris assembles his men to return to Gwyn," he said and turned to Idris. "Can we do that? Shouldn't take long, and I hate to think of leaving that behind us, like an open door."

"Who do you want with us?" Lleision asked.

"Rhodri. I don't see him here but I'll roust him out of bed if necessary. I'd like Mag, too, if she'll come."

Edern leaned over the two marshals. "Where is she?"

"Don't know," George said. He lifted his head. Can you hear me, he thought at her.

Greetings.

He told her the plan.

Agreement. Picture of terrace.

"She'll wait for us outside," he said. "I'll go find Rhodri."

Edern said, deadpan, "Tell him from me he's too old to be laying around in bed."

George blinked then smiled slowly as he heard the affectionate tease in his voice.

⌒‿⌒

He stood in the snow and looked at the new way with distaste. They were close enough to the manor to see the buildings through the bare trees. Much too close, George thought.

"I marked the spot for Lleision," Rhodri said, speaking softly to appease his obvious hangover. George saw the branches that had been dragged into a low line along the width of the way entrance, and the snow was unbroken from that point.

"No one's come through since it appeared, judging by the snow," George said.

Seething Magma moved closer to the entrance, leaving her odd signature in the snow behind her.

Picture of Granite Cloud. Picture of setting sun.

"Mag says Cloudie made it, and it points west."

Seething Magma straightened her body and oriented it south of west. George made note of the direction using his compass. "That's the exact direction," he said, pointing at her. "How far, Mag, can you tell?"

Picture of Shenandoah Valley to the west. Picture of north end of ridge in the middle of the valley floor.

"Comes from the north end of Massanutten mountain. That would be about thirty miles."

Edern said, "Can it be blocked?"

"Let's run a few tests," Rhodri said. "I see it as owned and closed. What can you see, George?"

"It's... blurry," he said. "I can see it from a distance just fine, but it's not very clear when I look at it."

"That's the 'closed' part. So, can you claim it?"

"How would I do that?" George said.

"It's an act of will."

George reached out and the way was... slick to his feel. He couldn't get a grasp on it. "I don't think so."

"Was the Archer's Way different?"

"I don't know. I didn't try to claim that. But it was already open, not closed. Does that make a difference?"

"We'll see what we can find out later this morning when we work with it," Rhodri said. "Let's concentrate on this one. Now, can you open it?"

George had no idea how, and unsurprisingly it remained closed. He shook his head.

"That's alright, that's normal. Do you remember how you sealed the Archer's Way? Can you do that here?"

George looked at it and tried not to predetermine an answer. A picture of a weave came to him, and this time he could feel the horned man stirring inside him, rousing a little at the challenge. He wondered if it had been the same when at the Archer's Way and he just hadn't recognized the feeling yet.

"Yes," he said slowly, "I think we can."

"You and Mag?" Rhodri asked.

"No," George said. "Me and Cernunnos." Edern and Rhodri turned their heads and looked at him.

"Do it," Edern said.

George nodded and visualized the way exit as a closed eye, He stitched the lid shut in a semicircle along the bottom, pulling whatever it was he was using as mental cord tightly through and knotting it somehow at the end.

Rhodri followed along with him and shivered. "I've never seen anything like that. Except for your seal on the Archer's Way."

Surprise. Picture of horned man?

"I don't know, Mag, I think he helped."

Edern asked, "Can you destroy this way?"

"Probably. Shall I do it?"

Lleision spoke up, "If it's truly sealed, then there's no hurry about it. We should save that for a more strategic blow and keep our options open."

"Mag, can you take over this way or open it?"

Frustration.

"Too hard a question, we'll have to break it into parts," George said.

"We'll leave it sealed and under guard for now," Edern decided.

❡

Idris and his guards assembled below the terrace steps while George waited on the terrace for the last of the messages he was supposed to bring with him. A bag hanging at his side held the bundles from Rhys and Edern, but Ceridwen was running late.

George spent the time filling Cydifor in on their activities earlier in the day. Rhodri, meanwhile, was looking over the entrance to Mag's way.

"Can you see what's different about this way?" he asked George.

George looked carefully, then tried to grasp the outer surface mentally. "It's not blurry, which means open, yes?"

Rhodri nodded.

George continued, "The outside feels different from the other one, I can get a grip on it."

"That's because it's unowned, unclaimed. In the old world, it's very unusual to find an unowned way. Here, I've found several."

"And claimed them, of course."

"Immediately." Rhodri grinned.

Warning.

"Mag says that wouldn't be a good idea."

Rhodri looked directly at her. "I had no such intention, my lady. This is your way. Can't you claim it yourself and prevent anyone else?"

Frustration

"I can't tell if the answer is hard to communicate or the action is hard to do," George said. "We'll have to get into this after we send Idris off."

Of the four of them there, only Cydifor couldn't see the way entrance and was letting his confusion show. George dismounted and walked up to it, casually sticking his arm in and letting Cydifor see it disappear, then using that visual aid to outline the whole entrance. I bet the couriers play games like this, he thought, when no one else is around.

Idris and some of the guards watched, too, from the ground level beyond the terrace steps.

George glanced up at Rhodri on his horse. "When I first looked at the Family Way a few weeks ago, I walked right through it. Here, I don't think I can walk through it without walking into it, into the passage, if you see what I mean. Though maybe from the other side…"

He put that theory to the test and walked through the way entrance from the back, with no effect.

Rhodri told him, "That's the difference between unclaimed ways and claimed ones that are open but require tokens. A way that's open and unclaimed, and all unclaimed ways are open, will take in anyone that approaches from the right direction. That's how we get humans stumbling into our world, especially here in the new world where we're still finding unclaimed ways."

"Oh," he interrupted himself as the thought struck him. "Of course. If Mag's people create the ways, then they're still being made, we're not going to run out. At least not over here where they live."

"Anyway," he continued, "Once a way's been claimed, then its behavior while open depends on the intent of the owner. It can be left open only for those with the right tokens, or a way-guide, or it can be left publicly open, like a road. In that case, the entrance is always very well-marked, to avoid accidents."

Movement from the manor house caught George's eye, and they all turned as Ceridwen opened the door with a large package of materials in her hand.

"Please accept our apologies for delaying you," she said. "Eluned and I have been scribbling since the early morning." She stood off to the side to watch them go.

George stuffed her papers into the bag by his side and made sure the strap across his chest was secure. He mounted up and raised an eyebrow at Idris, who nodded his readiness.

"Mag?" George said, "After you."

The small group on the terrace headed the party, and Idris's guards brought up the rear. In just a few minutes, they emerged into the river meadow, oddly empty since the bustle of people and wagons the day before had left their marks in the snow.

George rode right on without stopping to the entrance of the Archer's Way, and Idris's group came with him. Mag stood away with Rhodri and Cydifor to wait for him.

"I'll be right back," he called, and vanished into the way's passage with Idris's men.

Coming out the other side, he startled the two guards into attention as they saw Idris following.

One of them rode over to George. "Huntsman, my lord Gwyn asked me to deliver this to you if you should appear."

He took off a courier bag similar to the one George was wearing, and held it out to him. They exchanged their bags, and George saluted Idris casually as he turned to re-enter the Archer's Way.

Leave it to Gwyn to have a new mail drop organized, George thought, as he traveled the passage and returned to the river meadow.

Rhodri was waiting for him at the exit. "Let's start with the Archer's Way. It's probably going to be complicated."

George dismounted and joined him.

"What do we know about this way?" Rhodri asked his student.

"Well, Mag said Cloudie made it so we presume Madog owns it." He reached out to check that but the results were ambiguous, as though he could grasp it but not well. "I'm not sure, but I think I have some sort of claim on it. How could that happen?"

"You sealed it while it was open, and that may have compromised it. I thought that might have happened, since you were able to act as a way-guide. I wonder what the way you sealed this morning looks like now, since you did it."

"But that's not supposed to be possible, is it?" Cydifor asked. "If I understand what you've been saying."

"No," George said, "but I think I've been getting a little extra help from my, um, patron." He reminded Cydifor how Cernunnos handled the ways during the great hunt. "I think I must be something of a wild card."

"So," George said to Rhodri, "Does that mean I can close it? More to the point, can I keep Madog out?"

"I doubt that," Rhodri replied, "He's probably at least as much of an owner as you are and can't be blocked. Although I'm just guessing here—no one's ever heard of shared ownership of the same way or its parts. You might be able to collapse it altogether, and of course I would expect you could seal this end, and that would block Madog. After all, you've already proved that would work at the other end."

He turned to Cydifor and explained. "After the great hunt and the failure of Madog's schemes, he tried to escape through the Archer's Way but couldn't get past George's seal."

"Mag," George said, "Could you make a very small way for us, the kind that doesn't go anywhere? Rhodri and I would like to try claiming it and other destructive experiments, if you don't mind."

Agreement. Interest.

Seething Magma moved forward and progressively vanished, reappearing a few yards away. George watched while she made the way but couldn't detect what she was doing. The creation of the way itself, however, blazed through George's senses, so close as he was. It started with a light at the entrance which sizzled along the leading edge of the way as Mag built it, flaring up at the end when she finished. He could see both ends, as bright as for the large way she'd created yesterday to take them to Edgewood Manor.

"May I claim this one, my lady, for an experiment?" Rhodri asked.

Agreement.

"Go ahead," George said for her.

"Get comfortable, Cydifor. This could take a while, depending on how thick his head is."

George bent down and responded with a snowball.

Rhodri brushed off his coat and drew himself up into a simulacrum of a dignified lecturer. "Here's an unclaimed way. Let's pretend that it's a traveling way and I've just found the one end. Ah, the excitement." He grinned, breaking character, then sobered. "Seriously, though, this is a real luxury. Most way-finders don't ever see an unclaimed way, except when they're taught. There are a few minor ways that are used for teaching, which are claimed, unclaimed, reclaimed, and so forth as examples, and that's what we're going to do with this one. Watch what I do."

George could feel Rhodri reaching out and gripping the end of the way nearest to him. It flared where he touched it and its light changed. George struggled for a way to describe the change. He settled on color complexity, the color became somehow less pure.

When George reached for the same end, his grip now slipped on it. The other end, however, still seemed available, the color cleaner.

"You've claimed this end, but I think the other could be claimed by someone else."

"That's right," Rhodri said. "If we each owned one end, we'd have to cooperate to use it. The traveling ways that enter rock are usually claimed at one end, in expectation that the other end may someday become accessible."

"Do you know the history of the Travelers' Way?" he asked George.

George shook his head.

"Trevor Mawr discovered one end of it after a rock fall freed it from underground obscurity. He said that it blazed to the heavens before he claimed it for Gwyn. The other end was unclaimed, of course, because it ended in the new world, and none of us were there yet."

Picture of Granite Cloud, picture of short, small tunnel. Picture of Mag, picture of medium length, broad tunnel. Picture of Gravel, picture of long, giant tunnel.

"Mag says her folk make bigger and longer tunnels the older they get," George said.

"That makes sense. For the ways, the bigger they are, the less common. We only know of two between the old world and the new."

"How did Madog get here," Cydifor asked.

Rhodri turned to him. "That's the big question. Gwyn wondered if there might be another way that only Madog uses."

"Do you know, Mag?" George said.

Wait... Picture of Shenandoah Valley, overlaid with ways, too much detail.

She formed a pseudopod on the front of her mantle and struck her own surface, since she couldn't make a noise against snow-covered ground. Three knocks.

"She doesn't know. Rhodri, she showed me a brief picture of the valley beyond the Blue Ridge. There are dozens, maybe hundreds of ways there."

"Madog's creations? Or, rather, Cloudie's?"

"I don't see what else they can be."

"Where can they all go?" Cydifor said.

"Maybe they're experiments with Cloudie, like this." Rhodri said. "Back to this example. Can you take my claim away?"

George already knew the answer but tried again, without success. He shook his head.

"I'm going to close this end."

George saw the light become blurred.

"Can you open it?"

Just like Madog's way earlier that morning, George made the attempt and failed.

"Alright, I'm going to claim the whole way and then hide it," Rhodri said.

Question?

"Wait up, Rhodri. Mag, are you following our discussion of opening and closing ways?"

Picture of Mag, picture of way. Picture of mouse going through the way. Picture of water going through the way.

"Let me see if I understand. You make open ways. Animals go through them. Water goes through them."

One knock.

Rhodri said, "There are a couple of ways in the old world which are famous for having a stream running through the bottom of the passage. It's how they were discovered, the water vanishing or appearing unexpectedly."

George waited, but Mag didn't add anything. "Can you close the ways, Mag?"

Two knocks.

"Well, that's unexpected," Rhodri said.

"Why should it be?" George said. "They don't use them the same way we do. I don't think they can own them either. Otherwise, Mag could claim herself and confront Madog without fear. Right, Mag?"

One knock.

"Rhodri, can you hide the way? I'd like Mag to see," George said.

Rhodri stared at George. "I already did."

"Oh." The way looked exactly the same to him. "Can you see it, Mag?"

Amusement. One knock.

"Looks like she can see it, too," he said.

"I'm sure it's hidden," Rhodri frowned. "I know it's there because I claimed it, but I can barely see it. I'll change it back."

He walked over to a bush and broke off some twigs. "Let's try you on way-tokens. These are flimsy, but they'll do. Watch how I seal my ownership to a token."

George tried to reach out with his mind to watch but he couldn't see anything.

Rhodri looked up in satisfaction. "There. See?"

George shook his head. "Um, no. How should I watch?"

"The same way you did when I closed the way."

"That's what I tried. Nothing happened."

"Yes it did. If I gave another way-adept this token, he'd be able to open the ends I sealed—it's a master-token. Lesser tokens can be used by anyone." He handed it to George.

George looked at it. He had no sense of it at all. He looked at the way and the ends were still closed. He couldn't see how to apply the one to the other. It was just a twig to him.

"I don't think I can do tokens, Rhodri. This is just a bit of wood, for all I can tell."

Rhodri said slowly, "Apparently we're not the same sort of way-finder. This isn't how it usually works. Let me try one more thing. I'll give you my claim."

George reached out for the way again and found he could grasp it. He opened both ends. "That worked," he said. "I've claimed it."

They quickly ran through a similar list, this time with George at the helm. He was able to open and close the entrances and hide the way from Rhodri, though not from Mag.

When he tried to give his claim to Rhodri, though, he couldn't make that work. He tried to unclaim the way altogether, and was successful.

The horned man stirred inside him and stretched. "I want to try something," he said. He wasn't sure if this was a suggestion from within or his own idea, he wondered. Didn't matter, he wanted to see what the result would be, either way. Instead of reaching for the ends of the unclaimed way, he reached for the entire thing and, in some fashion, absorbed it.

"What did you do?" Rhodri asked.

"I'm not sure. Mag?"

Picture of George. Picture of George, larger.

Well, that fits, he thought. It feels like a really big coat. He mentally mapped the ends to his hands and moved his arms. The way's ends moved to match, and the passage in-between moved with them.

Rhodri gasped.

Cydifor looked at him. "What happened?"

"He's picked up the way and moved it," Rhodri whispered.

What if I can't take this off, George thought. What would happen if I intersected someone with a moving end? What if someone had been inside when I moved it? Can I bury it in the ground?

He pictured himself shucking off the coat, and the way settled into its new position, on the surface.

"That was unnerving," he said. A snort from the horned man as he settled back down.

Seething Magma shuffled several feet back from George, and he looked at her. "What?"

Picture of horned man. Respect.

"Don't do that, Mag, it's just me," he said.

Two knocks.

The implication made George deeply uncomfortable and he shied away from examining it more closely.

They walked over to the moved way and Rhodri marked its location in the snow for Cydifor, starting at the far end and coming toward them. As he reached Mag, his foot slipped and he instinctively reached for her to break his fall. When his gloved hands touched her, he cried out as if burned and fell back into the snow. Mag backed away from him.

George bent over him. Rhodri's face was ashen. "What happened?" George asked him.

"I don't know. When I touched her, it felt as if my hands were on fire, and then my mind." He took a deep breath and shuddered. "Can we go home now?" he said, in a plaintive voice very unlike his usual banter.

George was alarmed. He thought back and couldn't recall anyone touching Mag, everyone keeping a distance out of respect, or fear of her strangeness. He remembered all the children greeting Mag last night and felt light-headed for a moment. He helped Rhodri up. "We'll leave in just a moment."

Sorry. Sorry. Picture of children. Picture of Rhodri, in the snow. Sorry.

"He'll be alright, Mag," George said, though he imagined she could detect the uncertainty in his thoughts. "Was it something you did, by accident?"

Two knocks.

So, not deliberate. Maybe, he wondered, it's something you are. George took off his glove and reached out slowly, touching her with a fingertip. Nothing. He lay his hand flat on her surface, and then his other hand. No effect.

He lifted his hands and turned to look at Cydifor.

"Oh, no," Cydifor said. "I can see where this is going."

Rhodri, beginning to recover, appealed to him, and reluctantly Cydifor came forward. He gingerly tapped Mag with one finger and staggered back. "Very unpleasant," he said, "as if I were being drained somehow."

George said, "Thank you, Cydifor. I think this is very important to know."

He turned to Mag. "We're leaving, that's enough for now. We have a lot to think about. Can you destroy this way?"

Two knocks.

"No, I don't suppose there's any reason for your folks to do so, is there? Mind if I do? I don't want to leave it hanging around."

Agreement.

George reached out to feel the way, a little tunnel of order in a world that wanted to revert to entropy. He'd closed ways twice before, as gently as possible, since he didn't know how big they were or what to expect. This time he had an intimate feel for the entirety of this way and he clenched a mental fist quickly as if squeezing it into non-existence. It popped like a balloon with a miniature thunderclap, trapped air spurting out of both ends. Bits of snow and debris that had been tracked in by Mag fell a few inches to the ground, making a visible trace.

Cydifor and Rhodri stood their ground, their faces expressionless. He looked at them and wondered sadly if they were suddenly afraid of him, like Mag was for a moment. Well, nothing he could do about it except hope that it wore off.

Before remounting, he pulled out his pocket watch to check the time. He rubbed his thumb over the engraving on the back as he closed it.

Picture of watch. Question?

"It's a mechanism for tracking the time. The hands take a full day to go around the dial."

No. Picture of engraving. Question?

Ah. She wants to know about the engraving and why it means something to me. "This is an illustration from a legend where I come from. It's the story of St. George and the Dragon. A friend gave it to me, because of my name."

Picture of dragon, threatened by St. George's spear. Question?

"Is this because Ceridwen said the fae called your kind dragons once? Different worlds, different dragons. Don't worry, we're not enemies." He sent her a wave of affection. "You can read us better than that."

She paused, then *Agreement.*

She's as shaken as we are, he thought. He showed her the picture of mouse, deer, man, Mag, horned man, and told her, nothing is certain, but we can all of us choose our friends.

They mounted up and followed her back through her way to the manor.

⌑

George came into the conservatory from the outside with Mag for the afternoon council session and found the tables lined up again into a longer line, a return to the impromptu council table of the day before. He was the last to arrive.

He took a seat next to Rhodri who still looked unwell. "How are you feeling?"

Rhodri glared at him, then winced. "You say this does wear off, right?"

"Sure," he said, confidently. Privately he was worried.

Rhys asked Cadugan to report on the sorting out of travelers from the morning.

"Every one of them has been properly assigned to a village and a dwelling, in some cases to a shop or workshop. Most of them have started on the final leg of their journey, and the remainder will travel tomorrow."

"All of them?" Rhys asked, incredulous.

"All of them," Cadugan said. "It would not have been possible without the able assistance of Ceridwen and Eluned." He nodded at the ladies graciously.

Ceridwen laughed. "It was easy. We wouldn't let them into the hall for the mid-day meal until they'd gone through our line. The ones at the tail end were a bit grumpy, but they understood the necessity."

"We took the opportunity to appoint representatives for each location who will report back to us about education and health needs, through Lleision's temporary military outposts," Eluned said. "Some of them might be good choices for new mayors or part of the town councils."

Ceridwen said, "The only ones remaining are those whose special mission is to seek out relatives. The fae are working directly with us, but the korrigans will send out their own group tomorrow, headed by Tiernoc and Broch, and Benitoe and Maëlys have taken on the task for the lutins. They'll leave tomorrow, too. We have lists of names and information from all three groups, added to the names from the last two batches of settlers, as well as the names of all the people they're looking for. What we don't have is a list of names of the people already here when we came. We haven't found those records. Yet."

Cadugan added, "We've taken the lutins into our own employ, my lord. They were comfortable with the tasks, and it seemed the safest thing to do, to keep them near until we discover what happened to the others. The korrigans are more numerous and better-armed."

"Well done," Rhys said.

"The settlers will report on urgent needs once they look over their new houses, farms, and shops, and we'll discuss how to help each of them as individual cases. The small craftsmen can be adequately handled this way, but the larger establishments—I'm thinking particularly of the mines, the smithies, and the mills—will

123

need more coordinated work. The korrigans who came are involved in the mines and the smithies, and they understand the mills, so I've asked Tiernoc to help gather information about the state of affairs with all of the bigger industries as they move from place to place."

Edern said, "Tiernoc was eager to get some of his folk started in trade but I explained to him he may find that difficult until we solve the riddle of the deficits in the local fae. No customers, no trade. He'll understand once he gets out into the villages and sees for himself."

"Next, the news from Gwyn," Rhys said. "Our dispatches have been delivered through the Archer's Way, and George brought back the messages from my foster-father. My grandfather and I went through them this afternoon.

"I'm sure you'll be glad to hear that there's nothing of an alarming nature to discuss. All's well at Greenway Court." He looked at Ceridwen. "Gwyn asked me to tell you that your patient Emrys will be released back to Idris tomorrow. He's making excellent progress."

"That's the fellow who ran through the barrier, the one I told you about," George said quietly to Rhodri.

"I know how he feels," Rhodri said.

The light went on in George's head and he froze.

"What?" Rhodri asked. "What is it?"

George raised a finger to stop him while he considered what had just occurred to him. *Mag, he thought, you know the barrier around this place?*

Picture of Edgewood's land with a semicircle surrounding it, anchored on the Blue Ridge at each end.

Yes, that's right. Is that a way, a non-traveling way?

Picture of Granite Cloud.

He thumped his fist on the table in triumph, and everyone looked at him. "Oh, sorry. Mag just confirmed something. I think I know what the barrier is."

"Yes?" Edern said.

"Let me get to it in an organized manner," George said.

Rhys said, "You were next anyway. I've been hearing bits about your work today."

"Well, here's the current status. The newly-made way over there," he pointed west, "has been sealed. It's definitely Madog's, as if there were any doubt, and Cloudie made it. I can't take it over, but I think I can destroy it, and I think I should. The only evidence we have says Madog can't get through my seal, but I wouldn't rely on that, especially if he has Cloudie with him. The only other time that's been tested, he was alone."

Lleision said, "We're maintaining a guard on it."

"The Archer's Way remains open and unsealed. Madog still has an ownership in it, but apparently so do I. I can seal it from this end, but once I do so, you'll lose communications with Gwyn again. I'd like to transfer my ownership to Rhodri so that it can be maintained like the Edgewood Way, with tokens and so forth, but I don't imagine that can be done with Madog's fingerprints all over it.

"I haven't looked at the Edgewood Way and its problem, yet. That'll be first thing tomorrow."

He paused, wondering how much to discuss here. "We, Rhodri and I, discovered many things this morning, experimenting with Mag." He nodded to her.

"The most urgent thing we found is that she's dangerous to the touch." That caused a stir. He held up a hand. "She didn't know, and we've been lucky. We had an accident with Rhodri this morning, and the effects were very much like those on Emrys."

That made Ceridwen's brows rise. "So you think the barrier is… what?"

"I think it's a stationary way, a non-traveling way. I'm betting that the same thing that makes Mag dangerous to touch affects someone walking through a stationary way, across it, I mean. You don't use those, do you? Ever do the experiment? How would you know?"

Rhodri said, "That makes perfect sense. Who would deliberately walk through a way from the side? Only the entrance and exit are really present. You'd need a non-traveling way to try it."

"And we'll test that tomorrow. But I bet I'm right," George said. "Mag said the barrier was made by Cloudie—I just asked her. What would happen if you were surrounded with the same sensation you got from Mag when you touched her, diluted, from all directions?"

"Nothing good." Rhodri shuddered at the thought.

George hesitated, then said, "Now that we were finally able to take some time to run a few tests, we also confirmed that Rhodri and I are very different sorts of way-finders. It doesn't look like I can work tokens at all."

"No," Rhodri said, "You can move ways instead."

That startled everyone into attention. Edern said, "Excuse me?"

"I raised the question with Gwyn before we left," George said, "about how a third-generation descendant could have much of the fae powers. I mean, you've seen my glamoury, Ceridwen. Not impressive."

She gave a little smile.

"But you manage the hounds, you led the great hunt," Rhys said. "Mag can talk to you."

"Oh, I can communicate with the beasts, but then so can Cernunnos. And isn't he a master of the ways, too, for the great hunt?"

Ceridwen nodded. "I've wondered just how much you take after your father's line, whoever he was exactly."

"I haven't been able to learn the skills, the technology, you use casually for magic, the small wooden symbols, and now the way-tokens." He cleared his throat awkwardly. "I don't think I can *do* magic, Ceridwen. I think I'm like Mag, it's what I *am*. Or what my father was, anyway."

"The point of all this is I already knew I could move a way, a little. I widened the way I came in by, from the human world, to get back through it with my horse the first time I went back."

Rhodri stared at him.

"I didn't know that wasn't supposed to be possible," he said, sheepishly, looking at him, "so I didn't say anything." To Edern, he said, "This morning, we experimented with a small non-traveling way that Mag made for us. I picked it up and moved it a short distance. The, um, horned man helped. You know, from inside."

Dead silence. He tried to move past it.

"Now, look, here's what I propose. I'd like to take one more poke at that new way in the morning, to confirm a theory that Rhodri and I have about way ownership. Then I want to see if maybe I can untangle the Edgewood Way's entrance from whatever trap way has been inserted, by moving its end a little bit to separate them. If that works, I could seal the trap way and restore the Edgewood Way to use."

Edern said, "Ceridwen, I don't know how to evaluate this. Do you think it can be done?"

"I really have no idea," she said. "If Cernunnos is strong in him, then it may be so."

"I wouldn't bet against it," Rhodri said. "You didn't see the way move this morning."

Disturbed. Picture of storm tearing a way apart in the air, picture of landslide tearing a way apart underground. Picture of George crushing the experimental way, holding it in his hands like a toy.

He swallowed.

"What did Seething Magma say?" Eluned asked.

"How did you know…" George said.

"You get this look when she talks to you."

"Ah. Well, I can't be sure, but I think she just accused me of being a force of nature, like an earthquake."

Rhodri said, dryly, "Better not let Angharad hear that." The laugh echoed around the table and released some of the tension.

❧

Leaving dinner early, Rhodri made a point of seeking out Mag in the conservatory before George was done. He wanted to speak with her privately.

He found the room otherwise unoccupied except for Cydifor, sitting in a corner with some pieces of paper, writing. He paused every few seconds, looked off into space, and waved the hand holding his pen quietly along to something only he could hear.

Rhodri recognized the symptoms: Cydifor was working on a composition.

"What are you making?" he asked.

"I'm just trying to get the words for a song down."

"What about?"

Cydifor balked at telling him and looked down.

"Come on, now, you'll have to tell me eventually."

He raised his head and said defiantly, "Well, about the huntsman."

That stopped Rhodri dead. Were the instincts of a bard correct? Were they watching a legend forming? He'd often wondered what the contemporaries of famous figures thought about each other while the events for which they were known were unfolding. He didn't think you could tell, while it was happening, what was going to prove significant and what was not.

But maybe he was wrong.

In any case, this wasn't why he'd come in early, and George would be here soon.

"Can you help me talk to Mag?" he asked Cydifor.

"I'd like that," Cydifor replied.

Rhodri walked over to her, and she backed away as he approached. "No, don't do that, my lady. It was an accident this morning, not your fault."

She stopped and let him get closer.

"You know that I can't hear you, the way George does? That none of us can?"

One knock.

"But you can understand us."

One knock.

"Alright. May I have a few minutes of your time?"

One knock.

He bowed to her formally. "I speak for Rhys when I say we're very happy to help you however we can with the recovery of your child. We would do the same for anyone. I hope indeed that we will be successful.

"What I'd like to discuss with you is the possibility of continuing our friendship with you and your people, afterward."

Cydifor looked at him. Ah, he's forgotten that I'm also supposed to be a diplomat, Rhodri thought.

"Would you like that?"

One knock.

"Would others among your people like that?"

A pause. Three knocks.

No surprise, she doesn't know. That's not why she came, after all.

"Do you know whom we should speak to?"

One knock.

How was he going to get something specific out of this, he wondered. "Hold on," he said to her.

"Cydifor, there are games and toys stored along the edges of this room, under the window seats. Let's go see if we can find anything useful there."

A few minutes' work yielded a pile of toys, game pieces, and various odds and ends.

Mag moved over to a pile of pebbles, used for some game, and extended a pseudopod to make them into an isolated group.

"That's a person?'"

One knock.

Rhodri was stumped but Cydifor stepped in.

"What we need are a bunch of symbols. Let's start with that."

He rapidly sorted out several items and placed them along the top of a bench.

"This old dog collar, we'll let that be the huntsman. You understand?"

One knock.

"Good. This cup will be you." In an aside to Rhodri, he said, "Best I could come up with for a pool of lava."

One knock.

Soon they had established several stand-ins. Rhys was a small crown, Cydifor a miniature harp, and Rhodri a wooden sun.

"I don't understand that metaphor," he said, looking at Cydifor.

"Maybe that's what you look like to her."

One knock.

Mag moved her cup over to the next bench and added a bit of gray flannel on one side, and the pile of pebbles on the other.

"Oh, of course," Rhodri said. "That's you with Granite Cloud and Gravel."

One knock.

"So, Gravel is the one I should speak to, about long term relationships between our people."

One knock.

"Here comes a tough question. How would I do that?"

Mag made a vertical column on her bench, of Granite Cloud at the bottom, herself in the middle, and Gravel at the top. She made a scratching noise.

What did that sound stand for, Rhodri tried to remember "Ah, a question. Do I understand, you want to know?"

One knock.

"Can you give me any more clues?"

She made a second column with Rhodri's sun at the bottom, then Rhys's crown. She paused and then took a miniature metal star and a toy lion and placed them side by side at the top of the column.

Cydifor said, "That lion must be Gwyn and the star Edern, as brothers. Is that right, Mag?"

One knock.

She extended a second pseudopod and touched the symbols at the bottom of each column simultaneously, then the middle symbols, and then the top ones.

"I understand," Rhodri said. "We must bring our highest rulers to meet with Gravel. The relationships we're making today will help with that."

One knock.

"Well done, you two," Eluned said. Rhodri turned around to discover they had acquired an audience. Edern, Rhys, and George were standing there with her, and Ceridwen was just entering the room.

Edern addressed Seething Magma directly, bowing. "My brother and I will be glad to speak together with your leader, once we've gotten your daughter back."

George took on that abstract look he wore when Mag spoke to him. "She's thanking you, Edern," George said.

Rhodri let Eluned take over with George so they could map out additional symbols more efficiently. He was proud of himself for having gotten this far on his own, with Cydifor's help.

"She's pleased with you, Rhodri," George told him. "She likes this game."

CHAPTER 12

George stood in front of the entrance to the Edgewood Way and considered it. Earlier that morning he'd gone back to the new way near the manor and confirmed that he now had a partial grasp on it, a shared ownership. He wasn't sure if that meant his seal would hold against Madog if he brought Cloudie, but at least it was consistent with the Archer's Way.

Now he tried to understand what he could sense here.

"Rhodri, it feels like the Edgewood Way starts normally, but you can't see the other end of the passage, like you could before."

"It's not always easy to see the end looking in from outside."

"Yes, but now it's blocked right up front," George said.

He reached his senses past the Edgewood Way's opening to examine the end of the way that was inside it. "This isn't how the hidden branch of the Guest's Way works. That's just a fork, like a letter 'Y' with one branch hidden. This one reaches all the way across."

Rhodri said, "I can't see the inner one very clearly. Your sight may be better than mine, here."

Edern and Rhys watched in some frustration as Rhodri and George stared at what was, to them, empty space. The end of the Edgewood Way met an old flagstoned surface that had been built to accommodate traffic. The flagstones had been swept free of snow and the way entrance was well marked on the stones for about twelve feet, but the way itself was invisible to them.

"Mag, can you tell us anything about this?"

Picture of Edgewood Way, picture of a blue mountain cliff. Picture of the trap way, picture of Granite Cloud.

"She says the Edgewood Way was made by someone else altogether—Blue Cliff?—but the trap way was made by Cloudie."

He asked her, "Does it go the same place the other one does?"

One knock clicked off the flagstones.

"We already knew this," Rhys said.

"No, we only assumed it," George said. "It's good to check the facts."

He said to Rhodri, "It looks to me like the trap way intersects the side of the Edgewood Way right at the front, cutting into it at an angle so that its mouth occupies the passage, not the side of it. It's not open, but it doesn't feel exactly closed, either." He illustrated the relationship with his hands. "If it's open from the other side, the direction the messenger came from, what would it look like on this side? Are we somehow seeing it from the back?"

"I don't know, I can't picture it. This all sounds a lot like the tangle we discovered twelve years ago, when Rhys's parents were taken. We couldn't understand what we found."

George glanced at Edern and saw his clenched jaw.

"How do you want to approach this?" Rhodri asked.

"Well, maybe I can seal it, like the other one, even if it's facing the wrong way, but that might block the Edgewood Way, too. Let's try to move the Edgewood Way away from it, first."

"And how do you propose to do that?" Rhodri asked.

"Well, you just, um, put your shoulder to it and keep pushing. There's a lot of resistance, like moving a heavy object, but eventually it'll move. I hope." George tried to illustrate what he meant, but Rhodri just shook his head.

"Have at it," he said. "Can Mag help?"

Two knocks.

"This isn't something they ever have a reason to do," George said. "I'll need to own it, I think. Can you release the claim?"

"I'm the custodian of the tokens under Gwyn, so I should be able to."

George felt the change and claimed the way. He stood up straight and prepared himself, remembering how hard it had been to move the small Huntsman's Way a few weeks ago.

The trap way intruded from the left, so George mentally leaned his right shoulder into the Edgewood Way opening and started a slow, steady push. For several minutes nothing happened, and George settled himself for a long job of it.

Edern and Rhys stirred impatiently. Rhodri monitored the process and gave him occasional reports.

"I think there's a little movement," he said, after about ten minutes. "Get your back into it, now."

George smiled tight-lipped, but in truth it was a very strenuous activity. He tried to maximize the steadiness of the pressure without exhausting himself but he felt like a draft horse pulling on an overloaded sledge—it just didn't want to move.

With a sense of stickiness releasing he finally felt a bit of give along the bottom on the left as it pulled free. The break traveled the length of the lower edge, and the whole entrance started to move right, an inch at a time. After another few minutes, the entrance had shifted about eight feet and George was done, dripping with sweat and trembling. He sat down abruptly on the cold flagstones, breathing heavily.

"Was it enough?" he asked Rhodri, from the ground.

"I don't think so," Rhodri said. He leaned over to give George a hand up. They walked back to the middle of the entrance and looked into it.

To George's senses, nothing had changed. "Don't tell me I pulled both of the ways, not just the one."

"Looks like it," Rhodri said. "Now what?"

As George inspected the entrance to the trap way, it sharpened and lost its blurriness.

❧

Madog felt the sealing of his second Court Way yesterday. It amused him, since he could make more whenever he wanted. They didn't destroy it, which was unexpected. He assumed they couldn't, so did that mean the huntsman wasn't there? Or maybe there's some limit on what he can do? Now that was an interesting thought.

The Trap Way was proving a bore. They must not be sending any more messengers.

Time to turn it around and try from the other side. He reversed the entrance with his master-token and released the trigger stick.

❧

Edern watched George and Rhodri doing inexplicable things around the marked way entrance but there was nothing to look at to hold his attention. Gwyn had some way-sense, sharpened by the special powers of the annual great hunt, but Edern had none himself. He tried to stay alert but his thoughts kept returning to the capture of his son and daughter-in-law. Rhodri's remarks brought the whole scene back and fed his imagination about what had actually happened to them. The only witnesses had been no help, but now he was able to visualize better what the situation must have been like.

George had clearly done something before he collapsed, but Edern wasn't too clear on exactly what. It all looked the same to him.

Rhys was unable to hold himself still and paced about behind Rhodri and George who paid him no attention, deep in their discussion. Mag stood off to their left.

A clatter on the stones caught Edern's attention and he spotted a small, complex, wooden object coming to rest a bit to the right of the marked way entrance. Rhys was closest to it.

"Hey, what's this?"

It took a second for the question to penetrate, then George and Rhodri turned with alarm loud on their faces. "No! Don't touch that!" George cried.

Edern had started moving in that instant but he was too late. Rhys had already walked over and bent down to pick it up. As he touched it, his form shimmered and vanished.

George heard Edern's cry of anguish and his own stomach clenched in sympathy. He intercepted him before he could follow Rhys and forcibly held him back.

"The way entrance was moved, the stone markings aren't right anymore," he said, holding on to him. "Rhys didn't realize."

He spoke to Edern firmly, trying to penetrate his fixed desire to follow his grandson. "He entered it. The trap way twisted, somehow, and then winked open and shut. He's gone, Edern."

Rhodri joined them and held his weeping kinsman, keeping him back from the unmarked entrance. "It was some sort of spell-stick, and Rhys couldn't see the entrance."

Sorrow. Loss.

Edern stopped struggling. George released him and turned to seal the trap way, moving quickly now. Too late, he thought, too late.

"He didn't have a way-token," Edern choked out. "It shouldn't have let him in."

Rhodri said, "I had to give George the way-ownership so he could move it. It was open, no tokens needed."

The look of reproach Edern sent him stabbed George like a physical blow and he flinched back. He couldn't shake it off, even after Edern relented and grasped his shoulder. "You couldn't know."

George shook his head in denial and walked away. "Take it back and close it," he told Rhodri over his shoulder, relinquishing his claim. He walked on to the edge of the flagstone paving and turned his back on them both, unable to look them in the face.

After a few moments, he heard Mag approaching.

My cousin, he thought to her, without looking. My friend, my responsibility. His grandson, picturing Edern for her. Madog did this to his son and daughter-in-law, before.

Picture of Rhys, picture of Granite Cloud. Picture of both together.

Not for long, he thought. Rhys is unlikely to survive this. My fault, I should have known they couldn't see the danger. My fault.

He put a hand on her unconsciously, stroking the smooth mantle as if she were a consoling dog, and brooded, heartsick, trying to think what to do.

CHAPTER 13

"Are you sure you want to do this?" Benitoe asked Maëlys at the stables, before breakfast was completed.

"I didn't come here to settle," she said. "I came to find Luhedoc, and anyone else I can."

He looked over the two saddle bags she had filled. "Did you follow the list I gave you? Clothing for three days? Blankets?"

"Yes, and trail food, and bowls, and an iron pan. A small pot. Seasonings. You take care of the tent and externals, and I'll take care of the food. Enough for three days, in case we stay out an extra night," she said.

"Each of us needs fire-starters in our pockets, some food on our backs, and a good knife. A water bag. And a cloak."

"You've told me. Repeatedly," she said, exasperated.

Benitoe paused in his checking to look at her seriously. "Auntie, we're not going into the wilderness, but we don't know what we'll find here along the edges. Say we meet a bear, our ponies dump us, and I'm killed. You need to have the necessaries for survival on your person, not your horse. It may be unlikely, but only the prepared tend to live long enough to tell those stories."

She calmed down. "You're right." She rummaged in her saddle bags and moved a few items to the pack on her back, then tied a tightly rolled cloak around the outside edge of it.

She looked warm enough, he thought, with her full red skirt over the breeches and gloves on her hands. He wore the traditional red himself, which seemed strange after two months in hunt livery green. He wanted them both to be easily identifiable as lutins from a distance, in case any others were watching from hiding.

He reviewed the simple plan they'd settled on for this first investigation. Explore the market town just down the hill, then start on the outlying farms. If nothing turned up in this area, they were prepared to relocate to each of the other villages and try again from there.

They mounted up and took the road down to Edgewood village.

⌁

As they entered the town, joining its primary north-south street from the northeast, Maëlys took stock of her situation. How fortunate she was to have found Benitoe, to have him helping her. It was like finding a son, though he was a bit older than any she would have had with Luhedoc, had they been so fortunate. A nephew, then.

She wondered what had made him seek out his position as whipper-in to Gwyn's hunt, something no lutin had done before. She could understand the appeal of the hounds, that's why so many kennel-men were lutins, but how does he stand the melancholy end of the hunt, with the death of the prey? It had been a subject of much discussion with Brittou and his friends. She wanted to ask him about it but was shy of intruding.

Why was he so alone, a strangely solitary lutin? He was dignified and competent, reserved in his demeanor, keeping his grief private. You'd never know he'd recently lost his betrothed. Where was his family? Who supported him?

Whatever came of her quest, she decided, he was family to her now. She'd have to find a time to tell him so.

This village was smaller than Greenhollow, and oddly quiet. About half of the houses stood empty, and most of the shops, and they found few of the residents out of doors. As they walked their ponies down the street, no one turned to watch. Maëlys was normally annoyed by the interest the tall folks took in lutins outside of their customary settings, but here it was more disturbing to be ignored altogether. Only the children gave them an occasional stare, and there were very few of them about.

Benitoe paused to ask directions to the inn from one man, who looked worn and exhausted. He waved his hand indifferently down the road and pushed on by. Benitoe glanced at her with a raised eyebrow, and she shrugged in response. Everyone had warned them, you'll understand better when you meet the residents.

The inn was easy enough to find, but distressing. The sign, a crowing rooster, hung from one corner only, just one more good storm away from coming down altogether. It was empty, open to the elements.

Maëlys inspected the interior. The furniture and fixtures were still in decent shape. The building itself looked solid, the roof intact. What a shame, she thought. You could make a good living here, once the traffic comes back.

They found an active family of fae across the street from the inn, apparently claiming an empty house and the handsome stone craft-shop next to it. She recognized some of them from their group of travelers a few days ago. It was strange, seeing normal activity in these empty streets.

Benitoe raised a hand at them, and the leader beckoned them over. "How are you getting on?" he wanted to know.

"All our folk are settled at the manor for now, helping with the animals," Benitoe told him, "except for us. We're starting to look for our lost ones."

The fae nodded. "We began working on these buildings yesterday, and not one neighbor came by to meet us, or to ask who we were. So we went and knocked on their doors in the evening, three houses around in all directions, bringing food and seeking their welcome. No one would let us in. We asked about some of our own who'd come here, and no one admitted knowing the names, those who spoke to us at all."

"It's very strange," Maëlys said. "What's caused it?"

"My wife says, it's like a sickness. We shouldn't blame them if they can't help it."

Maëlys nodded approvingly at this common sense.

"We're going to settle in and treat them as if they were normal, and maybe they'll get better. They don't seem dangerous, anyway."

A woman came up while they were talking. "Yes, but what if we catch whatever they've got?"

The man made a face, "Aye, that's the problem. We'll go along for now, but already we're looking over our shoulders to see if any of us have started to change. Very disturbing, it is."

❧

They paused at the far edge of the village, at the crossroads where the street met the main east-west road through the district.

"We won't be finding them in that wasteland of empty houses," Benitoe said. "We've got to find places with animals, and that's going to be the farms."

He reached into his weskit pocket for a bit of paper, some highlights of the roads of the local area that he'd jotted down the day before from a reference Ceridwen had shown him.

Maëlys said, "Someone's coming from the west."

She pointed toward the Blue Ridge, only a few miles away, and Benitoe saw a party on the road, headed their way. He knew from the map that the road ended along the base of the ridge.

He could see, even from here, that they were mounted on ponies, not horses. "I think that's Tiernoc's people. They're doing what we are, exploring and seeking kin."

They waited for them to catch up, and the greetings were all the warmer for the chill of the village behind them.

"You've seen the town?" Benitoe asked Tiernoc.

"Yesterday. What a disaster it is," he said. "We went on to the mines at the mountain as quickly as we could. It seems less deserted when it's just empty buildings instead of empty people."

The lutins nodded. "What did you find?" Benitoe said.

"Fallen buildings and absent owners," Tiernoc said.

Broch spoke up, "But good signs, too. All the tools that could be easily carried were gone. I can't see those villagers having the energy to do that, can you?"

Benitoe said, "So you think they may be alive but in hiding?"

Tiernoc nodded.

"We're headed to the farms to seek our lost ones," Benitoe said. "We think they'll stay around the cattle and horses. There's a road running north a bit to the east of here that we wanted to try."

Tiernoc said, "We're going that way ourselves. There's a mill there, on our list of places to investigate, and your farms are probably beyond it. We'd welcome your company as long as our paths go along together."

Benitoe and Maëlys swung their ponies alongside Tiernoc and Broch.

"When the lutins go to ground, the stories say, they seek out herds and individual animals to care for and keep themselves to the night. We've been hearing stories about tended animals on the farms, and so we're hoping," Benitoe said. "What happens with your folk?"

Tiernoc was silent for a moment and Benitoe feared he wouldn't reply. "Ours go to the mountains," he said at last, "to caves and tunnels and holes in the ground. They dig in secret and

139

hunt in the woods. A few go to water, dwelling on the edges and living on fish and frogs. I'm thinking your folk may dwindle less that way than ours do. Without our tools and the skills to use them, we're lost."

Maëlys reached out her hand and patted him on the arm. "The fae in the villages have dwindled in their own way. We all of us have much to face."

⁓

Maëlys stood outside in the morning sun watching the korrigans and Benitoe swarming over the mill building. She'd never seen one so large. The wheel was still upright, as tall as the four-story stone structure beside it, but the axle was broken and it leaned crookedly. The flume above was empty of water, though plenty ran over the lip of the waterfall next to it. The mill pond above must be leaking or empty, she thought.

Benitoe came out of the bottom entrance, with Tiernoc.

"This was quite a mill, once," Tiernoc said. "I can see why it's a landmark. A backshot mill with internal gearing—you could do a lot with this once it was fixed up again."

"You mean this can be repaired?" she said.

"Not difficult at all, just a little digging in the muck of the mill pond to make it watertight again, and then some wood and iron work. The building's sound enough, and the race is still open." He pointed to the channel of water that held the wheel which drained out into the stream.

He laughed at her look of surprise. "All mills need maintenance, constantly. This one's been neglected a long time, but replacing all the wood at once is straightforward, compared to preparing the site itself or raising the building, or even getting the right gears. You just follow the existing pattern and, before you know it, you're done. Apprentice work."

He went on to join the rest of his folk, and Benitoe, last out of the building, walked over to her. "You know, it's not bad in there. The animals have been in it, of course, and part of one floor is down, but what's left would make a good shelter. If we don't find suitable hospitality where we're going in the afternoon, I think we should try to come back here for the night."

Tiernoc mounted his pony and rode over to them. "This is as far as we're going in this direction. We have more buildings off the main road to check. Are you two staying, then?"

Benitoe said, "I have a list of farms further north. We'll start there and take a look around."

"Good luck," Maëlys called to Tiernoc's company as they departed.

Benitoe gave her a leg up onto her pony, but before he mounted, he took something out of one of his saddle bags and tossed it into her lap. "What do you think?" he said.

She picked it up. A pair of crossed peeled sticks, maybe three inches long, were bound to two bundles of straw, of the same length, all held together with a wrapping of red yarn, like an eight-pointed star alternating wood and straw.

"What is this?"

"It's an old, old token, a call to assembly. It signifies a place where lutins are welcome and honored. I made a lot of these, yesterday, and I want to put them where they might be found."

"You want them to be curious," Maëlys said. "That's what you're trying to do."

"Well, I can't find them, if they want to hide, but we can make ourselves easy enough to spot, can't we?"

She reached for the red cloak bound to her backpack. "We'll make ourselves the most conspicuous lutins in Edgewood," she said, as she put it on in a blaze of color. Maybe the only ones, too, she thought, outside the manor.

141

CHAPTER 14

Rhys shivered in the dark and dreaded the time when he was likely to lose what clothing they'd left him, after stripping him of his coat, shoes, and the contents of all his pockets.

He envied his young sister Rhian who'd recently shown him how she kept a little three-inch knife tucked in under the root of her braid for emergencies. He'd thought her recent habit of carrying knives a silly sort of youthful enthusiasm, but now that they'd taken all of his, he'd wished he'd found more creative ways to hide one himself. He'd tell her so, when he saw her again, and make her smile.

If he saw her again. He knew it was unlikely. This was the man who'd murdered their parents.

They must be dead. Madog would never have had the patience to keep them alive all this time. Had they been in this very cell? Were they kept together? How long did they last?

What did Madog do to them?

He remembered vividly being ten years old and told he couldn't come with them this time, that he had to stay home with his baby sister. He'd resented it—visiting his grandfather was a treat he enjoyed.

Then something happened. The adults dodged him for days before Edern sat down and explained to him, with tears in his eyes, that his parents had been captured, that no one knew how to get them back. That no one was even sure they were alive. He'd felt his childhood stop on that day.

He'd nodded soberly as his grandfather explained to him that he must now look after his baby sister, that she was his responsibility. He didn't fully understand what had happened—that would come later—but he remembered being pleased, in the midst of everything, that Edern had told him the truth. That was a consolation he clung to in the years that followed, that someone he respected had judged him strong enough to bear it.

Now he'd come full circle and ended up where his parents did, as if he'd accompanied them on that journey after all. As if nothing that had happened since was quite real, just a temporary postponement of what was meant to be.

Rhys knew, in a distant way, that focusing on his parents' fate was a way of avoiding thinking about his own, something his mind kept shying away from.

Of all the fool things to do, picking up that spell-stick. When he heard George's shout he'd finally put it together, that George had moved the entrance to the way and he'd walked into it. He could still hear that cry ringing in his ears as he stumbled off balance into the arms of Madog's guards and saw the grins on their faces, the smoke of the torches on the wall—the disdain they had for him as two of them effortlessly bound his hands and disarmed him before he could even reach for a blade.

What worth was all that training with Hadyn when I can't defend myself when I most need to?

He knew, better than he wanted to admit, that this could only end one way. The faster he could resign himself to it, the better. Face that fact and square up to it, he told himself, regrets are pointless. They can only kill you once.

◡◠◡

Madog felt as full of pride as a tick. The partridge walked right into the snare, first try. It made up for the botched version of a few years ago.

It was going to be delicious playing with him. Young, just had a taste of rule, and in Creiddylad's domain, no less. Shame she wasn't here to see this, she'd appreciate the justice of it.

He'd have to keep Scilti from ruining him right away—he'd need him to bait Gwyn. Still, as long as the damage wasn't too permanent, that left a lot of room for fun and games. If he did have to give him back to Gwyn eventually, to entice him into a trap, how much better if he went back broken, a weakling for a foster-son.

He'd never liked him, too much a reminder of Gwyn. Let Gwyn see what he could do to one of his.

He could taste the possibilities. His possession of this piece would constrain Gwyn to at least meet with him, and he could control where. He started thinking about ambushes and angles, his mind humming. With Gwyn dead, nothing could keep him from Annwn.

⁓

Rhys looked up as his cell door opened and the light of the torches carried by three guards dazzled his eyes. He made himself stand up awkwardly, his bound hands impeding his movements. He wanted to meet his fate with whatever dignity he could, for as long as possible.

Madog stood in the doorway, looking like a genial host with that bland expression Rhys was learning to loathe. He stared at Rhys in silence, then a slow, satisfied smile spread across his face.

"I don't know if you ever met Scilti, here," he said, and stood aside as a tall, thin, cadaverous man stepped into the cell.

Rhys had never seen the man's face and knew he'd been glamoured when Rhian met him. "Is this the man who was bested by my little sister and her friend, before we defeated your last attempt? Why, I'm pleased to meet such a man." He put a juicy sneer into his voice.

Scilti scowled and strode forward, giving Rhys a vicious backhand blow that knocked him down and bounced his head off the stone floor. With his hands bound behind him he couldn't break his fall. As his head spun he heard Madog say, quietly, "Now, now, we want him to last quite a while, we do. I have much more satisfying plans for him. I want Gwyn to see him with his mind gone, before I kill them both."

The lights spun crazily as they left and the door shut, leaving him in darkness again. He couldn't quite tell up from down in the dark with his head throbbing, so he slowly scooted across the floor until he fetched up against a wall and leaned against it, working his arms to try and keep the circulation going.

I'm going to rot in here, he thought, or worse, I'll break. He didn't doubt that Madog might be able to do it. How strong could he be, in the face of hopelessness? He'd never been tested—he feared the failure more than the test.

He'd had a young man's confidence in his personal immortality but now he thought, I'm only twenty-two. I'm going to die before I really start my life. Never to have a wife or child. He hadn't expected to marry for decades yet—after all, there was no rush. And now it was too late.

Oh, grandfather, he thought. All that work to save me from my parents' fate and look what happens. I'm so sorry to bring this on you. I wish I could tell you so.

He knew his foster-father Gwyn would mourn him deeply. He understood the emotions under the public face he used for ruling. I mustn't be the instrument that brings him down, he thought. If I can't stand it, I must find a way to end it. It's the only way I can thank him now for his care of Rhian and me.

Rhian. I'm sorry, sister. I wanted to see you grow up, such a woman as you'll make. Don't grieve for me. You'll inherit all the wishes for both of us, and I know you can bear it.

He couldn't think about it anymore. The throbbing in his head reminded him that as long as they gave him this much freedom of movement, he could always run at a wall and dash his brains out. He promised himself not to do anything that would jeopardize that option. He thought he might be able to withstand whatever came, as long as that possibility remained open.

CHAPTER 15

Ceridwen rose to her feet at the council table in the conservatory and slapped her hand down, loudly. The noise startled everyone for a moment and even George looked up from where he'd been sitting, silent. "Enough! We must master our grief if we're going to be of any use to Rhys."

The tumult of the various reactions subsided, and Edern raised his hand for silence, the tracks of his tears still visible on his grim face.

"Thank you, Ceridwen. You are, as always, correct."

She sat down, looking prepared to do it again if necessary.

Edern said, "While Rhys is absent I take upon myself the office of regent on his behalf."

There were no objections.

"First question, are we sure he's with Madog?" he said.

Edern looked to George, but it was Rhodri who answered. "Yes, I'm sure."

George opened his mouth reluctantly. He'd said little since returning from the Edgewood Way's entrance. "We know the way ends in roughly the same place, over in the valley."

"So, we know who and where. Can we attack?" Edern asked.

George shook his head. "Remember the courier's tale to Gwyn. That trap way probably emerges into a secure area, like a dungeon." What about the other one, Mag, any idea what it's like at the other end?

Dark, underground.

"Mag says the other one also comes out underground."

Lleision said, "We'd be sending our men into certain ambush, my lord."

"Will Madog hold him as a hostage or kill him?" Edern said. George could see the effort it cost him to say it.

"We have no way of knowing," Ceridwen said, "but consider his previous actions. He's been trying to undermine Gwyn's rule for a long time. I think he wants Annwn itself, and for that he must defeat Gwyn. Rhys is more useful as a live hostage for that purpose."

Edern nodded. George could see that no one wanted to say, "but look what happened to Rhys's parents," though everyone around the table thought it.

"Let's operate on that belief. How can we rescue him?" Edern said.

Once again the room erupted into a variety of wild suggestions.

"I'll do it," George said quietly, almost to himself. In all the noise, no one heard him except Rhodri, next to him, who stared.

"What? How?"

"I'll cross the ridge. Madog doesn't think it's possible."

Their nearest neighbors quieted to listen.

"What makes you think you can?" Rhodri said.

George looked at him, angry. "Just like the hounds, remember? Like I can do this," he said, his voice rising as he slapped a hand on Mag, and Rhodri winced, clearly remembering what it felt like when he touched her. "I might as well be good for something."

By now the room was silent, listening to him. He rubbed his face and drew himself upright in his seat.

"I can cross the ridge. Probably. I know the land, at least the version in my world, and it's not that far, maybe thirty miles. There's a river to cross, the Shenandoah, but only the one. It shouldn't be hard to find where all the ways converge, and that's where Madog will be, in the center of his web. And where he is, I'll find Rhys." If he's alive, he thought.

"Mag, can you hear me, that far away?"

Picture of Cloudie, Picture of George.

"I think that was a yes. She can hear Cloudie that far."

Lleision said, "But no one else can understand our guest."

"No, that's not true anymore," Eluned said. "It's clumsy, but we're making great strides. We could keep in touch using Mag, if she's willing."

One knock.

"Cloudie will be in the same place, I imagine," George said.

"But to free her you'd have to get Madog to release his claim on her, if she's really like a way," Rhodri said.

"Or I could kill Madog," George said, matter-of-factly.

The room went quiet.

Edern said, "I don't know what it would take to free Rhys. He must be under guard."

"But killing Madog would be a good first step," George said, his face unchanged.

"Be serious," Rhodri said. "How would you do that?"

"I'll think of something." He roused himself. "Look, do you have a better idea? We can't leave them there, even if it's hopeless. We just can't."

Ceridwen said quietly, "Let's look at this as a possibility and explore how it would be done."

Lleision said, "We must secure our own borders first, and we must retain communications with Gwyn. If you leave, huntsman, who can use the Archer's Way?"

George said, "Here's what we can do. I'll kill that new way to the west and the trap way before I leave. We can send one more batch of messages to Gwyn through the Archer's Way this afternoon, then I'll seal that shut, just in case. Without the trap way, we should be able to use the Edgewood Way again, and that solves the communication with Gwyn issue."

He turned to Mag, "Madog might bring Cloudie to make more ways here. Is there anything you can do about that?"

Picture of Mag, picture of Rhodri. Picture of Cloudie coming, then going.

"I don't understand. You and Rhodri can keep Cloudie from coming?"

One knock.

"How?" Rhodri said.

"I don't know, ask her later," George said impatiently. "There's your defense, Lleision."

Edern said, "My boy, Gwyn will not thank me if I let you throw away your life on this. It's not your fault."

"Then whose fault is it?" George said. "Besides something like this had to happen eventually, for Cloudie's sake, and at least Madog won't expect it. Who knows, it might even work." Not likely, he thought, keeping his face straight.

He looked at Cadugan. "I'll go in at the nearest gap, on foot. so I can get through the woods on the slope. I'll need supplies for at least six days, that's three coming and going, more if I can bring Rhys out."

"Tomorrow," he said. "At first light. I'll kill the ways and then leave."

He stood up abruptly before they could try to talk him out of it and walked out, leaving the door open behind him.

⌒

George dismounted from Mosby in the river meadow at the exit to the Archer's Way. He'd made the courier delivery and picked up the message packets from Greenway Court and now it was time to seal it, just in case Madog's partial ownership in it still posed any sort of threat.

Mag had come with him, to take him through the way she'd made, but she'd said little to him since the council meeting. Now she stood motionless in the late afternoon sun, like a boulder that had recently been brushed clean of snow. Something in her posture caught George's eye.

"What?" he said.

Hesitance.

"Go ahead, spit it out."

Picture of George, picture of Madog. Picture of George shrinking and vanishing.

"You think Madog will kill me?" he said evenly.

Agreement.

"Well, it may be so."

Picture of Granite Cloud, picture of Madog. Picture of Granite Cloud, bigger. Picture of Madog shrinking and vanishing.

"If Cloudie waits long enough, Madog will die? Is that it?"

Agreement.

"That could be thousands of years. He might pass along his claim to someone else. And while he controls her, others will die." His manner was curt and grim. "Now, you picture this."

He portrayed for her a picture of Rhys laughing, a scene of his hunt staff all trying on their brand new livery. He pictured the scene with Rhys gone, then Rhys broken on the ground somewhere dark, with the ghostly images of his parents broken on the ground behind him, and Edern left standing. He pictured Rhian weeping.

"No," he said. "No. Not while I can help it."

She backed away from him, and he turned to the Archer's Way and began the weaving of the seal.

⌒

Cadugan had been a pleasant relief, George thought, treating his requests with impersonal coolness and efficiency. He was finally satisfied that the pack waiting on the bench in a corner of the main hall was as close to ideal as he could achieve, given the necessary trade-off between weight and supplies. He hefted it and estimated its weight at about fifty pounds, a heavy load, but he had food for a journey in and out, and extra for Rhys if he was successful, as well as adequate shelter for a winter trip in snowy conditions.

He could hear the post-dinner conversations in the other rooms but had no desire for company. Even Mag had picked up on his mood after her unexpected try at dissuading him this afternoon. He'd been able to avoid most other encounters, something in his face clearly warning them off.

He was grateful for it. He couldn't speak about why he found this attempt so necessary, and he would not be prevented from it.

But now he stood in the empty hall and thought of Angharad. When I leave in the morning, I may not come back, he acknowledged. He drew out the pendant and let it hang suspended, the arrow pointing south, firm as a rod. I have a duty to her, too, he thought, and his heart ached.

He tucked the pendant back under his shirt and walked down the hallway to the estate offices. As he expected, Ceridwen and Eluned were both there, helping Cadugan with his continuing search through the records. They looked up as he came in.

"Huntsman," Cadugan said, carefully. "Something we can do for you?"

His expression wavered before settling into its official mold, and George realized that his demeanor earlier had been his way of making things easier for George, not his genuine feelings.

"Yes, sorry to disturb you all," he said. "I'm looking for pen and paper. I'd like to write something for Angharad tonight."

Ceridwen handed him the materials and he thanked her, trying to ignore the sympathy on her face. He carried them up to his room and shut his door.

c⁓ɔ

Benitoe knelt before the main hearth at the mill while Maëlys prepared an evening meal for them both. She was frying sausage slices in a small iron pan and had promised corn cakes fried in the fat afterward.

He busied himself with preparing water to refill their water bags, from snow newly melted and boiled in their bronze bowls. He took the bowls by their handles, using cloths to avoid burning himself, and placed them on a convenient snowbank to cool, watching as they melted the snow around them to keep them from tipping over. When they had lost most of their heat, he poured the contents into the bags for tomorrow's journey. He kept back about a cup of water that Maëlys had asked for.

Reentering the mill building, he gave Maëlys the bowl with the remaining water, and she quickly added the dry ingredients for her corn cake batter from one of her small sacks and began frying them. The sausage slices had been removed to a clean piece of bark waiting for the bowls he brought back to be available. The corn cakes went on another piece of bark temporarily and she scrubbed her bowl with a wisp of dried grass after pouring the last of the batter into the pan.

She took the bowls and divided the sausage slices into them, then added the flat corn cakes, crisp and dripping with fat. She kept a few aside for toasting on a stone in the morning, and tossed the used bits of bark into the fire where they popped and flared.

While he dug into his meal, she added a bit more fat to the pan and sliced three of the apples she'd brought with her on top. She uncorked just a little honey to sweeten them and placed the iron pan far from the fire so that they could caramelize slowly and not burn while they finished the main meal.

"You're very good at this, auntie," Benitoe said, his mouth full. He wasn't used to having someone cook for him like this.

She smiled at him. "I've always liked feeding people. I hated to see that inn standing vacant in the village—what a kitchen it must have. I've been thinking about it all day."

"Running an inn is a complicated job. Things like that must have been among the first to be lost," he said.

"Yes, but if the fae recover, it's a good way to get them started again. A successful inn, a large one like that, needs lots of people."

"You should take it on," he said. "Sounds like you know what's required."

He was surprised to see her taking it seriously. "I've been considering it," she admitted. "If I don't find Luhedoc," Benitoe reached over and squeezed her hand, "I'm not sure I want to just go back. I think I might like a new challenge instead."

She looked at him. "Do you think the manor might invest in the inn with me as manager?"

Benitoe said, "I'm sure they want as many businesses established as possible. I'd be glad to help you make your proposal to them. They'll listen to you."

She dished out most of the honeyed apples from the warm pan into their bowls, saving a bit for the morning, with the corn cakes.

"What did you think of the farms today," she asked. "I confess I was frightened by what we found."

Benitoe considered the dirty and ill-kept buildings, the dull families, hiding inside when the lutins rode up to their doors. "Did you notice that the livestock was in better shape than the people? Less dirty, no sores. No empty water buckets."

"I saw you scattering those tokens around. You even hung one on that sty."

"Well, those were healthy looking sows, weren't they?" he said. "We'll go back in the morning and see if any of them were picked up in the night."

"Where did you learn to make those tokens? Who taught you that?"

He hesitated and looked at her consideringly. "I learned from the Kuzul," he said, "the Council."

She stopped chewing for a moment and stared at him before continuing. "But aren't you too young for that? Brittou told me you have to be at least fifty years old."

"Yes, but the members nominate juniors, sort of apprentices, and Ives, Gwyn's kennel-man, is my sponsor."

It was just another part of his life that separated him from his peers and he was used to having them withdraw once they discovered it, but Maëlys didn't seem to see it that way.

"What a mark of respect that must be from your elders," she said. "Did they select you for this journey, as their delegate, or was this your own idea?"

"Both. I could spare the time, since we can't hunt the hounds well in the deep snow, and of course the huntsman and I already work together. And I wanted to come, for personal reasons."

"Hmm?" she said, encouragingly, as she ate.

"My family, well, my mother died when I was born, her only child. My father, he lasted about seven years before he called me into his workroom one day and gave me the keys to his tool chests. He shook my hand silently and walked out, and that was the last anyone saw of him."

"Oh, you poor dear. What happened?"

"It's not that bad. I knew, all my childhood, that he was only partly there, that more of him was with my mother. He tried, he did, but I wasn't surprised when he finally gave up." He looked at her. "I don't think he's dead. I think he's gone to ground somewhere, to forget. Like our folk here."

"What did you do?"

"I was pretty self-sufficient by then. My mother's sister was in the habit of coming by every week or so to make sure I was alright." He paused, remembering. "It was ten days, this time. I managed the food and the animals just fine on my own, but I'll admit the laundry was a bit beyond me." He smiled faintly.

"She wanted to bring me into her family, her husband was a stout fellow and I was fond of him, but I wouldn't give up my father's house, the last of his line. I wouldn't go. They took me by force and I kept going back."

He was proud of his stubborn seven-year-old self, and she smiled along with him.

"It eventually came to the notice of the Kuzul, and they had a long talk with me." He remembered that well. By then he knew he was an unusual child, that he didn't fit in with everyone else. He wanted to go his own way, a most un-lutinish trait.

"What did you say to them?" she said.

"I told them I could take care of myself, well enough, and that I was fine where I was. And that they should stop bothering me."

"Oh my goodness. No one speaks to the Kuzul that way."

"You'd be surprised," he said, with a grin. "But no child, certainly. That stumped them. We were all rescued by my aunt. She barged into their interrogation and told them that she would take me on as an apprentice instead of a nephew, that apprentices were allowed their own living quarters where appropriate. Everyone looked at each other and decided to forget that there was a minimum age for apprenticeship."

"For the rest of my childhood, I slept in my father's house, but took most of my meals with my aunt and uncle, and helped them raise their family."

"It must have been lonely for you," she said.

"Not really, it's what I was used to. Still am used to." That sounded sad even to him, so he volunteered, "Isolda would have changed all that," and that made it worse. He stopped and stared into the embers.

"You'll find someone," she said, after a moment, "Not to replace her, just someone else."

He nodded without looking at her. He knew people wanted to see that conventional acceptance. He wasn't so sure himself. Isolda, even ten years younger, had been almost as different as he was in her quiet way, with her unconventional work driving teams of horses. He missed her, every day. He could feel himself building an outer husk of solitude, to make it easier to live alone again.

Maëlys startled him by rising to her feet and standing formally before him, her hands raised in the gesture of petition. She beckoned him up, and he stood in front of her with his hands palm-up in acceptance, puzzled, to listen and to honor her request, whatever it was.

She spoke in the slow measured tones of public testimony before witnesses. "Young Benitoe, hear me. With or without my dear Luhedoc, I am the mistress of my family in matters of relations and alliances. You have been of great service to me and I have a warm affection for you and interest in your life. You have lost your mother and your father and have been apprentice to your mother's sister, a cold relationship, and so I judge you to have no aunt or other near relations."

She lowered her hands and clasped each of her wrists with the opposite hand, binding her words.

"No man should be without family. I, Maëlys, would have you as my sister-son, by law and by custom, and not just by such nicknames as we use between us now. My hearth your hearth, my house your house, and my family your family, for our lives and beyond."

She grasped his open hands and pulled him forward, capturing his gaze with her own. "What say you?"

Mesmerized by her intensity, Benitoe nodded, without stopping to think about it rationally. She smiled radiantly and released him, and he stumbled back and sat down hard. This was an old custom indeed, and rare, an adoption into a clan, what they called a rebirth. Her words echoed through him, back and forth and back again. Something stiff and very old broke inside him, and he turned his face away while tears ran down it, silently.

She draped her heavy red cloak over him without speaking and patted his shoulder. Then she went to clean up the cookware and bank the fire for the evening.

⌒

Gwyn sat at his desk at the back of the council room in Greenway Court, alone. The two lamps on the desk and the remains of the fire were all the light he needed to stir a finger through the opened dispatches in front of him.

He knew he hadn't fooled Idris any, but his marshal respected his judgment and didn't push for the news, assuming Gwyn would tell him if immediate action was needed. Sitting through dinner with Rhian and Angharad had been intolerable. He'd tried to hold trivial conversations with the seatmates on his left instead, leaving the two of them to chat quietly together.

When he'd opened the courier bag the guards brought him late in the day, he'd checked for Rhys's handwriting, as usual, and was surprised not to see any messages from him. Then he turned to Edern's dispatches to read them first, as he usually did.

Over the centuries the brothers had grown ever closer together and developed a sympathy with each other that let them communicate in writing clearly, without misunderstandings. They would always be rather different people, but Gwyn thought their bond, slowly formed, was likely to last the remainder of their lives.

He smoothed out Edern's dispatch, marred where he had crumpled it in his fist as he digested the news of Rhys's capture. It comforted him to try and flatten it out again, as if he could mitigate the disaster it announced by reducing the creases. He could feel Edern's grief behind the simple factual narrative—it resonated with his own. He'd fostered Rhys for nine years. It would have been longer, but he well remembered the stubborn youth who wouldn't be parted from his younger sister and who waited for her to turn five, old enough to come with him. Gwyn loved him fiercely, he'd seen him grow into manhood, so promising. In his first rule at Edgewood he was doing well, fulfilling that promise.

Gone, all gone. And probably in pain for whatever remained of his short life. His stomach clenched.

He raised his head at a quiet knock on the door. When he didn't respond, Idris opened it, to see if anyone was there.

"Shall I go away, my lord?"

"No, stay. I have to tell someone, and you're the easiest, old friend," Gwyn said, pointing at a chair in front of the desk.

Idris closed the door behind him before coming over and sitting down. "What has happened?"

Gwyn took a deep breath and said it, all at once. Maybe that would make it easier, like ripping a bandage quickly off a wound. "Madog has taken Rhys. George is going to go after him. Alone."

Idris nodded, as if he'd expected something like this. He reached out his hand. "May I?"

Gwyn gave him Edern's wrinkled dispatch and stared off into space.

After a minute, Idris lifted his eyes. "I am sorry to read this, my lord. He's not very clear about what they intend to do."

"No. I imagine that was as hard for him to write as it is for us to read." He cleared his throat. "I have a thorough account of their plans from Ceridwen."

He gave the multi-page document to Idris, and rose from his chair to pace while he read it.

"Well, that's more understandable, but I don't like it, my lord. George doesn't stand a chance, much as I hate to say it."

"Oh, I think he can get to the general area of Madog's court, but how can one man alone do anything there?" Gwyn said. "I think they've sent my great-grandson to his death pointlessly, after my foster-son who's probably already dead."

"No, my lord, there I can't agree. Rhys would be an excellent hostage, and that's the right thing to fear. Madog would find him more valuable alive than dead."

"This is the man who killed his parents rather than keep them as hostages, remember."

"Yes, so we think, but we don't know what actually happened. It can't be easy, this business of trap ways and triggers. Maybe something went wrong."

Gwyn grunted noncommittally. Idris was right but he thought it a slim hope.

"I am sorry, though, about the huntsman," Idris said. "Madog must hate him personally. If he is captured…"

"Yes," Gwyn said shortly. There was little to say about it. "I have two messages from Rhodri. The first talks about diplomacy with this Seething Magma, this rock-wight you told me about. You can read that later. But in this one," he handed it to Idris, "he describes his work with George and the capture of Rhys, which he witnessed. It's clear they're not sending George. The problem is they can't stop him."

Idris read the document and put it down. "Well, you know how stubborn he could be."

Gwyn noted his unconscious use of the past tense and clenched his jaw. He's not dead yet, he wanted to shout. Neither of them are.

"'Advise me. Is there anything we can do from here?"

"I can't think of much. We can't cross the ridge though it may be true that George can. By now he'll have sealed the Archer's Way from the other side. I can't send anyone in to check that without him, but we'll know in the morning if the Edgewood Way is reopened, and that will give us options for reinforcing them if there's some sort of attack."

"But you don't think that likely," Gwyn probed.

"No. I think all the action will be in Madog's home ground, where we can't reach."

Gwyn raged with frustration. His great-grandson hadn't left yet, wasn't due to leave until the morning, but there was nothing he could do to prevent it. Assuming he truly wanted to—he admitted the forlorn hope of a rescue for Rhys, however unlikely, was compelling. There were no good choices.

"I can't bear just standing by, watching," he said. "But what else can I do?"

"You can be a rock for Rhian and Angharad," Idris said, quietly. "A source of hope."

Gwyn's shoulders sagged. "I haven't told them, yet. Let them sleep one more night in peace. I'll wait for the updates in tomorrow's packet. Then I'll know for sure that George has gone."

CHAPTER 16

As the sky began to lighten to the east, behind a veil of thick low clouds, George stood in the snow and looked at the exit of the intrusive way, west of the manor. Rhodri and Edern kept him company, with Seething Magma.

It was still closed, his seal undisturbed. He thought about where the end might come out. Underground, Mag said. Maybe there were guards there, unprepared this early in the morning.

The last time he destroyed the way that was standing here he'd simply unmade it, letting the world around it override the unnatural displacement. This time he wanted to use it as a weapon, if he could. He'd hardly slept all night, in rage and anguish about Rhys. One of the things that had occupied his mind was how to make the collapsing of the ways an attack.

He couldn't just pick it up, the way he did Mag's little non-traveling way in the river meadow. The other end was far away and he didn't fully own it. But destruction was easier than fine control, and that he could do.

"Alright," he said aloud. "I'm going to try and shut it down with violence at the far end, if I can."

He thought if he held the near end shut and collapsed it progressively, rather than all at once, he might build up a strong wind at the other end as all the air in the passage was forced out in one direction. He visualized it as a flexible tube of toothpaste, ignoring the banality of the image in favor of its familiarity. He removed the cap at the far end from his mental picture. The near end was already closed. He brought his right fist down in the real world, as well as his inner one, and shoved it away from him, squeezing the tube flat on an imaginary surface as hard and as quickly as he could.

There was a visible pucker in the air in front of him and the way collapsed. It seemed to him that the energy created by that had been successfully channeled in one direction, but there was no way to verify it.

He turned and they walked in silence to the Edgewood Way, a matter of a couple of hundred yards past the front of the manor. Rhodri clearly wanted to talk about what he'd done, but George let his expression discourage the attempt.

He looked at the scene of yesterday's disaster without comment. Then he placed himself several yards back from the entrance. He grinned mirthlessly at his audience. "You might want to move off to the side," he said. "That last one was fun, but I have some ideas on how to maybe improve it. Might be dangerous."

The way passages weren't typically very long, however much distance the way actually traveled. George thought the collapsing process, accelerated, gave him plenty of force to play with, but what he needed was more ammunition than the limited amount of air in the passage provided.

What he'd wondered, in the dark hours of the night, was whether he might be able to control the collapse, to start the process, let the near end lose its integrity so that it would be open to the air, and pulse the air from outside through the progressively compressing tube over and over until the whole thing died. He'd visualized the gestures his two hands might make on an imaginary tube, pumping it from the near end without squeezing it tight.

"Rhodri, I'll need to reach through the Edgewood Way to do this."

"It's yours," Rhodri said, releasing the claim.

George opened the Edgewood Way at this end but kept the far end closed. The last thing he wanted was some courier trying to come through while this was going on. He wasn't worried about any tokens they might have, since those wouldn't work while he owned it in Rhodri's place.

The end of the trap way was close to this end of the Edgewood Way, and still sealed by his hasty work yesterday. He thought the end would dissolve, sealed or not, as the way started to die, and left the seal in place to help make sure the end couldn't shift somehow when he started.

If this worked, it would be violent at this end, too, as air was sucked into the collapsing way. He glanced over his shoulder to check that Rhodri and Edern were well back, and found Mag close behind him, with two large pseudopods extended at the level of George's hips.

Picture of Mag anchoring George.

"You see what I have in mind? Think it'll work?"

Agreement.

"Alright, then. Let's get started."

She extended the pseudopods around him without pressure, a solid cage of rock for him to lean against while leaving his chest and arms free. An extension on each side ascended over his shoulders like a harness to hold him down.

He stood solidly, his feet apart, braced against Mag. He squeezed the near end of the trap way firmly enough to break the seal, forcing it open in the process, but held the collapse at that point, grasping the end mentally like a tube in his left hand. Then he used the image of his right hand to strip down the tube from near to far, squeezing lightly and releasing it at the end, and returning to do it again. His physical hands repeated the gestures, rather than caused them, an echo of the coordination his mind was attempting.

A wind began to build in front of him, roaring from his back and into the ways, passing through the Edgewood Way entrance into the collapsing trap way. He got a rhythm into his pumping actions, but the trap way continued to shrink slowly once the process started, making constant adjustments necessary. He wanted to make it last as long as possible.

When the way shrank enough that its opening ceased to block the full Edgewood Way passage, the air in that passage was sucked in, too. George had a momentary fear that the Edgewood Way would be compromised, but after the initial jolt, the situation stabilized and he was able to continue. Like a tornado that picked up a house but continued its destruction unchecked, he thought.

His back was pelted continually by debris, but his coat and Mag's embrace protected him from most of it. What he found most unnerving was the sound pulse that accompanied his mental gestures, the noise of the wind ebbing and blowing under his indirect control, like an immense breathing animal.

Inexorably the trap way continued to narrow despite his attempts to slow it down, and the suction effect lessened in the process. When it shrank to just a few feet across, he couldn't stave it off any longer and let it all collapse, grateful that Mag's support kept him from doing the same himself.

He sagged there for a minute, recovering from the effort while all around him he heard the quiet patter of small wind-borne bits falling like rain. Little gusts stirred them up and dropped them again, until the air settled down into stillness as if nothing had happened.

He straightened up and Mag released him. When he turned around, he saw Edern and Rhodri picking their way over the debris-littered flagstones in his direction. Edern's face was unreadable, frozen, but Rhodri could hardly keep his footing, so intent he was on trying to figure out just exactly what George had done.

"Take it back," he told Rhodri, to forestall discussing it with him. He released his ownership of the Edgewood Way and Rhodri reclaimed it.

"I'll bet that stung him," Rhodri said, turning him around and brushing the back of his coat clean and tousling his hair to shake the dirt loose.

George bore with him for a moment, then pulled away.

Edern stood at a small distance and bowed to him formally. "Thank you, kinsman."

George nodded in acknowledgment, tired rather than elated at his success. Time to pack up and leave, despite the low clouds and the threat of more snow.

Edern asked Rhodri, "Is the Edgewood Way back to normal?"

"You can restart the couriers anytime. They're probably waiting on us to verify it's alright, so we'd need to send the first one from our end."

"No. Before you do anything else, change the markings on the flagstones to mark the new location of the way entrance," George said wearily. "No more accidents."

～～～

Rhys passed from uncomfortable doze to wakefulness in the darkness of his cell. He couldn't judge how long he'd slept, or whether it was still night outside.

His bound hands and constricted arms were the source of a throbbing pain all the way to his shoulders but there was nothing he could do about that other than endure it. The worst was soiling himself helplessly. He had to make an effort to ignore the shame of it, and the smell.

His head felt a little clearer. What had woken him? Some change in the air?

He didn't know how many cells there were or how many "guests" Madog might be entertaining in them, but it was quiet enough that he could hear distant noise. That was new, he thought. A fight of some kind?

A stiff breeze blew in through the cracks in his cell door, and lifted up the dust. It was followed by gusts of fresh cold air, carrying the resinous scent of pine trees that overwhelmed the stench of the cell. It smells like dawn, he thought. What is this? The wind continued for several minutes before subsiding.

In the following silence he heard distinct noises of alarm. Whatever had happened, it was unexpected, he judged.

He wished the wind would return. It was cold, but it was clean. Some part of his military training came back to him, and he knew that warmth was more necessary to survival in extreme situations than comfort, but he missed it anyway. He smiled wryly to himself—he was truly Gwyn's foster-son, overly fond of cleanliness.

He might have dozed off again, but the next thing he noticed was footsteps marching to his cell, and the rattle of keys, the glow of torches coming through the cracks.

Madog followed his guards into the cell and looked down at him. Rhys was too stiff from a night in bondage to rise. He saw Madog dabbing at a shallow cut on his face which oozed blood steadily as head wounds do.

"What was that wind?" Rhys asked.

Madog regarded him sourly and didn't reply.

Rhys wanted to keep silent, but he couldn't help himself. "Was this how my parents died?"

⌒‿⌒

Madog was in no good mood, but the question brought a smile to his face.

"I never saw them die," he said, cheerfully but with a bit of regret. "The trap way I used for them wasn't well-anchored and the other end tore loose. I always assumed they ended up in the air somewhere. Before falling, of course. I wonder if their honor guard served them well, at the end."

He enjoyed Rhys's unguarded expression of horror. He said, conversationally, "It's been one of the hardest things for me to correct in my beast, this opening of ways into the air."

This was going to be easier than he expected, he thought. His prisoner was already too worn to look confused by that explanation. He wrinkled his nose. The smell rising from him offended him.

Edern, now, that would have been much more of a challenge.

He'd have to keep this one alive for a while to bait Gwyn. That meant keeping him from Scilti.

He assumed a magnanimous expression. "Cut his bonds and bring him some water and rags for washing," he told a guard.

He looked down at Rhys as the guard bent over him. "Can't have you dying just yet."

"What is it you want?" Rhys asked from the ground.

"Why, your foster-father's lands, of course, all of Annwn."

"Isn't there enough for you in the endless lands to the west?"

"It's Annwn I want, not empty wilderness. I will be the Prince of Annwn when I defeat him, and then we'll see what's next, when I stand from that base and look at the old world choices. Who will stop me? The absent Beli Mawr?"

"Cernunnos will never accept you," Rhys said.

Madog laughed at that. "He'll accept power, and the winner of the contest."

"No. He supports justice."

"My, you are young, aren't you? I keep forgetting." Madog left him, still smiling.

The smile subsided as he walked back through the chaos in the central hall of his dungeon. The wounded had been cleared away but there was still debris all over the floor along with the bloodstains.

The first gust, from the closure of his second court way, had blown out all except one of the torches but done little else. He'd come when summoned to see the situation, and that's when the trap way was closed, the one that did all the real damage. In the dim light, guards had fallen or been cut by sharp objects picked up by the wind. In the end, one fool broke his neck and several more were injured.

He wasn't concerned about the losses to his guards—there were plenty—but he wanted to know how the huntsman had done it. He had no doubt it was the huntsman, no one else could destroy the ways. It offended him that there were things the huntsman could do with the ways that he hadn't discovered, yet.

He reminded himself that it didn't matter. His recent ways into Edgewood may be gone, but he could make more whenever he wanted. Let them busy themselves there for a while.

⌀

Edern turned his horse back several feet to retreat from the discomfort near the top of the ridge, and Rhodri joined him, wincing. George looked at them both and half-smiled as he dismounted awkwardly with his heavy pack and handed his reins to Rhodri. He stood next to his horse, detaching the saber from his saddle to hang it around his waist instead and removing the long staff that had been tied on.

Edern said, "You don't feel it at all, do you?"

"Only the faintest twinge, enough to know it's there if I'm looking for it."

Rhodri frowned. "Hardly seems fair. It's just like when I touched Mag."

"I have a theory about that," George said, "When Mag showed me an image of the larger area map with all the ways marked, the ridge was full of them, underground. I think that's what comes out the top focused somehow and does the damage here."

Edern thought about it. "But surely that's not evenly distributed, everywhere along the entire Blue Ridge."

"That's the point. I don't think it can be. We don't have time now to look for any gaps, but there must be some. You should ask Mag about it…"

He broke off, and Edern filled in the missing part for himself, "in case I don't come back."

Ever since the disaster yesterday Edern had watched George withdrawing, disconnecting from his friends. He recognized it as his way of cutting ties to make this leave-taking easier. He wasn't sure if George quite realized what he was doing, but it was clear enough to him. He'd seen many men preparing to leave for battle.

Rhodri, he knew, didn't understand why George had been curt with him, not explaining much about what he'd done destroying the ways. It was too painful for George to resume the easy state of exploring their skills together, and so he cut Rhodri off, frustrating him. He'd explain it to him on their ride back.

George settled the pack more comfortably on his back. "Heavy enough," he said, "but at least it's downhill."

Edern watched him make himself seem cheerful, for their sake. He approved. Put a good face on it, kinsman, he encouraged him silently.

George walked over to him and put his hand inside his coat. He pulled a sealed document out, several pages folded together with a name written on the outside, and reached up to give it to Edern. "See that this gets to Angharad, will you, sir?"

Edern nodded soberly, then bent down and grasped George's shoulder for a moment. "Listen to me, nephew. Be careful. Take no unnecessary risks. Your family and friends want you back, whatever happens. All of us."

Rhodri said, "You know you need to return and give me some explanations, kinsman. How else can I learn if not from a master?" He said it with an irreverent grin, but Edern saw the sincerity behind it and expected George did, too.

George turned and began the short walk up the remainder of the wooded slope. He paused at the top and waved. "Wish me luck," he said. He crossed over and glanced back. Edern bowed to him from his saddle and watched him until he vanished out of sight on the other side.

He turned his horse to go and Rhodri joined him, leading Mosby. Edern looked at his woeful face, now that he no longer had to maintain appearances for George. "Don't give up on them, no matter what happens, and don't let Mag do it, either. There's hope here, whatever you may think."

He saw that Rhodri wasn't convinced. Hard to make the young take the long view, and even harder to keep his own heart from bleeding over Rhys and George, but he thought he perceived other forces at work here. Remember that Cernunnos is concerned with justice, he told himself, and this is his champion we just sent to the enemy. He worried that George might simply be a pawn in that game, something to discard after it serves its purpose. But then, wasn't Rhys one, too? And, no doubt, himself, he reflected ruefully.

George paused at the western slope of the Blue Ridge, George paused at the first break in the trees that offered him a view. The northern end of the Shenandoah Valley stretched out before him. North Mountain on the other side was barely visible under the skies with their threat of snow, and the nearby river he knew to be running at the base of the ridge was hidden from him by the swell of the slope, but the view of the mid-valley was clear. There was the ridge that rose up from the valley floor, Massanutten Mountain. In his world, a small city was at its base and a scenic highway ran down its spine. It was much too far away to make out any such details from here.

He expected this hike to take about three days, at ten miles per day. He had enough food that he wouldn't be delayed hunting, but the snow would slow him down. He wasn't sure how he would cross the Shenandoah River, but he needed to be close to see what his choices were going to be.

He took off one glove and pulled Angharad's pendant out. He hung it from his finger and it swung south and a bit east, pointing steadily. A link home he thought as he put it away.

Not his only one, either. Can you hear me, Mag, he thought to her.

Yes. Picture of George in snowy woods. Picture of George shrouded, hard to see.

Don't worry, I'll stay hidden, he told her. Like a very big mouse. He echoed back the same picture to her, but much smaller compared to the trees.

Amusement. Concern.

It was good to have company. Before continuing on, he gazed at the valley landscape before him from a couple of thousand feet up, looking for ways. He found them everywhere. Most were concentrated at the top and base of Massanutten Mountain, and those that weren't typically had one end anchored there. Hundreds, there must be hundreds of them, he thought.

He felt something on his cheek and looked up. Snow had begun to fall lightly. He picked up the nearest deer trail leading south and down. There'd be less snow under the trees.

CHAPTER 17

Seething Magma returned her attention to Eluned. She'd broken off to speak with George, raising a pseudopod like a hand to indicate a pause.

Here in the conservatory an entire end of the room had been given over to tables with impromptu symbols on them. Eluned and Ceridwen were working with Magma, ably assisted by Cydifor.

Seething Magma touched a pseudopod to the dog collar that represented George. She extended another one to the column of verb drawings Eluned had put together on a long strip of paper. She touched the side view of a mouth, and the symbol for past tense.

"George spoke?" Eluned ventured.

One knock.

"Is everything alright?"

One knock.

"Any news?"

Two knocks.

Eluned waited politely, but Seething Magma stopped there. How could she relay the little joke to them using objects and drawings, she wondered.

She sensed George's fatalism about this rescue attempt and it made her very uncomfortable. They live such a short time anyway, she thought. Some of this risk was on her child's behalf. How do they look at this? She couldn't see how to ask the question.

So frustrating to be limited to concrete symbols rather than abstract concepts. Still, she thought it was clever the way they worked together to tease meaning out of her, and it was getting more efficient by the hour, now that Eluned had some time to spare for it.

The symbol vocabulary had grown. The drawings that represented verbs were a great help, and they'd added some more people: a bit of antler for Cernunnos, a toy black hat for Madog.

That last had been George's contribution. She'd felt his amusement but didn't understand what was so funny about it.

Eluned resumed the conversation that had been interrupted. "So, my lady, all the ways we encounter are made by your folk?"

She knocked a yes, and a no, then touched the antler.

"Except for the ways made by Cernunnos?"

One knock.

"How are his ways different?" Eluned said.

Seething Magma waited for the yes/no list that would follow.

"Are they all traveling ways?"

One knock for yes, at least as far as Seething Magma knew.

"We believe he destroys ways, but your folk can't?"

Another single knock.

"Anything else?" Eluned asked.

Three knocks. Seething Magma didn't know.

She watched Eluned making notes. There was another interesting thing these people did, this business of reading and writing. She thought it unnecessary for her kind, with their long indelible memories, but she could see its use for short-lived people such as these. She remembered the taste she had of George learning from written archives as a student, instead of getting formal instruction from his parent, um, parents—hard to remember they had two of them. I guess if one dies, they still have one. Is that why?

Another question it would be difficult to ask. She thought she could convey her meaning to George, but didn't want to disturb him on his journey. She kept a light touch on him now, all the time, listening for his call.

She should tell Granite Cloud to expect him, she thought. She wasn't sure how constrained she was, maybe she could go and find him once he got closer. Would she be able to speak with him, too, or was she too young for that? No one had ever tried before, so Seething Magma had no guidance to draw upon.

It was fascinating what these people could do with the ways her people made. George unnerved her. It was like standing too close to an active lava tube. It could break through at any moment, and not even one of her kind would be safe. She was now certain that George, and maybe even Rhodri, could claim her, like a way. She wasn't really afraid of it. Realistically, she would outlive them and she was confident she could find a way to escape. More importantly, she trusted them both, that just because they had the power they wouldn't abuse it.

But George trusted her, too. She could have crushed him this morning in that cage of rock she built around him, and she never even tasted the thought in his mind. She knew these people here in the room would suffer if she touched them, but everyone did a polite dance of avoidance and never brought it up.

She'd never felt vulnerable before, not like this. She wanted to rescue Granite Cloud herself, but she had a vivid and discomforting fear of letting Madog capture her like her child and turn her against these new friends.

⌒‿⌒

Edern repeated his instructions to the courier at the entrance to the Edgewood Way. "Quick as you can, now, and don't forget to let them know on the other side that this end has moved a bit."

He had to raise his voice to be heard over the clang of chisel and mallet as the mason did a hasty extension of the colored stones on the pavement marking the way entrance. The craftsman pried up the embedded stones that were no longer correct on the left and used them as inlay for the new placement on the right. Rhodri had marked the new way edge for him and stood by for any questions.

The courier rode into the passage and Edern's eye was caught by movement as Benitoe and Maëlys came up the road from the village. They were a blaze of color, especially Maëlys in her red cloak. The two of them were deep in conversation with each other, Benitoe laughing at Maëlys's comments.

Edern hadn't seen much of Benitoe since the great hunt, but his own sense of fitness had made him pay attention to the man whose betrothed had sacrificed herself to save the life of his granddaughter. He'd vowed then that he and Rhys would take a special interest in finding the lutins that were missing at Edgewood.

He hadn't spoken much to Benitoe in his grief, but this was a different man he saw, his entire demeanor altered. There was still a deep sadness in him, but some of his self-containment was inexplicably gone. The two lutins were chatting like old friends, but the reserved Benitoe he remembered from Isolda's funeral would never have done that. He wondered what had changed.

The lutins looked up and saw the men at the way terrace. They cantered up, fairly bursting with news.

"The lutins are alive," Benitoe called, before pulling up. "We haven't seen them yet, but we left tokens for them and they've been taken. We're going to have to go back for a longer stay and try to coax them out of hiding."

"Is that why you're so conspicuously attired?" Rhodri asked. "I thought we had a couple of winter cardinals on ponyback when you turned the corner."

Maëlys smiled. "There must be several of them at this one spot, to tend the animals in all the farms we checked. And there are farms like this everywhere."

"Oh, and I promised my auntie here that I'd ask. My lord," he said, addressing Edern, "Maëlys would like to petition for the inn in the village, to run it. Where do we make that request?"

"I'm very pleased to hear your news," Edern said. "Let me know how I can help with the search, and go to Cadugan for supplies and assistance, with my authority. Talk to him about the inn, too, and he'll let you know how we're handling that. I don't see why Maëlys here can't get in line for consideration."

"Where's the huntsman? I want him to hear about this. Rhys, too." Benitoe stopped abruptly at the sight of Edern and Rhodri's faces. "What's happened?"

They filled him in, briefly. Maëlys hand rose to her mouth and covered it as she heard of Rhys's capture.

"And you let George go after him alone?" Benitoe asked, bristling.

Rhodri said, "We couldn't stop him, Benitoe. You know how he is."

"Yes, I guess I do." Benitoe subsided.

Edern said, "You mustn't let this stop your work with the lutins. You know neither of them would want that."

Benitoe nodded soberly. "Have you heard back from the korrigans, yet? We met them yesterday on the road and they had similar news—deserted sites but hand tools missing."

"And the fae?" Edern asked.

"Not good. We have a theory about that, Tiernoc and I. We think it's their version of hiding, their minds if not their bodies. Until we can be sure what the cause is, though, they're no easier to help than the missing lutins and korrigans. And some of the new settlers are wary of catching whatever this sickness is."

This was the task I needed, Edern thought, to keep my thoughts from my kin in peril. It's time to throw more people at this problem. He excused himself and headed off to the conservatory to check for news, occupying himself with plans to present at the evening council as he went.

❧⁓☙

Well, Gwyn thought, holding Edern's note. That's it then.

He wasn't surprised by the early courier. He knew Edern would want to tell him about the reopened Edgewood Way as soon as possible.

But the note confirmed all the bad news. Rhys taken, George gone off alone to attempt a rescue. A lot of hope that was. Edern had scribbled something about seeing Cernunnos's hand in all of this, but his brother had always been a romantic about Cernunnos. Gwyn's conversations with Cernunnos, few though they'd been, had left him with no illusions about compassion on the part of an immortal god. Our concerns and his are just too different, he thought.

I must tell Rhian now, there's no more delaying it. She should just be back from walking the hounds.

He picked up George's enclosure for Angharad and slipped it into his chest pocket. And then I have to go to one of my oldest friends and ruin her happiness for her.

❧⁓☙

Rhian and Brynach sat their horses in the kennel yard and finished sorting the hounds out, dividing them into their pen groups of adult dogs and bitches, and the young hound dog and bitch groups on the opposite side of the yard. Ives and his kennel-men Huon and Tanguy helped from the ground.

The outer kennel gates opened, and Rhian was surprised to see Gwyn walk into the yard. He rarely came to the kennels, and this was the first time he'd done it while she'd been left in charge.

She rode over to him and dismounted.

"How was the hound walk this morning?" he asked.

"It went well, foster-father," she answered, warily. Something was very wrong, she could tell. He looked deadly serious, even for him.

"May I speak with you?" he said.

Worse and worse, she thought. "Brynach, would you please take my horse for me?"

He dismounted and led over his own horse, taking the reins of hers in his other hand. "I'll put them both away," he said. His curiosity was obvious, but she was grateful for his restraint in asking.

"Let's use the huntsman's office," she said to Gwyn.

"Yes, that would be appropriate."

The office off to the side of the yard was little used in George's absence. After the long years of Iolo's tenure in the position, it already seemed as if it had belonged to George forever, rather than just a couple of months. He'd somehow marked it as his own, and she could no longer picture it any other way. Maybe it was because she'd joined the hunt staff under him, and so it meant so much more to her since then.

Gwyn followed her in and and closed the door. He gestured for her to take the huntsman's seat, behind his desk. She demurred, it wasn't respectful, but he insisted. He didn't sit down himself, which alarmed her even more.

"What's wrong?" she said, unable to hold her tongue another instant.

Gwyn stopped pacing and looked at her. "Rhys has been taken captive by Madog. Yesterday morning."

Both her hands flew to her mouth. Not Rhys, not her big brother. She forced herself to straighten in the huntsman's chair and shoved her hands into her lap. "How did it happen? Is he alive?"

"They were trying to fix the ways. I think George moved the end of the Edgewood Way in the process and Rhys walked into it and picked up some kind of trigger. The trap way took him."

He looked at her soberly. "We don't know if he's alive. We think Madog won't kill him, because he's more valuable as a hostage."

She couldn't help herself. "But our parents…"

"Even so, we think Madog will want to keep him alive."

But he might be wrong, she thought. She didn't think he was lying, exactly, but he wasn't telling her his true thoughts.

"Do *you* think he will survive?"

"I don't know. I hope so." His face was expressionless.

She looked at him. "What else haven't you told me yet?"

He paused. "George went after him."

Her heart sank.

"How?"

"He suspected he could cross the barrier at the ridge line, and he was right. He left this morning, headed for Madog's court on foot, about a three days' journey."

"All by himself?"

"No one else could cross. That rock-wight, Seething Magma, can apparently reach him, and so we're able to talk to him, more or less."

She sat still for a moment, trying to take it all in while Gwyn watched. She discarded her first impulse, to run into his arms for comfort. That was never an option with her dignified foster-father. She tried to think about it like he would, to make him proud.

If George failed to return, she would have to be her foster-father's huntsman. She thought she could do that, if she had to. But she could never replace her brother, never take his place. She couldn't bury her emotions like Gwyn did, but she could act as if she could.

She stood up. "Thank you for telling me, foster-father. Please keep me informed." She walked him to the door and let him out. As soon as he left, she stumbled over and sat on the old couch and shook, hugging herself, her breath catching with suppressed sobs.

After a minute, there was a knock and Brynach came in, brushing off some new snow. "Are you alright? I was worried."

She lifted her face. "Oh, Brynach, Rhys has been taken. George, too."

He looked at her, woeful on the old couch. "Come here," he said, looking bigger and older than his years. She stood, and he gave her the warm hug she needed while she sobbed dry-eyed for a few moments.

"What if Madog kills him? What will I do without him? He's looked after me all my life. I'm not ready to lose him."

"You have many friends and family, Rhian, and I'll look after you, too. We all will."

"George will be captured, too, I know it."

"Don't be so quick to assume the worst," Brynach said.

She nodded, but inwardly she thought, Rhys is gone, George is gone, Isolda... Even Benitoe is gone. Nothing is stable. She felt very young. She tried to pull herself together and pushed away from Brynach who released her carefully. It was colder when he let her go.

"It's alright, I'm better now." She put her grown-up face on. "You go on ahead. I'll be out in a minute."

He looked at her, then nodded and left her alone.

At least Brynach is solid, she thought. He reminds me a bit of George—knows just when to let me be.

❧

The snow had started to fall as Gwyn took the long path around to the front door of the huntsman's house. His heart was wrung by how bravely Rhian had tried to take the news. He felt like he was watching her shed the remains of her childhood before his eyes.

He would have liked to comfort her, but knew she had to face this challenge alone. He was proud of the way she'd ushered him out of the office so that he wouldn't see her cry.

This was going to be very different, he thought, as he climbed the two steps and knocked on the door. No hiding anything from Angharad.

As Angharad opened the door to him, he was engulfed by the scent of the warm balsam fir in the hall by the staircase. He paused to take a deep breath of it.

Angharad looked at him in surprise and invited him in. "It's good to see you, Gwyn."

"So this is George's famous tree," he said. Dozens of small brightly colored simple wooden ornaments hung from its branches, and four larger pieces, each about the size of an apple.

"I'm making him one item each day," Angharad said. "You caught me just as I was hanging today's."

She pointed at a set of nested hollow circles, each ring suspended between a larger one, the colors sequenced like a rainbow. It hunt free from the end of a branch where the rings could twist independently on their threads without hitting anything.

He bent over and admired it, delaying the moment he would have to speak.

❧

Angharad looked at Gwyn. As far as she knew, he hadn't been in the huntsman's house since Iolo's death. Her stomach clenched in fear.

"Why have you come, Gwyn? Is it George?"

Gwyn glanced at the study, and she led him into it where they could both sit down. Gwyn perched on the edge of his seat and Angharad fought to retain her composure.

"Well?" she prompted.

"Rhys has been captured by Madog and we don't know if he's alive or dead. That happened yesterday."

She knew what was coming. "And George went after him." He nodded. "Of course he did," she said, half to herself.

"This morning. He crossed the ridge-line. We're still in touch—that rock-wight is relaying messages."

"How far is it to Madog's... dungeon?"

"George thought it was about thirty miles, three days."

So he had three days of relative safety, she thought. And then what? Capture, likely. Death, likely. Oh, George.

Gwyn reached into his inner coat pocket. "He wrote this last night, for you." He gave her a folded packet of paper, several pages sealed shut.

She took it from him and held it tightly in her hand without looking at it.

"I'll let you know everything we hear," he said. He stood up and looked down at her. She didn't move.

After a moment he walked out of the room, and she heard the front door close.

She was afraid to open the letter. That would make it final, real. I was prepared to lose him to a lack of the long life, she thought, but not by hazard, not so soon.

She reached out with her mind for the pendant she'd given him. I can feel him, faintly. He's still alive. But alone in Madog's lands? There was a catch in her throat. What will I do if he doesn't return?

She looked down at George's letter and broke the seal. If he had the courage to do this, she thought, she could find the courage to read about it.

Angharad,

Dearest. Forgive me that I must do this, if you can. No one else has a chance. You know I can't leave Rhys to Madog, to suffer and die. It's my fault that the end of the way was unmarked and, even if it wasn't, I find I can't stand by and write him off. My cousin, my friend.

My charge. And then there is the matter of Granite Cloud, the little child enslaved by Madog. You remember the oak tree.

She put the letter down into her lap. George had once told her about the vision he'd had all his life, of a sheltering oak. It's how he saw himself. The great hunt a couple of months ago had ended at a spot that matched his vision, and she was working on a canvas of it for him.

She'd known he couldn't refuse this task, the instant Gwyn told her about Rhys.

I have some plans and it may work out. I haven't lost hope, and you mustn't either, whatever anyone tells you. But I must acknowledge the possibility of failure, that neither of us may come back. And so, I find myself writing my very first love letter to you, just in case it is my last.

I won't spend the time telling you what you mean to me, I think you know that. Instead I will tell you what I hoped we might do together. I wanted you to know, in case it never comes to pass.

Her eyes moistened and she had to put it down again. Just last night he wrote this, a few hours ago, before he crossed over the Blue Ridge. She blinked until her eyes cleared and she continued reading.

I hope I have the long life. I want to spend the centuries with you, not just a few years. But if not, I am grateful for what I get. I only regret that I'll pain you as I age and eventually die. But know that I will be happy, even so, and you needn't grieve for it on my behalf.

I hope we have children, many and many. I hope you want them, too. I think you do. I hope that children who need us, find us. I've come to realize that I have it in me to raise many children and I'm eager to start.

She put her arm across her belly unconsciously and then caught herself. No, it was far too soon to know. Will I lose him altogether, and no child? Let it not be so, she thought.

I have come late to my new family and the bond is all the fresher for that. My roots are sinking deeper every day, making up for lost time. Remember, it's not easy to kill a well-rooted oak.

How was I ever so lucky as to win you? I cannot believe that a man as lucky as I am can fail.

Be kind, if I'm wrong. I never meant to hurt you, and I hope you'll forgive me. Look after my grandparents.

George

Don't think about it, she chided herself, as her tears fell onto the paper. Think about it when it becomes inevitable, not before. Plan tomorrow's ornament instead. He'd like that.

She glanced out of the window as the new snow fell softly. How can the day be so lovely, and yet be so drained of joy.

She gathered herself slowly like an aged woman and rose to let Alun know.

CHAPTER 18

George examined the rock formation to see if it would do for shelter. Last night he'd been too exposed in the bare woods to dare the risk of a fire but he was determined to find someplace more sheltered for this evening, since he'd be leaving the protection of the woods in the morning. There were springs alongside the ridge here, near its base, and he'd hoped to find a cave or at least some large rocks behind which he could make a small fire.

This overhang he was looking at would do, he thought, open to the north rather than the west, into the valley, and with a rock outcrop in front that would partially block it. If he kept the fire low, the reflection shouldn't be noticeable. He hadn't smelled woodsmoke all day, but he'd have to take a chance and hope his wouldn't travel too far. He couldn't sense any people within a mile or so.

He hastened to set up his fire and get his meal cooking before it got dark. The fire would be far less noticeable in what was left of the daylight. He could eat some of his supplies cold, but he'd rather cook something to warm him before sleeping out in the cold again.

As he put a few sausage slices in his iron pan to sizzle in the lard, he felt something in the woods change. The animals became quiet. He listened again, and this time he sensed someone nearby, young. A boy? And something else. They weren't moving, probably watching him, he thought.

He let the smell of the food do its own persuading and called out, quietly, "Why don't you come on in and join me?"

He felt the consternation that offer created and hid his smile.

You taste like my mother.

"Granite Cloud, is that you? I've been looking for you." He stayed seated, tending the food, not wanting to scare them off. Cloudie was far more understandable than her mother, actual words instead of pictures and emotions.

Very cautiously, a boy of about eleven or twelve stepped away from the surrounding trees. He held himself like a deer, ready to dash off at a moment's alarm. George thought he looked rather like a wild animal, too, with his cast-off torn clothing and ragged hair.

"Who're you?" the boy asked.

"My name's George."

"Cloudie says you're alright."

"You can talk to her?"

"Sure. She says you know her mom."

"Her mother's very worried about her."

The boy stood and looked him over, his hands on his hip. "Can you get her home?"

"I want to try," George said. He put the sausages on the underside of a piece of bark and reached out to put it on the ground closer to the boy. He cut up a few more slices for himself.

"What's your name?" he asked.

"Oh, I'm nobody."

"You must have a name."

The boy sat down, out of reach, and drew the bark with the sausages over so he could begin eating them, hungrily.

With his mouth full, he mumbled, "Maelgwn."

George nodded casually. "Pleased to meet you, Maelgwn." He took out his sausages and added some corn cake batter to the greasy pan. "Where's your family?"

"Her boss killed 'em," he said, cocking a thumb back over his shoulder, "long time ago." The matter-of-fact way he said it made George's heart ache for him. No wonder he looked feral.

"Madog?"

"Yeah."

George turned over the corn cakes while Maelgwn finished wolfing down the sausages. "How come you're way out here? Won't you get into trouble?"

"Aw, he doesn't know about me. Don't you tell him!"

"I won't. He's my enemy," George said.

Can you take me home?

Something about her tone struck him as very young. "I'll try, baby. Does Madog hold you? Does he make you work for him?"

She came out into view. She looked much like her mother but smaller, about the size of a bull. After Mag's bulk, she seemed downright dainty to George.

179

I don't want to. People get hurt. I want to go home.

Maelgwn looked at George. "You're not afraid of her."

"I've met her mother." He cut up the the corn cakes in the pan and divided them with Maelgwn.

Picture of Seething Magma, picture of George and Granite Cloud together.

"That's her mom?" Maelgwn asked.

George nodded.

"She sounds nice," he said, wistfully. "How come she talks different?"

"I don't know. Cloudie's easier to understand."

Can you help me?

"I'm going to look you over for a moment. Don't be scared."

He examined her with his way senses, as if she were a way instead of a lost child. He could see that she'd been claimed and he could feel Madog's signature as the claimer, just like the ways in Edgewood. Reaching out, he felt a small open way behind her.

"Cloudie made a way for you both, just now?" he asked. "How did you find me?"

"Her mom said you were coming. I told her you'd be heading toward us and we could just wait for you but you know how kids are. She wouldn't leave me alone till I let her bring me here."

George asked gently, "Do you know how old she is?"

"Well, sure, she's about a thousand years old or something, but she's just like my baby sister was, and she was five. No more sense than that."

"Do you live with her?"

"Yeah, at his place. But he doesn't know about me. I got away," he said, proudly.

George paused before his next question. "Why did Madog kill your family?"

"'Cause we can see the ways, of course."

George was startled. This boy's a way-finder, like Rhodri. Madog must want to eliminate rivals.

"How do you live?"

"Aw, I made friends with Cloudie as soon as I met her. She was lonely and I looked after her. She helps me hide. There's this big place in his garden where I think he must have 'sperimented with her when she was really little. It's full of short ways that just go from one spot to another, a real tangled-up mess. It's so bad, he finally blocked it off. No one uses it."

George noted more evidence that Madog didn't know how to collapse a way, else he could have just cleaned that up instead.

Maelgwn boasted. "I live there. I've got food and clothes and all sorts of stuff, and no one thinks to look there."

"But how did Cloudie get away to come find me?"

"He can't keep track of her like that. He doesn't care what she does. He can make her come whenever he wants, he doesn't have to pay any attention to her the rest of the time. She has to do what he says."

He's mean. He hurts people.

"So if he summoned her right now," George said, "how would you get back?"

"I'd just use the way she made to bring me."

"Seems to me like you're taking an awful chance. He might spot you."

"I don't come out the other end unless I know he's not there." He was scornful of George's concern. "He's had her make so many ways, he never notices the new ones."

George considered the ramifications of all this. "Couldn't Cloudie make a way just for you and get you away from Madog, over the Blue Ridge?"

No! Don't go!

"I'd never leave her," Maelgwn protested indignantly. "We're family!"

"Alright, I'm sorry. I didn't understand." It was a close bond the two of them had, comforting each other, especially since the boy had no one else.

After a moment, Maelgwn settled down again. "So, how're you going to get her loose?"

"I'm working on a plan. I have another friend Madog just captured. I have to fetch him, too."

"Is that the one he got, the day before the big wind?"

George's hopes rose. The timing was right. "A young blond man."

"Yeah, that's him."

"Is he alright?"

"I heard the guards talking. They knocked him around but I think he's still got all his pieces." He looked at George consideringly. "You know, Madog likes to take bits off, a little at a time till there's nothing and then he throws what's left away. You better go get him soon."

Hearing those words from the mouth of a child made his hackles rise. He felt his ears move back on his head.

"Do you know where he is?" George asked.

"Maybe, but I'm not telling till you get Cloudie free."

George turned to Cloudie, still sitting at the edge of the firelight. "Have you tried talking to Madog?"

He can't hear me.

Maelgwn said, "So how're you gonna do it?"

"I'm going to break his claim on her."

"How?"

"Let me worry about that for now."

"Are you gonna claim her yourself?" Maelgwn asked, fiercely.

"Never."

Assurance. Picture of George, picture of Granite Cloud, together. Picture of Seething Magma, picture of Granite Cloud, together.

"How do I know you haven't claimed her mom and made her say that?"

Mom's alright.

Maelgwn subsided. "Sorry. They both vouch for you. It's just, she's had it tough."

George said, soberly, "I'm glad Cloudie has a friend like you, an older brother to watch out for her."

Maelgwn bobbed his head and sat quietly, watching George as he cleaned up from cooking dinner.

"Do you want to stay here with me?" George said.

"Naw, you should come back with us, to the garden ways. He won't find you there."

"I'd like that," George said.

Picture of Edgewood, picture of barrier. Question?

"Cloudie, your mom wants to know if you made that loop around the lands over there." He pointed east.

He makes me go all the way through it every month.

"Can you show me where the ends are?"

Sure. Picture of map.

Just like her mother's maps, this one had fine detail. George could see the nearest end, just south of them, up against the ridge line.

"Cloudie, that one hurts the people who live there. I want to shut it down. Do you mind if I try?"

Oh, good. Do it.

George wasn't sure if he could. Madog would know, of course, but he'd assume George was on the other side of the Blue Ridge. He reached for the end of the way. The full way was a passage many miles long rather than just a few dozen yards. It was… heavier was the best word he could find to describe the sensation, heavier by far than any way he'd tried to control before.

Alright, he told the horned man within him, how about a little help. He felt him stir. "Don't be afraid," he warned his guests.

He let the horned man out, and felt the familiar change in his senses. The woodsmoke and cooking aromas intensified, and the colors dimmed, but he was interested to discover that he could see better in the twilight in this form.

Maelgwn, he noted, stood up and backed away to join Cloudie, who hadn't moved. George stayed seated to make himself less threatening, cross-legged in front of the fire.

Together, he and the horned man grasped the end of the barrier way, a few miles distant, and let their senses run the full length of it in its outward loop until they came back along the far end, north against the ridge line. George couldn't have reached that far on his own.

He held that heavy fullness in its entirety for a moment, then let it quietly dissolve away, so slowly that it became porous as it went like a membrane, diffusing the trapped air calmly without so much as a puff out of either end.

Thank you, George. I hated that.

"You're welcome, Cloudie. Many people will be glad." Mag, be sure to tell them, back in Edgewood.

Picture of Rhodri dancing.

I guess they noticed, he thought.

My thanks, he said to the horned man as he pulled him back in. He thought he felt a casual wave of the hand in response.

He dropped his head and slumped, suddenly tired, and wanting nothing more than to just sit there a moment, but he took a breath and made himself rise as if nothing extraordinary had happened, and packed up the cooking gear. He kicked snow onto the fire until it was out, then he hoisted his heavy pack and walked over to join Maelgwn.

The boy hadn't seen him stand up until now and was clearly startled by his size. He looked as if he was reconsidering his invitation, until George smiled at him. Then George patted Cloudie absently as he went by and undid all his efforts at calming the boy.

"How did you do that? Doesn't she hurt you?" He hopped from foot to foot as if he would take off into the darkness.

"It's a long story, Maelgwn. Her mother doesn't hurt me either. Look, why don't you show me where you live, and we can talk about it all night if you want," he said.

Maelgwn nodded cautiously, and turned to lead him back into the woods.

George emerged from the way directly into a walled open space of about four acres. He saw the remnants of paved paths along the ground, but most of it had reverted to the sort of low bush and grass cover wasteland that he associated with treeless exposed ridges. The air was colder, and as he looked east in the twilight, he could make out the dark shadow of the Blue Ridge at a distance, near the base of which he'd been making his camp a few minutes ago. The top of the ridge was level with where he was standing. He must be on top of Massanutten Mountain, about 3000 feet above the valley floor, he thought.

He wasn't sure what was around them outside the wall, and feared that their voices might carry. "Shall I kill this way, so Madog doesn't find it?" he asked Maelgwn softly, as he came out.

"Yeah, sure."

George casually shut it down, gently, so no one would notice. He turned to look at the old garden with his way senses and gasped. The space blazed with virtual light, filled almost entirely at ground level with ways too numerous to count. Most seemed to be non-traveling ways—those took up the most room. A few were traveling ways, with both ends inside the walls. Ways went through other ways. It was complete chaos.

Almost all of them were open and unclaimed. I guess Madog didn't feel he needed to bother to claim them, George thought, not if he's killing off every way-finder he can identify. He could see at least three ways from here that had Maelgwn's claim on them. He wondered if the boy knew he had claimed them, or if it was an accident. How did way-finders grow into their skills? He wished Rhodri had told him. It had never come up.

If Madog ever looked in here, he'd see Maelgwn's claims. He's going to notice eventually, George realized. He looked down. Not to mention everyone's footprints in the snow.

I can see why he walled this off. A person susceptible to the effect of walking through the side of a way would be seriously hurt, maybe killed, trying to cross this space through so many of them. That must be how Madog got the idea of using a non-traveling way as a barrier.

"Maelgwn, can you see all these ways?"

"Sure."

"Does it hurt when you walk through the sides?"

"Yeah, like when I touch Cloudie. Madog can't touch her either."

The boy yawned and George joined him sympathetically. "Maybe we should get to bed and talk about all this in the morning. Can anyone see us in here?"

"No, this is the highest spot around. I can't make a fire in here, but they won't see us if we're careful."

Maelgwn led them to one of the short non-traveling ways he'd claimed, near the edge. His route was indirect, since he had to avoid all the other ways in between. To someone watching who couldn't see the ways, his path would have looked utterly random. He brought them in, Cloudie last. It was just tall enough for George to stand in, comfortably.

It had been transformed from a featureless curving gray passage about ten yards long and three yards wide to a cozy den with a series of divided spaces. Maelgwn had somehow learned how to close the far end so that the wind wouldn't blow right through it. There were scraps of padding and even worn rugs on the floor, and chairs that had been broken and mended. Shelving would have been a challenge since there was no way to attach anything to the walls of the passage, but George saw baskets and boxes of various kinds—wicker, wood, leather—that had been scavenged and turned to use as storage. At the far end was a pallet, clearly Maelgwn's bed.

It was dim but the passage shed enough of a glow to get around by. "What do you do for light?" George asked.

"I have candles for emergencies, but I don't like to use them. I don't want anyone smelling anything outside the walls or seeing the light and wondering where it comes from."

"And for cooking?"

"I can't make a fire here. Sometimes I take the food I find and Cloudie makes a way for me to somewhere else. Then I can heat it up."

"How long have you been living like this?" George tried to keep both judgment and sympathy out of his voice, but he was appalled—no heat and only cold stolen food. He was also impressed at the gumption of the kid, making this tidy nest for himself and getting by.

"It's been two winters, I guess. This is the third." He looked away. "It was really hard the first winter. I found a little way that went almost in a circle and blocked off the ends with bushes to cut down on the wind. I stole plenty of blankets, and that helped a lot."

"What about footprints? Didn't they know someone was here?"

"Cloudie takes care of that. This old garden is where she lives. Madog expects to find her here most of the time. She walks everywhere and tramples down the snow. Covers my tracks, too."

I can't let Madog find him.

"Good girl, Cloudie. You're taking great care of him." He could feel her glowing at the praise.

He set his pack down in an empty space near to the entrance and unfastened his ground cloth and bedroll. As he started to make up his bed, he asked casually, "How old are you, Maelgwn?"

"I guess I must be twelve," he said, "My birthday's just two days after Nos Galan Gaeaf, the start of the year, and we must be past that by now. Do you know the date?"

"It's the twelfth, of December." At his blank look, he dredged up the Welsh name. "Of Rhagfyr. Six weeks past the start of the year."

"My mom called me the start of the new year for the family. I was the eldest." His voice changed. "I guess I still am."

"What happened?" George asked quietly. He thought Maelgwn wouldn't answer, but then he spoke.

"They came at night, with torches, on horseback. Some of them had bows. My father took one look, and told us all to run and hide. My mom gave me the baby. He was so heavy." He was quiet for a moment. "She picked up one of my father's swords and joined him at the door."

George moved carefully, making his bed, not wanting to disturb his story.

"We went out the back. I had the baby in one arm and my sister held onto my other hand. They were really, really good, they didn't make any noise. It was cold and we didn't have any coats on." His voice choked. "There were more of them outside when we came out. Two of them shot my little sister, and she let go of my hand."

His voice continued, out of the darkness. "I froze, and they laughed at us. One of them tossed a knife, right into the baby. I felt him die."

George let him recover for a moment, then asked, softly. "What happened then?"

"I put him down and ducked under the house. They couldn't follow me. We used to play games under there and I knew every inch of it. They got tired of looking and set fire to the house, but I wasn't there any more. I got away in the dark."

George ached for him, but he knew any attempt to comfort him directly would be rebuffed. He began to empty his pockets conspicuously, hoping to entice the boy in his direction like a curious packrat.

"How did you get here? How did you meet Cloudie?"

"I followed them for two days." At George's look, he said, "They weren't in any hurry, and I had woods to hide in. I didn't have a knife, though, at least not a big one. I wanted to kill them at night, one by one, but I was afraid if I started, they'd wake up and I wouldn't get them all. So I had to wait."

A chill ran down George's spine as he listened to the childish voice.

"They met Madog in his village down below, where he was out in the field, and told him what they'd done. They boasted about how hard we fought, and said I was burned and buried in the house with 'the rest of the scum.'"

George would never have credited a twelve-year-old with so much bitterness.

"He laughed and thanked them for a job well done. I couldn't do anything about it. I should have killed some of them at least while I had the chance."

"And Cloudie?"

"She stayed behind when Madog left. I was watching from the edge of the woods, and then I stopped looking for a while, and then she found me."

He was very sad. I didn't want him to be sad.

"I'd never seen anything like her before. I like animals, my father taught me woodcraft. I reached out my hand to her, but it hurt when I touched her. She was real sorry about that."

Sorry, sorry.

"Oh, it's alright, you know that. You couldn't help it."

Maelgwn crept out of the dimness at the back of the passage to talk to her and approached George, seated on top of his bedroll. "She made a way and took me with her up to the old garden here. We protect each other."

"You could see the ways already?"

"My mom had started teaching me about them, but I couldn't really do much yet."

He was fascinated by George's saber, lying next to him on the ground cloth. "Can I look at that?"

"Sure. Try not to make too much noise."

Maelgwn picked it up and carefully pulled the sheath off. His arms weren't long enough yet to pull it all the way out directly. He had to lay it on the ground to withdraw the last few inches. He lifted it with one hand, but George could see it was too heavy for him.

"Try it with two hands. That's always easier when a weapon's too big."

"I bet you use one hand."

"Well, I've been training with it for a while and I'm a lot bigger. You'll grow into it," George said.

Maelgwn tried to swing it for a while, then put it back into the sheath. He pointed at the watch-chain with the compass at one end and the pocket watch at the other. "What's that?"

George showed him the compass first and explained what it was used for.

"What's the use of that? You can just look at the ways and tell what direction it is."

He's right, George thought. Sensing the ways was like having beacons on a mental map, hard to get lost any more once he'd started doing that.

Maelgwn picked up the pocket watch next. George opened it up and showed him how it worked and let him hold it up to his ear to hear the ticking. But it was the engraved back that really interested him. He tilted it to catch the dim light a little better.

"There's a story about this man on the watch. Would you like to hear it?"

"Sure."

"Well, I'm going to get comfortable while I tell it." He crawled partway into his bedroll and leaned his back against the passage wall. He patted the space next to him. "I'll have to talk quietly so no one can hear us."

The boy accepted the invitation and sat down next to him, leaning against him, his eyes on the engraved watch in his hand.

"You, too, Cloudie. Would you like to hear a story?"

Yes.

"Alright, come a little closer now." He looked down at the weary boy and the strange alien child, here in the heart of Madog's domain, and started to tell them a story from another world.

"Once upon a time, almost two thousand years ago, there was a soldier named George."

The boy sat up. "That's your name, isn't it?"

"That's right. He was very famous and many people are named for him. Now settle down."

George waited for Maelgwn to stretch out again. "Many things happened to him, but this story is about his encounter with a dragon. First I have to explain to you about dragons…"

He kept his voice low and quiet as he told the tale. Before he finished, stringing it out with invented incidents, he heard the even breaths of the boy as he sank down next to him, warm and sleepy. He drew one end of his blanket over him, wondering how he would react to this much contact with someone else after two years on his own.

Cloudie, he thought, I'll tell you the rest of the story this way, so we won't wake him up.

Alright. What happened after he rescued the girl?

George was tired himself, and he was never sure if he reached the end of the silent tale or not before drifting off.

CHAPTER 19

Ever since he'd left, Seething Magma spent George's waking hours monitoring his movements from the conservatory. Eluned had mounted a bell for her, in case news came in while no one else was in the room, and when Granite Cloud met George, she struck it sharply with the hardened end of a pseudopod.

She listened in on the conversation between Granite Cloud and George as the council members gathered, Cydifor the first in, as usual.

"What is it?" Eluned asked.

Seething Magma was becoming fluent in this strange hybrid method of communication. She plucked the dog collar and the gray fabric fragment from their spots and put them together on the table.

"George and Cloudie have met up?"

One knock.

"That's wonderful! Where are they?"

Mag turned to a map of the upper end of the Shenandoah Valley that she had made with Ceridwen, each drawing parts of it. Mag had learned to narrow and sharpen a pseudopod and dip it in an inkwell. It worked as well as any pen. She pointed to the western edge of the Blue Ridge about twenty miles to the south.

"So Cloudie came to him?"

One knock.

"Did you tell her where to find him?"

One knock.

"Can she get away from Madog?"

Two knocks.

Mag returned to the gray piece of fabric and moved it away from George. She flowed to the table where the unused symbols lay and poked through them with one pseudopod, then grasped a toy wolf and brought it back to join the Cloudie symbol.

"Cloudie has a pet?"

Two knocks.

"A companion?"
One knock.
"An animal?"
Two knocks.
This wasn't working. Seething Magma moved to yet another table with blank paper and ink. She delicately dipped a pseudopod into the inkwell and began sketching a schematic but recognizable man. She added deer antlers.
"That's George," Eluned said.
One knock.
Mag drew another figure, much smaller but otherwise very similar, without the antlers.
Cydifor said, "That's Cloudie's friend?"
One knock.
"A boy?" he said.
One knock.
She plucked up the cup that represented herself, and soon the sketches had the collar on the George drawing, next to her cup, and the wolf on the boy drawing, next to Cloudie's bit of cloth.
Cydifor said, "So as George is your friend, this wolf cub is Cloudie's."
One knock.
She stuck up a pseudopod in her gesture of "wait" and froze.
She set up a new tableau—wolf, tapped the symbol for speech, collar.
Eluned followed along out loud for the benefit of everyone in the room. "The wolf cub tells George…"
Seething Magma added the toy crown, Rhys's symbol.
"Is he alive, Mag?" Edern asked, from the outer ring.
One knock, then three knocks.
"She's not sure, but she thinks so," Cydifor offered.
One knock.
Tableau—wolf, the symbol for hearing, crown.
"The wolf cub heard Rhys," Eluned ventured.
Two knocks.
"Heard about Rhys?"
One knock.
Seething Magma was frustrated she couldn't tell them anything more precisely than this, but she could see they took this as good news.

Ceridwen said to Edern, "It confirms his capture but at least we know he wasn't killed out of hand."

Mother, he's changing. It's scary.

She held up her pseudopod again to catch the attention of her audience. She saw what George intended to do, and watched, fascinated.

Still holding her pseudopod up to forestall interruption, she reached with another one and added the antler to George's drawing, next to the collar.

Ceridwen said, quietly, "He's invoked Cernunnos?"

One knock. Wait, her gesture said.

⌇⌇

Rhodri lifted his head, turning away from Seething Magma who was frozen in place in an uncanny imitation of listening to something far away. He felt movement, at the very edge of his senses, progressing in an arc around him, from south to east to north.

It stopped, and suddenly there was a change in atmosphere, as if a fresh breeze had swept through the air without a breath stirring. Everything looked clean and bright, and even in the lamp-lit room he could see objects gleaming. The sounds of the fire and the movement of the people became clearer and more distinct, as if he'd removed plugs from his ears.

He felt remarkably well, as if a headache he'd hardly noticed had been going on for weeks and then stopped. Everyone in the room stirred, smiles breaking out.

"The barrier is gone," he said, realizing what it had to be.

One knock.

He did a little jig of euphoria, and Cydifor laughed at him. "You don't understand, I felt it go down. It was… remarkable."

He glanced at Edern's controlled face and sobered suddenly. Rhys and George were still in danger, and George no closer to Rhys than before.

Seething Magma picked up the three symbols for George, Cloudie, and Cloudie's friend and dropped them on the map on top of the mountain George had called Massanutten.

"That's where they're going?" Eluned asked.

Two knocks.

"They're already there," Cydifor said.

One knock.

Seething Magma pointed at the Cloudie cloth.

"Cloudie made them a way," Eluned said.

One knock.

Into the center of Madog's domain, Rhodri thought. Seething Magma added Rhys's crown.

              c⁓ɔ

Edern worked in the conservatory the next morning, composing his reports to Gwyn. He didn't want to stray too far from Seething Magma, the heart of his communications with George's venture.

Cadugan hastened in, his usually composed expression replaced by surprise.

"My lord, there are fae here, come from the village."

Edern looked at him blankly.

"Not our settlers," Cadugan said. "The original inhabitants. They want to know what happened to them."

Edern's heart rose. George and Rhodri's suspicions had been correct about the cause. Maybe these people could be saved after all.

"We'll have to take charge of this right away. There will be hundreds of them, all asking questions. Organize delegates and temporary leaders. Get the settlers involved, too, with their neighbors."

He wished Rhys were here to see this.

              c⁓ɔ

Benitoe and Maëlys walked their ponies past the mill at midday, clad in conspicuous lutin red. They'd felt the effects of the lifting of the barrier the night before, and Rhodri told them what had happened. Maëlys wanted to visit the lutins north of the mill again. Maybe this time they'd come out of hiding.

She took the opportunity to instruct Benitoe about his new family, and he listened carefully. He found the topic absorbing. He wasn't sure if it was the removal of the barrier's oppression or the aftermath of his rebirth into a clan, but he was thirsty as a sponge for knowledge, to learn where he fit in this extended family.

"So Herannuen's the one who married Corentin and had nothing but twins?" he said.

"No, that was Argantan. Herannuen's the one who scandalized everyone by picking up a hammer and learning smithing from the korrigans, leather apron and all."

Benitoe laughed. "Good for her."

Maëlys smiled back. "That's what I always thought. Now Luhedoc's family were altogether more respectable. Mostly. Except for him."

"What's he like, auntie?"

"He's a practical joker. He spared me most of it—wise fellow—but he bedeviled his siblings and his friends. Clothing would acquire knots, backsides would appear dusted in flour, and stockings would show up in the strangest places." She smiled fondly, reminiscing.

"We knew each other growing up, our families visited. I spotted his little traps and didn't give him away, and he didn't set them on me, in gratitude. We got to talking, in our teens, and discovered how much we had in common, how little we liked pompous meddlers, and how much we wanted to live our own lives. Like all young people, I suppose."

She looked at Benitoe. "Still, for us it stuck. He decided he wanted to raise horses, not just tend them. We married and started a place near Iona's. It was a wonderful life for a few years, except there were no children. I don't know why, but it's not too late even now. It made him restless, though, and he wanted to see if he could do better here, and then bring me to join him. He left me in charge and then went off for a few days to look things over. He never came back."

Benitoe reached over to her pony and patted her hand.

"I kept the business going for him for two years, waiting, but eventually I lost heart in it and had to give it up. I didn't want to live alone, so I made an arrangement with Iona. She absorbed the business, and I went to live with her, as a companion and a helper. It kept me from returning to my parents and being bothered by other men, wanting me to renounce Luhedoc and marry them instead."

She shook her head. "Until Brittou offered for me himself. Oh, it was kindly meant, but I won't give up on Luhedoc. I don't think he's gone."

"Don't fret, auntie. If we don't find him with this group, we'll keep on looking," Benitoe said.

He spotted movement at the side of the road ahead and drew up his pony. They were just approaching the first of the outlying farms past the mill.

A small figure dressed in rags stood in the road, cautiously. Benitoe dismounted and gave the reins to Maëlys. "Wait here." He walked up to the strange lutin and bowed. "I am Benitoe. We've been looking for those who live here, like yourself." He gestured at the stranger.

"I'm Berran." He looked confused but determined. "We don't understand what's happened, and I said I would find out. I remember the two of you with your assembly tokens."

"That's why we're here. Can we come with you and meet the others?"

⌇⟋

Edern called the council meeting together in the evening after dinner. He was struck by the change in everyone. The whole crowd was noisier and more cheerful than the day before, despite the fact that Rhys and George were still in peril. I hadn't realized just how depressed we had become, Edern thought. It crept up on us. Insidious

"Cadugan, please give us all a summary of what's been happening today."

The steward couldn't keep a smile of satisfaction off of his usually neutral face. "Yes, my lord. It's been a busy day."

That raised some laughter.

"Apparently our suspicion that the barrier caused the general malaise of the inhabitants was correct. Since the huntsman destroyed it last night, there's been a remarkable recovery throughout the population. Reports are still coming in from the other two villages but it seems to be the same there.

"Starting with the fae, as each family or neighborhood group identifies itself and begins asking for help, we've assigned temporary leaders to streamline the communications. Wherever there have been settlers nearby, we've recruited them to help their neighbors. The recovering people seem more bewildered than belligerent, and we're emptying our stores to get them back to normal as quickly as possible."

Ceridwen said, "The first thought, everywhere, has been to clean up. We're already out of supplies for that purpose, and the first dispatches we sent this morning were requests for more from Gwyn. That should arrive tomorrow."

Eluned said, "The next big request, after food—that's well in hand—is for clothing or at least cloth. They're all in rags, by and large, and cleaning will only go so far. That will take a little longer, we expect, but we've pressed Gwyn for that, too. Oh, and cobblers."

Cadugan resumed. "We expect that they'll soon begin asking about the empty buildings, their missing friends and family, and the new settlers."

Edern said, "Have each village select three or four people, and the farm clusters and hamlets one each. We'll organize true hundreds and tithings of ten but not right away. Send them here for Wednesday afternoon. If they need horses for travel, we'll provide them. I'll meet with that group and explain. Eluned, if you will help me prepare a statement, we can copy that and give each place a version to read, for those who couldn't come."

"Yes, my lord," she said.

"Cadugan, we're going to need good legal precedent for what to do about abandoned buildings and lands, beyond what we've done so far, and the process for claiming them. I want that included in my speech on Wednesday."

Cadugan nodded

"Now, what have we heard about the korrigans and the lutins?"

Rhodri said, "Benitoe rode in just a little while ago and sought me out. He's made contact with one group of lutins, and it's just like the fae. They want to come out of hiding and need guidance."

He handed Edern a note. "He asks you to send this to Ives, our kennel-master. It seems they're both members of the lutins' Kuzul in Greenway Court, and he's seeking the approval of the Kuzul to represent the needs of the lutins, until the members of their own Kuzul can be found."

That raised a few eyebrows around the table. Kuzul members were usually little known outside of lutin circles.

Rhodri continued. "He's already had the lutins in this one group meet with the fae at their local farms and explained to both what's been going on. They've agreed to resume mutual support and wait for further contact."

Edern said, "That was well done of him. Cadugan, we should encourage all the others that came with Mistress Rozenn to help him with this organization. Please help coordinate that. And we shouldn't be surprised if the Kuzul sends us a few more."

Cadugan nodded and made some notes.

Lleision said, "My lord, the korrigans, in the persons of Tiernoc and Broch, make their apologies for staying away to tend to their people. I have notes here sent in from my guards requesting supplies, and a proposal for civic organization that is much like the one you propose for the fae." He gave the notes to Edern who read them and passed them on to Cadugan.

"I approve of all of this," Edern said, "with one exception. I want representatives from both the lutins and the korrigans to join the fae who will be here on Wednesday, to hear the state of affairs officially and to re-bond with the others here in Edgewood. No huddling into tribal groups for the recovery. We'll all have to support each other and this court stands ready to help all of them. Lleision, you will have Tiernoc and Broch so informed. Rhodri, you are to tell Benitoe and Rozenn."

He stood to dismiss the council. "My lady," he called to Seething Magma, in her corner of the room. "Any further news from George?"

Two knocks.

That reminder sobered the everyone, and several of them promised to return and resume the vigil with Edern, once their tasks were done.

CHAPTER 20

Gwyn never liked the feeling of being behind events. Edern had started sending dispatches twice daily since George left, but it wasn't quick enough. Still, as he held the morning's messages in his hand in the early afternoon, he was delighted for once to share them with his council.

Angharad joined the rest of them, for at least as long as George was on his mission. Gwyn didn't have the heart to exclude her.

Their mood was hopeful, taking their cue from Gwyn.

"Yes, it's good news today." He watched them relax a bit. "Last night, George met the rock-wight's child, with some companion. They had news of Rhys. He's a captive, but unharmed." He glossed over the uncertainties in Rhys's well-being for now. "The young rock-wight took them to a hiding spot near Madog's dungeon, and tonight, George will try to locate him."

Rhian asked, "Who's the other person?"

"Seems to be a boy. Their nickname for him is 'wolf cub,' something about the symbol the rock-wight chose for him. It's hard getting detailed information from her, since George was the only one who could hear her directly. I understand that Eluned and Rhodri have some sort of translation workshop set up with her. There's talk of drawings and bells and toys—I have trouble visualizing all this."

"Excellent news that they're both alive and unharmed," Idris said. Gwyn could hear the unspoken "for now" in his voice.

"There's more," Gwyn said, "quite unexpected. George and Rhodri thought the barrier around Edgewood was a way, and they were right. George destroyed it last night, from miles away. The rock-wight thinks that Cernunnos helped."

That created a stir. "The barrier's gone?" Idris said. "For good?"

"Apparently so. And," he said, raising a finger for emphasis, "this morning the resident population started sending delegates asking what had happened to them. The people are waking up again. It looks as if the blight's been removed and they'll recover."

"The lutins, too?" Rhian asked.

"As of the time they sent this, there was no news about the effect on the lutins or the korrigans. But I expect it'll be the same for them. Why not?"

"Now," he turned to Ifor, "This last gives us something active we can do. Cadugan and Ceridwen say the first thing they wanted to do when they came to themselves was to clean up, and they need clothing and cloth, too. She speaks of a 'great scrubbing' going on."

That raised smiles all around.

"We are urgently requested for as much material as we can spare. I want a first shipment to go out today while there's still daylight, even if it arrives at night, followed by a larger one tomorrow."

He handed the lists to Ifor and stood up to close the meeting. "Let's get to it."

Only Angharad lingered behind. "George is going to search the dungeon tonight?"

Gwyn nodded. "That's what the rock-wight said was his plan."

"I have a very bad feeling about this," she told him.

He saw the distress on her face, instead of the usual calm. "It's natural to worry," he said, soothingly.

"No, it's not that. I don't know what it is," she said. "I wish, more than I can say, I wish that I could stop him."

⌒⌒

"Is she nice?" Maelgwn asked.

"Is who nice?" George said.

They were waiting for Cloudie to return. She'd been summoned by Madog this morning and had been gone for hours. George was trying to explore outside the garden walls without being seen, and Maelgwn had come along to show him around. So far they hadn't seen any patrols outside the manor walls.

"You're married, aren't you?"

"Oh," George said, understanding. "Yes, I am. She's wonderful." He smiled fondly. He recalled himself and looked down at Maelgwn. "She's about this tall," he said, putting his hand to his mouth, "and she has long, chestnut hair."

"Do you have any kids?"

"Not yet. Soon, I hope," he said. "She's been married before and has several children, but they're all a good deal older than you are, all grown up." Older than me, too, he thought, but he didn't want to get into all that with the boy.

"She gave me something to find her with, if I'm ever lost. Want to see?"

Maelgwn nodded.

George opened the top of his shirt and pulled out the arrow pendant. When it lost contact with his skin, it became visible, and Maelgwn's eyes widened. "It's magic," he said.

"She's very clever," George told him. He suspended it, and the arrow swung to the southeast and pointed there steadily. "That's where she is, miles and miles away." He tucked it back in and refastened his shirt collar.

They were sitting in a little woods looking down on Madog's buildings and grounds. George used his beast sense and confirmed no one was nearby.

He'd felt oddly bereft in the morning when he saw that Maelgwn had left the nest of blankets George had made for him the night before, but his heart lightened when his hand felt the body heat within and realized he'd slept there all night long.

He cleared his throat. "Maelgwn," he said, "I have something serious I want to discuss with you."

The boy looked at him.

"You know, if I'm able to free Cloudie, she's going to go back to her mom, and you won't be able to go with her."

"Yeah, I know," he said. "Besides, she's gonna be a little kid all my life, won't she? She doesn't understand about that."

"Yes, that's right." He paused. "Would you like to come live with me, afterward? For keeps?"

"Aw, what good is that kind of talk? We're not family."

"We can choose to be family. Sometimes those families are the best kind."

There was no answer from the boy.

"I'd really like it," George said. "You know, I'm a huntsman. I have lots of hounds. Horses, too."

"What would your wife think?"

"She'd be happy to have you. Truly."

George waited for a response.

"Could I visit Cloudie?"

George thought at Mag, well can he?

Picture of Granite Cloud, picture of Maelgwn. Picture of Granite Cloud, picture of Maelgwn, adult size.

"I think that means yes, forever, whatever age you are."

Agreement.

That silenced Maelgwn.

Picture of Seething Magma, picture of George. Picture of Seething Magma, picture of George bigger.

Well, let's hope I don't actually get any bigger, he thought to her, but I understand. Me, too, eh?

Agreement.

I appreciate it, he thought. I'm getting rather fond of you, too.

"When do you think Cloudie will come back?" George said eventually.

"Sometimes he keeps her all day long." Maelgwn looked grateful for the change in topic.

"Too bad. Alright, what can you tell me about these buildings? What do they hold and how often and where do you see any guards?"

After they exhausted Maelgwn's knowledge on this subject, George spent the rest of the daylight telling Maelgwn about the hounds, about his new Christmas tree, about how he came to Gwyn's world, and what he discovered about Cernunnos when he got here.

⌒〜〜⌒

Cloudie finally returned, just after sunset. She exuded crankiness. George thought, if she were a little girl, she'd be kicking the rocks out of her path.

"Where have you been?" Maelgwn said.

He made me do the long, long loop. I hate it. It goes on forever.

"Is there a barrier way around this place, sweetheart?" George asked.

She showed him a map like her mother's but this one covered more territory. A narrow line surround the upper third of the Shenandoah Valley, abutting against the western edge of the Blue Ridge.

"That must be two hundred miles. No wonder you're tired," he said, sympathetically.

If she'd had a nose, she'd have sniffed.

Madog's shoring up his defenses, George thought. I wonder what he thinks of losing the Edgewood barrier.

He gave her a chance to settle down, then he explained his plan to the two youngsters.

"I'm going to go inside and see what I can find. If I'm very careful, I can try and cast a glamour on myself. I don't do that very well, but I think I can aim for 'stone wall' and keep it simple."

He smiled at them, to keep them from worrying. "If I'm not back by morning, I want Cloudie to tell her mom, alright?"

Maelgwn put his hands on his hips. "We're coming along."

"No, not happening," George said.

"And how do you plan to stop it? Cloudie can just make a way in for us."

George tried to appeal to his sense of responsibility. "Maelgwn, I can't fight if I have to protect you, too. I'd be worried about you the whole time. And you can't let Madog see Cloudie make a way for someone else."

"No, *you're* wrong. Here's how it would work. Cloudie gets us in. You kill the way so there's nothing for Madog to find. Then you find your friend and she makes us a way out of there, and you can kill that one, too."

George opened his mouth and stopped. That might actually work. "I can do that without you, just me and Cloudie."

"No. Me, too, or it's no deal. She'll do what I ask her to."

He was probably right about that, George thought.

Maelgwn saw his hesitation and reduced his belligerence. "It's my fight, too. You have to let me help."

George admitted the justice of the argument, but his stomach crawled at the thought of letting a child do this. But this child had had years to stiffen his resolve, and just where did one draw the line that made this boy a man?

"If we do this—I say 'if'—then it will be like a military patrol, and I'm the commander. When I give an order, I don't want there to be any debate about it. If I tell the two of you to go, then it will be your duty to get yourself and Cloudie out of there, no matter what. Do you understand me?"

"Yes," Maelgwn said, resolved.

"Do you agree?"

"Yes." George saw that he took it seriously, not with the bravado of a child playing.

He made one more attempt. "I could die. You could die. This is no game."

Maelgwn nodded.

"Alright. I'll second-guess myself later, but something tells me I should let you have your way in this."

Maelgwn grinned.

"I already think it's a bad idea," George growled. "Don't make me change my mind."

⌇

It was late enough that everyone except guards should be asleep, and they'd be getting sleepy, too. Or so George hoped.

What sort of man builds a dungeon, he wondered, not for the first time. The sort of man who kills entire families that might rival him for power, he answered himself. He hoped this was where the ways he'd killed were anchored, that he might have done some softening up damage a couple of days ago.

There was no need to get close to the building, not with Cloudie providing an entrance. The three of them stood just inside the garden wall, in one of the rare unoccupied spots. George didn't want to risk detection by closing ways unnecessarily, or he might have cleaned up a bit in here while he was waiting for night.

"Are you sure you want to do this?" he asked, for the tenth time. Maelgwn was determined and just nodded his head. "Alright, we want a spot inside a corridor, as far from the center as possible. Can you do that, Cloudie?"

I'll show you.

She created a way and George entered it cautiously, in the lead, with Cloudie bringing up the rear. When he reached the end, he held up his hand for silence, It was dark, but Cloudie seemed to have successfully brought them out in a corridor and not, for example, in one of the cells.

He stepped out and discovered there was a little bit of ambient light, just enough to avoid the walls, if you were careful. He pulled Maelgwn out by the hand and told Cloudie silently to follow. When they were both next to him, he collapsed the way, very gently. Don't run into Maelgwn, he told Cloudie, he'll have trouble seeing you in the dark.

He cast his senses out as he stood there. Several way ends were scattered throughout the building. He suspected many of them were old. He was glad to find them, since it reduced the likelihood of Madog sensing a new one. He then used his beast sense to feel for man, not his most accurate skill.

The results appalled him. About half these cells were occupied, and there were at least ten people rotting in the dark, dying. From the smell, others had died but not been removed. He had no way to sense Rhys. He wasn't in the habit of looking for his friends that way and didn't know what to look for. A few of the people he could sense seemed in better health—fresher, as it were—and Rhys must be one of those, he reasoned. He wanted to free them all but it just wouldn't work.

He took Maelgwn's hand and put it on his belt. The boy got the idea and let him lead him through the darkness, one reluctant hand keeping in touch with the slimy wall. He headed in the direction of the nearest of the newer prisoners.

To get there, he had to turn a corner in the dark. He walked cautiously, afraid of stairs or other obstacles. He led them down the new corridor, trying to concentrate on just the cells occupied by the living. The corridor bent away from his target and he looked for another branching that would bring him closer to the newer captives.

When he found one, he followed it as long as it stayed straight. At each choice of corridors, he selected the more likely, as best as he could judge. It was a relief not to have to keep track of their route in the dark, since they would make a new way to get out again.

At his latest turn, he paused after he'd gone more than ten yards down to his left. He heard a noise, up ahead, a clang of a door being unlocked and a glimpse of torches, the people holding them coming down steps.

"Get out of here," he whispered urgently to Maelgwn. "Make a way and get in it. I'll be right behind you."

Cloudie and Maelgwn ducked back around the corner again. George turned to join them but was caught in the light.

"That's the intruder. Stop him."

A flung knife failed to penetrate when it hit his leg but it made him stumble on the slippery floor, and when he got up again, they were almost on him. Go, he told Cloudie, and he felt them use the way. He collapsed it behind them, then turned his attention to his attackers and drew his saber.

There were two guards and one other, directing them. George put his back to the wall and tried to hold them both off. He'd improved since he first started training under Hadyn, but compared to these professionals, it was a losing proposition.

The leader stood off to the side and commented, "I didn't believe him when he said we had an intruder. How about that?" He leaned on the wall casually as George tried to break through the two swordsmen facing him.

George tried to blitz one of them and lunged, slashing him deeply across his chest, but it exposed him to the other guard who brought the flat of his blade down on George's head. He dropped to the ground, his sword clattering out of his hand. He could feel the kicks in his ribs as he tried to get up, until another head blow flattened him completely.

Edern woke in the middle of the night to the sound of Seething Magma's bell.

He joined the group in the conservatory, where Mag was trying to make them understand something important.

Eluned, in a long woolen robe, raised her hand. "Silence, all of you." When she got the response she looked for, she turned to Mag. "Please, start again."

Mag drew an iron cage, and added a few next to it.

"Cells, a prison," Eluned said.

One knock.

She took the crown, Rhys's symbol, and put it on top of the cells.

"Rhys is prisoner there."

One knock.

Mag grasped the collar, the gray fabric, and the toy wolf and held them together. She moved them through space to the cells.

Eluned said, "Cloudie made a way to the prison and brought George and the wolf cub."

One knock.

Mag paused, as it trying to figure out how best to explain.

She picked up three toy swords and put them on another part of the drawing.

"Three guards?" Eluned asked.

One knock.

The collar, the wolf, and the cloth were marched in one direction on top of the cells, and the three swords were marched in the opposite direction until they met.

Eluned was silent. That didn't need a translation.

Mag dropped the collar with the swords and took the toy wolf and the gray cloth back out. The three swords and the collar went out the other side. That didn't need a translation either.

"Is he alive?" Edern asked.

One knock.

"Hurt?"

One knock.

"Can you speak to him?" Rhodri asked.

Two knocks.

They looked at each other in dismay.

Edern thought, this is what we all feared, that George would be caught or killed and nothing any the better for it. Although he's saved the people here, he remembered, destroying the barrier way. But at what a cost.

He looked to the house servants, woken by the bell as he was and standing clustered in the doorway. "Please have a pallet made up for me here. I'll be spending the night."

CHAPTER 21

George woke with a cry, the soles of his feet still stinging from the rods which had just pounded them. He was disoriented, his head throbbing and his vision blurred. He was stripped to the waist and barefoot, but for some reason his hands were free. His ribs were sore, and he thought some might be cracked.

He tried to stand up and discovered he was chained around the neck. It took him a moment to realize he had to move closer to the wall to create enough slack to make it possible to rise.

His skin felt dirty, slimy, from the floor. He blinked in the light of the torches along the wall. This wasn't a cell, it was too large. More like a workroom.

As his vision cleared a bit, he saw Madog seated comfortably, poking idly through his possessions lying in a heap on the table next to him. He raised a hand to his neck as if to feel the chain, but he was actually trying to find out if Angharad's pendant was still there. It was, undetectable except to him. He found the comfort that gave him out of all proportion to the knowledge that it was of no use to him here, that his remaining time was surely limited.

He looked around the stone walls and saw the gleam of equipment in the dark, things he shied away from examining too closely.

Madog spoke, with that bland voice that George loathed. "Well. Good to see you again, huntsman. I've been wanting a chat with you.

"Madog." George nodded his head civilly.

"I don't know if you've met my Scilti, or not. He's certainly heard a lot about you."

George looked over at the man who had commanded the guards last night. The man glanced back, with a crooked smile, anticipating a private pleasure.

"In fact," Madog said, "my people have been telling me lots of interesting things. I wonder if they're true? Let's find out, shall we?"

He waved a hand at Scilti and two guards grabbed his wrists and held his arms out and forced him to the end of his chain, despite his struggles. He watched Scilti pull on a pair of leather gloves.

Madog spoke again, and George turned his attention back to him. "For example, they tell me that it was you who destroyed my hidden way by the palisade. Is that so?"

Before he could reply, Scilti walked behind him and drove his fist into one of his kidneys. It exploded in pain. George's knees buckled but he recovered enough to stay standing.

"So," Madog said, "was that you?"

"What's wrong?" George said, "You lose that page in the manual?"

Madog didn't get the joke, but it didn't matter. Scilti pounded the other kidney and George sagged. If he fell forward, he would choke on his chain so he shuffled his feet under him and tried to stay up.

Madog said, "Let's take that as a 'yes.' You're going to teach me how."

George shook his head.

Madog laughed. "Oh, Scilti can be very persuasive. He likes it when I let him ask questions for me."

George tried to brace himself for another blow but it didn't come.

"And then there's the other matter," Madog said. "How did you get here?"

George muttered, "I flew like a little butterfly."

Madog shook his head. "Pointless, I'm afraid. You'll see."

He stood up and headed for the door. As he passed by Scilti he said, "Nothing too permanent yet. I may need to pick his brains for a while." He closed the door behind him.

Scilti advanced and began to work him over carefully, scientifically, laying bruise on bruise with concentrated pleasure. He said nothing. The only sounds George could hear were the blows he was taking, and those he heard both inside and out, his flesh resonating to the thuds. Sometimes the sound was wet. It wasn't long before his legs refused to hold him up altogether, and he sagged in the arms of the two guards until they dropped him to the floor. He never felt it.

George woke some hours later, every inch of his torso throbbing. He was so stiff he wasn't sure he could move at all, but eventually he was able to get his arms, which had escaped most of the punishment, into a position where he could push himself upright, sitting. Standing up was beyond consideration for now. Getting his head level helped make the spinning less of a problem.

Question?

Seething Magma was bespeaking him very quietly, as if not to hurt him, and George had the sense she'd been doing it for some time.

I'm here, Mag, he thought to her.

Approval. Picture of George. Question?

How am I, she means. What can I possibly tell her, he thought. Forget it, Mag.

Apologies. Picture of Edern, picture of Rhodri.

Ah, she wants a report. I guess she must be filling them in. Alright, what would they want to know?

Picture of Rhys. Question?

No, I didn't find him but I'm pretty sure he's here. Where else would he be?

Picture of black hat. Question?

The irreverent symbol George had assigned to Madog unaccountably cheered him, which is probably what she intended. Never mind, Mag, he doesn't want much. Just how to destroy a way, and how I got here. Which reminds me, how's Cloudie?

Picture of Cloudie, picture of Maelgwn, picture of old garden.

Well, at least they got away. If you ever get Cloudie back, try to save the boy, too.

Agreement.

He felt sick and started to shiver in the cold cell. He lay back down on the floor and curled on his side. The movement jolted his bruised kidneys and sent waves of pain down his back, and the pounding in his head took over the rest of his senses. Got to go, Mag, he thought, and passed out again.

❧

Seething Magma looked at the faces before her. They'd been waiting for news of George all day, ever since the first interrogation with Madog. She'd tried to tell them about it, but she didn't have the vocabulary.

Cydifor spoke with her quietly afterward and they framed more details, with a glove standing in for Scilti and a picture of a body showing damage, but when she saw the distress it caused them, she stopped and refused to elaborate any further.

Eluned defended her decision, and they stopped pressing her for more than she was comfortable giving.

She pointed at the collar and the symbol for speaking.

"You spoke with George, just now?" Eluned said.

One knock.

"Rhys?"

Three knocks. She didn't know anything more about Rhys.

"Do you know what Madog wants from him?" Ceridwen asked.

One knock.

She turned to Rhodri and pointed in the direction of the Edgewood Way. She made a cage of pseudopods like the one she held George in when he collapsed the trap way there.

"Madog wants to know how George destroys the ways, or maybe how to make them into weapons," Rhodri said. "Is that right, Mag?"

One knock.

"What else?" Ceridwen said.

Mag took the collar to the map and traced the path George had walked.

Cydifor said, "He wants to know how George got there."

One knock.

"Anything else?"

Two knocks.

"How is George, Mag?" Edern asked.

She started to answer, then stopped, then tried again, little interrupted movements of her body and pseudopods.

"Never mind," Edern said. "I guess I know."

She felt George's pain, and their pain at his suffering and probable death. So much sorrow in their short lives. They couldn't escape it, even in sleep. She'd felt Edern's dreams last night, whenever he dozed off for a while. No, not even when they slept.

⁓

The evening council was a subdued affair. Edern could barely make himself concentrate. He approved all the action for the recovering population that Cadugan laid before him and listened to

Eluned and Ceridwen's reports, but couldn't focus on any of it for very long.

Ceridwen offered to write his dispatches for Gwyn, and he stared at her for a moment, then nodded.

He knew one thing, though—this uncertainty wouldn't last much longer. Madog was like a cat. He tended to play with his food, but food it was.

Was Rhys getting the same treatment as George, or was Madog distracted by his newest prisoner?

CHAPTER 22

The splash of water on George's face woke him, and then he couldn't breathe. He panicked, feeling a hand clamped over his mouth and nose and woke up completely, struggling to reach it but unable to move. The hand was removed. and he drew big breaths, trying to still his heartbeat.

He opened his eyes cautiously, as if by keeping them closed he could put off what was coming. The reason he couldn't move became clear. He was strapped into a sort of chair, an open iron framework with arms and a seat. All his clothing had been stripped away.

The panic of immobility and vulnerability returned and drove his current injuries to the back of his mind. He had to force himself not to struggle, not to waste his strength.

It was hard to see since he couldn't wipe the water from his eyes. A face close to his moved back and he realized Madog had been leaning over him, watching his reaction. He shuddered with revulsion.

Madog reseated himself comfortably in front of him. He was clean and well-dressed, as always. George was conscious of his own stench.

"Ah, you're back," Madog said. "Good."

George couldn't turn his head far. Behind him, he could feel warmth on his bare exposed back and heard a sound that he belatedly identified as metal and cinders. An image came to him unbidden of iron pokers working in a fireplace.

In a moment of clarity, he thought, Mag, I'm sorry. You should go away. Now. I mean it.

Anguish.

Madog spoke. "So, how did you get here and how did you get into the cells?"

"I made a way, of course," George said.

"Sorry, I don't believe you. No one can make a way."

"You do," George pointed out.

"Ah, but that's my little secret."

"I made it myself, all the way from Edgewood," George insisted.

He thought Madog doubted him but couldn't quite rule it out.

Madog leaned forward. "How do you shut them down? That's a nice trick and I mean to have it out of you."

"Go pound sand," George said. He could see that the meaning penetrated the unfamiliar slang.

Madog looked at him in silence. Then he nodded to someone behind George.

Red-hot fire burned slantwise along half his back, and he screamed. It seemed to echo off the walls.

His breath came in gasps but he could hear, over that, the sound of an iron rod being returned to the fire behind him and stirred into the embers.

The pain it left behind was indescribable. It drew all of his attention.

Madog said, "Wrong answer, my boy. Our Scilti here can keep this up all day."

He nodded again, and George felt the heat of an approaching poker held near his back. He arched his back involuntarily to avoid it, and the heat receded, leaving just the original brand to throb and burn.

"One more time," Madog said. "How do you destroy a way?"

George just shook his head, all his bravado gone.

This time the poker struck with no warning, laying a line of fire across the first one. He managed not to scream this time. His back felt as if it had been exposed to the bone to bleed into the open air.

He sat there bound to the chair, his head hanging forward with his wet hair in his face, and panted.

"Hmm?"

George did not respond.

"Let's freshen these up a bit," Madog said.

Blows struck George's back, bursting along the burns and nearby skin. He screamed again at the first one, and soiled himself.

Madog's voice penetrated, delicately revolted. "Clean that up."

He heard the door open and a few moments later someone sluiced him down with a bucket of water.

"I'd like your full attention, huntsman," Madog said. "I may want to breed you to some of my stock and see what I get. After all, it'll be easy to control your offspring, they'll be less stubborn. But tell me, I understand you've already started that experiment with that cold bitch Angharad. How's that going? Do you think you'll get children out of her, or do you think it'll be fawns, popping out in pairs, like their father?"

George couldn't keep from shuddering at the vision.

"Ah, that's what I thought. Fawns it is. Still, they'll provide plenty of sport for you, won't they, when they grow up? With the hounds, I mean."

The hated voice was in his head and he couldn't get rid of it. He felt the horned man stir and told him, yes, do it now, but he subsided again.

"Go to hell," George muttered.

"You leave him alone."

George was horrified to hear Maelgwn's voice and lifted his head. He'd come through the open doorway, knife drawn to attack Madog, but Madog had twisted aside expertly and caught him in a firm grip, disarming him.

Maelgwn struggled to free himself. "You wait until Cloudie's mom comes."

George caught his breath. Don't let him notice, please, please, don't.

Madog held him effortlessly. "Cloudie? Is that my little beast?" Suddenly he focused his attention on the boy. "Is there another one? A bigger one?"

He turned to George. "Is that how you're doing it? You've got one like mine."

He was elated. "That would explain everything. With a big one, I could just take Annwn, encircle it like Edgewood. All mine. No need to worry about Gwyn."

Cernunnos exploded within George bursting some of the bonds holding him to the chair, but not enough to break free. He lifted his antlered head and glared at Madog. George's senses were assaulted by the full stinks in the room, including himself, but it was less personal, just animal scents.

The surprise made Madog loosen his grip, and Maelgwn freed himself, fleeing out the open door.

Madog turned to look after him, but dismissed him as unimportant. The greater prize was here before him. He faced the manifestation of Cernunnos, tied to the chair, feeling the implacability of the silent threat and shrugged it off.

"No, I don't think so," he said. "This one's mine now, he's not going anywhere. His beast will do me even more good than that Rhys hostage. Annwn's not yours any more. It's going to be mine. You'll come round, after it's all over, and maybe we can make a deal."

He nodded, and Scilti, behind the chair, reached around the great stag's neck with a narrow knotted cord and choked them into unconsciousness.

⌒

The tools fell from Angharad's hands when she felt the echoes through the pendant. Oh, George, what's happening to you? She leaned forward and gripped the sides of the table in front of her, bowing her head as he endured the next several minutes, before fading out. She drew herself up, shaking, and tried to calm herself.

That's it, she thought, and stood up.

In just a few minutes, she had packed a few thing and said goodbye to Alun, closing the door of the huntsman's house behind her.

She walked to the stable and left instructions to prepare her horse, then went on to find Gwyn in his chamber, waiting for the first news from Edgewood.

He took one look at her face and stood up. "What's happened?"

"I don't know, exactly, but it's very bad. I'm going to Edgewood, right now. I need a token." She held out her hand.

Gwyn reached into a drawer on his desk and put one in her hand, folding her fingers around it. "I'm coming, too, and bringing Rhian."

⌒

Gwyn and Rhian emerged from the Edgewood Way in the late afternoon at the head of several more wagons of supplies and made for the main hall. They were intercepted by Rhodri, wearing a very somber expression, and he led them around to the conservatory.

They found it a scene of chaos, with bedding piled at one end, an impromptu meeting table in the middle, and much of the room given over to tables with maps, drawings, and small objects. There was the bell, hanging on a wall, the one he'd read about in the couriers' reports.

Angharad had preceded them by a few hours. She rose to greet them and introduced them to Seething Magma.

The description Gwyn had read in the dispatches did not prepare him for her sheer size and strange featureless appearance. He'd been warned about touching her directly, and he appreciated how daintily she maneuvered her bulk to avoid accidental contacts.

He bowed deeply to her. "My lady, it's a great honor to meet you. I'm sorry that it took these melancholy circumstances to make it possible."

She dipped her leading edge to him, which he understood as a matching courtesy.

Angharad pointed at a small stuffed lion. This, he learned, was his symbol. Gwyn introduced Rhian to her. Rhian curtsied, and Mag led her over to the picture of cells with a small crown.

"Is that Rhys?" she asked.

One knock.

"That's yes," Angharad said.

Mag went to the table of unused objects and came up with a small pyramid which she dropped in front of Rhian.

Eluned said to Rhian, "Sometimes we don't understand her metaphors. Rhodri's a sun, for example."

"That's easy," Rhian said. "It's 'cause he's always sunny."

One knock.

Eluned shook her head ruefully. "That was too simple, we never thought of it."

Angharad said, "The pyramid's for Rhian, because it always lands right side up. It's solid, you can't knock it over." Rhian looked surprised, but Mag confirmed the guess with a knock.

Gwyn looked up as Edern came over and they clasped each other's arms. He was shocked at his brother's appearance. He clearly hadn't slept for some time. It had disquieted him when Ceridwen reported in his stead last night. Edern had to be deeply distressed not to be able to write. He reflected that his brother had never been as good as he was at walling off his emotions from his responsibilities.

Gwyn had waited for the mid-day dispatches before leaving, and he knew what Mag had been able to relay about Madog's interrogation, painfully, with many halts. He needed more details about Cernunnos's role in all of this, but that could wait until later.

He turned to her now. "Are they still alive, my lady?" he asked.

"You have to phrase it so she can answer yes or no, it's easier that way," Angharad said.

"George?" he asked.

One knock.

"Rhys?"

Three knocks.

"She doesn't know." This time it was Cydifor who spoke.

Gwyn made note of him. He'd heard, from Eluned and Rhodri's notes, how useful he'd been in getting details from Mag. He seemed to have a real empathy with her, a talent for understanding what she meant.

Edern pulled himself together. "Gwyn, I'd appreciate your help with this gathering tomorrow, all the delegates from the recovering people. It's the one good thing to come out of all this."

Gwyn had come partly for this purpose. He walked off with Edern and Cadugan to discuss their plans, leaving Rhian behind with Angharad to talk quietly with Mag.

❧

George woke, sometime in the night, to an empty room with a closed door. He was still strapped to the chair, and the straps that had been broken by Cernunnos had been replaced and reinforced. Some sort of metal framework had been added to the chair, jutting out above his head.

The pain in his back was insistent and he could feel it throbbing with his pulse. He'd had nothing to drink since his capture—he wasn't sure how many days it had been—and his thirst was the only thing more acute than his injuries.

His body had partially numbed to the unchanging position but everything ached and he couldn't move to make any small adjustments for relief. He tried to go back to sleep in the chair, but there was nothing to lean his head on and it hurt too much to just drop his head forward and let it dangle.

He tried anyway, and succeeded for a little while. But there were dreams, bad dreams. Dreams of death, but worse, dreams of Angharad's death, in childbirth, torn by unnatural creatures. He woke with a start, afraid to sleep again.

Mag, are you there?`

Here.

Sorry you saw all that, Mag. I hope you're alright.

Picture of George, crumpled. Sorrow.

217

Yeah, well, I thought something like this might happen. Don't worry, it'll be over soon. I can't give Madog what he wants. *Picture of Seething Magma.* That's right. He wants to own you, like Cloudie, and take over Annwn. Cernunnos couldn't stop him today, but you can. Don't come. *Picture of George, crumpled.* Doesn't matter. Don't come, no matter what. While Madog works on convincing me, he's probably leaving Rhys alone, in case he needs him as a second choice. The longer I last, the longer that should work. Madog thinks I've claimed you and can bring you here. Once that happens, all he'd have to do is kill me and claim you himself. Don't let that happen. That would be the end of Rhys and me, and eventually hundreds of people. *Agreement.*

The effort to convince her to stay away exhausted him. His head nodded forward and he tried to doze again, but the dreams returned, haunted with unnatural creatures and blood. From somewhere far away he heard a familiar voice humming a tune, a lullaby. It was soothing, and he followed it down, away from his thirst and his pain.

CHAPTER 23

Edern had dressed with care in the morning. He wanted to look reassuring and in command for all the Edgewood people who'd been living in darkness for so long.

He knew his own disinclination to rule made him rather different from others in his family. Gwyn had always been tougher, but they'd reached an accommodation over the centuries that suited them both. These last several days had been very hard on him, and he appreciated the work of Cadugan, Ceridwen, and Eluned in taking as much of it as possible out of his hands. Still, these people were in his care, as custodian for his grandson (don't think about him not coming back, he told himself), and all his breeding made that a sacred responsibility for him, one he didn't intend to shirk.

The speech was scheduled for the afternoon. Here, at the midday meal, he was stunned by the number of delegates that had appeared. There were at least a hundred fae, and a couple of dozen korrigans. The lutins had surprised him, sending more than twenty. More of all kinds were still trickling in.

He was determined to weld them back into a functioning domain, not a group of wounded animals trying to survive. They had it in them to restore their lives from this point forward, if he could just inspire them to try stay focused on rebuilding, not on dwelling on what they had lost.

❧

The opening of the door woke George from his doze. He watched blearily as Madog took his accustomed seat and Scilti moved behind him, out of sight, and fed more fuel to the brazier which had subsided overnight. One of the guards carried a tray with a pitcher and two glasses. Another guard walked around the chamber and lit the torches from the one he carried.

Madog said, "Perhaps you're wondering about the new iron roof over your head?"

George glanced up without comment.

"I thought some special preparations were in order. If your friend Cernunnos wants to join us again, he should break his head nicely."

George could feel the frustration, deep inside.

He laughed out loud, he couldn't help it. All that iron over his head when his very name, Traherne, meant iron-hard.

Madog looked disconcerted, but recovered his stride

"Now, I'd like to see that beast of yours, huntsman. You can sign it right over and I may let you live."

George opened his mouth, but his tongue was too swollen and dry to talk.

"Oh, so sorry," Madog said. "Let me get you something to drink."

He poured a glass of water from the pitcher and handed it to a guard. George gulped it down as the guard held it to his mouth, licking every drop he could reach.

Madog watched him with an unreadable expression for a few minutes.

George wished he could drink the entire pitcher, but the water helped. The face of Madog began to shine for him, to pulse. As Madog began speaking in an even, reasonable voice, George heard an echo behind the words. Drugged, the water was drugged, he realized.

The knowledge didn't matter. The hypnotic was reinforced by Madog's tone and he had to listen to him. Madog pulled him along on a smooth course.

"Now huntsman, just invite your beast here and give it to me. It'll all be over quickly, and then you can take a nice long rest. We'll see to your unfortunate injuries and you can have all the water you want."

The voice went on and on, soothing, liquid, and deadly. George's head nodded involuntarily but he kept his eyes on Madog's face, on his eyes.

A small voice inside him cried false, false, all false. Don't talk to him. It was very hard to obey, but he trusted it, it rang true to his own stubborn nature.

The seductive voice murmured some more. George tried to shut his eyes to break the focus.

"Look at me, huntsman." George obeyed. "Will you do this one thing for me?"

George could see nothing but Madog's eyes. He shut his own and shook his head. It was all he could manage.

There was blessed silence for a moment.

"Too bad," Madog said, with a sorrowful tone.

Scilti walked around to the front of the chair with a long thin red-hot needle of iron. He wrapped an arm around George's head to immobilize it and held the needle in front of his left eye with his other hand to give him a good long look at it, smoking, a few small cinders from the fire stuck to it. Then he delicately inserted it and blinded him. George couldn't remember screaming but he felt the echo of it in the room. The shock reverberated through and through him.

Madog leaned forward and patted him on the arm, consolingly. "Now, now, you still have one eye left. Don't you want to see your beast again? Why don't you bring it here?"

George curled himself up tight in a ball inside. Ignore him, he told himself. Why? Don't remember.

Somewhere outside of himself, he heard Madog say, "Hard to hunt the hounds if you can't ride, huntsman. Bring your beast and all this will stop."

George huddled inside and tuned him out. Silence was the only fight he could win.

His retreat was broken when Scilti smashed his left knee from the side with an iron sledge. With his remaining eye he could see bone fragments mixed in with the blood. He retched but there was nothing to bring up.

"So sad. One more chance. No?" Madog paused.

"Well, I think we can keep you a long time if we're careful. One more persuader, I think. If you can't see the ways, it'll be easier to manage you."

Scilti returned with the red-hot needle, smoking and sputtering. George watched him in terror and wept, but he refused to speak as he lost what remained of his sight.

⌒⌒

Seething Magma was alone in the conservatory except for Angharad. Everyone else was off listening to Edern in the main hall of the manor.

Mag wasn't completely sure about what was happening, but she understood that it was important to the recovery of the people here, and she knew their former state had been caused by a way her daughter had made, even if she'd had no choice in the matter. She felt responsible somehow.

She wished she could discuss this with Angharad. So, this was a second parent. She looked carefully and, sure enough, she saw the tiny new bud.

She rummaged through the unused objects and selected a magnifying glass. She placed it gently at Angharad's feet.

"This is me? What is it, someone who looks at small things?"

Cydifor walked in. "No, someone who sees clearly."

One knock.

"I thought you'd be at Edern's speech," Angharad said.

"I was there. Hard to make music out of politics, though, however well intended."

She laughed.

Mag went back to the table. Hard to choose for a bud, so she settled for good wishes. She found a small bell and brought it back to Angharad.

"I don't understand, what does the second symbol mean?"

Mag gestured with a pseudopod and Angharad put down the magnifying glass. Mag took the magnifying glass and the collar and put them together on the table.

"Yes, that's right. We're married," Angharad said.

Mag added the bell, below them.

Angharad blushed and Cydifor stared at her. "Are you...?"

"I don't know. This is a child?"

One knock. Mag didn't understand the fuss, but she tasted Angharad's deep joy and was satisfied.

She felt George wake up, but she saw he wasn't alone and decided not to distract him. She followed along and felt Madog's insistence on having her. She agreed with George's argument last night, that she couldn't let that happen.

It was terrible that she couldn't help him. She'd been pleased that her recollection of the woman's night song to her child, the one she'd learned after their evening of music a few days ago, had worked on him and let him rest. She'd have to try that again if it seemed necessary.

Pain. That's wrong. She heard Angharad cry out and tasted the echo she felt, too.

George's thoughts became strange and he listened to Madog. Mag worried. She thought George might be able to claim her, even from far away. She didn't completely understand the skills of these people, the ones who manipulated the ways. She trusted him but now he tasted different and she could feel him struggling to resist.

More pain. Were they killing him? And finally, the last blow. She didn't understand their senses, how localized they were, since her own were diffused throughout her body, but she had looked out through George's eyes and now she couldn't. Horrified, she realized he couldn't either. That's what blind meant.

She felt Angharad's distress.

"What's happened?" Cydifor asked. He held a weeping Angharad. Angharad shook her head, and he looked to Mag.

"Is George dead?"

Two knocks.

"Hurt?"

One knock. Pause. One knock. Pause. One knock.

"Badly?"

One knock.

"How? Show me."

Reluctantly, Mag sketched George. She drew two broad lines down and across his back in an "X" shape. She dropped a blot of ink on his left knee. She dropped a blot on each eye.

Angharad watched and moaned, shoving a fist against her mouth. She pushed away from Cydifor and walked over to a west-facing window and stood with her back to the room, shaking.

Mag headed slowly towards the bell on the wall to let the others know, but Cydifor stopped her.

"Don't. There's no point in interrupting, there's nothing they can do. Tell them afterward. That'll be soon enough."

She tasted his thoughts. Yes, he was right.

"Is it over?" Cydifor asked.

One knock.

"Thank goodness for that," he said. And then sat down himself in the nearest chair and wept.

Gwyn strode into the conservatory with Edern, congratulating him on the success of his speech. Rhys's council, now Edern's, followed hard on their heels, talking with each other.

Something was wrong, and Gwyn stopped. Angharad turned from the window where she'd been standing, tears on her face, and Cydifor looked up from his seat, in the same state.

Gwyn's heart sank. "What's happened?" he asked, in hushed tones.

Cydifor stood up. "No one's dead," he said, right away, trying to soften the blow. "But George…" He choked.

Rhian pushed past Gwyn and Edern and went to Angharad. "Come on, cousin, come sit down." Gwyn had never heard her call Angharad "cousin" before, though it was correct since George was indeed her cousin. And he'd never seen her take charge like, well, like an older woman making sure everyone was well looked after. She would be fifteen soon, he thought, irrelevantly. This is what she was becoming.

"Tell me," he said to Cydifor.

"We need to let Mag tell it, my lord, we just got the… the damage report." He picked up the sketch of George that Madog had drawn and handed it over. Gwyn glanced down at it briefly and closed his eyes. He felt Edern take it from his hand and he could hear the intakes of breath as it was passed around and each interpreted what they saw.

He reached for a chair at random and sat down. "Tell us, my lady, if you please," he said to Seething Magma.

⌁

Angharad sat stupefied by what had happened to George, listening to Gwyn and Eluned attempting to get the full story from Seething Magma by adroit questioning and occasional inspired guesses.

Why was Madog so insistent on this interrogation? She interrupted Eluned chasing another detail and asked Mag directly, "What is it Madog wants of George? Why is it so important to him?"

Mag stopped in mid-gesture and hesitated.

She moved to the map of Edgewood and picked up the little piece of gray fabric that represented her daughter. In another pseudopod she held the black hat of Madog. She put the two symbols together, west of the map of Edgewood, and then she moved Cloudie to the barrier way around Edgewood and traced the entire line, returning Cloudie to Madog at the end.

Eluned translated. "Madog makes Granite Cloud do things. He made her build the barrier way." In an aside to Gwyn, she said, "You know, the rock-wights are like ways. They not only make them, but they can be claimed the same way."

Gwyn said, "I had read this in your reports but hadn't fully considered the implications."

Mag somehow managed to express frustration. She turned to Cydifor and did a little rocking motion.

Cydifor explained, "This is her 'find me a word' request. Bear with us."

He ran through a list for Mag. "Noun... verb..."

One knock.

"Alright. Movement... action... state... abstract..."

One knock.

"Similar to... rhymes with..."

One knock.

"So, we want an abstract verb that rhymes with what?"

She moved to the sheet of human action and pointed at a mouth and cup.

"Swallow... hold... drink..."

One knock.

"Think," Gwyn suggested.

One knock.

Eluned drew a new symbol for Mag on the sheet of verbs, a head with a finger tapping the forehead.

Mag resumed her place and took up the story again.

She pointed at the little black hat, the new symbol, the gray cloth, and then put the cloth under Madog. Then she held up a narrow vertical pseudopod, like a finger.

Ceridwen said, "This is a logical proposition, my lord. Madog thinks Cloudie, what, belongs to him?"

One knock.

"And it's true." She said to Gwyn, "One for true, zero for false. George's idea."

One knock.

Mag pointed to the black hat, the new symbol, George's collar, and then put her own cup under George. She held up a pseudopod that formed a circle.

Ceridwen said, "Madog thinks George owns Mag. And it's false."

One knock.

Mag pointed to the black hat and the new symbol, then showed George giving Mag to Madog.

"Madog thinks George can give Mag to him, to own."

Seething Magma sketched quickly on a new sheet of paper. She ran a mountain chain down the middle left. On the top right, she did a recognizable miniature of Edgewood, complete with the barrier way. On the top left, she showed a barrier way running from the mountains west and down a great distance before rejoining the mountains.

She took Rhys's crown and Edern's star and dropped them onto the Edgewood portion. She dropped the black hat west of the mountains. Finally she picked up Gwyn's lion and placed it below Edgewood, east of the mountains. Most of the space on the map was his.

Gwyn said, "That's right. I didn't know Madog had a barrier way."

Mag picked up the gray cloth and ran it around Madog's barrier way.

"I understand."

Edern said, "It probably keeps his people in as prisoners, that's why he thought to do it here."

Mag paused. She pointed at the black hat and the new symbol.

"Madog thinks..." Eluned said.

Mag picked up her own cup symbol and moved it in a big loop east of the mountains, encompassing all the territory on her sketch, and off the paper as well.

There was silence.

Into that silence, Mag picked up Gwyn's lion, Edern's star, George's collar, and Rhys's crown, and dropped them all onto the floor. Then she found the piece of antler that was Cernunnos, and dropped that, too, with a clatter.

Gwyn said, faintly, "Thank you, my lady, that makes the stakes abundantly clear."

Angharad understood it as easily as he did. Rhys's capture was bad but this was worse. In Madog's hands, Mag would be a deadly weapon. And he would never stop trying to get her, never. Somehow he didn't know about her before, but now he did. There was no hope for George, then, as long as Madog thought he had to break him to get Mag.

Her whole body revolted at the thought. She refused to consider it. She'd trust her husband to find some way back, if he could just survive. So her job was to help him do that. And the first step was motivation, not comfort, as for a hopeless victim, but a reason to fight.

"Mag, is George awake?"

Two knocks.

"When he wakes up, I want you to send him a message from me, over and over, until you're sure he's gotten it. Will you do that for me?"

One knock from Mag.

Cydifor murmured, "She can only send pictures and emotions to him, George said."

"Fine. I'll make pictures she can use. That's what I do, after all."

She pulled a piece of paper out and inked a series of panels. In the first, she put herself and a recognizable corner of the conservatory with Seething Magma. In the second, she drew herself standing with outstretched arms reaching for a distant George. In the third, they had their arms around each other, with an obvious bandage around his eyes. In the fourth, she drew the two of them standing, a baby in his arms and his eyes still covered.

Cydifor mouthed quietly, "I'm here. Come home. I want you, the damage doesn't matter. You have a child."

She glanced at him. "Yes."

"Will you do it, Mag?" she asked.

One knock. Pause. One knock. Pause. One knock.

"Thank you."

A horrible thought occurred to her. "Can he still see your pictures, Mag?"

There was a stomach-clenching pause. Three knocks.

"I don't care. Do it anyway, something will get through." She stood up and walked to the end of the room with the pile of bedding. "Who's been sleeping here?" she asked.

Edern rose. "I have, my lady. Shall I have them make up a pallet for you?"

"Yes, and they can bring my food here, too."

CHAPTER 24

George drifted in blackness for some unknown amount of time. It seemed like hours. The remnants of the hypnotic he'd drunk made it easy to float but the pain kept him from sleeping.

He felt someone frantically tugging at the straps holding his left arm to the chair. He lifted his head in his direction.

"Your eyes," Maelgwn hissed. His movements stopped. Then he resumed working on the straps.

"Never mind," he soothed, "You're going to be fine. Just wake up, please. Now. You have to leave now."

Alarm penetrated George's haze. "Go away, you'll be caught."

"Quiet," Maelgwn breathed, ignoring him and unbuckling the last strap. "Cloudie and I have a plan. All you have to do is get into this way, right here."

With the removal of his bonds, George slumped in the chair, every muscle aching and tingling from inactivity. The slight movement sent fire up his left leg and he gasped.

"Water," he croaked.

The boy pressed a glass into his hand. "Here." He waited until George drained it and took it away. "Now stand up."

"Can't."

"Yes, you can."

George felt the voice resonate, realizing too late from the taste in his mouth that Maelgwn must have used the same drugged water that Madog left behind.

"Keep talking," he said. "Don't stop." He might as well go with the drug this time, the boy was trying to rescue him.

"I can't carry you, and you can't walk, but you can crawl to this way. It's real close. Don't you give up now." George felt him reaching for motivations. "Come on, Cloudie and me, we put ourselves into danger for you. You're not gonna let them catch us, are you?"

That worked. George focused on his voice and tried to stand up on his right leg, pushing with his arms. The muscles failed him part way up and he fell to the ground, agony flashing behind his dead eyes with bursts of remembered light. He clenched his teeth to keep from crying out and panted on the ground.

Maelgwn tugged at one arm. "This way. You can do it."

George rolled to his left side and pushed forward with his right foot, dragging the useless leg along with him. He lifted his torso onto his elbows and made his arms share some of the work, groaning at what the twist in his body did to his back.

"That's right," Maelgwn whispered. "Almost there."

George felt a way threshold and pulled himself forward into it. Movement was easier in the passage, less friction to drag at his leg, less grit to scrape his bare skin. The drug was seizing hold now and he was tempted to just give in to it and lie there. It felt so much better to lie down.

"Keep going," Maelgwn insisted. "You're almost at the other end."

His attention was still focused on the voice and he let it pull him forward as he doggedly crawled, a few inches at a time.

He felt the transition onto snowy ground and lay there shivering.

Maelgwn spoke to him frantically. "George, you have to wake up. You've got to kill this way or he'll know Cloudie helped you and find us here."

He shook his shoulder. "Can't you hear me?"

George heard him but it didn't penetrate. What did he want?

Maelgwn said, "Mother of Cloudie, can you hear me? Can you help?"

Danger. Picture of way. Picture of way destroyed.

What do you want, Mag. He tried to focus what was left of his attention on her.

Danger. Danger. Picture of way with George next to it. Picture of way destroyed.

You want me to kill it?

Yes, yes, yes.

Alright.

He collapsed the way.

Maelgwn spoke, relieved. "Just a little bit further now. We've got a place to hide you."

George let himself be coaxed toward another way. He crawled inside, out of the snow, and closed it behind him. He reached out and closed the other end, too, ignoring the protests of Maelgwn, outside. Then he curled up into a shivering ball and let the blackness take him.

⌒〰〜⌒

The sound of Mag shifting restlessly woke Angharad from her pallet in front of the fire.

"Is something happening?" she whispered, trying not to wake Edern.

One quiet knock.

She gathered a blanket around her and curled up in a small couch next to Mag. She heard Edern rise behind her, and he joined her, wrapped in his own blanket, his hair unkempt from a restless sleep.

"Show us," she said quietly, not wanting to wake the rest of the sleeping house.

"Shall I light some lamps?" Edern asked.

"No, the fire's enough."

Mag put George' dog collar on the prison drawing. Then she picked up the wolf toy and Cloudie's cloth and moved them together to George.

"It's a rescue," Edern told Angharad. He reached for her hand with his and held it tight.

Mag grasped all three objects in one pseudopod and lifted them outside together.

"It worked," Angharad said.

In the dim firelight, just awakened, it felt like a dream.

"Did you give him my message?"

Two quiet knocks.

"Why not?" She realized Mag couldn't answer that. "I mean, did you try?"

Two knocks.

"Was he too busy?"

One knock.

"Too hurt?"

One knock.

"Never mind. You just do it as soon as you think you can, and keep on doing it."

One knock.

Mag stopped moving.

Angharad leaned against Edern, reluctant to go lie down again. "Seems like old times, doesn't it."

Edern smiled at her. "And how do you like your new husband, really?" he asked.

"Oh, Edern, I don't know how to tell you. I'm alive again. I want him back, young, bold, stubborn, kind. I could kill Madog with my bare hands, I could, rip him to small bloody pieces."

"And me standing next to you."

She kissed his cheek and stood up to try and get some more sleep.

Edern said, "Is it true what your message says, that you're with child?"

"Mag says so, and I believe her."

"Congratulations, then, and may it be the first of many more with George."

She looked down at him. "Will you be guardian, if George..." She couldn't continue.

"My dear, with all my heart. You do me great honor."

Rhys was very tired of captivity. After the first interviews with Madog, they'd left him alone to rot. His only assurance that they hadn't forgotten about him altogether was the bucket of water he'd received yesterday. They weren't wasting any food on him, or blankets.

His teachers had talked about captivity, a risk for any warrior, especially for those that had a value for ransom. They stressed finding a way to occupy his mind, and they warned about becoming so lonely that his captors would come to seem like friends. He'd never understood that last one, until now.

It was dark all the time, so he couldn't truly count the days, not accurately, but he agreed with himself to call the deepest black "night." He wasn't sure how many days he'd been alone, but he'd started making marks on a wall whenever it seemed like a new day and that told him about a week had passed. That wasn't long at all, and already he found himself looking forward to his next contact. Rationally he knew he should be grateful that Madog wasn't devoting any attention to him right now, that no good would come of any more interrogations, but he wanted to see a face, any face. The last couple of days he'd heard random screams echoing through the corridors. That could be me, he thought.

He knew there was no way for his friends and family to reach him, but it was hard not to feel abandoned anyway.

He'd exercised the first couple of days to keep himself fit but after he realized they weren't going to feed him, he decided he needed to conserve his energy. He tried to invent mind games instead, running through old famous battles as exercises in tactics and creating new variants to see how that changed things.

With nothing else to do, he slept as much as he could, whenever he felt like it. This left him awake sometimes in the night, as he was now.

A puff of wind hit him in the face and he smelled a change of atmosphere. In front of him stood a boy, dimly illuminated by a nighttime snowy scene at the end of a passage. Something indistinct but large moved behind him.

"Are you him?" The boy had tears on his face.

"What?" Rhys said, rising from the floor. Was this some sort of dream?

"Are you the one George wanted to rescue?" He held out a familiar pocket watch in one trembling hand.

"George is here?" Rhys said, excited.

"He's hurt and he's sealed himself in and I can't get to him and he needs help." He sounded as if he were holding himself together by sheer nerve.

"Slow down," Rhys said. "You've got George, and you can get me out of here?"

The boy nodded.

"Well, let's start with that, then. My name's Rhys."

"I'm Maelgwn and that's Cloudie." He pointed behind him, warily.

Rhys smiled. "I do believe I've met your mother, young lady." He bowed, and thought he heard a giggle.

He let the boy guide him into the way.

⌣‿⌣

This time, it was Edern who was awakened first by Mag's movement.

"More news, Mag?"

One quiet knock.

He shook Angharad's shoulder and they resumed their places on the couch to watch by the light of the fire.

Seething Magma took the wolf and Cloudie pair and swept them back into the prison, to Rhys's crown. Then she moved all three near to George's collar.

"Rhys is out?" Edern said, his voice rising in disbelief.

One knock.

"He's alive?"

One knock.

"Badly hurt?"

Two knocks.

Edern bowed his head and wept unabashedly. Angharad put an arm around him and leaned her head next to his.

"How did they find him, Mag?" Angharad asked.

Mag put her cup symbol next to the crown, then moved it to Cloudie, then moved the crown to Cloudie.

"You knew what Rhys felt like and told Cloudie, is that it?"

One knock.

"You clever, clever girl," she said. "Thank you."

Mag showed Rhys's crown and George's collar meeting.

"This is happening now?" Angharad said

One knock.

Edern wiped his eyes and the two of them settled down to watch.

⌒

Rhys stood in the snow, barefoot and coatless. The walled space looked like a bare wasteland in the starlight. Maelgwn grabbed his arm before he could take a step.

"Can you see the ways?"

"No. Are there some here?"

"It's full of them. You'll have to let me lead you. The one we want is very close."

The boy took him by the hand and led him, with one sharp turn, to an apparently empty space. "Stay there. Don't move."

He walked about twenty feet away. "You're standing at one end, and I'm at the other. I brought him here to hide him, but he claimed it and closed both ends."

"Will he run out of air?" Rhys asked.

"I don't know. He's hurt bad. I don't think he's awake."

"Can't you open it?"

"I can't. I tried and tried."

Rhys could hear his voice rising in a panic. He said, "Can Cloudie open it?"

Maelgwn froze to consider that. "Cloudie, can you drill into the middle and make an opening for us?"

Rhys got his first good look at her as she walked up to the boy. She was several times his size, but her mother was many times larger yet. She seemed to lean against the empty space between them, then backed up.

"It worked," Maelgwn whispered excitedly. "Come here, I'll take you in."

Rhys took his hand, and they entered.

Inside, in the dim light of the passage, Rhys saw the body of a man lying a few feet away. He knelt beside it.

It was a horror. George was naked and unconscious, and a trail of blood marked where his ruined leg had dragged along the passage floor. His back was fully exposed and Rhys shuddered at the blackened skin and deep burns.

Pull yourself together, he told himself. They need you, both of them.

"Alright, Maelgwn. Don't look at him. Look at me. Can you get me water, food, cloth for bandages—all without getting caught? I need light."

"I've got candles."

"Good, bring them and something to hold them. A sharp knife, a small one. You've got his pocket watch, what about the rest of his things?"

"I got it all," Maelgwn said, "I'll go bring it. Wait here."

Rhys grabbed him before he could leave. "We're going to need shoes and blankets. If you can't find shoes, how about leather and laces? We can make moccasins."

The boy nodded and was off.

Rhys moved over to George's other side and knelt down. He didn't want to turn him over onto his back but he needed to see what else needed immediate attention. When he saw his face, he gasped and sat back on his heels. He had a good idea now whose screams he'd heard.

"Oh, cousin, what have they done to you? What will Angharad say? Your poor eyes."

⌁

Seething Magma showed Angharad and Edern that Maelgwn and Rhys had gotten into the way that George had sealed off. She confirmed they were both alive, and that Rhys wasn't much hurt, but she had to stop there. Granite Cloud was now attuned to Rhys, as she had to be to have found him, and she was very sad that he was so upset about his friend.

Mother, is he going to die?

Seething Magma knew she meant George.

I don't know, dear. We're going to try and save him.

If I hadn't run away, this wouldn't have happened.

It's not your fault. You're not the one who hurt him.

But Rhys is so sad.

I know. Why don't you leave them alone for a while and tell me about all the exciting things you've done today.

She turned and opened the door of the conservatory, headed for the night woods. She needed some time alone with her child and away from the short-lived and their sufferings.

CHAPTER 25

Rhys made a plan of action while he waited for Maelgwn. He'd had basic medical training, as any cadet would, but he'd never seen actual battle wounds before. The scars on his instructors were informative of just what sort of damage could be survived, and he was hopeful. He remembered his training—if the wounded man was breathing, then the next step was to stop the blood loss. After that, keep things clean and watch for fever. They didn't have a lot to say about how to treat fever.

He put his hand to George's forehead. George didn't stir. He couldn't feel any fever yet. He knew that burns cauterized the flesh, but infections came when dirt got into the open injuries. George's back was a mess, but not dirty, as far as he could tell in the dimness. That knee, on the other hand, was filthy from George's crawl to freedom. He needed more light, but the knee worried him. It was still leaking blood diffusely, not enough to help clean the site. He'd have to deal with that as soon as possible.

The eyes... well, there was little he could do about that but clean them up and hope they weren't life-threatening. Blind men died of head wounds, not loss of vision, and this had been done cleanly. Rhys had a fleeting suspicion that Madog didn't want to look at a butchered face on a regular basis, he wanted things neat and tidy. He lip curled at the thought.

Maelgwn returned with the first set of items in a lumpy sack, and a bucket of water.

"I brought cloth, and two knives, with a stone, oh, and a cup. Here are all the blankets, candles, flint and steel. Put these on your feet." He pulled out two long strips of wool that could be wrapped into makeshift socks.

"Any way to make a fire?" Rhys asked.

"Not without being seen or smelled. We're right next to Madog's keep."

He didn't like to use cold water, but there wasn't much choice. "Alright. See if you can bring his clothes, if you've got them. And

236

we're going to need some bowls or small buckets. I'll get started, and then you can help me when you come back."

The boy vanished again.

He lit the candles, fumbling with the flint and steel. We've gotten soft, he thought, relying on those human lighters. He cut the edge of the cloth and ripped off a strip from that start. He tore it into smaller strips about a foot long. He folded the first one into a pad and began cleaning the part of the knee he could reach without turning George over, to find out exactly what was still bleeding.

By the time Maelgwn came back, Rhys had cleaned George's face and wrapped a bandage around it, with soft pads over his ruined eyes.

"Good, I'm ready for you. We're going to have to roll him over to his other side and it's got to be done over his front, not his back. That'll be awkward. And we should move him at the same time to that blanket pad I've laid out. I'll pick up most of his weight at the top, but you're going to have to manage the bad leg. Can you do that? It'll be heavy and you don't want to put any stress on it."

Maelgwn looked sick, but he nodded.

Rhys straightened George's right leg which was drawn up supporting his balance on his left side. He bent over George's torso and lifted his left shoulder from the bottom, letting him rotate forward face-down and around until he had to put him down for the next step, this time on his right shoulder. Maelgwn held both legs together and tried to keep the left one from flopping. George moaned.

"Good job," Rhys said. "Now all we have to do is walk him up a few feet and lay him on the blanket."

Rhys couldn't just pick him up around the body without hurting the burns, so he bent over and lifted him by the right shoulder from below, high enough not to bump the drooping head, and slowly walked backward, Maelgwn holding the legs as best he could, until they could lay him on the doubled-up blanket, out of the pool of blood and off the cold passage floor.

The change in position of his knee brought George semi-awake.

Rhys had kept the water in the bucket clean so far by not dipping the cloths in it once they were used. He scooped up some water with the cup now and knelt behind George's head. He lifted it up and held the cup to his mouth. "Come on, cousin, have a drink."

"Rhys?" George said, confused.

"Never mind, just go back to sleep for a while, until we're done. You're safe now."

George obediently drank and dropped off again. Rhys spared a grim thought for the meaning of "safe," here in the heart of Madog's domain, but it was better than a cell.

They spent the next hour trying to reach every bone fragment in the ruined knee and cleaned it as best they could. Rhys was sure they hadn't succeeded, they just didn't have the tools. The joint was loose, and he knew what that meant. If George didn't succumb to infection, it would heal rigid, the bones fused and unbending. Impossible to ride, or even climb a staircase. He'd met a man in that situation, once.

"Maelgwn, you've done very well. One last task, can you find us some food and two long sticks I can use for the leg? And one more, for a staff."

The boy was pale and drooping, but nodded like a trooper and went off on the errand.

While he was gone, Rhys worked on the back, cutting away some of the dead blackened skin. He was relieved not to find any open oozing spots—this might heal cleanly. He'd need the boy's help to bandage it, wrapping cloth around and around George's chest while he lifted.

He stood up and stretched while he waited, to work out the kinks in his muscles from working in such an uncomfortable position. It felt so good to be free and useful again that he was grateful for whatever chain of events had brought George together with this strange boy. He sobered, fearing George had paid too high a price.

He rewrapped the woolen strips around his feet and started to give some thought to clothing in the cold exposed air. He'd been afraid to ask Maelgwn to close Cloudie's entrance while he was away. If George didn't wake enough to open an end and the boy was captured, Rhys had visions of being trapped inside this little passage with a dying friend. He'd make do with clothing in the meantime, until the boy was back for good. George would sleep in blankets tonight, so he borrowed his coat, much too broad for him, and drew it around himself for warmth.

When Maelgwn returned, lugging George's pack with difficulty, he finally let him close the entry. They splinted the leg and wrapped a bandage around the back, then covered George with two more blankets and let him be.

Rhys wrapped himself in two blankets and made himself eat the cold sausage and cheese from George's pack slowly, limiting the amount of this first meal. There was plenty, enough for them all for a day or two, even without a fire. As he dug through the pack wondering what else might be there, he fell upon the two spare pairs of socks with rapture, putting one pair on immediately, and the other pair onto George.

Dawn was breaking outside. Maelgwn slumped next to him in his own blanket, his eyes drooping. Rhys brushed away the last of the crumbs and said to him, "Now, don't you think it's time to tell me what's been going on?"

❧

Edern woke Gwyn at daybreak to deliver the news of the rescues, and they both went and roused Rhian. Gwyn was disquieted to hear that Seething Magma had left without explanation. Is she coming back, he wondered. We need her.

Maybe she's decided it would be best to make herself unavailable for use as a weapon. He could hardly blame her.

He came to the conservatory before breakfast with Rhian to visit with Edern and Angharad, getting all the details they knew. Angharad looked up as she saw Mag approaching from the outside, and opened the door for her.

"I'm so glad to see you back. Are you alright?" she said.

Pause. One knock.

Gwyn thought, she's probably appalled at our cruelty to each other.

An answering knock startled Gwyn as he realized she can read all our thoughts, if she chooses.

Mag confirmed that Rhys and George were alive and together, but refused to say more.

She relented only once, when Rhian understood that Cloudie must now be more fully aware of Rhys and thus all this adult worry. She stood and made a formal curtsy to Mag. "My lady, please thank your daughter for helping to rescue my brother. I'm in her debt."

Mag paused, then picked up the gray cloth, pointed at the picture of the speaking mouth, and the picture of the smiling mouth.

Rhian thought about it. "Cloudie says, she's glad?"

One knock.

Gwyn walked up beside his foster-daughter. "Our thanks to both of you, from all of us. Whatever happens next," he said.

❧

Rhys and Maelgwn spent the day alternately dozing and talking. They couldn't leave George alone. He wasn't responsive when Rhys shook him lightly, and he thought the best thing to do would be to let him sleep as long as he could.

The boy told him about meeting George. Rhys could see the impression he'd made. There was a certain curious way he had of speaking that already put him in mind of his cousin, though he had difficulty pinning it down.

He asked about his family and got a spare, laconic version of their deaths that wrung his heart. He tried to distract him by telling him something of his own life, though, when Maelgwn asked about his own parents, he admitted Madog had killed them.

"You, too?" Maelgwn said.

"There are probably lots of us," Rhys said sardonically, and was saddened to see his young companion nod wisely in agreement.

George lay quietly, though every now and then Rhys could see he was dreaming, nightmares. He uttered inarticulate protests and his hands clenched, but each time he subsided.

Around mid-day, something changed. George was rousing, but not completely, He plucked at his blankets, trying to remove them.

"Whoa there," Rhys said, coming over to stop his hands.

"Have to get up, I have to…"

"Hush, I know." Rhys had been expecting this, from his training about treating injuries. He reached over for a small bucket he'd put aside for the purpose. "Let me help."

After he covered him up again, he made him drink more water, and George dropped off into a deeper sleep.

Maelgwn took the bucket from him since Rhys couldn't see the ways outside to dispose of the contents safely. He returned in a few minutes, having cleaned it with snow.

Throughout the afternoon, Rhys checked George's forehead, but it was Maelgwn who first noticed him sweating and woke Rhys. He cursed. George was warm, some infection was loose. He knew it was almost inevitable but he'd hoped to avoid it. So far it was light, maybe it would stay that way.

And maybe it wouldn't. He needed to work on a plan on getting out of here himself with Maelgwn, in case George was incapacitated. Or worse.

⌣

At last, he thought. Benitoe lay the pen on the table and stood up. "All yours, with pleasure," he told the middle-aged lutin who took his place, the first member of the Edgewood Kuzul to come forward since the awakening.

Ives had confirmed his authority to take temporary charge of the lutins in Edgewood, and he knew it was a necessary task, but he wanted to be out with Maëlys, helping her find her husband. His uncle. It hadn't taken long for the sense of a deep and varied family clan to seem perfectly normal to him. All he had left to do was to match faces to the names Maëlys had entertained him with, whenever they rode out together.

He saddled his pony and rode to the village to talk to her. He knew he'd find her at the inn, setting things up.

She'd lost no time once Cadugan had granted her first rights, rent to own over ten years. Edern had guaranteed her character, on Benitoe's say-so, and funded her starting costs. He knew this was part of the debt Edern believed he owed Isolda, and he wasn't sure how he felt about that, but he was happy enough that Maëlys benefited.

Maëlys was determined to provide food, basic and simple to begin with, as quickly as possible as the village came to life around the inn. She'd named it the Golden Cockerel, and the freshly painted inn sign, rehung on a sturdy new bracket, was one of the first signs of the revival.

She had cadged buckets, mops, brooms, and all the things used to clean a house from the storerooms at Edgewood and gotten the inn scrubbed by the simple expedient of trading her materials for the labor of her neighbors. Everyone who borrowed a bucket spent some time cleaning the inn, too.

Carpenters for house repairs were in very short supply, but she hired one of the first to make himself known, a middle-aged fae, and arranged for lumber from some of the unoccupied buildings that were too damaged to repair. She shared both his work and the materials with her neighbors, and provided food for them as well. There were no regular channels for trade yet, but the manor kept a steady stream of wagons running to all the villages until ordinary trade resumed.

As she'd explained to Benitoe, her neighbors were going to get food from the manor anyway, but she could cook it for them in quantity more easily than they could themselves for now, and she was building up goodwill from all of them once the emergency was over. Already she'd had visits from grateful tradesmen who promised her first pick and favorable prices for their goods and services as they got restarted.

She'd appealed directly to Edern for the loan of the next mason to turn up. He'd appeared three days ago, with his old assistant, a korrigan. Unlike most, they'd hunkered down together instead of seeking out their own kind. They'd just gotten used to each other, was how they explained it. Both were still relatively young and, Maëlys was pleased to discover, not too proud to turn their hand to rough plastering in the kitchen once they'd seen to the main repair work. Like her carpenter, she'd offered to sponsor their work in the neighborhood, but they preferred to set up an independent establishment down the street. They came in every day for their lunches.

Benitoe rode into the inn's stableyard which was still a mess, and tied his pony in a ruined stall for a bit of shelter. He walked to the side door, ducking around a woman bearing a loaded platter of food.

The main room was bustling, even in the middle of the afternoon, and he saw more real tables, fewer improvised ones. People were sitting on chairs and stools and even, he saw, on boxes. He spotted Maëlys at the far end and wove through the crowd to reach her, his smaller size an advantage among the tall fae.

She hooked his arm and pulled him into a side parlor, not yet put back into use. "I'm free, auntie," he told her. "They've got one of the old Kuzul members back."

"That's great news. I'm stuck here for another couple of days, but we're making progress. No bedrooms or stabling yet, and only the one main room, but the kitchen's in full swing, as you can see. People have to eat. Laundry, next, I think."

Benitoe said, "I thought you might be tied down here. What I want to do is go looking for more lutins, and your Luhedoc among them. I want as good a description as you can give me of him. I have an idea."

"What?"

"I'm going to put up signs, everywhere, directing him here. If you can't go looking for him, maybe I can send him looking for you."

CHAPTER 26

George woke up gradually. It was still, where he was, and it felt like an enclosed space. He was lying down, not strapped to the iron chair. He was clean and warm. He felt wool blankets but no clothes. His knee throbbed, and his back, but as long as he didn't move it was tolerable.

Why can't I see anything? Then he had a vision of a red-hot needle with bits of cinder.

He lifted a hand to his face to remove a wrapping and someone stopped him.

"Better not."

"Rhys! What's happened? Where are we?"

"I don't know what you remember, but here's the tale as I've heard it from your protégé. Maelgwn and Cloudie broke into your cell and released you. They got you into a way and persuaded you to kill it afterward to remove the evidence."

"I don't remember that part very well. Mag was there?"

"She helped," Maelgwn said.

"You crawled into one of these ways in Madog's garden and locked yourself in."

"You closed both ends," Maelgwn said.

George could hear the remnants of panic in his voice.

"I'm sorry, I don't remember," he said. "I didn't mean to scare you."

"Our friend here was rather desperate and it occurred to him to look for me," Rhys said.

"And he found you. Are you hurt?"

"No, not really," he said. His voice changed. "But you, I'm afraid…"

"Never mind," George said, grimly. "I remember that part very well indeed."

Rhys was silent a moment.

"We've cleaned you up. How is it?"

"Blind, lame, and battered. Quite a prize for Angharad, don't you think?"

Rhys said, "She'll be glad to get you back in any form, believe me."

Picture of George crumpled. Picture of George, not crumpled.

Pleased to be alive, too, Mag, though I'm afraid I'm still pretty crumpled.

Maelgwn told Rhys, "He's talking to Cloudie's mom."

Picture of Angharad. Picture of Angharad drawing. Picture of paper.

You have a message from Angharad?

Yes. Picture of Angharad with Mag in the conservatory. Picture of Angharad reaching for me, my eyes bandaged. Picture of Angharad hugging me. Picture of Angharad and me, with a baby.

His sudden gasp made Rhys ask Maelgwn, "What did she say?"

He put a hand over his face reflexively, though there was nothing to hide that the bandage didn't already cover. He had no trouble translating the message. She's at Edgewood, she wants me to come back, she knows about my eyes, she's going to have a child.

Is this true, Mag?

Picture of Angharad, picture of bud inside Angharad.

"Sorry," he said to Rhys, "Mag just surprised me." His voice thickened. "You were right about Angharad."

"Of course. Never any doubt of it," Rhys said, trying to lighten the mood.

"Although," he continued, "we still have to get out of here, with the youngsters."

"More than that," George said. "Madog has to go down. Die, I mean."

"Impossible. We haven't the means."

"Doesn't matter. There's no other way to free Cloudie, and we can't let him live. He used Cloudie to run the barrier ways around Edgewood and his own domain. He wants to use Mag to do the same to Annwn. All of it."

Silence. "Is that possible?" Rhys asked.

"I don't know, but Cernunnos thought so. I can't let Madog live to try. He could claim Mag, just like a way—it's how he controls Cloudie."

"What are you planning to do?"

"I don't know yet, everything hurts too much to think." A thought occurred to him. "Maelgwn, did Cloudie make a way to Rhys's cell? Is it still there?"

"I closed it," Maelgwn said.

"Oh, no. Madog will know you exist now."

Maelgwn said, in a voice too bitter for his age, "He already knows, remember? From when I told him about Cloudie's mom." He was implacable in his determination not to forgive himself. "Besides, I couldn't let him follow Cloudie here."

"Not your fault. You had no way of knowing."

"I knew enough not to make stupid threats."

George left it alone. He'd have to come to his own terms with it. "Maybe I can kill it. He'll think it was me," George said. "I can't see which one it is. Can you point me to one end?"

Maelgwn took his hand and stretched the index finger in the right direction. "It's close," he said.

George felt for a way owned by Maelgwn, in that direction. Suddenly it was obvious, he could see that it was more recent than the others. When did I learn how to do that, he wondered. He collapsed it.

"Maelgwn, if Madog comes up here looking for you, those ways you claimed are going to stand out. You should unclaim them, and I'll do the same with this one."

"But then they'll be open and cold."

"A little cold air will feel good." He released the claim on the way they were in and the air temperature dropped.

Rhys leaned forward and felt his forehead. He was burning up.

"It's an infection," George said, unemotionally. "I can feel it."

"Just a wound fever, from the knee. It'll pass," Rhys said.

"Maybe." He asked for more water but refused food.

"I'm going to lie here for a while and see if I can't come up with some kind of plan. I've had enough sleep," George said.

Rhys recognized the grimness in his voice. "I'll leave you to it, then."

⌐~~⌐

Angharad looked up from her reverie when Mag tapped her drawing with the four panels.

"George is awake?"

One knock.

"You gave him my message?"

One knock.

"Did he understand it?"

One knock.

She wasn't sure how to phrase the next question. She wanted to know his mind, whether he would try to come back.

"What does he want?" she asked.

Mag picked up the black hat that stood for Madog, and dropped it on the floor.

"He wants Madog dead."

Mag picked up the toy black hat and George's collar. This time, the collar threw Madog to the floor.

"Oh. He wants to kill Madog."

"Is that possible?" Edern had come up beside her.

Three knocks.

~~

George lay on his side in his personal darkness all night long. He must have slept for some of the time, and much of it was spent in fever dreams, but in the lucid intervals he chewed on the problem.

He refused to think about his lost eyes. Instead, he welcomed the darkness as an aid to concentration. Better to think about a plan for attack than to dwell on what he'd lost.

For every year of Angharad's face, for the face of any child, for every painting she did that he wouldn't see—for each of these he wanted to exact his pound of flesh. He was infuriated that Madog could only suffer a single death. He couldn't think of his damage for his anger.

In one moment of clarity, he thought, I wonder if this is how Cernunnos feels, when affronted by injustice?

His fever put him through burning heat and bouts of teeth-snapping shivering, and it got worse as the night wore on.

He could hear Rhys and Maelgwn shift in their sleep and wake up, only to resume their even breathing a few minutes later. At least Rhys was free, and could look after Maelgwn. Something worthwhile came of this.

Mag sent him Angharad's message again.

Don't, Mag. It can't happen. I wish it could.

He put his hand down and felt the heat from his knee even through the thick bandage. I suppose blindness isn't really going to be the problem, after all, he thought. I would have liked to see the face of my child, though.

He forced his mind back to the problem at hand.

He never noticed the familiar voice humming a soft, soft tune as it sent him into sleep and kept him there.

George stirred uncomfortably while Rhys and Maelgwn packed away the remains of their breakfast.

"How are you feeling?" Rhys asked him.

"I've discovered that anger is very useful for blocking out unpleasant thoughts."

"Indeed, I've discovered that for myself recently," Rhys said.

He continued, "You know, it's morning, and Madog hasn't come here to search. It may be that he didn't look at my cell himself, and so the way was undetected. I think we've got to close this one again, it's just too cold otherwise."

George reluctantly agreed and re-claimed and closed it, including the little entrance Cloudie had made into its side, which was somehow separate.

"I have some business to take care of," he said. "First, I want to try something. Is there room behind me?"

"Yes, but for what?" Rhys said.

"Take the bandages off my eyes," he said, without explaining himself.

Rhys unwrapped them for him.

George raised himself on his right elbow, hissing at the stress it put on his back, and invoked the horned man. As he'd hoped, he could see again with the borrowed eyes, after a fashion, with colors suppressed. The heavy antlered head was hard to hold up in this awkward position. He could feel the bandages around his chest shift as his body contours adjusted.

"Rhys, unwrap this." He pointed at the bandage around his knee.

Rhys hesitated. "Maelgwn, can you sit behind him and help hold the antlers up, to make it easier for him?"

George understood that Rhys wanted Maelgwn far from whatever they would find under the bandage. "Light some candles," he said.

Rhys unwrapped the bandage. The knee oozed and stuck to the cloth as Rhys worked it free. George could smell the rot inside with the horned man's senses, but he wasn't sure if Rhys could.

George reached his free left hand down to his knee. It was hot under the skin. As he pressed it, wincing at the pain, he felt a sort of crackling inside.

He couldn't reach any further without stretching his back. "Feel below the joint. Warm or cold?"

Rhys lay his hand on George's calf. He looked up at the horned man's face. "Not warm." George could hear him suppress the alarm in his voice for the sake of the boy.

"Alright, that's what I thought. Let's wrap it up again."

Rhys said, slowly, "George, I don't think I can cut... Not without even a fire to cauterize it."

"I know. I think it's too late anyway. Nothing to be done about it." He tried to smile at Rhys using the alien face, to comfort him. "It just makes the deadline for our attack more urgent."

Time for the next item on his list.

"Maelgwn, please sit with Rhys where I can see you." The antlered head was heavy, but he wanted to be able to see their faces for this next bit.

"A few days ago I asked you if you would be my foster-son. Now I need to ask if you will go with Rhys instead."

"No, I want to go with you. I meant to tell you so," Maelgwn protested.

"Rhys comes from an important family. They have domains to rule. It would be better for you," George said.

"I don't care. You promised me, you said 'for keeps.'"

Rhys said, "He's right."

George said carefully, "Maelgwn, you need to hear something hard. I'm not going to get out of here. This," he pointed at his knee, "is gangrene, what Rhys calls 'wound fever.' The leg is dying. It's going to kill me as the toxins get into my blood." He paused. "It may not take very long."

Maelgwn drew his knees up and wrapped his arms around them. He rocked, with his head down, his face invisible. Then he lifted it up and said, "I'd rather be your foster-son even for a few days, if that's all there is."

"So be it," George said. "I want it, too. You'll abide by my arrangements?"

Maelgwn nodded.

⌒⌒⌒

Rhys listened as George spoke, numb with the ill fate of seeing George rescued only to have him succumb to his injury. He knew George was right. The wound fit the symptoms he'd learned. He was ashamed at his relief that he wouldn't have to try an amputation with George's saber, but it would never have worked anyway, without a fire to seal the wound and keep him from losing too much blood.

George said, "Rhys, I don't know the form. You'll have to help me."

"Doesn't require much, just a statement before a witness, and I can serve for that." He saw the grim lines of pain and determination on George's face as he prepared his words.

George looked at Maelgwn. "I, George Talbot Traherne, great-grandson of Gwyn ap Nudd, adopt Maelgwn as my foster-son, to share equally with any other heir of my body. If I should die before I see her again, I request my wife Angharad to take him in as her foster-son as well. I appoint my friend and kinsman, Rhys Vachan ap Rhys ap Edern, as his protector, to watch over him as an elder brother."

He looked at Rhys with a question in his alien eyes. For the first time, Rhys could see George behind the face of the horned man.

He nodded. "And so I will, and gladly."

"Anything else?" George asked.

Rhys said, "That'll do. We'll write it down later." Assuming there was going to be a "later," he thought.

⌒⌒⌒

George drooped and released the horned man so that he could fully lie down again, returning to the dark.

Maelgwn crawled over and knelt on his heels beside him. "Is there anything you need, foster-father?"

George was warmed by the pride in the boy's voice. "I need to rest and I need to work on an idea I have, with Mag. I'll open Cloudie's entrance so you can get in and out.

Rhys objected, and George said, "The cold air will feel good anyway." He could feel the fever building again.

"Whatever I'm going to try," he said to Rhys, "it has to be today, while I still can. Give me an hour or so."

Mag, I have an idea. Can you find Gwyn for me?

CHAPTER 27

Seething Magma knocked to get Cydifor's attention. He looked up from his conversation with Angharad.

"Something you want, my lady?" he asked.

She plucked the toy lion from a table and tossed it at him. He caught it. "You want me to find Gwyn and bring him?"

One knock.

He nodded and put the lion down, leaving Angharad alone with Mag.

"What is it, Mag, is it George?"

One knock.

She pointed at the collar, the drawing for speaking, and Angharad's magnifying glass.

"He wants to talk to me?"

One knock.

Mag repeated the tableau of George's collar throwing down Madog's black hat. She pointed at the sign for "one."

"He wants to kill Madog. That's number one."

One knock.

Then she picked up the collar, Rhys's crown, and the toy wolf, and moved them all to Edgewood on the map. She pointed at the sign for "two."

"They're coming to Edgewood. That's number two."

Mag returned the three objects west of the mountains. This time she only picked up the crown and the wolf and moved them to Edgewood. She pointed at "two" again.

"I don't understand."

Cydifor was back. "Gwyn's coming," he told Mag. To Angharad he said, "I think that was either all three come to Edgewood or only two of them."

One knock.

"So, Madog dies. Rhys and the wolf cub come to Edgewood. Maybe George."

One knock.

"What's the deciding factor?"

Cydifor said, as Gwyn walked in, accompanied by Edern and Rhodri, "George comes, if he can. Is that it, Mag?"

One knock.

"Is George worse, Mag?" Angharad asked, her voice steady.

One knock.

Mag picked up the drawing of George's injuries and added a bigger blot to the knee, then blotted the leg below and above.

"His leg is worse, it's infected," Angharad said, raising a hand to her face.

One knock.

Gwyn said, "Wound fever." The look on his face shook her. She knew it was a painful death.

"Is Rhys alright?" Edern asked.

One knock.

"You wanted me, my lady?" Gwyn said.

Mag lifted the collar.

"George wanted me?"

One knock.

She picked up the map of Madog's domain west of the mountains. She delicately covered it with little lines and stopped. She pointed at the barrier way, and pointed at her new lines.

"These are all ways within Madog's domain?" Gwyn said.

One knock.

"How many are there?"

She tapped the sign for one hundred, then tapped it again and again and again.

"There are hundreds of them."

One knock.

She drew a building with a wall around it south of Edgewood and put Gwyn's lion on it. She drew one thin line from Madog's domain to just outside the wall.

"That's Greenway Court and the hidden way Madog used," Gwyn said.

One knock.

She carefully scratched over the way, crossing it out. She pointed at George's collar.

"George collapsed that way."

One knock.

Mag pointed at the collar and the symbol for speaking.

"George says…"

She pointed at the sign for "one," then the collar, and started scratching out the barrier way and the other ways she'd drawn.

"First he will kill all the ways," Cydifor breathed.

She pointed at the sign for "two," then picked up her own cup and brought it to George's collar. She added Madog's black hat and Granite Cloud's cloth.

"Then Mag will come to George," Cydifor said, "and Madog and Cloudie will be there."

She pointed at the "three," then picked up George's collar, the crown and the wolf and moved them to Edgewood.

"Then they will come here."

She pointed at the sign for "four," then picked up her cup and the black hat, and threw the hat to the floor.

"Then Mag will kill Madog," Cydifor said. The room was silent, following along.

She pointed at the sign for "five," then picked up Granite Cloud's cloth and her own cup and brought them to Edgewood.

"Then Mag will come back with her daughter."

"This is his plan?" Gwyn said.

One knock.

"When?"

Mag made a pseudopod with its end curved in a circle. She moved it from near ground level on the east over her body to almost ground level on the west.

Cydifor said, "That's the sun, I think. Today, Mag? At dusk?"

One knock.

"It has to be today," Gwyn said. "He doesn't have much time, not with wound fever. Did he have a question for me?"

One knock. She drew a thick line from Madog's domain over to the eastern edge. She drew a similar thick line from below the drawing of Greenway Court over to the eastern edge. Finally she drew a thin line from Greenway Court itself in the same direction. The three lines looked like they would eventually meet, if the paper were large enough.

"That's the Travelers' Way and the Family Way," Rhodri said. "The other must be Madog's way from the old world. We knew that it had to exist."

One knock. She touched the collar and the symbol for speech.

"George says…"

She crossed out the thick line from Madog's domain. One knock, pause, two knocks. The scratching noise that meant a question.

Cydifor said, "Should he destroy that way, too, yes or no?"

One knock.

Angharad saw Gwyn considering the strategic importance of a third way from the old world. It only took him a moment. "Kill them all. Leave the bastard no way to escape," he said.

One knock.

Rhodri and Gwyn started speculating on how this plan could possibly be accomplished. It was impossible for Mag to communicate that level of detail.

While they explored the question, Angharad was lost in more personal considerations. If George's plan worked, he'd be coming back tonight. "If he can," she reminded herself. And if the wound fever was too advanced, he would die of it, she knew this. Either way he would be very ill and there was little she could do for him.

Then one thought occurred to her. She scribbled a note, folded it, and gave it to Edern. "Can you see that this gets to Idris, right away?"

"I'll send it with the latest dispatches, in just half an hour or so. Mark it urgent."

George waited for the response to the plan he'd sketched out from Rhys and Maelgwn.

Rhys said, "Lay this out for me again. I want to see how many holes I can poke in it."

"The crux of the matter," George said, "is that Cloudie can't be freed while Madog's alive. We three can't kill Madog."

"Ruling out unreasonably lucky assault," Rhys said.

"Followed by immediate death," George said. "Yes, I think we can rule that out."

He continued, "I could ask Mag to come, but Madog would claim her. I could claim her first, with her permission, but then Madog only has to kill me and then he can claim her himself. We'd be no better off.

"So, what I need to do is figure out how to bring an already claimed Mag in, and then get out of Madog's reach before he kills me." Or before I die anyway, he thought, and leave her in a jam, to be claimed by Madog.

Maelgwn said, "Cloudie could make you a way."

"Madog won't let her, she'll be controlled."

"Mag could make a way ahead of time," Rhys suggested.

"That's a good idea, but you don't realize how something like that would stand out to Madog. He'd spot it in an instant, and it would be open when it was made. Either Madog would claim it ahead of me, or he'd be warned and never come near.

"No, what we have to do is set a trap, and look trapped ourselves. You two need to be hidden, and I need to be the bait. And then we need to hold him there long enough for an attack.

"I think we need to bring Madog here, to the old garden. The two of you can hide in a way that Maelgwn claims—Madog can't go through them all, there are too many of them.

"Then I can provide a distraction that will keep him from escaping."

Rhys said, "What can you do?"

"Kill all the ways he has, except these right here. With violence. I think Cernunnos will extend my reach, like he did for the Edgewood barrier way."

"That's gone?" Rhys said.

"Didn't I tell you?"

Rhys shook his head but George couldn't see it.

George felt light-headed but he was looking forward to this part of the plan. "So, I kill all the ways except these. He looks for his ways, sees that these are the only ones left, comes up to find out why, and catches me."

"No!" Maelgwn and Rhys said, together.

"Hold on, he can't bring any guards here. He and I are the only ones who can walk here safely, except for you, Maelgwn. I can't run away or fight, so he'll feel safe. He'll love it. He'll be infuriated at the loss of his ways and blinded to anything else.

"He'll try something and I'll bring Mag. Then I'll dive into one of these ways and claim and close it. He won't be able to reach me."

Rhys said, "Why not claim one first?"

"Same reason Mag can't. My signature will stand out just like hers. I'll have to release this one before we start. Maelgwn's signature looks a lot like Cloudie's to me, maybe Madog doesn't notice his."

He faced Maelgwn's voice. "You'll have to make a pack of everything you want to take with you. You won't be coming back."

Rhys was still trying to puzzle out the impact of the way rules on the tactics. "What happen if Madog claims the open ways first? Won't that lock you out?"

"In that case," George said, "I'll kill all of them except yours. Your way will be exposed but he won't be able to do anything about it if it's claimed. I don't think he knows about Cloudie's trick that let her break into this way."

"Or maybe he does," Rhys said. "Remember the trap way?"

That gave George pause. "You're right. But if I throw enough problems at him and bring Mag, maybe she can kill him first."

Maelgwn said, "It would be better if you just made a way yourself and got us all out when Cloudie's mom came."

"I don't know how," George said.

"Cernunnos does," Rhys said. "Will he help?"

"I don't know. I can't tell."

Rhys said, judiciously, "There are so many ways for this to go wrong, and just the faintest possibility it might work."

"I think our only alternative is to give up. I don't like the risk we run with Mag, but it's the only chance I see to free Cloudie and maybe survive." He shivered as the fever resumed its attack. "And I can't wait—it has to be today or not at all."

"What does Mag say?" Rhys asked.

Agreement. Picture of Madog, picture of Seething Magma crumpled. Picture of Seething Magma, picture of Madog crumpled

"She says now that Madog knows about her, he has to die, or she won't be safe."

"How can she kill Madog?" Rhys said. "How would Mag do it? She's big, but she's not that quick and I can't see Madog hanging around while she tries to crush him."

"I gave her a suggestion," George said. He shivered uncontrollably again and lay down in his blankets and let the fever cycle take him, trusting they would rouse him before nightfall and help him get dressed.

⌇⌇

At the afternoon council session, Gwyn reviewed their plans for George's attack at nightfall.

"If this works, we should expect a way to appear, but we won't know where ahead of time. That's your job, Rhodri, of course."

Ceridwen said, "Eluned and I have prepared for them, especially since we know George may need serious help. Wherever they arrive, we have to get them to the infirmary here as quickly as we can. If George's leg has turned bad, we may have to remove it to save him."

Gwyn glanced at Angharad who was staring at nothing and holding herself together. She clutched a package that Edern had given her from the afternoon courier.

CHAPTER 28

George's fever completed its cycle and relinquished its grip for a
while.

"What time is it?" he asked Rhys, weakly.

"Almost dusk."

"Help me outside, then find a way behind me that Maelgwn can
claim and close it. Once this starts, Madog might get here fast."

Rhys got him partly dressed, cutting off the left leg of the
breeches at the thigh to get them over the bandaged knee and the
splints. Boots were impossible, but then he couldn't walk on it
anyway, and a sock would have to do. He took a shirt but refused
his coat. Rhys reached for his forehead to feel for fever, and
George shook him off. "You wear it."

They got him upright with considerable difficulty, and George
unclaimed the way. With Maelgwn guiding them around the
tangled ways, George leaned on Rhys and was half-carried to a
broken stone bench. Rhys lowered him down, trying to keep the
splinted leg straight.

"Good luck, cousin," Rhys said.

Maelgwn gave him an awkward hug, then led Rhys off to a
nearby way. George felt it being claimed but there was something
imperfect about it. Maybe he didn't close it completely, to watch.

George sat as straight as he could on the bench, feeling for its
edge with his hands to shift himself to the center. The fever's
abeyance wouldn't last for very long, and he wanted to get this
started while he was still relatively lucid.

He invoked the full form of Cernunnos. With his eyes, he saw
that it was twilight. What better time for his patron?

Are we in agreement that Madog must pay?

Justice, came the reply.

Then help me extend my grasp, George thought.

Only one way left the valley, as far as he could tell—the way to
the old world. He started by sealing it, to keep the rat in his trap
with no way to escape.

With that taken care of, he decided to work from the outside in. That meant that the barrier way would be the first to go. It was also, by far, the way with the largest interior passage, since it wasn't a traveling way.

He started with a bang. The barrier way exploded down its length as the air was forced out of a rip down the top line. The boom had length, like a curtain of sound. It bounced off the Blue Ridge and off of North Mountain, and echoed back and forth across the valley. It didn't die off quickly, as thunder mostly does, and George realized that since the sound source was at ground level, it would be slower to rise and dissipate than thunder in the air. All the better, he thought.

Before the reverberations had ceased he was busy squeezing ways shut all along the outer periphery, his fists mimicking what his mind was doing. There were so many different methods of shutting a way explosively. He worked in random directions, but cleared entire rings before moving inward.

The thunderous noise began to roll in from all directions, resonating oddly off the snow-covered ground. He thought his fever must be amplifying the sound, but maybe it really was that loud. It grew, echoed off the Blue Ridge, and the echoes made echoes until it was a grand cacophony of noise rumbling from one side of the great valley to the other.

He pumped the ever-closer ways as if the noise were a swing which he kept filling with energy. Random gusts blew from all sides as the local vortices of collapsed air coalesced or reinforced each other.

There were just so many ways here. He felt as if he were trying to disassemble the girders from a skyscraper by hand, bolt by bolt. It took forever. He made a point of locating every last little way that Cloudie had ever made. He swept up a few older ways in the process, from before Madog's time.

It was full dark, maybe an hour later, before he finally reached the inner few miles. These were dense with ways, and they included the great prize, the way from the old world that had first brought Madog here.

George circled around it popping the small ways like balloons, and then released it. It was wide and took a moment to fully collapse, folding like a blimp before losing its integrity. Being a traveling way, its passage wasn't particularly long, and George was disappointed he couldn't get a great boom from it. He thought it deserved better.

He smiled inwardly, the deer head expressionless, and admired the evening for a moment. It was likely his last. Then he took a breath and finished the rest of the ways—the ones in Madog's buildings, in his dungeon, in his nearby villages—leaving nothing but the old garden untouched.

He tilted his head up, with the great crown of antlers, and listened to the last echoes rumbling to a close, and waited.

c——ɔ

Rhodri stepped outside the conservatory and stood on the terrace facing west as the sun sank over the Blue Ridge. Seething Magma joined him.

The first roll of thunder was loud and long, and Rhodri thought it had to be the barrier way.

One knock.

Of course, he thought, she was watching it happen through George.

"It's started, then?"

One knock.

He called the others out, and they stood in the snow together and listened to the rumbles that made it over the mountain, wondering how loud it must be on the other side.

They spoke little.

After about an hour, silence returned to the woods around the manor. Then, abruptly, Mag vanished. Ceridwen started forward and Rhodri grabbed her. "No, there's a way here." He claimed it and closed it, lest Madog do it first.

c——ɔ

Maëlys stepped out into the ruined stableyard with Benitoe so that she wouldn't have to shout over the noise of the diners in the inn. He told her about the posters he had asked Lleision's guard to distribute to their posts around Edgewood, where they were helping to round up the newly awakened.

They were interrupted by the first boom from the west over the mountain. As the thunder and the rumbles continued, the door to the inn opened, and diners began to pour out, drinks in hand, to listen. Eventually several dozen people stood in the snow in wonder.

Benitoe turned to Maëlys. "Auntie, this must be a fight against Madog. I bet it's George."

He ran for his pony, sheltered in the collapsed stable, and took off at a gallop for the manor.

❧

George's peaceful evening ended when Madog arrived. He posted guards outside the garden walls and called Cloudie to him, mentally leashing her there.

He contemplated the figure of Cernunnos seated on the bench, staring back expressionlessly.

"Centuries of work," he hissed. He was livid with fury. "I promise you, you will be sorry."

George watched with Cernunnos's expressionless face.

Madog casually claimed all the unclaimed ways in the old garden.

Rhys was right, George thought. He's been doing this a long time. With one more effort, he collapsed all the ways in the garden, but he did it in a sequence, ending with the ones furthest from where he was sitting, hoping to hide Rhys and Maelgwn for a few moments more by directing Madog's gaze away from him. It worked, he turned his head.

With Cernunnos's help, George reached out to claim Seething Magma and she roared out of a way at his feet, facing Madog and sheltering George with her body.

George's fever was kicking in again. He killed Mag's way lest Madog try to use it, and then tried to stand with one leg and fell. Rhys grabbed him, threw his right arm over his shoulder, and forced him to hop on one leg, trying to back up while keeping Mag as a shield.

George heard him shout, "Get us out of here," and Mag opened a way for them. Maelgwn tried to support him from the other side and they tumbled together out of the garden and into the snow, somewhere else. George hit the ground with a cry and faded out.

❧

Rhys was horrified to realize the way had a very brief passage and they were still fully exposed to any efforts of Madog to kill George.

He knelt by George in the snow. "Wake up, you've got to kill this way." He shook him and got no response. He felt his forehead—he was burning up.

"Lord Cernunnos, please. We have to kill it."

The horned man manifested, and this time there was no trace of George to be seen in him. He killed the way and withdrew again.

Rhys watched the scene on the other side vanish and caught a glimpse of Madog bloody and falling but he couldn't see exactly what happened.

Maelgwn knelt beside him and shook George, trying to wake him. "Foster-father, wake up, please."

George mumbled, "No, you can't have him." He started waving his arms about feebly, alarming Rhys who recognized this fever as worse than before. Where were they? They had to find shelter.

He saw lights in the distance coming towards them. All he could hope was that they'd gotten out of Madog's domains, because they couldn't run any further now.

CHAPTER 29

Rhodri called to the people on the terrace. "There's a new way, out where the other two were." He pointed west. They took off on foot and passed a guard's post, a perimeter Lleision had established for a little extra defense. Gwyn and Edern grabbed lit torches from it as they went by.

Rhodri tried to catch up with them but they were faster. He swore under his breath. He'd just have to lead from behind, tell them if they started going in the wrong direction. To his left Ceridwen was keeping up well, her long woolen skirts hoisted in each hand to lift them above the snow. A mounted guard cantered up on their left and Ceridwen shouted, but he didn't hear her. She whirled in the snow, dropped her skirts, and with a gesture stopped both horse and rider abruptly. That got his attention. "Bring a stretcher," she cried.

"Yes, my lady." He wheeled and turned back.

The way was unclaimed and Rhodri feared Madog might use it. He tried to claim it, but it was slippery somehow, he couldn't grasp it. It winked out. By then they were close enough that Rhodri was able to point Gwyn and Edern directly to where it had been.

They stopped, standing over bodies in the snow and holding up their torches. Rhodri finally caught up to them, breathing hard. Rhys stood up, filthy and haggard, but otherwise in reasonable shape. A feral, black-haired boy kneeling in the snow must be the wolf cub, but the mess lying next to him, talking deliriously and twitching in the snow, could that be George?

Ceridwen dropped to her knees in her skirts and took charge of George on the ground. When Eluned arrived, she oversaw the stretcher and commandeered the torches for light. With the help of more of the guards, arriving on the scene, they scraped George up out of the snow and bundled him onto the stretcher, bearing him off to the infirmary as quickly as they could. Angharad followed behind them.

As Rhodri watched, Rhys restrained the boy from going with them by main force. He walked him over to Gwyn. "Sir, this is my foster-brother, Maelgwn. He rescued both of us."

He turned to Maelgwn. "This is my foster-father, Gwyn ap Nudd, Prince of Annwn."

Maelgwn's eyes widened and he managed a creditable bow, but Rhodri could see he was dying to go. He looked at him more closely and realized he might be another way-finder. That would explain why he was Cloudie's companion.

"Sorry, my lord," Maelgwn said, "but I have to go." He ducked Rhys's hand and ran off to follow after George.

Rhodri thought, just a few days and he already sounds like George.

Rhys was wearing what must be George's coat, much too big for him, and carrying his pack. He looked exhilarated to be back. Edern couldn't speak, and Rhodri noted how Gwyn gave him time to recover.

"I am more pleased than I can say to see you back safe," Gwyn said.

Rhys nodded, but then he walked over and hugged his grandfather. Still speechless, Edern wrapped him in his arms and rocked him for a moment. He pulled back and looked at his grandson, tears on his face. "I feared you were lost like your parents."

"I know. I'm so sorry I was careless and made you worry like that."

Rhian walked slowly out of the darkness where she'd been standing and into the ring of torchlight. "Don't you ever, ever do that again," she said, and punched his arm. Then she hugged him.

"I'm sorry, sister," he said down to the top of her head. "I thought of you often while I was there."

Gwyn gathered them up. "Is the way closed, Rhodri?"

"Yes, sir, but not by me. It's gone."

"Then let's get you cleaned up, Rhys, and find out how my great-grandson is doing. And your new relative."

"He's really George's foster-son. It's a long story."

"Yes, I imagine it is."

⌁

Angharad stood several feet off and kept out of the way while Ceridwen and Eluned quickly and efficiently stripped George, cutting the clothing off of him, and started to clean him and remove the bandages. The room was ablaze with the light of several oil lamps on the wall, and assistants brought more light closer as needed. Two fireplaces kept it warm.

He'd been placed on his right side. When they cut the knee bandage off and got a good look, they froze. Eluned put her hands on it and on the skin above and below and looked at Ceridwen, who was biting her lip. George shivered in the warm room, semi-conscious.

"Let's get the fever down, anyway, and he needs water. We can clean this, some, but it may not make any difference now. Why put him through it?" Ceridwen said. She looked at the dark traces ascending George's thigh, and patted him on the hip in an absent gesture of comfort as she moved up him to cut the chest bandages off and look at the burns on his back.

"Ugly and painful but not urgent," Eluned said, and Ceridwen nodded.

"Are you her?" a young voice asked.

Angharad looked down. A dirty boy of about twelve had come in unnoticed and stood at her shoulder. It had to be Mag's wolf cub.

"Who would I be?" she asked, quietly.

"His wife." He said it tentatively, preparing to be defensive.

"Yes. I'm Angharad. What's your name?"

"Maelgwn." He hesitated for a moment. "He said I was his foster-son."

"Why, then, and so you are," she said, calmly. This boy needed mothering but she knew better than to offer it directly.

He looked at her. "What do you think about it?"

"I think George has excellent taste, and I think we should get to know each other better. Would you like to stand here with me while Ceridwen and Eluned finish cleaning him up?"

Maelgwn said, "He thought he was going to die." He didn't look at her.

"I won't let him," she said fiercely, "Not without a fight."

"Good." He stood there and kept vigil with her.

⌒～⌒

After several minutes of suspense, Ceridwen came over to Angharad. She looked at Maelgwn, but Angharad put an arm over his shoulder and said, "He can listen to anything you have to tell me. This is our foster-son, Maelgwn."

Ceridwen nodded.

"It's bad news, I think you knew that. The leg's gone bad and it's too advanced. We can't save it and I think it's too late to try and remove it. I'm sorry."

Angharad swallowed hard. "You have an idea, I can tell."

"I do, but it's not very likely to succeed. You can watch, but don't disturb us. We're going to try and reduce the fever and bring him around first, so you may be able to talk with him."

Eluned had gotten a febrifuge infusion into George and covered him with a blanket. Angharad and Maelgwn pulled up chairs to sit next to him so that he wouldn't have to lift his head. The eye wounds were exposed and unbandaged, but Angharad ignored them.

"Welcome back, love," Angharad said, and she took his hand.

"I'm here, too, foster-father," Maelgwn said.

George smiled to hear their voices. "I'm so sorry, sweetheart," he whispered. "Forgive me?"

"I'm not done with you yet, husband, don't you believe it."

"What do you think of my Christmas present?" He nodded in Maelgwn's direction. "You know, he rescued us."

"A son any mother would be proud of. I'll be glad of him, if he'll have me. But he needs a father." She stood up and placed his open hand on her belly. "So does this one."

"Then that was true, what Mag showed me?"

"I'll never lie to you," Angharad said.

"Well, foster-son, looks like you'll have a young brother or sister to protect. Do me proud."

"I will, sir," Maelgwn said.

❧

George heard Angharad and Maelgwn push their chairs back, and Ceridwen faced him in their place.

"Now, George, I'm planning to have a talk with Cernunnos. Try not to interrupt. We're going to have to seat you upright so he has enough space, but I'll give you something that should dull the pain of moving you again. Do you understand?"

"Good luck," he said. "I think I've exhausted his list of favors."

She lifted his head and gave him something to drink. In a few moments, he recognized the blissful feel of an opiate. It dulled the edge of the pain as several hands sat him upright and lifted him to a chair, stretching out the left leg straight in front of him. The pain of moving the leg was given a bit of distance by the drug. They draped a cloth across his lap for modesty.

He felt someone stretch a rope across his bare chest and flailed his arms at it. He cried out, his speech blurred, "No, don't!"

Maelgwn shouted, "Don't tie him to a chair, my lady, don't."

The hands hesitated then took the rope away, and he breathed again. "Alright," Ceridwen's voice said, "Stay as upright as you can, George."

Ceridwen moved to his front, standing clear of his leg. "My lord Cernunnos, I would speak with you."

George felt her power and tried to invoke Cernunnos for her. Cernunnos rushed up from the depths and George stepped aside instead of sharing his space.

He bent under the the weight of the antlered head and concentrated on holding it up. He watched out of Cernunnos's eyes.

Cernunnos shifted to the horned man so that he could speak. "Yes, my daughter?" he said in his deep bass voice, so much lower than George's baritone.

"I'm no daughter of yours, beast-master," she replied, tartly. "You have my respect but I serve Senua.

"What is it you want, daughter of Senua?"

George, standing apart, caught a glimpse of the great force of nature that was Cernunnos, chaos and will, balanced, and a merciless search for justice, to maintain that balance.

Ceridwen said, "This man has served you well. Would you see him broken and discarded like a worn out rug?"

"All creatures die."

"Is this your justice, lord?" she said.

George heard the outer door open, and through the horned man's eyes he saw Seething Magma and Granite Cloud come in together, followed by Gwyn. Cloudie went to stand by Maelgwn, and Mag joined Ceridwen, who moved aside to make room for her.

He heard Gwyn murmur to Ceridwen before retreating to stand with Angharad, "Sorry, she insisted."

This is wrong, great one.

George marveled to hear her accurately, the way she must sound to her own kind and to Cernunnos.

You should heal him and let him serve again. Where do you think to find another such?

Yet he enslaved you, Cernunnos thought to her.

We agreed upon it together, for the sake of my child and the death of the abomination Madog. Which you wanted.

The horned man looked at her. His thoughts were opaque to George. Then he spoke out loud. "Huntsman. Given one request, what would it be?"

George surfaced and said in his own voice, sleepy from the drugs, "Let me release Mag."

"She'll be free in any case, when you die. Don't waste the gift."

George said. "That's what I want. I promised."

There was silence for the space of several moments.

"So be it," said the horned man. He withdrew back into the depths, and George took his place. He felt a boiling and bubbling in his knee and gasped, despite the drugs. He could feel a tugging at the skin and realized Ceridwen must have sliced it open to allow for drainage. He was grateful he couldn't see it, he could smell it all too well. Liquid dripped off the injury, and he felt large bits which he took for bone and dead matter being expelled. His lower leg tingled and pulsed in a welcome if painful return to feeling. He could dimly perceive something scrubbing at the impurities in his blood and drying his mouth.

"Water," he croaked.

He drank glass after glass of it, held to his mouth. His own arms were occupied trying to hold him to his chair. Eventually the last of the damaged material was expunged from the gash in his knee, and he felt the ends of the joints, and then the patella coming more and more to match the other leg. Bone, cartilage, tendons, blood vessels, nerves, and muscle were all involved, with the most disconcerting sensations.

Someone stitched the cut, and bandaged the knee, and the whole leg from heel to hip was immobilized.

"Still with us, George?" Ceridwen asked.

He nodded weakly, panting.

"Good. Lean forward now, we need to reach your back."

He bent at the waist and someone knelt in front of him to help support his shoulders against the work going on behind him.

The opiates were beginning to wear off with the cleansing of his blood and he could feel them cutting away the dead flesh, but they suddenly stopped and he heard them back away. He felt the burns age, all at once, as if they were decades-old wounds. Ceridwen put her hand on his back, and it was tender and scarred, but it was far from the damage of a few minutes ago.

"Let's leave this alone for now," she said uncertainly.

They leaned him back in the chair carefully and for the first time in a while he put some weight against his back. Not too bad. He smiled.

What were they standing around waiting for, he wondered. Ah, his eyes. Didn't look like Cernunnos was prepared to go that far. Well, he thought, can't have everything. He'd think about it later, he was very tired.

"Mag," he called. "Come here, please." He heard the slur in his speech.

He felt a pseudopod take his hand and turn it upright. It dropped a small object into his hand, and he realized this was the toy hat for Madog, crushed. He closed his fist around it. Good.

"Did you do what I suggested?" he asked Mag.

Yes. Very satisfying.

He could still hear her clearly, a legacy from her conversation with Cernunnos.

"Thank you, my lady." He released his claim on her.

Thank you for my child.

Cloudie came up and held his other hand. *Thanks for bringing my mother.*

With a wincing pain, George doubled up again and matter poured from his eyes to drip upon the floor. Hands returned to hold his head, pulling his own hands aside, out of the way. Hot wet cloths soaked the last of it out, and then he felt his eyes regrowing from the inside out until they pressed lightly against the cloths. Someone lifted his head and gently washed his face, and he blinked several times. Couldn't see much, but at least he saw light.

Someone poured another glass of water down him. It had a peculiar taste. "Go to sleep George, you'll be fine." It took little persuading. He was out before they lifted him from the chair.

⌀〜〜⌀

Angharad sat by George's bed. He was sleeping restlessly. She felt his forehead, warm to the touch but not burning hot like before. Eluned had warned her there would be residual fever, possibly for days.

His face twitched as he wandered in some nightmare. She opened the package she'd asked for from Idris and removed an orange. Gwyn's human agent, Mariah Catlett, had given the messenger what she had in her refrigerator at Angharad's relayed request. George had courted her with oranges and Angharad thought he'd associate the scent with better times. She scratched the peel with a nail to release the volatile elements and held it under his nose.

George breathed it in once, twice, and sighed, his face visibly relaxing. Until next time, she thought.

He looks so strange with this beard growing. She wasn't sure what she thought of it. It was starting to hide his sunken cheeks.

Maelgwn had his own pallet in the room, next to hers, but he had trouble sleeping. Now he came up to stand by her chair. He'd been scrubbed raw, and someone had given him clothes in the right size. She ran her fingers through his clean hair and thought, I need to give you a haircut.

"How is he?" he whispered.

"He's doing fine," she said. "Maelgwn, do you know when he last ate?"

"He wouldn't touch any food after we got him, said the fever wouldn't let him. Last time I saw him eat was just before we tried for Rhys the first time. That's..." he paused and counted back on his fingers, "five days ago. Maybe Madog fed him."

Unlikely, Angharad thought.

"Lie down and try to get some sleep," she said. "It's late."

She watched him climb back into his blankets and turned out the lights. She dozed in her chair.

Sometime in the dark of the night, George cried out. Angharad reached for a lighter and lit the lamp on the table beside his bed. He stared at her wildly. "I couldn't see." His new eyes, in the lamplight, were a dark green with flecks of gold now, subtly different from the lighter green she remembered.

"I'm sorry, dear, I turned the lamp out. I won't do that again," she said. "Go back to sleep."

He looked at her, gradually settling down, and a sheepish expression crossed his face. "Sorry to be so twitchy."

He reached for her hand with one of his and brought it up to his nose. "Mmm... Oranges. Where did you get them?"

"I have my methods," she said.

271

He smiled at her and held her hand loosely, never taking his eyes off her face.

She stroked his bearded cheek, and gradually he fell asleep again and released her.

Maelgwn waited until his breathing was regular, then spoke out of the darkness where he lay.

"Do you know why he couldn't bear the rope to tie him down?"

"No. Will you tell me?" she asked quietly.

He told her about the iron chair and the torture George endured in it, strapped to it by the arms, chest, and legs.

She couldn't speak for a moment after he finished, then she said, "Thank you, foster-son, for getting him away."

He choked. "If I hadn't threatened Madog with Cloudie's mom, it might not have been so bad."

She sat down beside him on his pallet and pulled him against her, wrapped in his own blanket. He wept in that safe cocoon while she crooned to him quietly. Then he pushed back and wiped his eyes, looking anywhere but at her.

She patted his shoulder to spare his embarrassment and went back to her chair. George was lost in another nightmare.

CHAPTER 30

Rhys felt much improved for a bath, a couple of meals and a good night's sleep. There seemed to be no fear of counterattack so, since Angharad had Maelgwn in tow and George was... occupied, by tacit agreement everyone had decided to postpone business until morning.

After Gwyn's update on George, they'd left him and Maelgwn to Angharad and the healers overnight. Rhys was planning to go see him as soon as this first meeting was over.

Benitoe was there, at Rhys's request. He'd appeared last night on ponyback and joined the tail end of the mad scramble to the returned travelers. He'd just missed seeing them bear George off on his stretcher but stayed to give Rhys a warm welcome back, once his grandfather had finally released him.

Rhys took his accustomed spot, trying not to let his foster-father's presence fluster him, and called the council to order.

"There will be a second session this afternoon to discuss policy regarding our neighbors to the west, but for now I'd like to keep this fairly short and local. First, what do the healers say about George?" He looked to Ceridwen and Eluned.

"We expect him to recover fully, in time." That brought smiles and some surprise around the table. "Cernunnos was persuaded that justice was better served by a healing."

"Excellent news. And unexpected." Rhys pulled the broad smile off his face and returned to business. "The next item is to report what intelligence I was able to gather while I was captive."

He turned to his Edern. "Grandfather, I am sorry to tell you that Madog convinced me that my parents, and all those who traveled with them, are certainly dead. Madog had Cloudie build a trap way like the one here, but the other end wasn't anchored properly, it was in the air. They fell to unwitnessed deaths and we are never likely to recover their bodies. I don't think even he knew where they were."

All hung their heads at the sad confirmation.

Rhodri said, "Don't tell Mag, it wasn't really Cloudie's fault."

Rhys continued, "George knows more than I do about Madog's original plans and what he's done to his poor people. He should tell that part when he can"

He looked to Gwyn. "I understand you already know about his intent to take Annwn by force. You should also know that he had Scilti with him." Rhian looked sharply at him. "Scilti did most of Madog's dirty work on me, and I expect George will confirm the same for himself. He is very, very dangerous, and now he has no master. He would not have fallen in that final confrontation with Mag, because he wouldn't have been able to stand where Madog was. That's a long story in its own right, and we should save it for George, it's not relevant for planning. Just know that he's out there.

"One last thing. We never saw your sister Creiddylad while we were there. She's unaccounted for."

"No sister of mine," Gwyn said quietly, with steel in his soft voice.

Rhys rubbed his hands together. "Now, tell me all about this awakening that's been happening since George destroyed the barrier. It's the most wonderful news."

⌒‿⌒

"Someone's asking for you, mistress."

Maëlys looked around from her discussion with the two cooks about the day's menu. "I'll be right out," she called.

She wiped her hands on her apron and dodged the dishes coming back with the serving boys, ceding them the passage through the doorway since the plates were breakable and she wasn't, at least not so easily. She expected to see the man the carpenter said he would send, to start putting in piping for both baths and laundry.

She looked expectantly at the main door to the inn. This was a lutin, not a fae, and one she didn't recognize. His clothing was ragged and he was worn and faded like his clothes. He held a piece of paper in his hand, and stared at her. Then he smiled, a crooked smile that stopped her heart.

"Luhedoc?"

She ran to him and seized him, in front of all these people, both her workers and her guests. Let them look, she thought.

He grabbed her face in his two hands and stared as if he would eat it. "I don't understand, you're no older."

"What does it matter what I look like, you great fool?" That set him to laughing and he sounded like her husband again. The room exploded into laughter and applause with him, and she blushed.

"Alright, come with me." She pulled him into the side room, still a shambles. "Where have you been? How did you find me?"

"This was posted in the place where the manor guards were handing out food and taking names."

He showed her a notice that said the lutin Luhedoc could find his wife Maëlys at the Golden Cockerel in Edgewood Village. It included a description.

"I walked all night," he said, simply. "I thought you might vanish." He looked at her greedily. "I thought I'd never see you again."

"Benitoe said he sent something to all the guard posts. He'll be so happy it worked."

"Who's Benitoe?"

Maëlys said, "He's my new sister-son, and yours. He looked after me. It's a long story."

"Are you working here?" he said, listening to the bustle in the next room. "Won't you be missed?"

She laughed at him, this time. "It's mine, husband. I'm the new mistress of the inn." Her smile faltered. "Unless you don't want to stay, after your troubles?"

He looked around the room, where much work was needed but the structure was sound. He beamed at her. "Why, you'll be needing an hostler, then, won't you?"

He sobered, "How long has it been, my sweetling?"

"Eighteen long, long years," she said, wearily.

"They passed in a fog for me." He looked at her shyly. "Will you take a worn out fellow back?" he said. "There's no one else?"

"There never has been, you old fool. Come here."

❦

George's dreams turned dark. Madog's words still echoed like a stain that couldn't be removed. Fawns, deer children from Angharad, death in childbirth, hunting his children with hounds.

He woke with a start in the morning light to find Angharad shaking him gently.

275

"Looked like you needed some outside help with that dream," she said. "What was it? You said something about... fawns?"

Her skirt had a protective cloth over it and her lap was full of wood shavings. He could smell the new-cut wood, a clean scent. She put her knife and a small object down on the table next to his bed, and Maelgwn came up behind her chair and looked over her shoulder.

George mumbled that it was just a dream. Maelgwn said, "No it's not, you had that one before."

Angharad regarded him insistently.

He stammered through an explanation, avoiding her eyes. "It was just a taunt Madog made, about using me for breeding, and suggesting I would sire, um, deer, like Cernunnos. It made me think of our child-to-be, of its birth, and your death. Madog put an image in my head of hunting it with the hounds when it was grown."

She was silent and he was afraid to look at her. He was embarrassed, but the horror of it was also fresh in his mind.

He dreaded her response. What if he'd made her fearful about the coming birth?

"George Talbot Traherne," she said distinctly, standing up and brushing the shavings off her skirt. "You look at me."

He obeyed.

Her voice began to rise. "Fawns. You wooden-head. It's ridiculous you are to fear such a thing. You know that was malice not foresight."

He blinked. This wasn't what he'd expected. He watched, riveted, as her temper got the better of her. He'd never seen it happen before.

"And I'll tell you another thing." Behind her, Maelgwn's mouth hung open as he backed up. "If something like that should ever happen, that I bore fawns to you, why they'd be the best fawns in the world and we would cherish them like the wonders they were."

Her voice rang in the room. "Do you hear me?"

He marveled that she hadn't stamped her foot yet. He said, meekly, "Yes, ma'am."

She swept out of the room, muttering under her breath. She left a stunned silence behind her.

Maelgwn grinned at George.

"She's had a hard night, she's just tired," George told him.

Maelgwn's grin broadened.

George started to chuckle, it was irresistible. Soon they were both laughing uncontrollably.

Rhodri stuck his head in the door and raised an eyebrow at them, but George just waved a hand feebly and wheezed, winding down with a hiccup or two.

"I came by to talk to Maelgwn for a moment first, to see about way-training for him." He looked at George. "And to welcome you back, big fellow. You're looking much improved."

"Feeling it, too," he said. "What was it like over here, when the barrier went down?"

Rhodri's eyes shone. "I can't do it justice. It was like the world started over. A film you couldn't see just vanished. And if we newcomers felt that way, imagine what the people who've been here all that time, hundreds of years, felt like."

He paused. "You know, we heard the ways collapsing over the mountain. We stood and listened for an hour. I've been told that there were people all over Edgewood gathered outside, listening to the thunder."

"It seems like a long time ago," George said.

"Only yesterday," Rhodri said.

The door swung open again, and Rhys came in, looking thin but vibrant, humming with energy. "Hey," George said, "What's happened to you?"

"I don't know. I just woke up delighted to be clean again. Maybe I needed to lose a few pounds," he said with a grin. "I expect it won't last, by afternoon I'll be dragging, but I'm enjoying it now."

He looked over at Maelgwn. "Foster-brother, I've come to take you on a tour of the manor."

"Hey," Rhodri said, "I was here first."

Maelgwn was bewildered at the attention. George said to him, "Think of them all as a pack of older brothers. You've got a lot of them, now. You can choose which you'd rather do."

Maelgwn bowed to Rhodri and said, "Thank you, sir, but my foster-brother has a claim on me." He walked off with Rhys who grinned at Rhodri in triumph.

"How do you do it, George? A few days in your company and he already sounds like you."

"Does he?"

"He does." Rhodri took Angharad's vacated chair. "Now, since you're awake, tell me all about the ways over the mountain. Tell me what you found."

⌇

Gwyn looked in before opening the door all the way. George waved him in from his bed, interrupting the conversation with Rhodri.

"I saw Angharad outside just now..." he said. "What happened?"

"She scolded me, and rightly," George said, laughing. "I imagine she's a bit embarrassed about losing her temper."

"You must have been done something very bad," Gwyn said, solemnly. "It doesn't happen often."

"Better get used to it. I was an idiot, and I don't expect that to change anytime soon. I'm sure to set her off again."

Gwyn smiled down fondly at him. "It's good to see you so much better. I was there last night, for the healing. I can hardly believe the difference."

"Yes, I remember."

Gwyn brought another seat up to join Rhodri. "Seething Magma must have returned and gone straight to the conservatory. I think she couldn't find you."

"Cernunnos had me, it must have confused her."

"She picked up that dog collar she used for your symbol and thrust it in everyone's face, looking for you. When she reached me, I felt she had every right to come."

"It was the best thing to do. It's what convinced Cernunnos to keep me around," George said.

"No, you're wrong," Gwyn said. "You did that. You executed justice for Seething Magma, and he judged you worthy."

George was taken aback by that interpretation. He'd have to think about it, later.

A thought struck him. "Rhodri, what about the way Mag made coming back with Cloudie? You've claimed it, haven't you?"

Rhodri leaped to his feat, chagrined. "In all the excitement, I forgot. Fixing that now." He ran out of the room.

Gwyn asked, "What are you worried about?"

"Mag makes open, unclaimed ways. Anyone can pass through them until they're claimed."

"You're thinking about refugees from across the mountain?"

"I'd like to know where Scilti is," George said, darkly.

"Hmm," Gwyn said. There was silence for a moment. "I have a question, if you're up to it."

"Feel free."

"Just how did Seething Magma kill Madog? Last night you asked her if she took your suggestion."

George smiled fiercely. "We lured him into an old bare garden with a wall around it. He had to come alone because it contained hundreds of ways no one else could see. Then we killed those ways. That left him no way to escape quickly, though he could dodge around. You understand?"

Gwyn nodded.

"Mag didn't think she could catch him, when we worked on the plan. I suggested she open a way through him, a non-traveling one."

Gwyn's eyes widened.

"She's really good at that, of course. Quick, precise. Deadly, too, I expect." George laughed coldly. "That's the only way left in Madog's domain, now. The one that killed him. Other than the one Mag used to leave. Too bad it was so damn quick."

Gwyn shuddered. "How... appropriate."

George looked at him. "That's one thing I'm not losing any sleep over. It was long overdue."

Gwyn nodded.

"I need to tell you some of the things I learned over there," George said. He talked for a few minutes about Madog breeding captives, about killing way-finder families, about the general state of what he'd observed.

"What's going to happen to the place now? Can they be helped? Will it just collapse? You know, I killed their barrier way, too, so they're going to have their own version of the awakening, and eventually they'll realize they're no longer hemmed in."

"We haven't decided what to do yet, but we can't have chaos on our borders," Gwyn said. "Why weren't Madog and Creiddylad affected by the barrier ways? Or any of the people they brought to my court?"

"Scilti, too," George said. "I don't know. It has to be some sort of technology that Madog developed, but I don't know what. The barrier doesn't affect me either, but that's different. I know that Madog had the same limitations Rhodri does, he couldn't touch

Cloudie, for example. But he's had many hundreds of years to marry his way skills to his magic ones, and I'm not the right person to tell you what's possible. Remember those spell-sticks he gave to Cyledr Wyllt for the great hunt. He seems to have been very inventive."

A thought occurred to him. "You know, the barrier was much further away from Madog's court than our barrier was, here. Maybe there's a simpler explanation, maybe it's just a matter of distance."

Angharad pushed open the door and looked into the room. He was very happy to see her, and very tired. "Forgiven me yet?"

She stalked in and told him, mock-severely, "I'm considering it."

She looked at Gwyn who was already rising. "Out. He needs his rest. You can come back later."

Gwyn bowed to her, and turned to George. "Thank you, great-grandson. We'll talk again."

George barely heard him, his eyes on Angharad. She sat down and held his hand. "Anything you want?" she asked quietly.

"Got any more oranges?"

She picked one up and rubbed it on her hands. When she let him inhale the mingled scents, deeply and repeatedly, he could feel some of the tensions within fade away, comforting like a deep massage. He remembered nothing after the fourth deep breath.

CHAPTER 31

George was up again in the afternoon when Benitoe came by, sitting at a table with the remains of a meal.

"You just missed our late breakfast. Bacon and eggs and orange juice." He laughed at Benitoe's blank look. "May sound exotic to you, but it's a taste of my human life. They asked me what I wanted and I told them. Angharad provided the oranges."

He was even more pleased to be able to sit down. Eluned had submitted when he insisted on removing the splints immobilizing his knee. He had to exercise the leg to strengthen the new bone and muscle, he told her, and she agreed. A soft wrapping protected the joint from accidental knocks, and he felt liberated. The robe he wore was too small, but at least it covered him.

He looked down at Maelgwn who was slowly finishing his orange segments and smelling his hands. "His first orange," he said to Benitoe.

"I've never had one either," Benitoe said. "They smell good."

Maelgwn stood up and offered him a segment. The two of them were much the same size. "I've had plenty, sir, please take one."

Benitoe thanked him and tried to bite it in half, cautiously, then blinked as it sprayed him with juice.

George laughed and gave him a cloth to wipe his face. "Well, what do you think of it?"

"Juicy. Sticky, too."

Even Angharad laughed at that. "They're common enough in the human world, but hard to transport in ours."

She piled the dishes on one corner of the table and brought out a cloth, a comb, and a pair of scissors.

"Sorry, Benitoe," she said, as she stood behind George, "but haircuts are next on the agenda. You can talk at the same time, if you don't mind."

George said, "I hear the lutins are found. I want to hear all about it." He listened as Benitoe recounted some of the story. As Benitoe talked, George tried to puzzle out what was different about his whipper-in since he'd last seen him. He'd always been, what, solitary I guess is the word I'm looking for, despite his betrothal to Isolda. He doesn't look that way anymore.

He interrupted Benitoe's account. "What's happened to you? What's changed?"

Benitoe looked down a moment, then met George's eyes. "You remember Maëlys?" he said.

"Of course."

"She, well, she's adopted me into her clan. She's my real auntie, now." George wasn't sure exactly what that meant, but he could see its effect on him. That was it, he thought, he didn't look solitary any more.

"Like my foster-father adopted me," Maelgwn said, proudly.

"That's right." Benitoe smiled at him.

"Congratulations on your new family," Angharad said, as she trimmed George's hair.

"Maëlys has taken the inn in the village. She's restoring it while we look for her husband."

George blinked. "That's a big job."

"It is, but she seems to have it well in hand. I think she welcomes the challenge."

George heard Angharad's muttered, "I should think so," behind him and suppressed a smile.

"Well, I'll leave you some privacy and come back later," Benitoe said, heading for the door.

It opened in front of him and Rhian came in, tentatively, letting him out.

"Eluned said you were up…"

"Come on in. Maelgwn, this is Rhys's sister, Rhian. She's just a couple of years older than you, and she's the junior huntsman for Gwyn's hounds."

Maelgwn stood up from the table and bowed very politely. Then he looked at George. "Does that make her my foster-sister, like Rhys is my foster-brother?"

"I suppose that's up to her." He caught her eye and smoothed out her startled expression.

"Yes, Maelgwn, I'd like that. I've never had a younger brother before."

"I had one once, and a little sister, too." George hated to hear him speak of it and his muscles tensed, but Angharad's hand squeezing his shoulder stopped him from saying anything.

Rhian sat down at the bench along the table across from them and patted the spot next to her. "Will you tell me about them?"

Maelgwn began his story.

Maybe Angharad was right, he thought. These are his ghosts and he has to come to terms with them, not remember them only in their deaths.

Angharad finished his haircut and tousled his hair to release all the stray bits. He ran his fingers through it, pleased.

She turned to Maelgwn, who'd reached a pause. "What about you, young man?"

He looked at her, alarmed. His hair was tied back with a thong and had clearly been hacked off with a knife from time to time, blindly. He'd been washed, but it was still a mess, if a clean one. "I don't know. I just... It's been a long time."

"You can cultivate warrior braids, if you want, Some do. Or you can keep it short, as most of Gwyn's family do, and George, too."

"Your choice, foster-son," George said.

Maelgwn decided. "Like you, please."

Angharad nodded and pushed George from his seat, summoning Maelgwn in his place. George walked over to sit next to Rhian on the other side, slowly and carefully.

"It's so good to see you walking like that, cousin. Yesterday..."

"Yes, I know," he said. "That's past now." He didn't want to dwell on the sorry sight he must have made.

"I was surprised to see you here," he said.

"Angharad came on Tuesday, and Gwyn and I joined her later the same day."

Angharad looked at him over Maelgwn's shoulder with an unreadable expression.

Oh, no, he thought, working it out. That was the first day in the iron chair. Did she feel some of that? He must have looked stricken, because Angharad said, "Never mind, dear, it was just an echo."

"I'm so sorry, love."

"Not your fault. And it brought us all here." She went back to her haircutting and closed the conversation.

Rhian had her hand over her mouth as if she'd given away a big secret. George patted her other hand on the bench. "Don't worry about it."

"Who's looking after the hounds," he asked, to change the subject.

"Brynach."

"All by himself?"

"Ives is helping," Rhian said. "I thought it was a good thing, it keeps him busy. And it's just within the palisade, Brynach can't really lose them."

"No, I approve, as long as it works for them. That was good thinking."

She relaxed again, pleased to have her judgment confirmed.

"There," Angharad said. "What do you think?"

They turned to look at Maelgwn while Angharad searched for a mirror. Rhian said, "Why, he looks like you now, huntsman, just a little… curlier."

Maelgwn brightened at that, and looked at himself in the mirror for a long time, clearly trying to reconcile himself to his new appearance. George wondered how long it had been since he'd seen his own face. All at once he yawned, and then did it again. A shiver ran through him.

"Alright, Rhian, time to say goodbye for a while," he heard Angharad say. "This man's going back to bed."

She was at his side then. "Alright, you, no arguing." He pulled his robe tighter around him and shivered some more. He stood up and she steadied him as he slowly walked back to his bed. He crawled under the covers, still wearing his robe, but Angharad stopped him before he could fully lie down and took it off of him. He shivered down under the blankets "I wish this would stop," he said.

"Soon, if you'll let it. Now go back to sleep."

Edern sat at the council table in the afternoon watching in deep satisfaction as Rhys took charge, still fired up with the euphoria of being free again. Too thin, too energetic, he thought, he'll never last much past dinner, but that was alright, that was to be expected. He seemed to have taken no permanent harm, and to have come back toughened somehow.

As Rhys ran down the list of items that needed discussion and decision, Edern watched him visibly not deferring to Gwyn, here in his own place. That was so like Gwyn as a younger man, Edern thought. Rhys takes more after him than he does after me, and isn't that often the way of foster-children, after all? That was fine, Rhys could use Gwyn's political insight and connections. He didn't doubt that his own character would manifest in him over time—he already liked the strong moral man he was becoming, like his father before him.

Gwyn asked Rhys, "Did you witness Madog's death?"

"I caught a glimpse, before the way was destroyed, but my view was blocked by Mag. There was a lot of blood, and Mag is here, but that's all I know."

"My lady," Gwyn said, turning to Seething Magma, on the periphery of the room, "My great-grandson told me he made a suggestion to you, and you followed it."

One knock.

Gwyn said, to the council, "She opened a way through Madog, a non-traveling way. As George pointed out, it's the only way left in Madog's domain."

That brought startled laughter and then they each rose and bowed to Mag, some applauding in approval. Granite Cloud at her side looked at her mother as if asking her to explain.

When everyone was seated again, Gwyn looked at Rhys who nodded his permission to take over.

"We have several items of strategy to discuss, and I asked Rhys to invite Cydifor and Benitoe to this session for a purpose. George and Angharad can't join us yet, but I'll speak separately to them. I'm sure we'll see them here soon.

"First, there is the matter of our guests, Seething Magma and her daughter Granite Cloud. We are very glad they've been reunited, and we thank them for the death of our mutual enemy. Edern and I would like to speak with your mother soon, my lady, and explore how we can assist each other. Will you be with us for long?"

Mag held out George's collar.

"You're waiting for George? To say good-bye?"

One knock.

"How will we reach you, after you leave?"

She dangled the collar again.

"Ah, George can reach you. All the way from Greenway Court?"

Two knocks. She pointed at the map and drew a line from Greenway Court to the base of the Blue Ridge in Edgewood.

"You'll make a way he can use to reach you easily."

One knock.

"Thank you, that will be fine."

Gwyn turned back to the council and looked around the table, not excluding Cydifor and Benitoe, seated a rank back. "Here in this room is everyone, with the exception of the huntsman's family, who knows that these rock-wights, our guests, are the creators of the ways. We cannot hide their existence—far too many people have seen them—but this knowledge must be kept quiet."

Benitoe spoke up, "But my lord, many of the travelers coming from Edgewood saw that Mag created a way from the river meadow here to the court."

"We will have to put it about that she revealed a way to George, not that she made it. We must keep this suppressed."

Edern spoke to the council. "The knowledge that the rock-wights are the way-creators is lost in the old world, if it was ever known, as the beings themselves have become scarce. We would put them all in danger from such as Madog. And it would spur an invasion of the new world to try and control the only known population, to use them as weapons. It would greatly disturb the peace we've enjoyed for many centuries. Do we want a horde of ambitious fae here, with their way-adepts and their armies?"

"My brother is correct," Gwyn said. "I do not say that this knowledge can be hidden forever, or even for long—that is not the nature of the world—but it needs thought and much preparation. I will discuss this with my grandfather, Beli Mawr, as soon as possible."

That caused a stir around the table. Beli Mawr was largely withdrawn from the world, and some already considered him halfway to some undefined place between fae and god.

"Do I have your oaths to follow me in this?" he asked, looking sternly at each of them.

"Aye, my lord."

"I so swear, my lord."

The verbal oaths came from every person in the room, down to Rhian, the youngest.

"Thank you. Now, there is one final matter—what shall we do about our neighbors over the mountain? We've cut off their head, but what next? I want your opinions."

Rhodri said, "They have no ways out, except for the one Mag made when leaving, and that's been claimed for Gwyn. They can't cross the Blue Ridge any more than we can, but their barrier way is gone and nothing prevents them from spreading in other directions. As George mentioned, they'll be undergoing their own version of the awakening we've had here."

Edern said, "George was of the opinion when he crossed over that the barrier along the Blue Ridge wasn't intentional, that it arises from the activities of the rock-wights within the ridge. He thought there would be natural gaps, therefore. I don't think we can assume it's an unbreachable boundary any longer."

"Our choices are stark," Rhys said. "We can leave them to rule themselves, with some new strong man rising to the top who may continue in enmity to us. Or we can seat one of our own there, with troops to support him, as our own strong man. Or we can help select one of their own and ally with him. All of these are uncertain and assume knowledge we don't have, and two of them need us to extend troops, supplies, and possibly a ruler."

"Did Madog have family, other than whatever arrangement he had with our one-time sister?" Edern asked.

Silence. Then, two knocks.

Seething Magma pointed at her daughter, then at the symbol for speech.

"Cloudie says…," Eluned translated quietly.

Mag walked over to the pile of unused symbols and found a black rock. She drew a black hat and put the black rock on it.

"She gave the toy hat to George," Gwyn said. "Is this the new symbol for Madog?"

One knock.

She put the black rock next to a generalized picture of a woman, then tapped the picture of a child.

"Madog made a child," Eluned said.

Mag dipped a pseudopod in ink and dropped a blot on the child.

"The child died."

Two knocks. Mag dropped the black rock on the blotted child.

"Madog killed the child?"

287

One knock.

"Did he have any other children?" Gwyn asked.

Mag dropped another ink blot on the drawing of the child, then another, and another, until the image was entirely black.

"He killed them all?" Eluned said, shaken.

One knock.

"He didn't want to raise rivals," Gwyn said.

"Does he have any living relatives that you know of, Mag?" Edern asked.

Two knocks.

Edern looked at his brother. "What about his family in the old world? What do we know about it?"

Ceridwen said, "We'd only started to look into that at the time of the great hunt, and then we put it aside for a while."

"We'll have to pick that up again, and find out for sure." Gwyn said. "But I think we can assume we can't just elevate a natural heir to that domain. So, should we expand and absorb it? That's a question of both means and security. If it were a trusted ally, that would be one thing, but how can we be secure with it as it is? I think we must try to take it over. But can we create an army sufficient to the task, and will there be resistance in the population?"

Silence around the table. "We can't leave it as it is for long. If we so intend, we must put our presence there quickly."

He turned back to Seething Magma. "My lady, if this is the course we must take, then our task of mutual alliance becomes more urgent. We would want to request ways into the heart of Madog's domain, and of course we would want to know what we might offer you in return."

Mag turned and pointed at the little pile of rocks that represented her mother.

"Yes, I understand. We would need to speak with Gravel."

Cydifor suggested, "George would be a good translator, my lord."

"Indeed," he said. "I think he'll be fit for it, soon."

"Thank you, my lady," Gwyn said to Mag. "We'll speak about this again before you go."

One knock.

Edern watched Rhys smoothly resume control of the meeting and wind it down. He stood up and walked over to his grandson for a private conversation.

"How are you holding up?" he asked.

"I'm beginning to think a nap before dinner would be a fine thing," Rhys admitted.

"And so I was going to advise, but you're beyond the age where I can send you to your room."

Rhys smiled at his grandfather, and the two of them strolled out together.

CHAPTER 32

Angharad stood up and stretched, then walked over to the window on Sunday morning. The snow had begun in the middle of the night and was still falling steadily, drifting down with no sign of stopping. Maelgwn was out in it, somewhere, working off some steam with Rhian.

She liked the boy's fierceness and his loyalty to George. She thought he had the makings of a good man. She put her hand over her belly, where another life was forming. Both of these children might outlive George by centuries, if he didn't have the long life.

Don't be greedy, she thought. George might have died already, if his friends hadn't helped get him back, if Ceridwen hadn't dared to stand up to Cernunnos, if Cernunnos hadn't been merciful. No, it wasn't mercy, she corrected herself. If George hadn't chosen Mag's release over his own life, Cernunnos would have discarded him in his cold search for justice and freed her that way.

George was still sleeping behind her. She'd made him get up and eat something in the early evening, but he'd been hard to rouse since then, rising twice to hobble away half-awake to relieve himself, but otherwise lying unmoving on his bed. All she could do was keep him warm and make him drink when she could, and wait.

When Eluned came around earlier, they talked about it. Eluned said the small pockets of infection that weren't cleansed by Cernunnos had to work their way out of his system, and his body was busy finding them and attacking them. That's what caused the intermittent fevers and shakes. The sleep was just his body's way of keeping him still in the process. That, and concentrating on the replenishment of the demands made upon it by the sudden healing.

They agreed to let him sleep as long as possible. There was no heat from his knee, which was the main thing, as long as the rest was improving.

Angharad went to the table near the bed from which she could keep an eye on him and returned to her work. She'd brought carving knives and small blocks of wood with her from Greenway

Court, and she was working her way through her daily quota of ornaments for George's tree. Several completed ones were already tucked away, waiting for paint. She kept a cloth nearby to throw over her work in case George woke up—she wanted to keep it a surprise.

Back behind her, the door opened cautiously and Maelgwn walked in, trying not to make any noise. His cheeks were glowing from the cold and the exercise.

"Did you enjoy yourself?" she asked, softly.

He nodded excitedly. "Rhian let me ride her horse a little bit. That was fun. I've never been on one before."

"One of the great pleasures of life," Angharad agreed, making a note to get him started with learning to ride in earnest, as soon as they returned home.

"Did he wake up yet?"

"Not this morning. He might sleep all day, it's the best thing for him."

Maelgwn surprised her by going to George and feeling his forehead expertly. He must have learned from Rhys, she thought. George didn't stir.

Maelgwn came back and looked at the block in Angharad's hand which was starting to take the form of a deer's head.

"Can you show me how to do that?"

"Did George tell you about his little tree?" He nodded. "Well, this is going to be an ornament on that tree in a few days. It's a surprise for him." She looked down at his somber face. "Would you like to make him one?"

His face lit up. "Do you think I could?"

"Why not? It should be about so big." She held her hands apart as if to cup a large orange. "What would you like it to be?"

"Anything?" he asked.

"Anything."

He walked over to the bench where George's spare clothes were folded and picked up his pocket watch. He brought it back to Angharad and pointed at the engraved dragon on the back. "I want to make a dragon. Is that too hard?"

"I'll show you how." She propped the watch up in front of them so they could refer to it, then she took a block of wood about three inches square and one inch thick. She quickly drew on a piece of paper a simplified profile of a dragon sitting compactly and squarely, to largely fill the space available. Maelgwn could roughly carve out the shape, she thought, at the very least, and maybe carve some muscle shapes and other surface decoration, if he has the knack.

He liked her drawing, so she showed him how to lay it over the wood block and make little marks through it to transfer the drawing to the wood, on both sides, and left him alone to do that himself. She returned to the detail work on her own carving, but kept a watch on his progress out of the corner of her eye.

He was quick to catch on to the transfer work, leaving a line of prick marks. When he held it up for her judgment, she nodded.

"Now take this larger knife here. It's for the rough work, where we take away the unnecessary material outside the drawing."

She showed him how to hold it and how to control it as he cut. He busied himself for quite a while whittling the block down to his marks, careful to leave just a little bit extra. She noticed his forethought and approved.

He looked over at the living deer head forming under her hands and sighed. "I'll never be able to do that."

"There's no need. I've been doing this a very long time, and if you want to learn I can teach you. But today, all we need is a simple blank in the right shape. When we get back, we'll paint it. Did you know that dragons come in all sorts of colors?"

He cheered up at that, and they chatted cozily as their little blades bit into the wood, a clean smell of shavings rising around them.

⁓

Benitoe ran his fingers through his hair and brushed off the residual snow that still clung to him before knocking on the door to the private dining room at the Golden Cockerel. He was about to meet Maëlys's husband for the first time, his new uncle, and he wanted to make a good impression.

At the response inside he opened the door and took a couple of steps in before stopping. An astonishing transformation had taken place. On Friday it had been a wreck, not yet repaired, with holes in the walls and a filthy floor. Less than two days later, it had been cleaned and repaired, the floor and walls scrubbed. It needed paint and polish, but otherwise it was almost respectable.

The fire yielded a cozy, welcoming warmth, and the table was decorated with evergreen boughs and candles that helped brighten the wan snowy light coming through the clean windows, their broken panes boarded up for now.

"What a change," he said to Maëlys, and she beamed with pride.

"I decided the laundry could wait one more day. I wanted to set this room in order for private feasts and ceremonies. It's not done yet, of course, but it'll do for now."

She turned and took her husband's hand to draw him forward. Benitoe recognized the walk of a fellow horseman. "This is Luhedoc, of course."

Benitoe bowed deeply. "I'm very pleased to meet you and to find you well."

"Welcome, nephew," Luhedoc said with a half-grin. "I believe this is yours?"

He handed Benitoe one of the posters Benitoe had caused to be placed everywhere that Lleision's guards had gone.

Benitoe noted that it had been folded carefully to fit in a pocket. "I couldn't be happier that you found it. Auntie has been so worried about you." He gave it back to him.

Luhedoc said, "When Maëlys told me of the adoption, I told her we should do it properly, that you missed the clan feast. We're going to make up for that now."

Maëlys opened the door, and some of her new staff came in, bearing platters of steaming food. "Nothing fancy," she said, "but plenty of it."

After a few minutes of filling their plates and catching up on events, Benitoe paused to tell them, "You know, I'll have to go back with the huntsman when he leaves, but I can come back regularly to see you both."

Luhedoc said, "I may see you first. Maëlys has told me how my original herd was folded into Iona's. I'm minded to go back and bargain with her for some foundation stock to bring to Edgewood, both horses and ponies." He looked Benitoe over. "Think you could help me bring them back here, through the ways?"

Benitoe approved the scheme, and they passed the afternoon trading stories and approving Maëlys's recipes, until the light started to fade. The snow continued to fall lightly.

❧

George stretched in bed. The raw new leg felt better and even the bruises from the beatings were reduced to background noise. His eyes popped open. "What time is it?"

"Late afternoon, sleepyhead," Angharad's voice came from behind him.

He turned over to look at her, and kept right on going, sitting up and swinging his legs over the edge. "I don't understand. And why is it still snowing?" he said, looking past her out the window.

"You've slept all day," she said.

"Really?" He stretched his arms out behind him. "I feel like I may never sleep again."

He reached for the robe over the foot of the bed and stood up to put it on. He stood there barefoot with his feet spread, tying the belt. Then without shifting position he lifted his arms to chest height and began twisting left to right, stretching the sides of his back. It felt wonderful.

He bent forward at the waist, trying to curl between his spread legs to stretch the length of his back. It was tight, but pain-free.

"Are you sure you want to do this?" Angharad asked.

"I feel well. I need the exercise."

She grabbed his spare pair of knee-breeches from the bench. "Put these on instead and let me get something for that back."

George pulled on the pants leaving them unfastened below the knee and shed the robe. All this time, Maelgwn had been staring at him silently. He winked at him, and the boy grinned. "Want to join me?"

Angharad protested, while she rubbed some ointment on his back.

He said to her, "He may be hurt someday. It's good for him to know how to handle it."

"So, listen," he told the boy. "I got my leg back, but it's brand new. The bones need to be worked and the muscles are weak as a kitten's. That's no good. Not only does it make me limp, but the effort of the rest of my body to compensate will twist it and make everything else hurt. You understand?"

Maelgwn nodded.

"So I have to strengthen it as fast as I can, and I have to use it as if it were normal as much as I can, to keep my posture straight."

"Have you got a mirror?" he asked Angharad.

She found two and held one for him. He looked at the reflection on his back, and then reached back and touched the part of the scars he could reach.

"My back, now. Scars can cripple you if you don't keep them supple and stretched, especially when they're new. Deep ones can make adhesions of flesh on the inside sometimes, like tying your skin together. The marks don't matter, but the lack of flexibility and reach, that matters."

Maelgwn nodded solemnly.

"So I must twist and stretch my back until it feels as good as before, or live with that weakness forever. And I have to start now."

Angharad said, tartly, "What he's not telling you is that recovering from a fever means you don't have any stamina. If he does too much of this, he's going to fall right over. But until them, being a man, he's going to try anyway."

Maelgwn grinned.

"So, sit here beside me on the edge of the bed," George said, ignoring her.

George went through a series of lower leg lifts, slowing both the up and down phases as much as possible. He broke a sweat after half a dozen of them, but it was a start. He waited a few seconds, then started again. He knew deep knee bends were out of the question for now, but he did a series of shallow squats to start building those muscles. He was immensely grateful to have a working knee at all, however weak, to climb stairs, to ride a horse, to sit down like a normal man. Strength would come.

Maelgwn beside him had all the suppleness of youth, and a fraction of his weight. Still, he would add strength training as he grew to maturity and learned to handle weapons. Didn't hurt to start him now.

George stood and began a series of focused back stretching exercises. Angharad stopped him partway through to lay him flat on the bed and massage his back, rubbing in more of her ointment. "No pain?" she asked, as she kneaded the deep muscles.

"It feels wonderful," he growled. "Don't ever stop."

She swatted him and let him up again, and he ran through the stretching set two more times before calling it quits.

His muscles trembled from the unaccustomed exertion, but his body felt more his own, like it belonged to him.

He needed to bathe. He rubbed his hand over his beard of several days. "Well?" he asked Angharad. "Beard or not?"

"Shave," she recommended.

"On one condition," he said. "Find us somewhere else to sleep tonight. I'm very, very tired of a sick room."

Dinner was well begun in Edgewood Manor's hall when Rhys at the high table was struck by a tableau at one of the entrances. George stood there, fully dressed, wearing the coat Rhys recognized as the one he'd borrowed for emergency clothing while they huddled in one of Cloudie's way passages. His clothes were clean, and he'd even managed to don his boots. He looked scrubbed and alive, if rather worn.

Maelgwn stood behind him with Angharad, looking apprehensive. Rhys thought this might be the boy's first time out in public, with so many people. George leaned over him, no doubt offering some encouragement.

They entered the hall, George with a cane moving slowly and carefully to accommodate his weak healed leg. Angharad and Maelgwn walked behind, letting him set the pace.

As he headed toward the high table, the people at the first long table he came to on the main floor looked up and began to whisper. Some of them were recently come from Greenway Court and beyond, and others were newly awakened, here at the manor to resume their old positions or to find new ones. George's destruction of the barrier way had freed them. As he passed and the word spread about who he was, the diners at that table rose and bowed to him. They stayed standing.

Rhys felt the hairs rise on the back of his neck. Gwyn, next to him, was motionless, hand frozen to his glass.

As George walked by the end of the next long table, the people seated there rose and bowed, as well. Silence spread through the hall as people stopped talking and only the noise of George's footsteps and the people standing up could be heard.

About halfway through the hall, he started up the stairs of the dais, still moving slowly. When he reached the top, the people at the far tables, which he hadn't reached, stood and joined the others. When they bowed, too, in silence, George flushed red with embarrassment and acknowledged them all with a jerky nod.

Rhys rose, and was joined by everyone at the high table. They made their own bow, even Gwyn and Edern. Rhys could see George's jaw muscles clenching as he held his face still and bowed back.

George had Maelgwn sit next to Rhys, and then he joined them, with Angharad, sitting down very carefully and looking down at his plate, overwhelmed.

Rhys leaned over and whispered to the astonished Maelgwn. "That's your foster-father they're honoring. Always remember this day."

CHAPTER 33

By Monday late in the day, George was getting restless.

Contrary to his expectations, he'd not only slept again the previous night, but had already taken two brief naps today. Seemed like he couldn't get enough. But in all other ways he was feeling better by the hour. He wanted to go home, but there was still unfinished business in Edgewood.

He'd spent much of the day, when he was awake, chatting with Mag in the conservatory. His ability to understand her clearly had lasted, and he provided clean translations of her responses to Eluned and Ceridwen's questions.

Now he had a question of his own for her. "It's clear there are many things for us to value from your people—your knowledge, your ability to make ways. But what do we have to offer you, besides our friendship?"

You are looking for something to trade?

Yes, I suppose so, he thought. It's one basis for a long and healthy relationship.

Remember the night you told me about how the earth is formed and how it changes?

Of course.

That is knowledge we would treasure.

George considered that. She meant true knowledge, not just the layman's overview that he'd provided. Geology would be needed, but also chemistry, physics, even biology. Perhaps astronomy. And yet, why not? They had plenty of time. The knowledge was available, in his human world.

Human evolution, if it came to it, would be a shock. We've only been around a blink of an eye, from her perspective. I bet the fae are no older, he thought. He'd have to ask Ceridwen.

"Think you could learn how to read?" he asked. He fetched a book and a piece of paper and started to show her some of the basics.

∽

Seething Magma didn't take long to understand the system of phonetic writing that George showed her, but translation was another matter. She heard thoughts directly, even when people spoke, so she needed to learn the spoken language without the thoughts in order to read, and that was going to take a little while. Once George understood the difficulty, they put it aside for another time.

Are you well, George asked her.

I am very pleased that you have survived and that Granite Cloud is back safe.

She felt his pleasure at her response, and then a bit of curiosity that amused her.

You want to know more about Madog's death?

He admitted it.

He didn't understand at first that I was claimed, that he couldn't take me himself. He was... disappointed.

George appreciated her humor.

He threatened to hurt Granite Cloud, to send her at me.

She reverted to pictures to describe what happened next, a series of moments. A picture of a way, small and focused like a laser, dissolving the clothing of his coat. The way expanding into a circle the width of his body. Madog's expression of disbelief, dying before the pain could reach him. Madog's lifeless shoulders and head collapsing onto his legs in a pool of blood. Granite Cloud's release and joy as she danced around her mother, tracking carelessly through the remains.

Satisfaction.

George heaved a sigh beside her. Well done, he said.

George woke with a start in his chair in a darkened corner of the room and realized in horror that a council session was already underway. He'd dozed off again, clearly, and they'd let him sleep. Hope I didn't snore.

Mag, don't let that happen, he thought.

You needed to sleep just then.

Perhaps, but it's humiliating.

Benitoe was asking about Madog's domain, would Gwyn try to intervene?

George sat up straighter to hear the response.

"I will set an interim government of some kind into place there within the week," Gwyn said. "Longer range plans will require more thought."

Rhodri spoke up, "About George's new foster-son, he'll need way-training. He's definitely going to be skilled."

George caught movement in a chair behind him in the dark and realized Maelgwn was there. *Keeping an eye on me?*

George spoke up, "It can wait until you're free again, Rhodri. Then we can ask him what he wants to do."

What time was it, anyway, he wondered. He saw Angharad smile at him from a seat in the lighted half of the room. *Must be after dinner, they're all too relaxed to be hungry. I must have dropped off for a while.*

Eluned said, "I would like to offer a formal commendation to Cydifor. His translations for Seething Magma have been very perceptive, better than anyone but the huntsman. He has greatly helped Ceridwen and me with our scholarship."

"Well done," Rhys said.

George was pleased to hear Cydifor so well thought of. *His venture here would be successful, after all.*

It's time for us to go. We only waited to say good-bye to you, friend.

George stood up. "Our guests are ready to leave," he told them.

They rose from the table and gathered in front of Seething Magma and Granite Cloud. Rhian helped Cadugan turn up the lights in the room.

Speak for us, friend.

"Mag asks me to speak for them," George said.

We are sorry you think of us as dragons, as monsters.

"She believes we see her as a dragon," he told them. "You're wrong, Mag. You weren't the dragon in the story at all."

He pulled out his pocket watch and showed her the engraving again. "Madog was the dragon, and Cloudie was the young maiden. You were St. George, come to the rescue."

Maelgwn followed along, fascinated.

The spear, maybe, or the horse.

George laughed out loud at the notion of riding a sentient creature her size.

We have a gift for you, something to remember us by.

Mag and Cloudie each extruded a pseudopod and pinched off the tip of it, dropping a piece of rock about the size of half a fist to the floor. George picked them up, and then Rhodri was brave enough to try touching one. There was no reaction, they were safe to handle.

"These are gifts, part of themselves," George said.

For you to recall how we taste.

She turned and George walked in front of her to open the outside doors. Gwyn followed them both out onto the terrace and bowed deeply.

"We will be contacting you through George about our next visit and about meeting your mother, Gravel. Our most heartfelt thanks for your help these last two weeks."

And our gratitude for our child.

"She thanks you for getting Cloudie back."

Bye-bye, Maelgwn. Thanks for being my friend.

George let that be private for the boy's ears only.

Maelgwn said, his voice thickening, "Travel safely, baby sister. Listen to your mother." He walked off to the edge of the terrace, out of the light, and George let him be.

With that, Seething Magma made a way, and the two of them entered it. After a few moments, George collapsed it behind them.

They walked back into the conservatory, a subdued group. The quarter of the room that was filled with tables, maps, toys, and scraps of paper looked empty and forlorn without the rock-wight. Cydifor walked around it, picking up all the symbols and papers Mag had used. Ceridwen and Eluned joined him, and George overheard Cydifor ask Eluned to take him on as a student.

George thought, alone in my head at last, with Mag gone. He felt Cernunnos stirring in the depths. Alright, be quiet and leave me my illusions, he amended.

Rhys came up to him in Mag's corner and gripped his arms with his own. George knew he was thinking of the long hours trapped in the way passage plotting destruction. Against all expectations, they had survived.

Cydifor walked over to Rhodri and murmured something.

"Really?" Rhodri said. "By all means, let's have it."

He turned to the rest of them. "Cydifor has a praise-ballad he'd like to perform, for this moment."

Rhys said, "Let it be so."

They sat themselves down in a small semicircle in front of the fire, and Cydifor stood off to the side, without any instrument, and began to sing.

George thought, it's a catchy tune, I'll give it that. Rhodri's already got some harmonies going for it. But it's preposterous. I'm not this ballad hero, it wasn't really like that. He looked at Rhys. I expect my face is just as red as his at this moment.

Maelgwn at his feet smiled proudly. I can't live up to that, he thought. He looked to his wife next to him for balance, and she gave him just the right raised eyebrow of skepticism. It was the perfect antidote, and he grinned at her.

He leaned down and whispered into her ear, "Can we go home now?"

CHAPTER 34

"Keep an eye on him, Benitoe," George said, from his seat in the back of the high open wagon with the rest of the luggage. Benitoe, mounted, was on a level with him and winked. They watched Maelgwn sitting as carefully as he could on George's large half-draft horse. Mosby was a gentleman, as horses go, and not inclined to mischief, but the size difference couldn't help but worry him.

"I've got my mind on Mosby, and it should be fine, but..." he was embarrassed to continue.

"But you might drop off during the journey," Benitoe responded matter-of-factly. "Angharad and I will keep him safe, and besides, look at him."

Benitoe was right. The boy's face was glowing, his first time on a great horse, after his initial work with Rhian on smaller steeds the last two days. Everyone was mounted except for George, and pleased to have a wagon for their gear so that they didn't have to carry it themselves.

"Would you see to his lessons?" George asked Benitoe. "You ride well, and he'll need to start on smaller horses anyway, until his first growth spurts kick in."

"My pleasure, huntsman. He could come hound-walking with us to get some experience."

They started off for the Edgewood Way, everyone who had come from Greenway Court recently, except Gwyn who would follow tomorrow. Rhian and Angharad chatted together while Ceridwen rode alone wrapped in silence. Maelgwn was quiet, trying not to be noticed so as to prolong this treat as much as possible.

George settled himself into a comfortable position, sitting propped up against the side of the wagon with bags and bits of gear holding him in place against the jolts of the road. He monitored Mosby, but there was no need. The horse placidly ignored his light-weight passenger and kept the other horses company on the road, plowing easily through the newly-fallen snow.

He remembered entering the way with his companions, but he'd already dozed off by the time they came out the far side.

George carefully climbed the steps to his own front door and paused before going in, savoring the moment. The wagon driver had offered to drop him at his house but he'd insisted on walking the short distance from the stables, sorry though he was to slow Angharad and Maelgwn down.

The boy hadn't stopped looking around since they'd exited the Guests' Way. Greenway Court was bigger than Edgewood, and fortified, with its palisade and curtain walls, the stone-built manor house with protective bastions at the front corners.

Behind him, he heard Angharad murmur to the boy, "This is your home now."

George opened the door and smelled the balsam scent, still heavy in the air after two weeks.

Alun emerged from the kitchen at the sound of the door. He smiled delightedly to see George, then recalled himself and greeted him with a dignified, "Very good to see you, sir."

"It's good to be back."

They dropped their bags in the front hall and George drew Maelgwn forward. "Alun, this is my foster-son Maelgwn."

"I've prepared the room on the left for him. It's all ready."

Of course, George thought, Angharad and perhaps Idris had kept him informed.

He glanced at the tree, which was looking rather bare. There was a network of small painted ornaments, but he saw only a handful of larger ones, clearly Angharad's work before she left. He was touched that she'd thought to do that, to make her own contributions to the custom he was trying to introduce. I'll look at those more closely later, he promised himself.

What's the date, he wondered. He worked it out quickly, why, tomorrow would be Christmas Eve.

Angharad showed Maelgwn the study while George lingered in the hall and he heard her promise to tell him the story of the painting with the archer shooting at George, later.

"Let's show you your room," George called, and they all went upstairs. George took the steps carefully, forcing his left leg to bend and lift properly. He made it halfway up before he was forced to lean on the banister and his cane for assistance. Too slow, he thought to himself, there's got to be a faster way to strengthen this. Hadyn might have an idea, he must have advised people recuperating from injuries. Tomorrow, I'll ask him tomorrow. The wall of family photos was clearly too much for Maelgwn to absorb right now and George didn't try. That could wait for another time.

Alun opened the door to the front guest room that had been given over to Maelgwn and let him walk in first. George followed, and Alun and Angharad left them alone.

George stood in the doorway and watched the boy's first tentative steps into his room. He walked to the side of the bed and sat down. He looked around at the clean, warm, safe place and gulped, his face crumpling.

George walked over slowly, sat down next to him, and put an arm over his shoulder. "You'll never forget your family, Maelgwn, never. This isn't a replacement, it's an expansion. More family, more friends. No more living alone."

Maelgwn made no noise but George could feel him shaking next to him. He let him work it out of his system until he calmed down again.

He stood up to go, but his leg wouldn't hold him and he fell back onto the bed. The room faded and started to spin.

He dimly felt Maelgwn shaking him but couldn't respond. He heard the boy's voice, in the hall, calling, "My lady, um, mother, he needs help."

When he focused again, he found Angharad bent over him. With Alun's help she pulled him upright. "I told you not to overdo it," she scolded him, gently. "Let's get you into your own bed."

❦

Benitoe knocked on Ives's door in the kennel-men's rooms. He'd picked a time when Huon and Tanguy were usually out to have a private discussion with Ives.

"So you're back, are you?" Ives said.

Benitoe stood squarely before him, as always. He'd been writing the Kuzul through Ives ever since he'd arrived in Edgewood, and now he handed the most recent correspondence to him directly. He expected Ives would have questions about how he'd managed things and was prepared for it.

"How's that new family of yours?" Ives asked. "Is Luhedoc settling in to the work at the inn, then?"

That wasn't what he'd expected. Since Isolda's death, their relationship had withdrawn into formality, and Benitoe had gone along with it to ease the pain for her father, since he seemed to want it that way.

"Well, don't just stand there. Sit down and tell me all about it." He leaned back in his own chair. "I haven't heard of a clan adoption in years. Everyone's talking."

Benitoe smiled back at the welcoming smile on Ives's face, glad to see it return. He's going to be alright, he thought. He sat down as bid and launched into his story.

❧

Rhian brought Maelgwn in through the main gates of the kennels. "You know, your foster-father has his own entrance, we call it the huntsman's alley. We'll go out that way and bring his own dogs back to the house with us, but I wanted you to see it like everyone else does, first."

She watched him as he stood boldly in the inner courtyard and sorted out the hound arrangements for himself. When he's quiet, you forget he's so much younger than me, she thought. It's something in how he stands, in his face. She'd lost her own parents, but she didn't remember them and there'd always been family around to take care of her. His story was far bleaker, and he'd managed to survive on his own in a hostile land.

She wasn't about to tell him, but she admired what he'd done. He's been tested, she thought, and he knows what he can do.

And then, he was so fierce sometimes, it was like having a young wolf standing guard over George. She very much approved of him as a foster-brother.

She knocked on the kennel-men's door, and went in to introduce Maelgwn to Ives who was deep in conversation with Benitoe.

"This is Ives, our kennel-master," she said. "He's in charge of everything in the kennels. You'll learn a lot from him. Ives, this is George's foster-son, Maelgwn."

Maelgwn executed a proper bow, and then grinned when Ives waved it away.

"Well, young man, and are you interested in hounds and hunting?" he said.

"I don't know, sir. I've hunted alone and set traps, but I can't really ride yet. Can you teach me about the hounds?"

Benitoe said, "George and I decided to fix the riding part right away. Every morning after the hound walk, I'll be giving you a lesson, and as soon as you're fit enough, you can come help us walk the hounds, if you like."

Rhian watched Maelgwn's face light up. "Yes, sir, thank you."

Ives told him, "Benitoe will take you in hand for a while and then you can decide what you want to do, once you see what's what."

Rhian thanked them both, and brought Maelgwn back out to the courtyard. "Would you like to see where your foster-father works?" she said.

"Shouldn't I be going back?"

"I think they'll be fine without us," she said. She knew George was probably asleep again. Maelgwn had told her, in a worried voice, about his collapse earlier. She made light of it, for him, but it worried her, too. They'd tried to keep it from her but she knew George had been near death only a couple of nights ago. *I guess we can't expect him to just bounce back immediately, even after a healing. A healing that serious did its own damage,* she realized. *What a strange concept.*

She opened the door to the huntsman's office, and lit some of the lamps. "Your foster-father can show you everything himself, but here are the logs of the hunts, and the breeding of the hounds."

She had him sit behind the desk in the huntsman's chair and look at the open hunting log's entries in George's handwriting, and her own. *What if he can't read,* she suddenly wondered. She was relieved to see him flip backward through the log and read some of the entries.

They both looked up at a knock on the open doorway. Benitoe and Brynach stood in the entrance.

"I'll trade you the big one for the smaller one," Benitoe joked. "Would you like to come with me and start to meet the hounds?" he asked Maelgwn.

The boy popped out of the chair and followed him eagerly. "I'll bring him back to the house," Benitoe called to Rhian, over his shoulder.

"Don't forget George's dogs, too," she said, and they were gone.

Brynach hadn't said anything yet, and suddenly Rhian felt a bit shy of him. She didn't feel as young as she did a couple of weeks ago. She'd been more carefree, then, she thought. She looked at Brynach speculatively as if he were someone else she could lose, too, and she didn't like the feeling that gave her.

His sober regard disconcerted her, and she broke the silence. "So, how did the hound walking go without us?"

"It was fine. Ives came out to help, and nothing much went wrong." He looked uncomfortable, himself, she noted.

"How are you?" he asked.

She tried to sort out an accurate answer to that and couldn't. He walked over and hugged her. "I'm glad to see you back," he said, quietly.

He was getting larger by the day, she thought, absently. It felt right to stand there, his arms around her, no demands made. Secure. Warm. She was grateful for it.

"Oh, Brynach, I almost lost them both. What would I have done?"

He just held her and let her burrow into his warm cocoon to find comfort. Eventually she backed away, shy again.

"Brynach..." she started, then stopped. "I don't know what I want."

He kept his distance. "I know. There's no hurry, don't worry about it."

His intense gaze was making her nervous and, as if he could sense that, he turned away to go.

"No, stay," she said. "Sit down and tell me what's been happening here."

❧

Angharad reseated herself in Iolo's old workshop at the back of the huntsman's house. George was still sleeping. It was hard to adjust to his recovery cycle—there was so much improvement that he seemed almost his old self again, but these sudden crashes showed how little stamina he had. The demands of Cernunnos's healing must have been bone-deep.

They'd clearly moved him too soon, but she'd sympathized with his wish to come home, and echoed it. This wouldn't do him any lasting harm, they'd just have to take it slow for a while.

He hadn't had the energy to look into this room so far, and she meant to keep it that way until tomorrow. She expected he would

308

think the smell of paint normal, if he noticed it at all. She usually kept that sort of work for her studio, but this time she hadn't wanted to leave the house and had made an exception.

She'd talked to Gwyn again, before she left, about the Christmas traditions from George's home. She had a surprise arranged for him, tomorrow, and smiled to herself, running over the plans.

She turned the object in her hand and added a broad red stripe to it. It was time she got busy and finished her part.

CHAPTER 35

Ives closed the gates after the hounds as they went out with Rhian for their early morning exercise and walked back toward his office. It was quiet without them. On a hunting morning, some would be left behind, howling their protest, but the daily walks took every hound that wasn't injured with them, and the peace always seemed a bit unnatural to him. Huon and Tanguy were already in the pens, cleaning them while the hounds were out.

He looked over as George came into the courtyard, up through the huntsman's alley from his house. At a distance, he seemed unchanged, until Ives noticed how slowly he was walking, taking care with each step, even with the cane. He'd heard about his healed injuries and realized that leg must still be very weak.

He changed course to greet him, and waited, respecting his effort and giving him a chance to close the distance himself. Up close, he was shocked at how gaunt and worn George looked, and there was something different about his eyes.

"Good to see you, Ives," he said.

Well, at least he sounded like himself. "Welcome back, huntsman."

"Have you heard the news about Benitoe's new family?"

"Yes, and isn't it splendid? A touch of the old customs, that was." We've been caught in the same isolation, Benitoe and I, he thought, and it's good that he's been jolted from it. Maybe I can look forward, too.

"Makes me smile just to see the change in him," he spoke his thought aloud.

"I had the same thought when he told me, and I can see it reflected in you," George said, with a penetrating look.

He looked around the kennels with disappointment. "Rhian must have them out already."

"They're no great distance. Why don't we take a little walk and watch them?" Ives heard himself suggesting. He wasn't entirely sure George could walk that far, looking at him, but he could tell he wanted to see his hounds. Why not let him try?

"I'll bring you your kennel coat, and you can meet me at the gate."

Ives turned and let George start his slow walk while he fetched him his kennel coat to keep his clothing clean, once he reached the hounds. He caught up to him well before he reached the gate and opened it for him.

"Leg bad?" he asked.

"No, it's been fixed, but there's no strength in it yet."

Or in much of the rest of you, Ives thought, judging by his movement. He approved of George's efforts to keep exercising it to build it up, but he changed his plans about where to take him.

"I have the perfect spot," he said. They walked slowly through the curtain gates to the front of the manor house and around to the main terrace. This brought them to the top of the terrace steps with their broad view of the grounds inside the palisade down the slope.

Ives stopped there, intending to go no further, and watched George's face light up at the sight of the hounds exercising at the far end, Rhian moving them from spot to spot. Brynach and Benitoe were both out, flanking the pack in their usual positions.

Ives waved an arm and caught Rhian's attention. She smiled to see George there, then made a sitting motion with her hands at Ives. He understood her meaning.

"Huntsman, let's get you seated here. See, it's dry, they keep it swept." He brought George down a few steps and made him sit with his back to the side wall and his bad leg stretched out along the broad stone step.

Once Rhian saw him take his spot, she brought the pack up the slope and halted a few yards below him. All the hounds were watching him and quivering, but obedient to her control. "Ready, huntsman?" she called.

"Send 'em in," he said, a glad note in his voice.

Like an irresistible flood, George was immediately mobbed by the hounds. Ives stood a couple of steps above and watched him bespeak them into sobriety and better manners, but he could see the joy with which he greeted them, calling each by name and rewarding it with a touch. They sat as closely as they could get to him, on every side, and the closest lay down next to him and just looked at him.

"They've been waiting for that," Benitoe said to Brynach. "Look how they've missed him."

Ives didn't move and, as he half-expected, George's movements ceased as his head dropped against the flank of a hound on the next higher step and he dozed off. Each hound wanted a part of him, so they carefully oozed in closer, propping him up and covering him, and joined him in a sunlit nap.

Rhian smiled at the scene. "You two should go on in. He's been doing that a lot," pointing at the sleeping George.

Benitoe said, "I'll do that. I've got a riding lesson with Maelgwn this morning." Brynach followed him up the remainder of the slope and through the curtain wall.

Rhian kept Ives company for a while and they chatted about Benitoe. Ives had missed their casual conversations and realized Rhian had been avoiding him since Isolda's death. Had he driven her away? "Will I see you this afternoon?" he said, nodding at George.

"Of course. You'll be there?" Rhian said.

She hadn't expected him to come, Ives saw. It was time for that to change. "Wouldn't miss it," he said, gladdened by her smile in response.

"You go on in," he told her. "I'll wait for George. We can handle the hounds."

George was roused from a dreamless nap by the twitching of his lumpy blanket. As he opened his eyes, puzzled, he realized he was deep in a nest of warm hounds. Several of them lifted their heads as he woke and he grinned to see all the eyes staring into his at eye level. Or even higher, as he realized they were on the steps both above and below him. Golden eyes, amber eyes, honey, and chocolate.

He raised his gaze further to Ives. "Sorry, I do seem to keep dropping off this way. I expect that will pass, eventually."

Ives waved it off with a smile. "Made the hounds happy, not that that takes much."

George shooed the comfortable hounds off and cleared enough space to stand up. "Let's take them back," he said.

He kept the hounds packed up behind him as he made his slow steady way back to the kennel gates. They obeyed him without demurral.

Inside the kennel courtyard, he sat down on a stone bench. As Ives came up to start putting hounds away, he waved him off. "Just open the dog hounds' gate," he said. Ives sent Tanguy over to do so.

One by one George called each dog hound out of the pack around him, looked him over, and made much of him. Then he sent him over to Tanguy at the gate to his pen, bespeaking him individually and getting instant obedience, even from the normally unruly hounds such as Cythraul. Dando, when it was his turn, rose up to look into his face for a moment, then dropped and licked his healed knee before joining his pack mates in the dog hound pen.

George went through the bitch hounds in the same way, looking over each hound in her turn. He commented to Ives, "We'll have to think about breeding them soon. I'll start working on that."

Eventually only the young hounds were left, not quite full pack members and housed in their own pens on the other side of the courtyard. George gave each of them his individual attention, and they squirmed with delight.

As he dismissed the last one he looked down at his kennel coat in dismay. "Guess I'll need another bath," he said. "Not the cleanest of blankets, those hounds."

"But they warm you, inside and out," Ives said, and George laughed in agreement. Forty souls, happy to see him. Well worth a little dirt. And fleas.

~~~

"Angharad said you wanted to see me?" George said, standing at Ceridwen's door in the early afternoon. He was pleased with himself for having completed the brief walk down the lane without needing to use the cane he was carrying.

"Yes, huntsman. Come in."

She brought him into her library study and joined him as he took his customary seat in the comfortable chairs facing the fire. "I have something for you," she said.

She reached into a pocket of her skirt and pulled out a small object that would fit inside a closed fist, especially in a large hand like his. She held it for a moment. "Someone like me collects a

313

great many objects over a lifetime, many of them by accident, much the way this library collects books. They find their way to me, strangers hand them over, they appear in the road before me. This one fell from the sky, in another land. Someday I'll tell you the story."

This was an odd mood for her, he thought. She was usually more... brisk.

"Mostly they come to stay and live here quietly," she said. "But once in a while they call for my attention and remind me that they have other places to be."

She glanced down at the object in her hand. "This one came to my mind yesterday." She gave it to George.

He examined it. It was an old carving, smooth and worn. It looked like bone. It was roughly cylindrical, and symmetrical, two identical ends and a small central shaft between them. He held it up to his nose and smelled old bone and eastern spices he couldn't identify. It felt indestructible, despite the material, and very old. It fit his hand perfectly, no wider than his palm.

"What is it?" he asked.

"It's in the form of a thunderbolt, in the eastern style, but I don't think the shape matters. What it contains within is... not visible to me."

She tilted her head. "I don't know if this is a gift from Taranis or a stray thought in my own mind, or just an odd paperweight, but it seemed to me that this belonged to you now. I've learned to heed such impulses, even if I don't understand them. Perhaps especially so, in that case."

"What should I do with it? What's it for?"

"I have no idea. Tie a cord to it and hang it on your tree, if you wish," she said. "But it's yours now. Don't lose it, it's very old."

He could feel nothing within, no hint of the presence Ceridwen suggested. "Is it dangerous?"

"I don't know. It's not hostile, I'm sure of that much. Treat it with respect and pass it along to your heir, if you never figure it out."

He put it carefully into an inner chest pocket in his coat. What would he tell Angharad, that Ceridwen just gave him a thunderbolt? This place was a constant surprise.

"I had a question for you," he said.

She waited for him, attentively.

314

"I think I know what we can trade to Seething Magma for help with the ways. I talked to her about it before she left." He looked at Ceridwen. "You'll like this. She wants books."

Ceridwen laughed.

"Not just any books, mind you," he said, "but books about geology, the history of the planet. Apparently, they may be very long-lived indeed, but not quite on a geologic time scale, and they have theories that need data. We talked about it late one night, when she caught a stray thought of mine."

"Those would be human books, you're suggesting?"

"Unless the fae have a history of studying geology," he said.

Ceridwen shook her head. "Our technical scholars concentrate on magic more than science, though there are works of engineering. We designed our larger buildings after human exemplars, your Romans and some others."

"And this is my question," George said. "I'm afraid of introducing knowledge where it hasn't been... earned. For example, let's pretend that what the rock-wights learn lets them, oh, produce gold and silver on demand. Those who earn their living from mining, like the korrigans, would find their prices reduced, and disruption would follow. Just an example."

He frowned. "I know this is the wrong attitude, that no one can control knowledge. Our experience in economics tells us that it's a dangerous illusion to think you can, that it invariably causes harm. There's no way to know what the impacts will be. And it's wrong to try and control it, I believe that. Who am I to dictate what people can and can't learn, even if I could."

Ceridwen said, "But you don't want, you yourself, to be the agent of change, is that it?"

"I suppose so. I guess that makes me squeamish rather than principled."

"Yes, it does. You can't bury knowledge, once known. Like life, it will out. You couldn't not think about the information that Mag found so enlightening. There are few real secrets."

She gestured at the shelves of books all around them. "I know dangerous things. I don't make it easy for the unqualified to learn them, but nothing can stop a determined scholar with evil intent."

"So you think I shouldn't hesitate to let some of the human knowledge seep in, as requested or needed."

"No more than if it came from a foreign land instead of another world," she said. "Change will come and not everyone will adapt, but that's how life works."

He sat and thought about it for a few minutes, and then he found himself waking up again in his comfortable chair, a lap robe thrown loosely over him and the fire diminished. Ceridwen was still in her seat, and she lifted her eyes from the book in her lap when he stirred.

He rubbed his face. "I am so tired of this constant fading out. When will it stop?"

He meant the question rhetorically, but Ceridwen surprised him with the intensity of her response.

"You don't understand." She gave him a hard look. "Cernunnos's healing may have been brutal, but I assure you without it Angharad would be a widow today and your new foster-son would be fatherless again."

George flinched. She was probably right.

"If you think about it," she said, "it's a miracle he did it at all."

George lifted an eyebrow.

"Hasn't it occurred to you how dangerous you are? That if you can kill a way, you can likely kill a rock-wight, too?"

He felt the blood drain from his face as she continued.

"Cernunnos probably thought it a good idea to just remove you as a threat to them. Seething Magma's intervention made him reconsider."

George was appalled. "I would never... It never crossed my mind," he whispered.

"I imagine they both know that. But Cernunnos might have insisted on certainty instead. You're very fortunate that Mag felt she could trust you, and even more fortunate that you made the right choice when Cernunnos tested you."

She stood up and looked down at him. She seemed to age before his eyes and assume an authority she usually masked. "Once you collapsed Madog's hidden way after the great hunt and Gwyn realized what you could do, don't you think he had choices to make, too? What do you think would happen to him and all of us if you killed the Travelers' Way or any of the other ways around which our settlements and trade are based? How could he stop you?"

He was shaken by this description of Gwyn's assessment and defended himself. "I never thought of it. Just because I can doesn't mean I ever would."

She waved a hand dismissively. "There are many men of power who would eliminate a future threat by destroying a present ally," she said. "If you want to be an active agent of change, go to the old world and collapse every other way, and watch us descend into bitter and bloody war over what remains. Those are real choices, not a few books."

She looked down at him sternly. "That's why Madog was so interested in how you could kill ways. He would have taken Annwn and then used that as a base against the old world, and done just that, or threatened the ways for ransom."

George was speechless.

"You're lucky to be alive. If Gwyn weren't a man of honor, you would surely be gone, family or no. You can't afford to remain this naive about the power you represent." She sighed, looking at him, "Sometimes it's easy to forget just how young you are, just Rhodri's age."

He didn't know how to react. What she'd said put everything in a different light. He replied, quietly, "You're saying I need to understand the politics and economics of this world, and I don't— that's true. I've set myself a private life, and you're telling me I can't do that. But that's all I ever aimed to do."

She relaxed her severity. "Oh, George, I know that, and Gwyn does, too. We truly are your family and friends. But we need your active participation. You can't be sitting on the sidelines, a threat to all and an aid to none."

"Alright." As simply as that, he dismissed his dream of a quiet private life. Nothing she'd said was wrong, and he bowed to her superior argument. "How can I help?"

"Gwyn will have a great deal of planning to do, with Madog's death and our discovery of the rock-wights. He and I will have to give you an accelerated prince's training, like Rhys and Rhodri's, as quickly as possible, since I'm sure you'll be involved in whatever the next steps will be."

She beckoned him to stand up and took away the lap robe. "You're not the first to fall asleep in these chairs," she said, smiling, as she folded it up.

"Angharad's going to be looking for you. I'll walk back with you."

CHAPTER 36

George heard the noise of a gathering inside before he came to the door of his house with Ceridwen. He glared at her.

She shrugged, "Angharad wanted you out of the way for a while, and we had things to discuss."

He rolled his eyes, then opened the door and waved Ceridwen in.

"Good, I was beginning to worry." Angharad greeted him, with the dogs, and Alun took their outer garments. She looked at his face with a bit of apprehension.

George made himself join in with the spirit of the occasion. "Ceridwen gave me something and then followed it up with a pretty good talking to which I think maybe I needed. I'll tell you all about it, later."

Angharad gave Ceridwen an unreadable look, then brought him over to the tree, still standing handsome but rather bare in the hall. "I invited a few people over to finish decorating this tree. I'll need your help to reach all the spots."

George was surprised to see rope garlands of evergreen boughs around the banister. "Where did all this come from?"

"Oh, Rhian and Brynach have been busy." She pointed to the fireplace mantel in the study, where holly cuttings surrounded a brightly painted carving he couldn't quite make out from the hall.

He was distracted by the people spilling out of his study into the hall. Rhian and Brynach were there, grinning, and Benitoe and Ives, even Gwyn, on the edge of the crowd. He must have returned just today, George thought. He nodded to him thoughtfully, thinking of Ceridwen's words..

Alun had provided drinks and food for everyone while he'd been napping in front of Ceridwen's fire. Looks like the party started just fine without me, he thought.

Angharad showed him the few ornaments she'd added to the tree before she left for Edgewood. He admired them sincerely—

they were clever or witty, or just miniature works of art. Each was made of wood and most were painted.

"Gwyn gave me the idea for some of them. He described this sort of tree in your world." She nodded at Gwyn who was standing quietly next to his foster-daughter, a drink in his hand.

"But I thought it looked rather empty," she continued. "I wanted to make something for each day since you brought the tree into the house." She reached into a bag she'd left on the staircase and handed him a decoration. "Think you can find a spot for this?"

He held a palm sized version of his own oak tree, in a wooden silhouette. This was the sign he'd adopted for his family, after choosing to leave the human world. He smiled to see it. He hung it high on the tree, so it could shelter the ornaments below.

He turned and held out his hand for the next one. She gave him the toy wolf that Mag had used to indicate Maelgwn. He looked for the boy and called him over. Angharad told him, "Did you know this is how Cloudie's mother referred to you? 'Wolf cub,' we called you, before we knew your name."

George gave him the toy, to which Angharad had added a ribbon. "Go hang it somewhere where we can see it every day."

Maelgwn proudly tied it on the tree, then went and stood by his foster-father.

"This one was my symbol," she said, and gave George a small magnifying glass on a ribbon to hang. "I tried to find yours, but it was gone."

Gwyn stepped forward and gave him something wrapped in a sky-blue cloth. "That's because I already had it. I took it before you had the chance." George unwrapped the cloth and found a silver miniature version of the dog collar Mag had used.

This unexpectedly hit him, like having his human grandparents there. He thanked Gwyn, his voice choking a little. He remembered his grandfather Talbot talking about an old king who'd called one of his ancestors, "Talbot, our good dog." It was like an echo out of history.

Angharad's hand dove into the bag again and came out with something that tinkled. "Mag had another symbol for my family, but I wanted to add my own to it." She gave him a little wooden cradle, with a bell inside. He almost dropped it, then hung it under his oak tree, for protection. Those who hadn't heard the news yet congratulated them.

She blandly handed him the next ornament, a pair of sleeping fawns. Maelgwn burst out laughing, and after a moment she joined him, while George somewhat sheepishly found a place to hang it. Every family accumulates private jokes, he thought. This is one of ours. He refused to explain it to his guests.

Next was a vibrant carving, the miniature head of an antlered red deer. This time he did glare at her but she shrugged it off, and he hung it for her in a place of honor.

"Maelgwn has something for you," she said.

The boy flushed, but he went into the study and returned with a small cloth-wrapped bundle which he put into George's hands.

George unfolded the cloth carefully. It was a gaily painted silhouette of a dragon, quite recognizable. He looked more closely. Someone had painstakingly taken the toy black hat that George had given Mag to use as a symbol for Madog, and tied it onto the dragon's head. George's last memory of that hat had been Mag putting it into his hand while he sat blind and dying, ridden by Cernunnos. He'd crushed it in his hand at the confirmation of Madog's death. He glanced from the dragon to Maelgwn.

"I made that," the boy said, somewhat unnecessarily, George thought.

"Where did you find the hat?"

"You dropped it," he said. "I wanted to make sure you knew this was Madog, not Cloudie's mom."

My deadly enemy, no, our enemy, reduced to a boy's colorful ornament, he thought. He approved. "Let's hang this one together."

They placed it as high as Maelgwn could reach.

Alun stepped up shyly then, with a bag of painted wooden birds, in several sizes. George remembered his hobby of making birdhouses and other items. He thanked him and waved him at the tree to start tying them into place. They brought the tree to life.

"I don't understand how all of you found the time to do this," he said. Angharad and Alun shared the smile of conspirators.

Ives had been watching quietly all this while, comfortable in the crowd. He came forward now with a dog made of bound straw tied in places with red cord. It reminded George of the straw horses they made in Sweden. "From the hounds," he said.

"Be sure to thank them for me," George said dryly, and Ives grinned.

Benitoe followed. He bowed to George and presented him with a summoning token, like the ones he'd left for the lutins to find in Edgewood, all made of new straw and red yarn. Ives gave him a stern look at that, but Benitoe said to him, "Why not? When he killed the barrier way at Edgewood, were we not summoned? Our folk would still be huddling in caves and windfalls without him." Ives made no response.

Angharad reached into her pockets and pulled out two more items. "Our new friends," she said, handing him one.

George realized these were the bits of Seething Magma and Granite Cloud that they had extruded as farewell remembrances. Angharad had set them in cages of wood and wire. She told him, "We'll keep these on our mantel the rest of the year."

He reached into his own chest pocket and looked at Ceridwen. She shrugged. He begged a bit of spare ribbon from Angharad and tied the thunderbolt to the top of the tree. No star of Bethlehem here, he thought, but something strange and unknown. I suppose that star was, too, once upon a time.

Angharad led their guests back into the study and Alun started to offer them hot cider and stronger drinks. George lingered in the hall to admire the tree, full and colorful. It was far better than he'd imagined three weeks ago, no longer just a sign of intent in his hall, but covered in meaning and memory. So much to have happened in such a short time. Children.

Ceridwen's words lingered. He expected they'd burn in him for a while. She was right, he'd been living his life blindly, thinking he could just go along like a child himself, without ambition. It was comfortable, but unrealistic, an unexamined habit he realized he'd brought from his old life, where the decisions of private life, even in adulthood, had little consequence to anyone else, to any larger community. He'd wanted a more "real" existence, and now he'd gotten it. It brought responsibilities he barely suspected yet.

He considered Cernunnos. The notion that he might have just let him die out of cold prudence, that shook him. He'd reached an uneasy *modus vivendi* with his occasional presence in his mind, but this disturbed that status. He doubted he'd ever be comfortable with him again. Was his every thought from now on to be monitored for threat, as if he were a dangerous weapon that might go rogue? It felt as if someone with obscure motivations had put explosives in his head and held the trigger.

It took real effort to bring himself back to the pleasures of the moment. I won't let him ruin it, he thought. I can't control the rest of it, but I can control that.

He walked into the study where his guests were talking and went up to the mantel. What was that, bright between the holly branches? When he got close enough to see it clearly, he chuckled. It was Angharad's work, obviously. She'd made a large carving of a cornucopia spilling fruit, but instead of a horn of plenty it used the bottomless cauldron of legend, lying on its side, and instead of meat and drink or harvest fruits it poured out... oranges. Lots and lots of oranges, all sizes.

He turned around to seek her in the crowd, and there she was, standing by the door to the library, watching him. She smiled when he did, and they shared a private moment. She filled his heart. To hell with Cernunnos. If this was all he got, it was worth it.

He joined her and gestured at the empty room behind them, the huntsman's library. "Did you get everything?" he asked quietly. His life had been derailed before he could think of a suitable present for her, but he wanted Maelgwn, at least, to benefit from the traditional association of Christmas and gifts. He'd gone to the armory with Hadyn earlier today for his, and he knew Angharad had something in mind.

"All ready," she said, "and something from Rhys, too, which Rhian will present."

He turned and faced his friends and family. "Well, folks, I'm sorry not to have little keepsakes to give you in return, but I thank you, more than I can say, for yours and for coming today. I call that a proper Christmas tree now." He waved his hand in the direction of the hall.

Ceridwen remarked, "You've been a little busy, we understand." They all laughed at that.

"It's also a tradition where I come from to give gifts to each other at this time. Maelgwn, please come here."

The astonished boy got up and walked over to stand next to his foster-parents. "I've already received my gift," George said, as he put an arm around Maelgwn's shoulder and gave it a squeeze.

Angharad murmured, her arm curled around her belly, "And I, mine."

George broke off to smile broadly at her. "But Maelgwn hasn't gotten his yet. It's time to fix that."

Angharad fetched him, from the library, an object about a foot long, wrapped in a cloth. He took it and presented it to Maelgwn. "Every man needs one, sometimes more. Your foster-sister Rhian can talk to you about that."

Maelgwn unwrapped the belt and sheathed hunting knife, practical and unornamented. He swelled with pride and bowed to his foster-father in thanks.

Angharad gave him a flat package of her own. He opened it and found a set of wood carving knives in a box. "In memory of a very pleasant day together," she said to him. For the first time, at least that George witnessed, the boy threw his arms around her and hugged her.

Rhian stood up and whispered in Angharad's ear, and she ducked back into the library for something. "Foster-brother," she said, "Rhys charged me with a task when I left, since he couldn't be here himself. When he was your age, he received his first sword. He can think of no one he'd rather see it with than you. He thanks you, and I do, too, for the saving of his life."

Angharad handed her a plain boy's saber with a belt wrapped around it. It was small, suited to his size, but in all ways a real weapon. Rhian unwrapped the belt, knelt, and buckled it on him.

Maelgwn held his ground at these unexpected events, but he couldn't manage anything beyond a stammered thanks. George kept his face appropriately dignified so as not to spoil the moment, but smiled inside, remembering that Rhys was only ten years older than Maelgwn even now, though that probably seemed like an immense distance to the boy.

George caught Benitoe's eye, and the lutin rose to speak from where he was sitting next to Ives. "One more thing, Maelgwn."

The dazed boy turned his head.

"As soon as he can ride again, your father and I will take you to Iona's to get you your own horse."

That did it. Maelgwn lost his composure and fled the room, and everyone laughed.

George looked down at Angharad, "Well, that was a success." He caught himself in a yawn. Not again, he thought.

That was the cue for the party to wind down. He stopped Gwyn for a moment and said quietly, "Ceridwen gave me an earful. I'd like to speak with you, in the next few days."

Gwyn smiled and gripped his arm. "Merry Christmas, my boy, it reminded me of your grandmother." He glanced at Ceridwen. "Yes, we'll talk, later."

Ceridwen and Angharad lingered in the hall, speaking of nothing important, but George could feel an unspoken undercurrent of communication, that way women had of conveying much more than their words alone would indicate. He couldn't tune in to that channel, but he'd lived long enough to recognize it. He ask Angharad about it later, but meanwhile he had one last thing to do.

He took Angharad's pendant off and stood on a footstool to tie it to a beam in the hall. It spun and pointed to Angharad. He stepped down and moved the stool out of the way, standing directly beneath the hanging arrow.

"Now, Ceridwen, I wonder if you're familiar with the human seasonal customs surrounding the hanging of mistletoe?"

As he'd hoped, that piqued her interest, and she broke off her conversation with Angharad to focus on the question. Angharad drifted his way while she talked, just as he'd planned. It was like waiting for a trout to take his fly as he floated it by on the current.

"Gwyn mentioned something. I believe you hang it up and then exact a kiss from someone as they pass beneath it?"

He reeled Angharad in as she got within reach. "That's right." He leaned down to kiss his wife, and forgot about Ceridwen. The sound of the door opening and closing barely registered.

⟡

It was quiet in the great hall for dinner, none of the fuss they'd made in Edgewood, for which George was very grateful. He stopped by Eurig's place at the head of one of the floor-level tables, and bantered with him for a moment.

"Going to pick up that honeymoon again?" Eurig asked.

"He's a fast worker, dear," Tegwen said over her shoulder as she congratulated Angharad. "I think he's got the hang of it."

Brynach made room for Maelgwn to join him. Five years was an intimidating distance for him at first, but soon George heard him telling Brynach all about his second riding lesson with Benitoe today.

George accompanied Angharad to her seat on the dais. A child, he thought to himself, still listening to Maelgwn, fondly. How did that happen? And another one coming.

He took his seat next to Angharad feeling blessed. The extended healing he was enduring, the marks it had made, all of that faded to insignificance.

He leaned to Angharad and spoke quietly. "You know, I always regretted not finding a suitable wife and starting a family when I was younger. Well, I hate to remind you of my excessive youth..."

She smiled.

"...but I'm barely old enough even now to be Maelgwn's father. It's as though I haven't lost any time at all."

He put a hand over her stomach under the table edge. "I don't deserve this, I know I don't." She lay her own hand on top of his.

⁌～～⁍

Angharad sat in bed, reading by lamplight while the banked fire flickered companionably. Maelgwn was tucked into his own room for the second night and seemed to be settling in. She smiled to herself. She'd bet he was stalking around his bed waving Rhys's saber in the air, if she knew boys.

George dozed lightly next to her, lying face down to spare his tender back. The room was warm enough that he'd pulled the covers down to his waist to cool off, intending to raise them later.

She put her book down and caressed his back with its scars. They were livid with newness, but the skin was welted and thickened as if they'd been there for a decade. She traced the thick lines with her fingertips, remembering what his back had felt like, that last night in this room before he'd left for Edgewood.

It's a very small price to pay to get him back, she thought, a very fair trade. The real honeymoon is getting to keep him.

She made an involuntary noise at the thought of how close he had come to not returning.

George opened his eyes and smiled up at her, not changing his position. "I remember the last time you did that," he said.

"So do I."

"Do you mind it, very much?"

"Everyone has scars." She leaned down to kiss the back of his neck "It's the price we pay for life."

GUIDE TO NAMES & PRONUNCIATIONS

MODERN WELSH ALPHABET

A[1], B, C, CH[2], D, DD[2], E[1], F[2], FF[2], G, NG[2], H, I[1], J,
L, LL[2], M, N, O[1], P, PH[2], R, RH[2], S, T, TH[2], U[1], W[1] [2], Y[1]

[1] These letters are vowels. The letter 'W' can be used either as a vowel (when it is said 'oo' like in the Welsh word 'cwm' (coom) meaning 'valley') or as a consonant (when it is said like it is in English, for example in the Welsh word 'gwyn' (gwin) meaning 'white'). This is the same with letter 'I' which can also be used as a consonant (when it is said like an English Y like in 'iogwrt' (yog-oort) meaning yoghurt.

[2] Letters that are not in the English alphabet, or have different sounds. CH sounds like the 'KH' in Ayatollah KHoumeini. DD is said like the TH in 'THere'. F is said like the English 'V'. FF is said like the English 'F'. NG sounds like it would in English but it is tricky because it comes at the beginnings of words (for example 'fy ngardd' - my garden). One trick is to blend it in with the word before it. LL sounds like a cat hissing. PH sounds like the English 'F' too, but it is only used in mutations. RH sounds like an 'R' said very quickly before a 'H'. TH sounds like the 'TH' in 'THin'. W has been explained in the sentences before about vowels.

It helps to remember how Welsh is pronounced in order to translate the unfamiliar orthography into familiar English sounds. The language has changed over time and so has the spelling. People with very long lives tend to be conservative in how they spell their names.

Some nicknames are descriptive, occupational, or locational, as they are in English (e.g., Tom Baker, Susan Brown, John Carpenter, Meg Underwood)

Bongam - Bandy-legged
Goch - The red(-haired) one
Owen the Leash
Scilti - The thin one

PRINCIPAL CHARACTERS & PLACE NAMES

HUMANS

Conrad (Corniad) Traherne
Father of George Talbot Traherne, husband of Léonie Annan Talbot.

George Talbot Traherne
Huntsman from Virginia. His parents are Conrad Traherne and Léonie Annan Talbot.

Gilbert Payne Talbot
Father of Léonie Annan Talbot, husband of Georgia Rice Annan.

Georgia Rice Annan
Mother of Léonie Annan Talbot, wife of Gilbert Payne Talbot, daughter of Gwyn ap Nudd (Gwyn Annan).

Léonie Annan Talbot
Mother of George Talbot Traherne, wife of Conrad (Corniad) Traherne.

FAE & IMMORTALS

Alun (AL-an)
Servant to the huntsman of Gwyn ap Nudd.

Angharad (ang-KAR-ad)
Artist affiliated with Gwyn ap Nudd's court.

Beli Mawr (BEH-lee MA-oor) - Beli the Great
Father of Lludd Llaw Eraint (Nudd) and Llefelys.

Bleddyn (BLE-dhin)
Artistic mentor of Angharad.

Brynach (BRIN-akh)
Great-nephew of Eurig ap Gruffyd.

Cadugan (kah-DUG-an)
Steward to Rhys Vachan ap Rhys at Edgewood.

Ceridwen (ke-RID-wen)

Scholar, healer, magician at Gwyn ap Nudd's court.

Cernunnos (ker-NOO-nus) - Master of Beasts
Deity takes the form of an antlered man (the horned man) or an antlered red deer.

Creiddylad ferch Nudd (krey-THIL-ad verkh NIDH)
Daughter of Lludd Llaw Eraint (Nudd), sister of Gwyn ap Nudd and Edern ap Nudd, one-time wife of Gwythyr ap Greidawl. Lady of Edgewood (Pencoed) to Gwyn ap Nudd.

Cydifor (KEED-ih-vor)
Musician seeking employment at Edgewood.

Cyledr Wyllt (KIL-eh-der WILT) - Cyledr the Mad
Son of Nwython. Warrior of Gwythyr ap Greidawl.

Edern ap Nudd (EE-dern ap NIDH)
Son of Lludd Llaw Eraint (Nudd), brother of Gwyn ap Nudd and Creiddylad ferch Nudd, father of Rhys ab Edern, grandfather of Rhys Vachan ap Rhys and Rhian ferch Rhys.

Eiryth (EI-ryth)
Wife of Rhys ab Edern, mother of Rhys Vachan ap Rhys and Rhian ferch Rhys.

Eluned (e-LII-ned)
A master scholar and healer to Rhys Vachan ap Rhys in Edgewood. Grandmother's sister to Eiryth, mother of Rhys Vachan ap Rhys.

Emrys (EM-ris)
One of Idris's guards.

Eurig ap Gruffydd (EI-rig ap GRIFF-ith)
Husband of Tegwen, great-uncle of Brynach. Vassal of Gwyn ap Nudd.

Gwyn ap Nudd (GWIN ap NIDH) - Gwyn Annan
Son of Lludd Llaw Eraint (Nudd), brother of Edern ap Nudd and Creiddlyad ferch Nudd. Father of Georgia Rice Annan. Prince of Annwn.

Gwythyr ap Greidawl (GWI-thir ap GREI-dul)
Ex-husband of Creiddylad ferch Nudd. Gwyn ap Nudd's opponent each Nos Galan Mae.

Hadyn (HAY-din)
Weapons-master to Gwyn ap Nudd.

Huw Bongam (HUE BON-gam) - Hugh Bandy-leg
Innkeeper of the Horned Man in Green Hollow.

Idris ap Hywel - Idris Powell (IH-dris ap HIH-wel)

Marshal to Gwyn ap Nudd. 2nd in command.

Ifor ap Griffri - Ifor Moel (IH-ver ap GRIFF-ree), (IH-ver MOYLE) - Ifor the Bald
Steward and administrator to Gwyn ap Nudd under Idris Powell.

Iolo ap Huw (YO-lo ap HUE)
Huntsman to Gwyn ap Nudd. Iolo is a diminutive of Iorwerth.

Iona (YO-na)
Breeder of ponies and small horses.

Lleision (LHEI-shon)
Marshal to Rhys Vachan ap Rhys. 2nd in command.

Lludd Llaw Eraint (LHIDH LHAU er-AYNT) - Nudd/Lludd of the Silver Hand
Son of Beli Mawr. Brother of Llefelys. Father of Gwyn ap Nudd, Edern ap Nudd, and Creiddylad ferch Nudd. King of Britain.

Madog ab Owen Gwynedd (MAA-dog ab OU-ain GWI-nedh)
Son of the Prince of Gwynedd. Discovered a way to the new world around 1100.

Maelgwn (MYLE-goon)
Young way-finder, friend of Granite Cloud. Adopted son of George Talbot Traherne.

Meilyr (MYE-lir)
A leader of the new world fae on the Edgewood expedition.

Morial (MOR-yal)
Weapons-master to Rhys Vachan ap Rhys.

Nudd
See **Lludd Llaw Eraint**.

Rhian ferch Rhys (HRII-an verkh RHEESE)
Foster-daughter of Gwyn ap Nudd, daughter of Rhys ab Edern and Eiryth, granddaughter of Edern ap Nudd, sister of Rhys Vachan ap Rhys. Junior huntsman to Gwyn ap Nudd.

Rhodri ap Morgant (HROD-hrii ap MOR-gant)
Distant nephew to Gwyn ap Nudd, cousin to Rhian ferch Rhys and Rhys Vachan ap Rhys. Diplomat to Gwyn ap Nudd. Musician.

Rhys ab Edern (HREESE ab EE-dern)
Son of Edern ap Nudd, husband of Eiryth, father of Rhian ferch Rhys and Rhys Vachan ap Rhys.

Rhys Vachan ap Rhys (HREESE VAKH-an ap HREESE) - Rhys the younger, Rhys Junior
    Foster-son of Gwyn ap Nudd, son of Rhys ab Edern and Eiryth, grandson of Edern ap Nudd, brother of Rhian ferch Rhys. Earl of Edgewood under Gwyn ap Nudd.
Scilti (SHIL-tee) - The thin one.
    From Irish Cailte, Caolite.
Senua (se-NOO-ah)
    A goddess of springs and wisdom.
Taranis (ta-RAN-iss)
    A god of thunder and strength.
Tegwen (TEG-wen)
    Wife of Eurig ap Gruffydd.
Thomas Kethin (KETH-in) - Thomas the Swarthy
    Son of Thomas, Lord Fairfax, and Dilys
Trefor Mawr (TREH-vor MA-oor) - Trevor the Great
    A famous way-finder.

KORRIGANS (KOR-i-gans)

Broch (BROCKH)
    Elder, community leader for Gwyn's korrigans in Edgewood.
Tiernoc (TEEAIR-nok)
    Elder, community leader for the old world korrigans in Edgewood.

LUTINS (LOO-tanh)

Argantan (ar-GAN-tan)
    A relative of Maëlys.
Armelle (ar-MEL)
    Betrothed to Tanguy.
Benitoe (BEN-ih-toe)
    Whipper-in. Betrothed to Isolda.
Berran (BERR-an)
    A dweller in Edgewood.
Brittou (BRIH-too)
    Stable manager to Iona.
Corentin (COR-en-tin)
    A relative of Maëlys.

Herannuen (her-ANN-wen)
Relative of Maëlys, a smith.
Huon (HOO-on)
Kennel-man.
Isolda (i-SOL-da)
Daughter of Ives, betrothed to Benitoe.
Ives (EVE)
Kennel-master. Father of Isolda.
Luhedoc (LOO-eh-doc)
Husband of Maëlys, missing in Edgewood.
Maëlys (may-EL-iss)
Wife of Luhedoc, works for Iona.
Rozenn (ROH-zenn)
Matriarch of a family looking for relatives and opportunities at
Edgewood.
Tanguy (TAN-ghee)
Kennel-man. Betrothed to Armelle.

ELEMENTALS

Granite Cloud
Daughter of Seething Magma, granddaughter of Gravel.
Gravel
Mother of Seething Magma, grandmother of Granite Cloud.
Seething Magma - Mag
Daughter of Gravel, mother of Granite Cloud.

HORSES

Eleri (eh-LEH-ri)
Pony for Benitoe. Bay mare.
Gwladus (GLA-dus) - Ruler
Pony for Benitoe. Gray mare.
Mosby (MOZ-by)
George's horse. Dapple-gray Percheron/thoroughbred gelding.

HOUNDS – CŴN ANNWN

Cŵn Annwn (COON AN-nun)
The Hounds of Hell. See **Annwn**.

Cythraul (m) (KEH-thral) - Devil, Demon
Outsider.
Dando (m) (DAN-doe)

DOGS (OTHER)

Cabal (KA-ball)
A terrier owned by Angharad.
Ermengarde (ER-men-GARD)
A terrier (puppy) owned by Angharad.
Hugo
A blue-tick coonhound owned by George.
Sergeant
A yellow feist owned by George.

EVENTS

Nos Galan Gaeaf (noos GA-lan GAY-a) - The night of the calend
of winter
The first day (night) of winter. October 31, the eve of
November 1, the eve of All Saints' Day (All Hallows),
Hallowe'en. (Celtic dates begin in the evening).
Nos Galan Mae (noos GA-lan MAY) - The night of the calend of
May
The first day (night) of summer. April 30, the eve of May 1.

PLACES

Annwn (AN-nun)
Part of the Celtic otherworld, traditionally the underworld. See
Cŵn Annwn.
  Daear Llosg (DEI-ar LHOSK) - Burnt Ground
  The meadow on the slope north of Greenway Court where
  funerals and cremations are held.
Dan-y-Deri (dan-ih-DEE-ri). Also **Danderi**. - Below the Oaks
A village visited by the great hunt.
Dyffryn Camarch (DEH-frin KA-markh) - Broad valley of the
winding Horse River
The Shenandoah Valley.

Llys y Lon Las (LHIIS eh LOON laas) - Greenway Court (Court of the Green Lane)
   The name of Gwyn ap Nudd's manor, later borrowed (before 1750) by a human visitor, Thomas, 6th Lord Fairfax, as a name for his wilderness estate and hunting lodge at White Post, in the Shenandoah Valley.
Pant-glas (PANT-glaas). Also **Pantglas**. - Greenhollow
   The name of the village below Greenway Court.
Pen-y-Coed (PEN-ih-KOID). Also **Pencoed**. - Edgewood
   The name of Creiddylad's estate, granted by Gwyn ap Nudd. Now in the charge of Rhys Vachan ap Rhys.
Tredin (TRE-diin). Bottom Farm
   The name of Cydifor's home village.

IF YOU LIKE THIS BOOK...

You can find illustrations of George's pocket-watch, family arms, and the text of the song he sings at: PerkunasPress.com/wp/books/the-hounds-of-annwn/the-ways-of-winter/

Please tell your friends about this book. You can link to it on my website and let people know on Facebook or Twitter.

The next book in the Hounds of Annwn series, **King of the May**, is scheduled to be released in Fall, 2013. Find out more: PerkunasPress.com/wp/books/the-hounds-of-annwn/king-of-the-may/

Sign up for my newsletter to stay informed of new and upcoming releases: PerkunasPress.com/wp/about-us/

You can contact me at PerkunasPress.com. You can also follow me on Facebook: Facebook.com/PerkunasPress

If you let me know about any discussion groups or fan-fic on other sites and provide a link, I'll link to them on my website.

Please consider writing a review wherever you bought this book, or on sites like Goodreads, or on your own blog.

Please help me make this book better for everyone by reporting any errata to me. Since page numbers vary by format, let me know what Chapter contained the problem and some nearby sentence. The first five people who report more than 5 errors (typos, formatting) will receive a free trade paperback edition, suitably corrected. If you would like to be credited in a corrected edition, just let me know when you contact me.

EXCERPT FROM KING OF THE MAY

Creiddylad knelt at her father's feet and waited for his response. She surreptitiously watched from her humbly lowered eyes, a subtle smile on her face as he took the bait.

Lludd, the King of Britain, stiffened in his great seat in his private audience chamber. "Can this possibly be true? The wizards were right that elementals made the ways we use, and my son Gwyn knows this and keeps it from me?"

"He's found a method of controlling them, father," she said, rubbing salt into the wound. "I fear my friend Madog paid with his life when he challenged Gwyn's authority." The fact that Madog had been experimenting with the elementals, had even kidnapped a young one, was carefully omitted.

Lludd ruminated on this treacherous and independent son. Prince of Annwn, indeed. Only by my will, he reminded himself. It was time he took that back and made something more useful out of him. Annwn would be better served by an ambitious deputy who owed everything to him, one who had proven his loyalty.

It would be a shame to hurt him too badly, but he could always breed other children. That's what they were there for, after all—the glory of his line.

$\backsim$

"Gwyn truly wants four litters from this year's breeding? Where will we put them all?" Ives, kennel-master to Gwyn ap Nudd stood next to the huntsman's desk and shook his head.

George glanced over at the lutin, all four and a half feet of him in his traditional red jacket, hands fisted on his hips, and thought about how much to tell him. Gwyn had pulled him aside a couple of days ago with the request.

"He plans to draft out the least promising as alliance gifts. Not to rival the great hunt, of course, but to serve as foundation hounds for other packs, as goodwill. Two litters from fourth generation breeding, and two litters for us, from the fresh outsider hounds."

He turned to his new foster-son, twelve-year-old Maelgwn. "Do you remember which hounds are the current outside breeders?"

"That would be Cythraul and Rhymi, sir," he said, leaning over the breeding books till only his curly black hair was visible. "They came to the pack three years ago and I've been told they've proven to be good hounds."

George nodded and turned to the last person in his office in the kennels, Gwyn's foster-daughter fifteen-year-old Rhian, his junior huntsman. "And why shouldn't we just mate them to each other and keep the outsider blood undiluted?"

"Because we don't know how they're related," she said, passing the test. "When Iolo brought them back after that year's Nos Galan Mai, they were just two whelps. If he knew anything about their breeding, he never told us or wrote it into the hunt logs, and now he's taken the knowledge with him." Rhian referred to George's predecessor as Gwyn's huntsman, murdered three months ago.

"Right," George said. "So we treat them as full siblings, just in case, and try to spread their blood into the pack as a whole over time. If you look over the records you can see that Iolo did the same. The closer all the pack members are to a first generation outsider hound, without unnecessary inbreeding, the better. It keeps the pack healthy and capable for the great hunt, and it helps make a level pack, where no hounds are too slow or too fast compared to the whole."

After another hour's work discussing the bloodlines, referring to breeding books spread all over the desk, George and Ives settled on the pairings they wanted to use.

"We'll have to take over a couple of stalls in the closest stable for a month or two," George said, in answer to Ives's original question. "If Gwyn decides to make this an annual request, we'll set up something more convenient and permanent for next time."

George and his own two dogs left the kennels by the private huntsman's alley that exited onto the lane across from his own house. When he walked up the porch between the holly trees and opened his back door, he could still smell the lingering scent of the balsam fir that had served as his Christmas tree. He'd taken down the seasonal decorations a few days ago, but some still lingered on shelves and mantels and one of them, the old bone "thunderbolt" Ceridwen had given him, rested in his pocket, tied to his belt.

Angharad called to him from the study in the front of the house. His glance traveled automatically to her belly but nothing was yet visible in her form. Something was different in the room and a new painting on the wall caught his eye. He grinned when he saw it.

She'd finished her scene of the oak tree, from the end of the wild hunt a couple of months ago. When he'd met her, he'd told her about the vision of the oak that he'd carried all his life, spreading its strong branches and providing shelter. They'd seen it in reality, together, at the end of the great hunt where justice was served on Iolo's murderer, and she'd promised to paint it for him.

"It's wonderful," he told her, admiring the autumn colors in the moonlit scene, the oak prominent at the top of its upland meadow. All the chaos of the wild hunt, the hounds and hunt field, the criminal at bay, had been removed. Just the oak remained, serene and permanent in the landscape, caught in the moonlight in the upper right, and the fading light pooled down to bosky darkness on the lower left, leaving the oak with its promise of protection glowing, drawing the eye.

He drew her into his arms for a kiss. "How did you make the leaves match your hair?" he said, tickling her nose with the end of her long auburn braid.

"Put that down and I'll show you," she said, kissing him back before letting him go again.

"Did you get the hound breeding sorted out?" she asked. "I know you have a deadline, if you want the dams to be ready for six-week-old whelps by Nos Galan Mai."

"Yes, I had to back into that," he said. Nos Galan Mai was the night of the first day of May, fae calendars starting their days in the evening. May 1 was the mid-year festival, when Gwyn would face his rival Gwythyr ap Greidawl for their endless recurring battle.

"I wish Iolo had written a description of what it's like, when Gwyn wins and opens a way for him into Cernunnos's realm." Cernunnos was Gwyn's patron, the great antlered god of the beasts. "All we know is that he brought back two whelps, dog and bitch, each time. I wonder what else he saw there."

"You'll know soon enough, if Gwyn wins again," she said.

If, indeed, he thought. Gwyn didn't always win, he understood, and then there was no new blood for the pack. Hounds that were more than three or four generations from the outsider blood weren't fit for the great hunt, that pursuit of justice initiated by Cernunnos each Nos Galan Gaeaf, the night of the first day of winter, October 31. The hunt through the ways that Cernunnos opened for the quarry and his pursuers needed special hounds, able and willing to mete out justice at the end and restore ritual balance to the world. It was the foundation of Gwyn's rule as Prince of Annwn, under Cernunnos.

Iolo had been murdered in an attempt to prevent the great hunt from happening, to overthrow Gwyn, and George's coming from the human world to this otherworld version of the Virginia Piedmont had prevented disaster when he took over as huntsman. If Gwyn lost consistently at Nos Galan Mai, it would cause the pack to dwindle in effectiveness, and that would be another way to destroy the great hunt.

"How's the knee?" she said, as he dropped into a chair.

"Hardly feel it at all. Riding out with the hounds was no problem." George had recently recovered from serious injuries, and then from the healing itself which was severe.

"So, what's the matter?"

He gave her a look, and sighed. "You're right. It's just, I can control the hound breeding, that's part of my job. It's all the rest of this that has me worried. Ceridwen drops this bombshell on me a couple of weeks ago about being dangerous, along with dark hints that Gwyn wants to use me for something and then—nothing happens."

Ceridwen liked to describe herself as a scholar but George was beginning to recognize that a better term might be "wizard."

"She's right, you are dangerous. Anyone that can kill the ways would be a disrupting force. You're a walking threat."

The ways, passages that connected two distant locations, functioned as a sort of road network, even crossing the ocean. Most long-distance travel was organized around them. They were scarce resources, much fought over. Specially-skilled fae known as way-adepts could control them, but no one could create one or destroy one, until George manifested the latter ability.

"Not my fault," he protested. "Tell Cernunnos." Cernunnos opened and closed ways for the great hunt, and George's father Corniad Traherne, about whom little was known, was some sort of descendant or avatar of the god that George now carried as a passenger within him.

"Maybe a solution to this will come from the meeting with the rock-wights, now that we know they're the way-makers," she said.

Finding the elementals here in the new world a few weeks ago had been a great surprise and the next steps toward diplomatic relations would be starting this very afternoon.

"Ceridwen's been giving me this crash course in fae politics and history, but it's such a tangled web of relationships. I used to think my rural Virginia towns had dense relative and feud networks, but they don't hold a candle to the fae. Makes the hound bloodlines look simple." Between their long, long lives, several thousand years in some cases, and their habit of fostering their children to other relatives and allies, it was very difficult to identify the important family ties for any key ruler. "How do you keep it all straight?"

"Well, don't forget, I've had hundreds of years to digest the changes as they occurred instead of trying to do it all at once. Give it time."

Time was what he didn't have. He was only thirty-three, and Angharad was more than 1500 years older, not even middle-aged by fae standards. There was some possibility that he had inherited the fae's long life from his great-grandfather Gwyn but it wasn't likely since his grandmother, Gwyn's daughter, had not.

No one had any idea what the effect of being Cernunnos's avatar would be on his lifespan, but they had to assume that he wouldn't have the long life himself. They'd know for sure when he began to show the effects of later middle age on a human timescale, but until then Angharad and George tried to treat every moment as fleeting and precious.

He saw from Angharad's face that she regretted the slip of the tongue that reminded them both of what was likely to come, and he smiled back at her to console her. "How can I keep my mind on my studies when I have that to think of?" he said, pointing at her belly.

As he expected, the reference to the child coming in late summer distracted her. If he had to leave her in a few decades, at least he'd provide children to carry on.

⌁

George and his foster-son Maelgwn walked the full width of the back grounds behind the manor, from the kennels at the south end to the orchards tucked into the north bend of the living palisade that surrounded the manor and its extensive acreage. All of the land rose to the west, to their left, along the lower slope of the Blue Ridge mountain.

"Will Cloudie be there?" Maelgwn asked.

"I don't know. Seething Magma may bring her, as I've brought you," George said. "Now remember, you and I will be the only ones who can hear them clearly, so I expect you to be helpful with translations for everyone if they ask."

"Yes, sir."

"This is likely to go on for hours. It could be pretty boring,"

George warned.

"That's alright." Maelgwn looked up at his new father. "Thank you for letting me come."

George draped an arm over his shoulder and gave him a quick hug. He'd found the orphaned Maelgwn as a secret companion to Granite Cloud, the very young daughter of the rock-wight Seething Magma, when he snuck into Madog's domain a few weeks ago. Madog had been using the kidnapped elemental child to make ways for him, and George's rescue had begun the relations between the rock-wights and Gwyn's people that they were formalizing today.

They were the last ones to reach the rock outcrop just within the palisade where they had decided to anchor the way Seething Magma would be creating. Gwyn and Edern were deep in conversation with Ceridwen. George's friend Rhodri waved them over.

"You're here in a dual capacity today?" George teased Rhodri.

"Just call me Ambassador," Rhodri said with a straight face. "I doubt we'll have that much use for way-adepts in this crowd."

"Maelgwn," George said, "I want you to stick close to Rhodri if he and I are separated."

The boy nodded.

"Good," Rhodri said. "I could use your help."

Ceridwen looked up at the sun. "Mid-day, everyone. George, why don't you take your spot. The rest of us will give you room."

George stood in front of the rock outcrop and watched them all back off a good distance. The winter-bare apple trees nearby loomed like scarecrows. This part of the arrangement made him more than a little nervous. Seething Magma was going to home in on him like a beacon, since she knew his feel best, and make the exit of the way come out upslope in front of him. If she miscalculated he'd probably never feel it. Wouldn't be his problem any longer.

Can you hear me, Mag, he thought. I'm in place.

Greetings. I'm coming.

When he'd first encountered her, he could only pick up

emotions and images from her, but that changed after she spoke with Cernunnos inside him during his healing, and now she was as clear to him as Granite Cloud had always been to Maelgwn. He wasn't sure what to expect from any of the other elementals that would be participating.

He faced the outcrop to watch. Until a month ago, no one had ever seen a way made before. Of the group there today, only Rhodri, Maelgwn, and he, and to a lesser degree Gwyn, would be able to see it happen.

A glow appeared on the ground between him and the rock face and widened to about twenty feet, marking a semi-circular opening, a passage slanting into the earth at a gradual angle. Most way entrances were above ground like invisible tunnels, but since they had a choice Gwyn had suggested this underground approach for greater ease of defense.

Rhodri's face lit up as it completed, and George backed away to give Seething Magma room to emerge. She was the size of a large pickup truck, a featureless flexible slab something like an animated boulder, propelled by short pseudopods on her lower surface.

Location correct?

"Perfect," George said. He walked up and patted her upper body.

Maelgwn waved at her. "How's Cloudie, my lady?"

Greetings, friend of my daughter. She's waiting to see you.

George looked over at Maelgwn repressively and he made himself into a dignified miniature of his broad foster-father and subsided.

You are well?

"Much better, all recovered," George said.

Rhodri walked up and bowed. "May we offer you any hospitality, my lady?"

We are waiting for you at the other end.

"She say they're all waiting for us on the other side."

Gwyn and the others joined them and bowed, keeping a careful distance away from her. "We are very glad to see you again, my lady," Gwyn said. "Please lead on, and we will follow."

ABOUT THE AUTHOR & PERKUNAS PRESS

Karen Myers writes, photographs, and fiddles in the picturesque foxhunting country of the Virginia Piedmont. She can be reached at KarenMyers@PerkunasPress.com.

A graduate of Yale University from Kansas City, Karen has lived with her husband, David Zincavage, in Connecticut, New York, Chicago, California, and for the past several years in Virginia, where they both follow the activities of the Blue Ridge Hunt, the Old Dominion Hounds, the Ashland Bassets, and the Wolver Beagles.

Perkunas Press, founded in 1993, is pleased to enter into a new era of independent publishing in ebook and trade paperback formats

Made in the USA
Charleston, SC
06 January 2013